BE JUBILANT, MY HEART!

A Novel by
ELIZABETH RICHMAN

Star Song

PUBLISHING GROUP

Nashville, Tennessee

Star Song Contemporary Classics is committed to publishing titles that address real life issues in a dramatic and memorable fashion and are as edifying as they are entertaining.

Star Song Publishing Group, a division of Jubilee Communications, Inc. 2325 Crestmoor, Nashville, Tennessee 37215.
Printed in the United States of America.

First Printing, May 1993

Library of Congress Cataloging-in-Publication Data

Richman, Elizabeth.
    Be jubilant, my heart / by Elizabeth Richman.—1st ed.
        p.   cm.
    ISBN 1-56233-039-X : $9.95
    1. Family—New England—Fiction. I. Title.
PS3568.I3447B4 1993
813'.54—dc20   93–10926
                                                  CIP

1 2 3 4 5 6 7 8 9 10 — 99 98 97 96 95 94 93

BE JUBILANT, MY HEART!

ONE

"Dear God! Dear loving God!" Abigail whispered as she stood petrified at the window. How fragile her children were. The big black car bore down on them as they ran back and forth across the road. It was a game they played, to see how many times they could run across the road in front of an approaching car. Abigail closed her eyes and prayed, for there was not enough time for her to reach the children or even to shout at them.

"I'm a wild thing, a bird," cried Carla, her daughter, as she ran across, then turned to cross again. The approaching car whirled through the dust, drew closer and slowed but did not stop. *I must win, I must,* the refrain throbbed in her heart. The car drew closer, and no one stopped the keyed-up child. The old man at the wheel, cursing the strange behavior of farmers and their livestock including children, leaned on the horn and trod with all his might on the brake.

The boy, Howard, paused. *I should run across once more to show her, but I'd get run over, I'd never win.* He was always the one who stopped first, "chickened out," she called it.

The car slowed but did not stop. Carla dashed across once more. "I won!" she exulted.

Their father, walking across the field with an axe over his shoulder, was dimly aware of all this, but he had other things on his mind—food, taxes, and more immediately, firewood. As he drew near the road, the car sped away, and the two children stood side by side watching its dust. He went into the house.

He was a tall man and bearded, but light of step, and the wooden floor did not give at all as he strode through the kitchen. His wife stood by the open window, quietly sobbing.

"Why Abigail!"

"Why Abigail indeed!" she cried. "Did you see, Josiah Wingate, did you see? They could both be killed. I won't stand for it. And you had better support what I'm about to do!" She whirled from him and ran outside to the children. Josiah stood at the window and watched as she chastized the children.

"Well," he said and went outside. "You, Carla, don't let me see you doing that again, and Howard, go get that wood into the kitchen."

Carla will hide in the hay and sulk, he thought, and Howard will get the wood. He went back to to the kitchen to reassure his wife. She came in, her eyes glistening with anger and went to the stove. Gaily she sang a nursery rhyme as tears suddenly ran down her cheeks, "Polly put the kettle on, put the kettle on, And we'll all have tea."

He went back out. A sudden change of mood! Well, he was used to that, for she was like quicksilver, always had been.

That night at the Wingate farm the moon shone full upon the fan-shaped elm and danced among the autumn yellow leaves. It reflected off the rosy Duchess apples in their uncovered barrels; it glistened on the wood neatly stacked by the road; it reached the big field and picked out the faded plants in the broad field of unharvested potatoes. Its rays found beauty in the clapboard siding, which seemed to have been painted white years ago, and it softened the gray of the shingled roof. The magic of the moon, as yet untouched by the foot of man, for this was 1923, made attractive even the ragged spot where shingles were missing. The light entered the larger of the downstairs bedrooms, and neither Abigail nor Josiah needed a lamp to see the determination in the opposing face. She was a short, slight woman in her thirties, her long dark hair hanging in one neat braid down the back of her patched flannel nightgown. Gold-rimmed glasses half concealed her eyes, her lips were quivering, her hands clenched into fists. He was somewhat older, tall, angular, balding, and his grizzled beard flowed luxuriantly over his ragged longjohns.

"Woman," he said, "I'm doing all I can. You're just upset over those kid games."

"It's not that. I've handled a roomful in my time. I thought I made myself clear. Things can't go on like this."

"What do you want from me? I've raised the crops, got in what potatoes I can sell and six barrels of apples that nobody wants; I've broken my back sawing cordwood that nobody will buy; I've milked the cows and made the butter and walked my feet off in town trying to get rid of it. I tell you there's no money left in Maine."

"Why can't you admit your way has failed? We go from bad to worse. The house is falling down, we live on swill, Carla is in rags. I'm ashamed to send her to school."

"Take down those curtains and make 'em into a dress. We're doing nothing the whole world can't see."

"And there's Howard, his overalls! Even if I could sew, I couldn't make pants out of pink-flowered chintz."

"You can't this and you can't that! You can't sew and you can't milk the cow."

"You always said that wasn't woman's work."

So he had, so he had, like a fool. He tried to divert her. "What's that old chum of yours doing here day after day?" he demanded.

"Miss Abbott's been in the neighborhood, just dropped by."

"You used to call her Jennifer. You were in school together."

"I know, but think of her position."

"So what if she is some high muckamuck?" A terrible thought came to him. "You haven't been talking to her about," he hesitated, then spat out the word, "charity?"

Abigail took a step backward, frightened by his anger. "She did notice, I couldn't help it. She saw the deplorable condition of Carla's teeth."

"I don't want her coming here."

"Did you get her letter?"

"I did and I filed it where it belonged. That and one from some county office." He'd torn them in bits without reading them and thrown them in the toilet.

If he hasn't read the letters, thought Abigail, he doesn't know, but he has to be there. Still she dared not speak to him of the forces she had set in motion. She took the attack. "You *must* go in to town and look for work."

So that was what she wanted him to promise. How many times had he told her that it was no use? Go into town and look for work; move into town and she could find work too—oh he was sick of her talk. Yet she did have reason to complain. He saw her lip tremble. "Enough of this for tonight," he said, his voice now gentle. Once in his arms she'd relax, and so would he. He moved toward her and would have embraced her had she not jumped away like a skittish colt.

"No," she said. "We'll not kiss and make up. We'll make up and then will be time enough for kissing."

His tenderness vanished with her rejection. *I'm surely within my rights,* he thought, *but has it come to this, that I must stand on rights? There was a time. Ah, but that was when I was somebody, a dashing political figure, when they were talking of running me for the Maine state legislature, and since I knew Teddy Roosevelt—who can say what else?* He'd given up the chance to go to Augusta because she was pregnant and afraid to stay alone at the farm. Opportunity never knocked again. And now, now, what was he?

And her thoughts dwelt on the two living children in want, the horrors of one stillborn, another dead in infancy. And there she was, a wretched, nagging frump—she who but yesterday—ah, don't think of yesterday. That they did not speak their thoughts made matters worse. Their silence was no longer a sheltering chamber but a wall dividing them.

Insolent woman, he thought, she glories in my humiliation.

And to herself she said, he doesn't care how I suffer.

Yet within each there was an understanding of the other's needs and a shame at not meeting them. Oh bitter, bitter shame!

"Am I so repulsive?" he cried. "Is there no love?"

"Would I be here in this squalor if there were no love?"

"Where could you go?"

That did it. Abigail drew herself up as haughtily as her small stature would allow and marched into the other bedroom, which was small and dark, quite untouched by the moonlight. There was a bed but no bedding. After bracing the door with the straight chair, she lay down, covered herself with a small rag rug, and lay there shivering. When Josiah came and rattled the door, she leaped up in a frenzy. "Don't you dare come in!" she cried.

"Abigail, I want to talk to you."

"We've already talked."

He rattled the knob, shook it fiercely, and it came off in his hand. She laughed scornfully. He flung it against the door, but the door was solid wood, and the knob bounced off and fell back with a thud.

"Abigail!" he roared.

She shivered. He might still have strength to break down the door. But he made no such attempt. He retreated to the other room. No sound came from him and no sound from the rooms above where the children surely were sleeping. There was no sound, not even crickets or the yowl of a cat—a dead blank silence. There was no voice telling her what step next to take. "I must do something, something, something," she whispered to herself.

Bone weary he lay and swallowed his anger, anger at the unreasonable Abigail and anger at himself because, after all, she wasn't so unreasonable. *I shouldn't have married*, he decided. *I was too old. How pert she looked in her frilly white blouse holding forth in her schoolroom! How I'd admired that clever tongue of hers!*

But that was long ago. He sighed, turned his tired body and slept after a fashion. He rose while it was still dark, pulled on his blue denim shirt and his faded overalls, took a piece of bread from the kitchen, and went to the barn. He got himself a cup of milk, warm and frothy direct from Rosy the cow, and standing in the barn doorway, he ate his breakfast and felt his spirits lifted. It was a sweet day in the dying time of the year. On the rise to the west the maples, touched by the early morning sun, blazed red and orange. They'd soon be bare branches etched upon the sky with a gray November beauty, and then would come the snow.

Leave the farm? Take his kids into the city? It'd be a cold day in the bottomless pit when he did that. Howard, puny even now, would sicken and die, of that he was sure. And Carla? He shuddered at what might await her there. Abigail was right about Carla's needing clothes, not that a couple of patches on her little plaid gingham dress would hurt her, maybe do Carla's high and mighty spirit good; but she'd outgrown the thing so that it already gave an indecent exposure to those too mature legs. Abigail never worried about that. She was such an innocent! As for that idea she had that she could find work in town, impossible! She wasn't up to it, and even if she were, he still had some pride. He finished his refreshment, scowled for a moment at the six barrels of apples and then at the stacked cordwood. His eyes rested for a moment on the elm by the driveway, golden in the clear day. Comforting thing, he thought, a big tree. It spread a mighty fan and never needed painting or shingling or a new dress. He hurried back into the barn, milked the cow, took the pail into the kitchen, and left before anyone else was around. He'd walk in to Amsterburg, catch a ride to Bangor.

Abigail waited some five minutes after she heard him close the door, then rose, dressed, and went into the living room. The air was cool from the night. The sun crept through the window and lit up the opposing wall, where the wallpaper had long since faded and been smoked into a shabby gray. Yet there were the pictures. She'd miss them. She stood there trying to look at the room as a stranger might, trying to make it alien, not wanting to admit that it was home, something she'd miss, long for. *No, I will not long for it. I will remember it as something from which I have risen.* Still, if she could take the pictures. Framed alike in raw wood were the two with religious themes. The first showed the Shepherd Jesus leading His off-white flock out of a pure white, swirling snowstorm. The second portrayed a Rock of Ages rising from a tumultuous green sea to furnish a refuge for a wave-tossed, struggling woman whose long dark hair floated out upon a wave. The other, larger and framed in polished walnut, was a print of El Greco's "View of Toledo," that great melancholy landscape with trees sharp against the grass and the eye of the beholder drawn by the winding wall and the tower upward to the stormy sky. To take them would be impractical, and she must strictly avoid the impractical.

The ray of sun lit up the "Rock of Ages" so that the cross and the despairing face were illuminated. Abigail knelt and placed her hands on a roughly made sewing basket which stood on a small table under the picture. She closed her eyes and began to pray, her low voice vibrating with a muffled sob. "Dear God, Almighty God, lead me, tell me what Thou wouldst have me do." She hoped with all her soul to achieve contact with the Infinite One, a hope so tremendous she scarce had faith. "Oh my babies," she cried. "The load, dear God, is too much. No, no, I am strong. Just guide me, God. The whole road I do not ask to see, just one step. Lead me, God." If one could see the whole road, would it ever be possible to traverse it? She'd already taken the first step, but it was not too late to turn back. "Help me, guide me!" With all her heart she prayed. Still she did not know God's will.

As she stood, the children came clattering down the stairs. "Last one down's a sissy," shouted Carla. "I'm a boy," she cried. "I'm first, I'm a boy, my name's Carl!" She was a sturdy eight-year-old with light brown braids, large gray eyes and rosy cheeks, and was dressed in the green plaid gingham dress which had offended Josiah by the shortness of its skirt.

Howard ran in behind her. A year older, he was somewhat shorter, a slender, tow-headed boy with triangular face, gray eyes much like his sister's, a prominent nose, and a small chin. He ran and confronted his mother. "She's not a boy," he insisted.

"Okay," said the girl, grinning at her angry brother. "I'm not a boy." If she were a boy, she could learn to swing an axe and go to the woods with Papa, like Howard, and not have to stay behind to do the dishes. She looked toward her mother, wanting her smile. "Mama," she cried with sudden awareness, "you're dressed up!"

Abigail's dark hair was piled high after the Gibson Girl style, and she wore a neat dress of lavender cotton made with puffed sleeves and a long full skirt brought in tight at the waist, a style elegant enough but outdated. It was indeed her very best dress. There was both question and accusation in the child's eyes. Abigail stood straight, her upswept hair adding inches to her height and an immeasurable something to her dignity. Her face had regained perfect composure, and her brown eyes behind the lenses of her gold-framed glasses were calm and clear.

"See, here I am with Faith, Hope, and Charity," she said. It was a family expression of long standing, and it helped her keep her emotions in check. The sheep in the storm represented Faith, the cross on the rock, Hope, and the sewing basket which Abigail had bought from a wandering Indian woman was Charity. She'd tried to work the Toledo painting into the saying but had never succeeded.

"Come," she directed. "Have your breakfast."

She herded them briskly until they stood before her, their stomachs filled, their hair brushed and Carla's braided, their clothes straightened, their lard pail lunch containers in hand. The darlings, oh the poor darlings! And oh those wretched black stockings on Carla!

She handed the girl a brown paper sack. "Here are your pretty little socks," she said. "Change under the bridge."

The stockings were worn by Josiah's command. Abigail had connived with Carla to evade the decree, and so far Howard had respected their secret. Carla took the packet and flashed her mother a cheerful smile, displaying front teeth half eaten away with cavities. *I have my answer,* thought Abigail as she stood in the doorway watching the two figures trotting down the road. *Those disgraceful, rotting teeth! In my baby's pitiful mouth!*

The children walked quickly until they came to the bridge, then scampered down the path beside the wooden frame and found their favorite big flat rock behind a willow tree. There they stopped, and Carla removed her shoes and stockings while Howard stood by the brook watching it splash over the rocky bed.

"Something's up," Howard asserted. "Do you know what?"

"No," she admitted.

"It ain't good," he said.

"Look," she cried, "there's a green bottle." Carefully balancing herself, she drew a dark green bottle from the brook. It was tall, slender, and graceful. She held it to the sun and the light glowed through. "Bottles like this have messages," she said.

"There's nothing in it."

"Not that you can see. Maybe it washed here from the ocean."

"Upstream?"

"Anyway the brook goes to the ocean. Let's follow it."

"Whatever's up with Mama is up," said the boy. "We'd better get to school." He hated school, and she loved it, yet it was he who felt compelled to leave the brook.

A frog sat on a rock and stared at her. Carla tensed to spring at it, but Howard pulled her back. Slowly she put on her socks and shoes and hid the bag with the black stockings behind a clump of bushes. They went back to the road, over the bridge, up the hill. They came to the house where Edmond and Robert lived, but their father, who was hitching up his ox team, said the boys had already gone. Carla and Howard continued, past the house where they had the screaming geese, but the geese were penned up for a change. They passed the little weathered meetinghouse where Abigail took them whenever some wandering evangelist came to preach; they passed henpecked Henry's; they trudged on into an oak grove to the one-room school, newly painted white and standing out sharply against the dark red trees. They joined the alphabetical file of children and marched on into the schoolroom.

It wasn't until after the morning Psalm, the Pledge of Allegiance, and the singing of "America" that Miss Phipps noticed the green bottle on Carla's desk. The teacher stood there, tall, gaunt, and gray, and demanded in her no-nonsense manner, "What is that old bottle doing on your desk?"

"It's mine," said Carla stubbornly, like a three-year-old.

Miss Phipps glanced at the others, twelve in all. She guessed the bottle wouldn't be a problem if she didn't make it one, and she certainly didn't feel like starting the day off with a Carla hassle. She'd never seen anything like that child, so well-behaved, quiet, almost shy, but when crossed, a demon. She was also the school's star pupil. Funny, the brother was a slow learner, definitely a slow learner, but willing, always willing. The family was so desperately poor, though respectable, certainly respectable; too full of long words, even she admitted that, and at the same time impractical or maybe just unlucky. Josiah Wingate wouldn't want his child to have an old wine bottle sitting on her desk. Miss Phipps shrugged and went on with her day.

"Carla," she asked, "have you learned your poem for the United Columbus Day program?"

"I'm studying it," said the child. She fixed her eyes on the book, then looked out the window and in her mind was reciting: "Behind him lay the gray Azores, Behind the Gates of Hercules." She had read about Hercules. "Before him not the ghost of shores; Before him only shoreless seas." How wonderful to be on the great ocean! They should have followed the brook.

She recited her geography, blushed when Howard made a mistake, and forgot lessons when Miss Phipps rang her bell dismissing them for lunch. She huddled on a mound of leaves with a couple of other girls and hurriedly ate her sandwich and apple and the cookie which Mama had cut in the shape of a leaf. The afternoon bell rang. After reading class, Carla settled down to studying her poem. She looked away and out the window and mouthed the words: "Why, now not even God would know—Should I and all my men fall dead."

God, her mother's God, how could it be He wouldn't know?

At the front of the room Howard was stumbling through his reading. Then he stopped. Everything was quiet, strangely quiet. The door had opened, and through it had stepped a man, a big middle-aged, black-moustached man wearing khaki clothes with a silver star near his heart. The Sheriff! He pulled off his hat and became less impressive by reason of the sweaty bald spot with its fringe of wiry black hair.

Miss Phipps faced him sternly. "Well?" she asked.

"Sheriff Kingsbury," he introduced himself.

"I know," she snapped. "If you will recall, I taught you your ABC's." Having thus cut him down in return for his having interrupted her class, she stood waiting.

He produced a note. "I am authorized to take these two children," he said.

Every eye was fixed upon the man, and there was absolute silence as the teacher read the note. "Bless my soul!" she said. "Howard and Carla."

Trembling with fear, yet proud of being the center of attention, Carla came and stood by Howard. She was clutching her precious green bottle. The Sheriff waited patiently until the children were formally excused by their teacher. "Carla," added Miss Phipps, "take your reader."

Frightened, yet sustained by the ordinariness of the teacher's command, the children followed the Sheriff's khaki trousers out of the room.

"You got nothing to be scared of," the man said as he pushed aside some boxes and a suitcase to make room for them in the rear seat of his black Ford touring car. *I ought to cross my fingers when I say that,* he thought. He drove for a couple of miles, then led them across the porch of Mrs. Whittemore's big house. Mrs. Whittemore, a stout widow somewhat past middle-age, came to let them in. She stood for a moment looking stern, then led them into the big kitchen. There sat Abigail drinking tea from a blue willow cup at the table by the window. She wore a long black coat over her lavender dress, though the day was warm. A black straw hat, decorated with an artificial white rose, perched uneasily on her head. Her big brown purse lay on the table. She stared for a moment at the children as if she didn't know why they were there, then bade them be seated. Shyly they moved toward the table.

"Why Carla," said Abigail, "whatever are you doing with that dirty bottle?"

"It's mine," said Carla.

Howard scuttled behind Carla and found a seat at the back of the table, while Carla stood facing her mother.

"You will leave your book here," said Abigail. "Mrs. Whittemore will take it back to the school. And throw that dirty bottle away. Mrs. Whittemore, where can she put it?"

"It's mine," said the girl.

"Mrs. Wingate," the older woman interposed, "let her keep the book. I'll make it right."

Abigail hesitated. "Well," she said at last, "maybe it will help. But the bottle. I don't want the Sheriff to think we've been drinking."

"I got other things to worry about," said the man.

Mrs. Whittemore hurried over with tea for the Sheriff and apple juice for the children. "Sugar? Lemon?" she asked. "Another cookie? Excuse me, I must fix tea for the old ladies."

The old ladies were two poverty-stricken octogenarians who were boarded with her by the County, the only two left now that the old gentleman had died. The people of Amsterburg referred to her establishment as the Poor House, but she called it Whittemore's Boarding Home.

"We'd best be on our way," said the Sheriff, getting to his feet.

"You can still go back," said Mrs. Whittemore.

"That's right," the Sheriff agreed. "Get in the car, and I'll drive you home." Abigail turned to the man. "You think I'm wrong?" she asked.

Over his shoulder he said, "I ain't paid to think."

"He doesn't know," said Abigail. "He tore up the notices. He won't be there."

"A fine mess!" the man grumbled as he took his seat behind the wheel. "I guess I *am* paid to see he shows up or at least has a chance to."

The children huddled in the car's backseat, trying to figure out where they were going. They drove by houses strange to them, and a neat white church, and a country store. There was an apple orchard, and a great bank of goldenrod, and then a hedge of blackberry bushes, laden with fruit. They could feel the wheels rolling on and on and on. The wind blew stinging dust into their faces.

They were coming into a town at last. Houses stood close together, and there were many cars. The sun had already set. It was getting dark, and everything seemed to be closing in. Slowing down, the Sheriff drove past a red brick building with many windows, each with vertical iron bars. He stopped in front of a one-story annex. A big black dog chained near the entrance barked ferociously. "Shut up, Nero," the Sheriff commanded, and the dog was quiet.

A smiling woman in blue-checked gingham came out to greet them. She glanced inquiringly at the little woman who bore herself with such an air of dignity despite her quaint costume; at the sturdy, rosy-cheeked Carla; at slender Howard in his faded blue overalls, his scraggly hair tousled by the wind. A sharp gust whipped their clothes about them. They were shivering with cold and fear.

"Poor darlings," she said. "Come sit by the fire."

The children clung to their mother's coat. A young man in uniform came quickly through an inner door and beckoned to the Sheriff, who went with him at once.

"Now what?" Mrs. Kingsbury asked. "They always call him just when a meal is ready. I never saw it fail."

They could hear the heavy tread of the men walking down the hall, receding out of earshot. When they returned, the Sheriff was scowling. "Old Jack Cleaver thinks he owns the place," he grumbled. "If he wanted a fancy hotel he shouldn't have—" He checked himself and turned to the younger man. "Take those boxes and that suitcase out of my car and put them in Number 24," he ordered.

There followed a dinner, which Carla refused to touch. Howard shoveled in the victuals as if he feared it might be his last chance, while Abigail ate politely, praising the cooking. She talked compulsively, mostly about her youth on a potato farm in Aroostook County, while the others were silent, except for an occasional monosyllable. Finally the Sheriff wiped the blueberry pie off his moustache, rose, put on his hat and billyclub, and said, "We'd best be getting you stowed away for the night."

He led them through the door leading off the kitchen, down a short, dimly lit hall, unlocked a heavy wooden door, and motioned them to go ahead of him while he carefully locked the door. They were in a long, narrow, pale green hallway, dimly lit by unshaded electric bulbs which hung from the ceiling. They marched down the corridor, the Sheriff in the lead, then Carla and Howard, with Abigail bringing up the rear as if to protect the children, or perhaps to prevent their running away. They came to a stairway which was somewhat lighter, having been recently painted white. It was cold and damp and still smelled of paint. Up the stairs they went to a landing. Their way was blocked by a heavy door, which the Sheriff unlocked. After they had passed through, he locked this door as he had the first. They were in a brightly lit corridor with doors at intervals on each side. They heard a woman's voice mumbling something incoherent, then all was still. The Sheriff unlocked a door and motioned them to enter. "Here you are, ma'm," he said to Abigail.

It was an ordinary dark wooden door, except that near the top was a glass window about a foot square with two vertical iron bars set into the casing. "We're in jail!" screamed Howard. He tried to push by his mother, but she held him by the arm.

"Children," she said firmly, "Miss Abbott, you remember the State lady who visited us, has arranged for us to spend the night here because we must be in Halsey early tomorrow, and we have no other place to stay."

The children were propelled by their mother into the whitest room they'd ever seen. They heard the bang of the closing door and the click of the lock. For a fleeting moment they saw the Sheriff's face in the little window, then they were alone.

There were three white beds in the room, and opposite them a small table with three chairs, also painted white; there was a closet with no door and in it, some boxes and a suitcase. In the far corner stood a white flush toilet and a washstand. There was one window with a white shade. The whole room was lit by an unshaded overhead light. All the necessities, thought Abigail, and yet the most depressing room she'd ever seen. In a cave they could have snuggled together and comforted one another.

"This will be my bed," she said with forced cheerfulness. "The one nearest the door is for Howard, and Carla, you will have the one next to the window. And, oh yes, Howard, I have a piece of rubber sheet in my box."

The boy hung his head in shame. Every once in a while he wet the bed, big boy of nine that he was. Why did she have to bring it up, the boy thought. He went and sat on his bed with his back to the others. He could hear the wind howling outside, and he wished it would blow him away where no one would ever find him again.

Abigail took from her suitcase the blue woolen sock she was making for Howard and sat down with her Bible to knit and read as she always did at night.

"Where's my reader?" asked Carla. "I'll study my poem."

"You must have left it downstairs. You should have brought it instead of that dirty bottle."

"I'll go get it. I'm sure I can find my way." She ran to the door but it was locked fast. "Let me out!" she cried. The outrage of being locked in flooded over her. Refusing to listen to her mother's common sense, she screamed, "Let me out, let me out," and beat on the door with her fists until one was bleeding.

Carla heard an angry woman's voice ordering her to shut her trap, then she heard a man's slow, heavy footsteps. Still screaming, Carla ran behind her mother. The Sheriff's face filled the pane of glass. He wore his hat, and he was holding his finger to his lips. As Carla became silent, he walked away.

"Why!" cried Abigail, scandalized. "He could look right in no matter what we were doing."

They remained hushed until they could no longer hear the steps, then Carla spoke to her mother. "Mama," she asked with trembling voice, "are we here because Papa is dead?"

"No, no, certainly not."

The child jumped away from her mother. "You're lying," she cried. "Papa's dead. He's been killed."

Abigail quivered with anger. To think that a child should accuse her of lying! A child accuse her own mother! She struggled to control her own over-wrought emotions and physical exhaustion. In the end all she could manage to say was, "Everything is going to be fine. You must believe me. Now I want both of you to behave." She had established a command, a tenuous command; there would be no more unseemly outbursts, at least no more that night. The two children were doggedly quiet, Howard convinced that somewhere in that big building Papa was locked up, heaven knew why, and Carla sure that Papa was dead. It was clear to both that Miss Abbott, the State lady who had tremendous powers, had gotten Mama and them locked up in jail. But why? why? why?

TWO

By the time the Sheriff let them out of jail the next morning, Howard had convinced his sister that Papa was alive and in the jail, but he was no longer sure himself. Maybe Carla had been right and Papa was dead, maybe run over by a car or gored by a bull. They clung to each other, sobbing quite openly, while Abigail herded them out onto the sidewalk, fooling no one with her gush of cheerful talk. Miss Abbott got out of her car and strode toward them. She was a tall woman, her suit an exact match in tone and almost in texture of her russet brown sedan. She wore sturdy walking shoes and a close-fitting hat with an iridescent feather band. She smiled at the children with a great display of large even teeth.

Poor Jennifer never was pretty, thought Abigail. Her hair and eyes are not dark enough to be brown; her complexion is sallow. Perhaps under other circumstances. Abigail could see her as she might have been two generations ago in buckskin skirt striding across the prairie, her hair blowing in the wind, her face a healthy tan, her firm voice encouraging the horses, the man, the children. But now she would never marry. Abigail, who despaired of her own marriage, sat and pitied the successful Miss Abbott who would never marry.

Miss Jennifer Abbott thought her own thoughts. Look at Abigail, forlorn, old before her time. And her clothes! And those children! How small the boy is for his age. She looked at Carla childishly clinging to some brown bag.

"The children will be provided for," she said. "As for you, we'll have to get you a job. First some clothes. Of course what you're wearing gives you a certain style, but it isn't up-to-date, not at all."

Abigail brightened at the mention of a job. "I don't expect to be a fashion model," she said. "Just a school teacher."

"I'd give you some of my own things, but I'm built on such different lines."

"I'd be taller if they hadn't turned so much under for feet," Abigail joked nervously.

"Even now you can joke!" cried Miss Abbott. "Marvelous, Mrs. Wingate, er Abigail, simply extraordinary. It's that kind of gumption that'll be your salvation. I wish more of our clients—" She broke off quickly at Abigail's sudden gasp of distress at the word.

From the restaurant they proceeded to the Amherst County Court House, a dignified one-story building, its generous portico upheld by six classical fluted columns. It stood in deep shade, its appearance made more solemn by the dark pine trees at either end of the portico. Miss Abbott led them through the heavy door and down a wide hall to a somber room occupied by a massive table and a half dozen heavy chairs.

"Your mother and I will be back." Miss Abbott's words of comfort frightened the children.

"First they got Papa," cried Howard. "Now they've got Mama!"

"Let's go find her!"

The door opened and in walked the Sheriff. "You'll stay here," he said.

"Yes sir," mumbled Howard while Carla kicked at the table leg.

"Okay, Carla," said the Sheriff. "What's in the bag?"

"It's that bottle and a book," she answered sulkily.

"You both need a bottle, you babies." He stood looking at them. "Sit down at the table," he commanded. "You've got a book. Read!"

"Poor little tikes," he muttered as he closed the door firmly behind him.

In the meantime Abigail, becoming more and more dizzy, had followed Miss Abbott. She sank into the chair as directed. The room was reeling, but she fought to remain conscious. Miss Abbott dragged her to her feet; the room whirled; a tall black figure floated before her, towered above her. There came a booming voice; for a moment the shape materialized into a man with snow white hair, then dissolved again into a blur of black. Abigail managed to sit down.

"Mrs. Wingate, Abigail," she heard Miss Abbott whisper, "are you all right?"

And then she was fully conscious. There across an aisle sat her husband, Josiah, his light hair neatly combed, his beard brushed, his old blue suit shabby with clumsily patched elbows.

Bidden by the judge to speak and prodded by an insistent Miss Abbott, Abigail stood and at first hesitated, but once started, she had no control; she could only plunge and gallop like a startled horse. Words came in a torrent, and her voice grew shrill. "No matter how badly off we were," she wound up, "he'd do nothing about it. I can't let my baby's teeth rot, I can't let my children go in rags!"

Josiah Wingate started from his seat and was rebuked by the judge. "Last year he even sold the horse. How is he to take the apples and potatoes to market, I ask you?" She glanced nervously at Josiah.

"You may continue," the judge prodded her.

"Things can only get worse." She hesitated, and for a moment it seemed she would be silent, but she stood there resolutely and went on. "I've two children now I can't look after, and I've buried two, one stillborn and the other dead a week after his birth. I can't face having more children! But will he listen?"

Josiah Wingate could no longer restrain himself. "Shame on you, woman!" he shouted angrily. "How can you talk in public of what goes on between man and wife? Have you no sense of decency?" He stood quivering with rage.

"As I understand it, Mrs. Wingate," said the judge, "you're charging non-support?"

"Yes, your Honor."

"You may be seated. Mr. Wingate, you have heard the charge. How do you respond?"

"I'm not proud of the way things are." His cheeks and his forehead and even his bald head were crimson with shame. "But I've done my best. There's food and a roof over our heads."

"Food!" Abigail scoffed.

Josiah turned upon her. "Yes, there's all the potatoes and apples we can eat, and eggs and milk and whatever else we can scratch together."

"As I understand," said the judge, "the complaint had more to do with medical care and clothing."

"We make do for that as best we can," Josiah responded.

"Hmm. What about her suggestion that you go into town and find a job?"

"I've tried that too," Josiah muttered.

"Hmm. Perhaps a little job counseling might help you to understand your full potential."

"I pretty much know what I can do. I can shear a sheep, fell a tree, plant potatoes, prune an apple tree, can read and write." Then becoming excited Josiah went on sarcastically, "And I know the Mosaic Code, thought once I'd be a lawyer, and who knows, even a judge."

The judge rapped ever so gently with his gavel. "And perhaps you are a carpenter? You farmers do a bit of that."

"Sure I'm a carpenter, in a rough sort of way."

"That might be an opening."

"Have you ever gone about a city trying to get a job as a rough sort of carpenter, I ask," Josiah cried, "have you ever?"

"The Court would advise Mr. Wingate to be more restrained," growled the judge. "Not contempt of court as yet, matter of fact rather flattering to suggest the Court, who has two left hands, should be able to do any kind of carpentry. But the tone, my good man!"

"Are you making fun of me?" demanded Josiah.

"No, no, just trying to offer some kind of practical suggestions."

"Such as?"

"Well, pull yourself together, spruce up," the judge encouraged.

"The day I find a suit of clothes on a spruce tree, I'll dress so fine even my wife'll take notice."

"I had more in mind the beard, something you could do without cost," the judge spoke tactfully. "Beards aren't in style you know, things like that do make a difference."

"You get me a job where it matters and I'll shave it off. In the meantime it keeps my throat warm."

"Come, come, Mr. Wingate, I sense in you a too-ready disposition to take offense."

"Do you think I have nothing at which to take offense? I tell you I'm not a salable commodity, and what's worse my potatoes aren't either. Can't compete with the big farms. A one-horse farm that's lost its horse."

"Yes, yes, the horse. Why did you sell the horse?" questioned the judge.

"I sold the horse to pay my taxes, my blasted high-as-the-sky taxes," cried Josiah. "At least we kept the farm."

What more could he say? He stooped and seemed to grow shorter. It was hopeless. Non-support! Maybe it was. He sat down.

Miss Abbott was standing, quietly answering questions put by the judge. "We recommend," she said at last, "with Mrs. Wingate's full concurrence, that the children be placed in the custody of the State, pending disposition of her divorce suit."

Wingate jumped to his feet. "No, no! I won't sanction it," he cried, but he knew he was spitting into the wind.

He was the first to leave the courtroom. Under the guidance of the Sheriff he came to the room where the children sat. They ran and clung to him, but he pushed them away.

"They've done it," he said despondently. "Howard, old man, they've done it." He handed Carla a brown paper package. "I guess you'll need these," he said. It was the bag with the black stockings.

He sat down and took her on his lap and kissed her, his curly beard tickling just as it always did. Howard pressed close to his father, and the man embraced him. The boy was sobbing uncontrollably. "You'll need me to help cut the wood," he managed to say.

"I'll try to get you back," Josiah said at last. "Right now they've got me surrounded."

The children's whole world had crumbled. Until this day they had been protected by people stronger than themselves, but now there were no protectors. When Miss Abbott came back with Abigail, Josiah hurried out the door. Howard sought refuge in a corner where he cowered flat on the floor.

Miss Abbott decided it was time to put her triple-A, well-shod foot down. "This won't do," she said.

"It won't do," agreed Abigail sadly. She stood up, managed to pull Howard to his feet, wiped both sad little faces, stooped to pick up her wretched hat which had fallen off, and fainted quite away. She recovered consciousness almost immediately.

It was exactly as Miss Abbott had foreseen. Abigail was too sick to work. Miss Abbott must go ahead with the contingency plan, an alternative that she had never doubted would be the route they must travel. "The immediate thing," she said, "is to go where you can relax and not worry."

"Where would that be, unless I die and go to heaven?"

Howard set up a loud wail but was quickly hushed by Miss Abbott. Carla sat sullenly in her chair, kicking at the table leg. Miss Abbott turned to their mother. "I have made the necessary inquiries," she said, "suspecting from what you had told me and from my own observation that you are indeed quite ill, obviously anemic, though I, not being a doctor, shouldn't make a diagnosis."

Abigail stared at her, at the long, serious face, at the compassionate eyes, at the strong hands which lay calmly on the table, at the smartly tailored suit which carried authority in every well-pressed line. "It's not working out as I had planned," Abigail moaned.

"I have made arrangements," Miss Abbott continued, "for you to go today to Mrs. Whittemore's."

"The poorhouse! Oh no."

"You can still go back to the farm."

Abigail hesitated and the children brightened perceptibly. Miss Abbott said firmly, "One place or the other."

"But the poorhouse! What about the children?"

"I will be responsible for their care."

Abigail broke down and wept. "Where will it end?" she said at last.

"The girl has intelligence and drive," said Miss Abbott "There is no telling what she might do if she had the chance." She paused, then turned to leave. "I must go out now. When I come back in a half hour, I must have an answer. The, er, Mrs. Whittemore's or back to the farm."

The door closed gently. "My baby Carla!" cried Abigail as she held the girl. Then she disengaged herself. "Your hair is coming undone," she said. "I do believe you've been tugging at it." The girl sat silently while her mother stood brushing and combing and braiding the wavy brown hair.

Abigail's tongue worked without ceasing, for there was so much to tell them, and this might be her last chance. She told how as a girl she'd lived in the big farmhouse out in the Happy Corner District. It had been a happy family with the hard-working father and the teasing brothers and the mother who knew how to do everything from baking a fancy cake to cleaning out the barn to making a stylish dress, and the older sister so like her mother, and of course Abigail herself, who was considered the scholar of the family, the bookworm.

She told them about the corn huskings and the quilting bees and the barn raisings. And the hanging of May baskets, and the hayrides, and the swimming in the lake. And the skating and skiing and the wild bobsleds flying down the hill. But it was all gone now, everyone scattered.

She paused, thinking of the next town where she'd lived, the place where she'd been the respected teacher, the place where she'd met Josiah Wingate. Oh she must talk of him, must not tear him down. "I invited your father to my school to speak," she said. "He was the leading political figure thereabouts, and they were after him to run for the State Senate. He knew Teddy Roosevelt too."

Carla was amazed. Theodore Roosevelt was in history books, and Papa was nobody, yet he had known Roosevelt. Mama called him "Teddy"!

Miss Abbott came in at this juncture. "Well," she said, "what is it to be?"

"I see it now," said Abigail. "I see the whole plan, not just the dark days. Not just the poorhouse. After I'm well and get a job we'll be together, that's the best of it," she cried. "The children and I."

"And Papa?" asked Howard.

"Oh yes, yes!" cried Abigail impulsively. "Yes, yes, Papa too."

Wingate won't ever accept that, thought Miss Abbott. When they went outside the sun was shining on the white courthouse and lighting up the green pine trees so that the needles glistened and danced. *Why*, thought Abigail, *did I think it gloomy?* Sheriff Kingsbury was waiting in his car. Desperately the mother embraced the children, then broke away and climbed into the black car. Miss Abbott held Carla firmly with her right hand and Howard with her left. They were too stunned to cry.

She put them in the back seat of her car as if they were packages and drove to another part of town. Here the air smelled of the sea, for Halsey sat upon a bay, and this street was on a hill above the piers. "I have to call on someone here," she said. "You children may walk a block each way, but you must not wander."

The children stood motionless until they saw Miss Abbott's brown skirt disappear through a doorway. Then they ran down the street, which they found dead-ended at the edge of a cliff.

Below they saw the beach and the pounding breakers rising ever higher and higher until they whirled themselves over in a great splash of foam. A footpath meandered along a steep incline to the beach, and they ran down it to the sand. On this most unbelievable of days they had actually arrived at the ocean. A quarter of a mile to their right they could see the pier with boats tied up, small boats, some with masts, some without. Men were moving about, busy on the boats, busy on the pier. A sailboat was coming in, so slowly that it seemed hardly to move. And the air had a strange smell, the salt ocean smell. They trotted along the sand, running after the receding waves, scurrying back to escape the incoming breakers. They looked up at the jagged cliff and at the saw-toothed row of fir trees atop it. They gazed at the swooping sea-gulls, then they ran upon the sand and came to a place where there was no sand, the rocks extending to the water. Clambering over the rocks, they found themselves in a ravine and down this ravine tumbled the waters of a swiftly moving brook.

"I'll bet it's our brook," said Howard.

"We could follow it home!" cried Carla.

Then they heard, mixed with the cries of the gulls, their names, clearly their names. Looking up they saw Miss Abbott twenty feet above them on the rocks of the ravine. Furiously she beckoned them, and slowly they walked to meet her. "You gave me a scare," she said. "I thought you'd run away."

They'd missed their opportunity. Back to the car they went.

Meanwhile Sheriff Kingsbury, on the way to Amsterburg in his Ford, looked straight ahead and kept his mouth shut. Flurries of dust irritated Abigail's nostrils, dried her lips, and she felt her stomach rolling like the dust cloud. As they approached the farm, she saw first the barn and then the house. She noticed the barrels of apples, and she thought how refreshing one would taste, but they were no longer hers.

Josiah opened the front door and stood there in his white shirt and rumpled necktie scowling fiercely at the Sheriff. "What'd ya come for this time?" he asked.

"Mrs. Wingate's trunk," said Sheriff Kingsbury. After a closer look at Wingate he asked, "Say, have you been drinking?"

"Now why should I be drinking?"

"Reason enough, I guess, but I didn't expect it of you."

"Don't see why not."

Kingsbury stood silent, appraising the man. There was something about him that suggested he might have been capable of great things—the fire in his blue eyes, the resonance of his voice, the way he stood straight as a ramrod even now. And yet there was no denying that he was drunk.

"Man alive, Wingate!" the Sheriff exclaimed, "You used to argue that whoever sold that rotgut ought to be horsewhipped, and here you are doing business with him. I won't ask who."

"If you knew, would you have him horsewhipped?"

"No. Jailed if I could."

"That's different."

"There's one other thing." The Sheriff hemmed and hawed, actually the man's being drunk made this part easier. "You're a decent sort," he said, "and I hate to tell you this. Mind it isn't me saying it, it's a court order. You're to stay away from your wife and kids until after the divorce."

"Where are the kids?"

"I don't know. Ask the judge."

Without further talk Kingsbury took the small trunk by its leather handles, carried it to the car, and stowed it in the back seat.

"Maybe I should stay." Abigail had noted Josiah's condition.

"Mebbe." The Sheriff sat behind the wheel and hesitated.

"Should I? What do you think?"

"Ma'm, I'm here as County Sheriff and there's things the County can't tell you and not even the State of Maine and not the Feds. It's your responsibility."

"But he's been drinking. Don't you enforce the law?" she demanded.

He eyed her warily.

"I mean should he be left there like that? Drinking and selling and buying, you know it's illegal."

"Sometimes the law uses a little common sense. As for you, ma'm, sit or jump out."

"Take me to the poorhouse."

⚘

Josiah waited until they'd driven over the hill, then went to restake the cow. She stood in the field in the pleasant autumn day, a brown Jersey, dehorned, with white markings on her face. If he'd known how gentle she'd be, he thought, he never would've dehorned her. He pulled up the stake, moved it to another part of the field and pounded it into the ground with a rock. He went over and patted her head and then her soft, gently moving cheeks; then patted her head again, where the horns would have been, then walked, stumbling a little, back toward the house. In a day all the neighbors would know of his disgrace. He could only withdraw into himself, stay on his farm. He'd be safe enough on his farm; no one would stick his nose in there, or at least he'd soon enough send him on his way. He came to the apple barrel, took one from the top, bit into it. Surprisingly enough it was good.

He went into the living room and sat in the rocker eating the apple down to the core. *I should've known I wasn't a marrying man,* he thought. *And yet,* he sighed, *she is a wonderful woman. I can't understand what has gotten into her. Now I must face divorce proceedings, charged with failure to support. Merciful heavens, if only she'd charged me with beating her or adultery or drunkenness. Any one of them would have been less of a disgrace.*

It was chilly in the house, and he went out into the sun-warmed yard to feed the chickens. The hens crowded about his legs and the rooster, a big Plymouth Rock with a black-and-white barred body and shiny red comb, stalked around the flock, pompous as a victorious politician, fierce as a bare-knuckled fighter. Funny critters, chickens, thought Josiah, as he finished scattering the grain and went back to the front stoop to sit in the sun. He looked at the row of maples across the road—big, flaming trees. He sat and watched the dropping of leaves, the gentle peaceful dropping of leaves. If only he could drop silently like a leaf and be no more. The sun beat down upon his head, no longer soothing but fiercely burning. "My babies!" he said, his chest heaving with misery. "What has become of them? Why aren't they with Abigail? God have mercy on those innocent babes!"

✹❡✹

At about that time, the two children, after a long ride through strange country, were being deposited by Miss Abbott at the Stoughton boarding home in Augusta. Miss Abbott led them up the porch steps and tugged vigorously at the rope of the ship's bell which hung near the door. A big red-headed boy motioned them into a dark shut-up parlor. From the depths of the darkness issued a voice, the source of which, once their eyes were adjusted to the dim light, they saw to be a stout woman dressed in black and seated by a table playing solitaire. "I was expecting you," the voice said. "Douglas, put them in the nursery." He led them to a big room where some fourteen children were being supervised by a sad-looking young woman, who was neither glad nor sorry to see them.

They stayed there several weeks, during which time they were fed and supplied with a new wardrobe far surpassing anything they'd ever had. Carla saw the dentist, whose thumb she bit, and one morning they got into a fight. One of the boys was taunting Howard, who'd wet his bed, and soon others joined in, hissing, derisively shaking their fingers, holding their noses. Carla with her head down came rushing at the leading tormentor and butted him in the belly. He yelled bloody murder while Howard stood nonplussed on the sideline until one of the girls started shouting at Carla, using the teasing rhyme, "Carla go darla, go farla, Tee-legged, ti-legged, bowlegged Carla."

When one of the boys joined the verbal attack on Carla, Howard, who'd been too shamed to defend himself, now sprang into action. Considering it beneath him to strike the girl, he launched himself at the boy. Howard was small, but he was a strong country boy and blood flowed from the other's nose. Every child there had some pent-up hatred to vent, and it became a free for all. Douglas and the sad young woman screamed to no avail. Mrs. Stoddard, however, put an end to it, using both her powerful voice and her sturdy arms. The children were subdued; they escaped into various corners and crevices, all except Carla and Howard who faced the angry woman, secure in the belief that they had been absolutely in the right. Mrs. Stoddard didn't care who was in the right, only that order was restored. After that none of the children teased the Wingates; some even condescended to play with them. They didn't go to school, being only "temporaries."

One day not long after, Douglas, who never went to school if he could get out of it, located Carla and instructed her to get packed. "Miss Cunningham is coming to take you away," he said.

"Who is Miss Cunningham?" she asked.

"She's a cat," said Douglas.

Carla moved about pondering the nature of the cat Cunningham. Finally she presented herself in the parlor as per order, neat in a blue-and-white-checked dress, conscious of her newly capped teeth and her neatly cut hair. She wished the visitor had been Miss Abbott, for Miss Abbott at least was a tie with Mama. Miss Cunningham was a tall woman like Miss Abbott but of heavier build and judging by her gray hair somewhat older. Her clothing, all of it an identical shade of pearl gray, was softer. She wore a hat like a tam-o'-shanter with ripples in it and a dress with full skirt which billowed above her pearl gray stockings as she walked briskly across the room toward Carla.

"Get your things," the woman said. "I'm taking you away."

"What about Howard?" asked Carla.

"He's been assigned to a different boarding home."

Carla, sensing the futility of protest, ran upstairs to Howard, whom she found doing a jigsaw puzzle. "They're taking me away from you," she told him. "Do you want my book? Or my green bottle?"

"No, no thanks," he murmured. "How will we see each other?"

"I don't know. We can write."

"Me? Write a letter?"

"You must, you must," Carla pleaded.

"But I won't know where to send it."

"Maybe if we both wrote to Papa—"

Miss Cunningham swept into the room. "What on earth is taking you so long?" she scolded.

Then disturbed by the sad faces of the children, for she was not an unkind person, she went herself to strap the suitcase. "Come Carla," she said, "let's go." Turning to Howard she said, "Good-bye, Howard, be a good boy."

Howard stared at her, wiped his nose on his sleeve and went back to the jigsaw puzzle. Carla, dragging her suitcase, followed the gray skirt down the stairs and out into the street. While the woman was stowing the gear, Carla cried suddenly, "I didn't kiss Howard good-bye," and dashed back to the house.

She found Howard near the bookcase calmly and methodically banging his head against the wall. Bang, bang, bang. She ran to him, "No, no, Howard, don't. Don't turn crazy, don't!"

"Might as well," he said, but he stopped the banging and stood looking at her, blankly staring at her. Hurriedly and awkwardly, for the Wingates were not a kissing family, she kissed his cheek.

"I'm glad you came back," he said and returned to his puzzle. "Don't forget me."

On the sidewalk Carla found Miss Cunningham pawing the ground with a pale gray foot. "No more nonsense," she said. "Get in the front seat."

Thus the child set out on another stage in her journey, carried farther and farther, so far she could never get back. *If I should die, Mama would cry*, the words were like a ringing in her ears. She was pleased that it rhymed and though she had but a dim perception of death, she was comforted by the thought that someone would care. *If I should die, Mama would cry*, Carla repeated in her mind, and once she whispered it, ever so softly, and the wheels took up the refrain and for miles they sang the couplet *if I should die, Mama would cry; if I should die, Mama would cry*. But if she were to die, perhaps Mama and Papa and Howard would all live at the farm. It was her fault, she hadn't brushed her teeth and they'd rotted, and—oh! That was what did it. *If I should die*—but she was a bad girl, she didn't want to die.

THREE

Carla glanced out of the corner of her eye at Miss Cunningham. Douglas had said she was a cat. Long ago when there was a home, they'd had a cat named Jezebel, Mama's pet. It caught mice, little gray balls of fur, and it played with them, claws unsheathed till red blood stained the fur, but Mama wouldn't ever let Carla save the mouse. *If I try to run,* thought Carla, *she'll catch me with her claws.* It startled her when Miss Cunningham spoke.

"We are now in Hambledon West," she said. "Out in the Galamander District."

She slowed and pulled into the driveway of a neat white house. An old man sat in a rocking chair on the porch, puffing on a corncob pipe and looking far into the distance.

A robust gray-haired woman came out and took charge. Carla stood silently evaluating her. She was not a cat, more of a bulldog, with a pushed in face and overlapping lower teeth. As she talked, the teeth flashed white as milk. They clicked once in a while, not being of the best fit, and for a moment this fascinated the child and she forgot to cry, but the woman, Mrs. Hubbard, noted the tear streaks upon the little face.

Miss Cunningham in a flurry of gray skirt hustled the suitcase onto the porch and greeted Mr. Hubbard, who was hard of hearing and ignored her. She stood for a moment looking at the girl. "My, my, you are a pretty child!" she said, noticing it for the first time.

"Come Carla." Mrs. Hubbard set about putting her orientation routine into operation. "You must call me Aunt Beulah. Mr. Hubbard is Uncle Mark. Now follow me."

There were cookies and milk which Carla refused, half-grown kittens from which Carla drew back, a brown horse in the barn, and down in back beyond the rocky pasture a brook with reeds growing at the edge. After a moment at the brook, Aunt Beulah, inwardly lamenting the child's sulkiness, led her back to the parlor which had, wonder of wonders, an organ, like the one at the meetinghouse. Amazing, thought Carla, a house with a real organ! Aunt Beulah played just one song, which Carla believed to be a hymn, and then went on with the "mustn't give her time to think" routine.

"Come child, I'll show you Millicent's piano. Maybe she'll let you play it."

It stood in the corner of the dining room, a small, dainty piano with a cabinet of highly polished light wood and keys as white as Aunt Beulah's teeth. Carla touched the keys with the tips of her fingers. An organ and a piano! Holy cow!

"I can't let you play it now because it belongs to Millicent," Aunt Beulah explained. "Come into the kitchen. I have to do some cooking and you may help."

"Please, ma'm, do I have to? I don't know how to cook. Please could I take a walk somewhere?"

Aunt Beulah looked at the upturned sorrowful face. The poor dear wanted to go off somewhere and cry, get it out of her system. "Why yes, child. Just don't go too far. If you follow the brook you can't get lost."

If I follow the brook, if I follow the brook, thought Carla, as she ran past the low spreading junipers in the rocky pasture and down the steep slope toward the stream, *if I follow the brook I'll come to the ocean and if I follow the ocean I'll come to our brook. But I wouldn't recognize it anyway and it's a million miles away.* She stood there on the bank in the midst of the reeds, mingled brown and green, and she watched the slow moving stream. It wasn't at all like the Amsterburg brook, which danced and sparkled and jumped over the rocks. She stepped back and threw herself onto the grass and buried her face in its roughness; she clung to Mother Earth and cried from the depths of her broken heart. *I'll just stay here till I die,* she thought. *They won't even notice I'm gone.* Once she turned over and looked up at the sky, but the brightness of it hurt her eyes, and she buried her face once more in the grass.

"Hello," said a voice above her. "How old are you?"

Carla raised her head; her eyes traveled upward, from the slender shapely legs, up past the blue skirt and the white blouse to the girl's face, looked into her blue eyes and noted the fair complexion set off by a halo of jet black curls.

"Cat got your tongue?" the girl asked. "How old are you?"

"Going on nine."

"You'll be awful big when you grow up, just like Aunt Beulah," the girl tossed back contemptuously. "But I'll be exactly five-foot-three and perfectly shaped. I'm thirteen now and almost grown."

Carla pulled herself to a sitting posture.

"I suppose you're the new boarder," the girl continued. "There are two boys here, Woodie and Willie. Horrid brats. State kids, you know. But I'm not a State kid, my father pays my board. My name is Millicent and don't you ever call me Millie."

"Oh, you're not Aunt Beulah's—"

"I'm not her anything. I'm here alone."

"Alone? Like me?"

"For three years, but I'm not afraid."

"What's it like to be alone for three years?" Carla's voice was filled with apprehension.

"You grow up. Why I was a baby like you. Well, not quite. At least I have a father."

"You get to see him?" Carla asked.

"Once, a year ago. But he pays for me. Who pays for you?"

"I don't know."

"That's a lie," Millicent challenged. "You're a State kid."

Carla had to face it. "Yes, I guess so," she said.

"Aunt Beulah says you want to play my piano."

"Oh could I?" Carla jumped up eagerly.

"I told Aunt Beulah yes, but if I were you I wouldn't."

"Oh."

"Just let on you don't want to, and I'll teach you something good. I'm not saying what, but I will."

"I don't really care about the piano, not if you'd rather I didn't."

"Let's get back to the house. There's going to be a big to-do. Woodie's going to catch it. He stole a dollar."

Millicent ran lightly across the field with Carla trailing behind, hating the older girl with all her might, yet fascinated by her. They went around to the back porch and tiptoed to the kitchen window. Carla could see a boy, maybe seven years old, standing wide-eyed before Uncle Mark, who held a razor strop in one hand. The boy reminded Carla of Howard, tousled tow hair, homely face, slender body.

"Bend over that chair," commanded Uncle Mark.

The boy did as he was told. Uncle Mark raised his sinewy old arm and lambasted the child's behind with the leather strap. A howl of pain was followed by wild appeals to stop. Again the old man laid on the leather, then paused, breathing a bit harder, his face calm and unmoved, not even angry.

Carla couldn't stand it. She tore open the kitchen door. "Stop, stop!" she yelled.

Aunt Beulah came running in and pushed Carla back onto the porch. Millicent had disappeared. "Be quiet, child," Aunt Beulah commanded.

Carla stood there sobbing and begging that the boy be spared. She could hear him screaming. Aunt Beulah sat down on the steps and drew Carla to her. "It's over," she said. "Woodie always howls a long time after. Ten minutes from now he and Uncle Mark will be laughing over a game of checkers."

Carla watched the clock. It was more like five minutes. "See?" said Aunt Beulah. "Some children respond to spanking and some to scolding and some you can't do anything with no matter what."

The wretched weekend passed. On Monday Carla headed for the strange school alone, for the others had run on ahead. She scuffed her shoes in the dust; she stopped to tie a lace. She tried hopping on one foot, then walking with tiny baby steps. But at last she entered the schoolyard. Millicent was gaily talking to a couple of girls. Boys of various ages were playing tag. It was a school much like the one she had attended in Amsterburg only a little larger. The teacher, young, freckle-faced and red-haired, came out of the building. "You must be Carla?" she said pleasantly. "What grade are you in?"

"I don't know."

She heard Millicent's derisive laugh and blushed red as a beet but kept the tears back by saying to herself over and over, *Millicent is a pig, I will not cry.* She went inside with the teacher, who after some questioning learned that Carla had indeed not been assigned to any one grade but had done work as she was able. After administering cursory reading and arithmetic tests, she decided that although only eight years old Carla belonged in the fifth grade. The girl went to her assigned seat, and head bowed she waited for the others to take their places. The desks were in double rows, and the one next to her was vacant. How she hoped no one would be sitting there, but the seat had been assigned to Roger Thorfinnson, who was a few minutes late that morning. He was a gangly, dark-haired boy, and at first he busied himself with arranging his books. Boys don't like to sit next to girls, thought Carla. But Roger greeted her casually, offering her a licorice coughdrop. He'll be nasty later on, thought Carla.

Ignoring her, he amused himself drawing faces on a sheet of paper. She noticed that he had drawn similar faces on his arithmetic book, which was exactly like hers. Carla doodled fill-ins in the corners of her papers, but she never drew in her books. Roger proceeded to make a row of square faces on the page he was studying. His own face was square like that. He saw Carla's apprehensive glance, and he smiled, a big-mouthed, good-natured smile.

At recess the teacher set about organizing games. Miss Phipps had never done that, thought Carla, she'd just let them play. Carla wondered who had said the poem at the school program. She stood there thinking about the poem, but Miss Parker would not allow such daydreaming. Recess was recess and this new girl must play the games. She must run in the relay race, just like the others; the teams were picked, it wouldn't be even without her. Miss

Parker lined the pupils up in two lines. Carla was third on her team and Roger was fourth. The first boy on each team ran to the turning post and dashed back; a couple of girls ran. Carla's heart pumped painfully, her knees wobbled. The girl was running towards her with the stick, was handing it to her. What if she dropped it? But her hand grasped it. She must run. She told her feet to run, but they refused to move.

"Run, run!" the children were shouting, and over at the end of the other line Millicent was doubled over with laughter.

"Go ahead, child, go ahead," the teacher directed.

"I can't, I can't!" she cried.

"You can," Miss Parker said firmly.

Carla stared about her in alarm. In her line they were all waiting for her but in the other they kept on running in turn. Still Carla's feet refused to budge.

"Carla," the teacher said, "you must run!"

By now the girl was in tears. Then Roger stepped forward. "Don't mind, Carla," he said. "I can't run either. Or at least I run crazy."

He took the stick from her and started toward the goal. He capered clumsily, his legs seeming to go in every direction, and by the time he had reached the goal and started back, the race was over, Millicent ending it triumphantly for the other team. Roger capered wildly until he fell, and all the time he was laughing at himself. At first Carla thought it was an act, but later she learned that he really did have difficulty running due to an illness from which he had not quite recovered. The bell rang and Carla started to run toward the building, but her feet again refused to run. So she walked. This pattern continued throughout the sunny fall weather, making every recess a torture. Frightened and abashed, she shied away from the others and made no friends.

No friends, unless you counted Roger, and Carla reasoned he couldn't exactly be a friend because he was older than she and a boy. Yet they played together in the field between their homes, he insisting that he must teach her to run again. And then one day Roger's mother phoned to invite Carla to lunch. "Hmmph!" snorted Aunt Beulah. But one didn't say no to Julia Thorfinnson.

Carla tramped through piles of leaves by the wayside, and she walked dustily along in the middle of the road. It was a calm clear day, and she wore the dark blue, checked dress she liked so well. Everything was perfect, the fallen leaves, the chipmunk on a log, the cows in the pasture, and now here was Roger coming to meet her. She stopped to wait for him. In the distance she could see the Thorfinnson place.

"Let's run," Roger challenged.

Carla stood still.

"Come on." He was capering about.

Frightened, she stood there.

"Oh well," he said, "we can get there walking."

They approached the house which was even larger than it had seemed from a distance. Beyond loomed the gigantic barn.

"I'll show you the barn first," said Roger. "Dad raises horses, mainly those fast horses for sulky racing."

Carla had never heard of sulky racing. Several of the horses were in their stalls munching hay. Roger's father, a tall, broad-shouldered man in blue denim work clothes, was hitching one of the horses to a little two-wheeled cart, a sulky, Roger explained. Thorfinnson greeted the children perfunctorily, patted the horse tenderly, got in the sulky, and whirled away in a cloud of dust.

Next to the barn was a white dairy shed, with big tin cans of milk and a wooden churn and a bowl of cream and another of butter, and a rich enticing dairy smell. Then they went to the kitchen where they found Mrs. Thorfinnson just putting her broom away. Julia Thorfinnson was of medium height and build, with dark hair and a lively pleasant face. She was wearing a loose-fitting bulky gray sweater and blue denim pants. A woman wearing pants! Carla would have given anything to exchange her neat blue-and-white dress for an old sweater and pair of pants. Mrs. Thorfinnson moved about with quick easy strides. Carla had never seen anyone so wonderful.

"Come," said Roger, "I'll show you my den."

He took her into a small wood-paneled room off the kitchen. One wall was covered with diagrams on heavy white paper. Another wall was lined with floor to ceiling shelves on which were books and boxes and various bric-a-brac, mostly animals carved from wood. They were the handiwork of Roger's Grandfather Thorfinnson.

Roger pointed to the diagrams on the wall. "Those are my drawings," he explained.

Carla looked thoughtfully at them. They were black lines drawn on white, mostly angular, though some went in circles and ellipses. She followed the lines trying to form some shape from them, but had to turn to him and ask what they meant.

"They're plans," he said.

"For what?"

"Machines mostly. And here in the corner is something I built."

"What is it?"

"Well, if you strike this knob here," he demonstrated, "it pushes that bar up, which causes the marble to drop into this cup which upsets the balance. I'm not sure what it is, but I think it generates power."

"Marvelous!"

"I think so too. And this is a galamander. You know this is the Gala-mander District?"

"So that's a galamander. Why it's just a cart, and I thought a galamander was some kind of animal, you know like a salamander."

He laughed, but the laugh didn't cut like Millicent's laugh. He explained that it was the kind of cart used years before to haul out granite from a nearby quarry which had long since been mined out and closed.

"You know so many things!" she said admiringly.

"Grandpa told me. He knows everything about Hambledon history and Maine history too and, well, he just knows everything."

This was the beginning of the many days she spent with Roger, who be-came like a brother to her, or a cousin, a magnificent brother-cousin. Ward Thorfinnson was always busy with the horses, but Julia Thorfinnson smiled and made her welcome. After a while Grandfather Thorfinnson, who'd been visiting relatives, returned home; and Carla found that Roger was right, he did know everything. What stories he told! How proud he was of the collection of books which lined his room! Why it was like a library! He noticed at once the rapt attention which Carla gave to his every word, and several times he encour-aged her to actually take one of his precious books in her hands. He told her to call him Grandpa, and once she even did.

The leaves fell completely from the trees and snow covered the fields and the road. The children had to allow extra time for the walk to school, often being the ones to break the path, though sometimes the Thorfinnson horses took their exercise early in the morning, usually hitched to light sleighs. One Saturday Carla and Roger rode squeezed beside Mr. Thorfinnson. The harness bells tinkled like fairy chimes, the slender strong legs of the horses moved in easy rhythm, snow banks lined the road, and the air stung their noses. Ward Thorfinnson kept urging the horses to go faster and faster and laughed at Car-la's fear. The next day Mrs. Thorfinnson, dressed in elegant woman clothes, took them to Sunday School. The bells tinkled, the snow sparkled, the horse's dark brown flanks glistened in the sun. "We'll go every Sunday," said Mrs. Thorfinnson.

Their Sunday School teacher was an enthusiastic young man who brought very close to them the wonderful Christ figure who once had walked the coun-try roads of Galilee. By Christmas time Roger had vowed that he would be-come a minister. Carla, not to be outdone, declared that she would some day become governor of the state, and that when she was governor, no one would ever be poor.

Christmas came and they had a tree at the Hubbards', a green fir covered with red and white glass balls that shone like stars and must on no condition be knocked off.

Carla got letters from both Papa and Mama. Papa sent her a dollar, and his handwriting was hard to read. Something about taking long walks. Mama was still staying with Mrs. Whittemore. She sent a present, a Bible, a used, somewhat battered Bible.

"A secondhand present," scoffed Millicent.

And Carla got a letter from her brother. "Do you know what a recorder is?" he wrote. "It's a wooden flute. They have one here, and if I don't you-know-what, they will teach me to play it. Cunningham had to go and tell them about that. The doctor fixed me so I won't."

For Valentine's Day Carla worked long hours on a Valentine for Roger. Using red pencil on white paper she made fantastic lines, curling and angling, forming various designs, just as they happened, not at all planned. Here a face with large almond eyes peered from a square, there a bird perched on a whorl. An intricate lattice formed the frame and careful lettering begged Roger to be her Valentine. And Roger did one for her. He drew a square face, then with a crayon gave it unruly brown hair; and beside this he put a longish rectangular face with big eyes; and he made little bodies, the square face a boy in pants, the other a girl in a skirt. The figures were holding hands and were framed in a heart-shaped outline. Around the edges he made a lacy doodle, such as he had seen Carla make, and neatly printed "From: Roger To: CARLA." That was a good touch, he thought, printing her name in caps, and to make things perfect she noticed it, and said she'd always keep it

The days passed, and Carla cried less. She still couldn't run, but at least the teacher no longer pestered her about it. March came in with fierce gales, then April melted the snow. On the road were wagons and autos, and the Thorfinnson horses got their exercise with the sulkies. The children had a week off for Easter, and Carla went out one day with Woodie and Willie to build a dam in the brook. Tiring of this, she wandered off to look for violets. The sky was clear and blue with soft clouds like little lambs; the air still held the freshness of the previous day's rain; the trees were putting forth their leaf buds, pale green and delicate rose. Finding no violets, she broke off some pussy willows and ran back to the house to give them to Aunt Beulah. How she wished she could send them to Mama!

Aunt Beulah was in the driveway talking to Mr. Tompkins, the fish ped-dler, who was standing beside his wagon. He was a middle-aged man with sandy hair just visible under his greasy felt hat. His straw-colored moustache straggled over his lip obscuring his mouth.

"Well, well, here's my sweetheart," he exclaimed. "Hello, Carla."

She wished he hadn't found out her name. "Hello," she muttered.

"Come, Carla," he said, "come and show me the pussy willows."

Obediently she walked over and held them out for him to inspect, but he didn't even look at them. "What a pretty girl you're getting to be!" He looked down and smiled. "Give us a kiss."

Aunt Beulah cut in sharply. "She's much too old to be kissed."

"How old is she?"

Aunt Beulah ignored the question. "Here's the money for your fish, and you, sir," she snapped, "had better get on with your fish peddling."

He settled his hat on his forehead, climbed into the high driver's seat, slapped the reins on the back of the old gray horse and drove off.

"You didn't have to jump down the man's throat," Uncle Mark chided.

"Sometimes you hear too well," she replied. "I can smell the evil in that man."

"I never heard any bad of him."

"Of course not. Most of the time you're deaf as a post. You never saw him before a couple of weeks ago, you probably don't even know his name."

"You got me on all counts," he conceded. "Do you know his name?"

"Tomcat," Beulah said as fish in hand she went on into the house.

Carla giggled. The name suited him. When he looked at her, she felt like a mouse being stalked by a cat ever so much more frightening than the cat Cunningham or even the Jezebel cat.

The fish peddler came several times, and then for a fortnight there was no sign of him. "Good riddance," said Beulah.

That same day there was a long letter from Miss Cunningham. Beulah ground her teeth, she snorted audibly, she tore the letter in two, but the fact remained that Miss Cunningham had instructed her to keep Carla home from school the following Wednesday. "I suppose I have to," thought Beulah, "but for the rest, Cunningham can do her own explaining."

On the appointed morning Beulah Hubbbard went about the house doing her work with an extraordinary amount of banging, with her face set hard and grim. The three other children went to school, and Carla, who'd been kept home, got out the schoolbook from Amsterburg to see if she still remembered that poem. Aunt Beulah had put in her teeth for the occasion though she usually didn't until afternoon, and every once in a while Carla could hear her grind them. Her lower jaw jutted more than usual, and she looked like a most unamiable bulldog. Once she said quite audibly, "I'd like to skin him alive!" At ten o'clock Miss Cunningham drove furiously into the yard and with a high-pitched squeal braked just in time.

"I'm on a tight schedule," she said. "Is Carla ready?"

"No, she's not."

"You didn't tell her?"

"I did not," replied Aunt Beulah. They had gone into the living room, and Aunt Beulah had chosen to perch on the organ bench, tall and straight and stern.

"You should have."

"You are making a big mistake, and I'll not be a party to it," Aunt Beulah replied.

"Do you have any reason for thinking it a mistake?"

"You might call it a hunch, or say I've a sharp nose."

"That would go over big with my supervisor," said Miss Cunningham.

"You have orders from above?"

"Yes, but if you have any information, any real reason for saying it's a mistake, I will listen."

"I know what I can sense, what I should think anyone could see," Aunt Beulah insisted.

"It seems to us to be a great opportunity."

Carla stood trembling. Miss Cunningham came and put her arm around the girl. "Someone wants to give you a good home," she said.

"My mother?" Carla could feel the hastened beat of her heart.

"Not your mother, she hasn't the means. But it's someone you know." Carla looked at her in wonder. Someone she knew? Could it be the Thorfinnsons?

"Someone who has no children," Miss Cunningham continued.

There went the Thorfinnsons.

Miss Cunningham cleared her throat. "Mr. Tompkins has seen you and talked with you and is so impressed that he wants you to come and live with him and his wife and be their little girl."

"Tomcat! Oh no!" cried Carla.

Miss Cunningham was surprised at what she took to be a pet name. But why the negative? She supposed the child had gotten used to being here with the Hubbards. It was one of their better homes, but it certainly wasn't what you would call opportunity. "Go pack your things," she commanded. Carla looked appealingly at Aunt Beulah, who just sat there grinding her teeth.

As they drove along, Carla whispered her tear-restraining magic words, "Millicent is a pig, I will not cry," but the magic was gone. The car drove on and there she sat, a rosy-cheeked girl with neatly combed, wavy brown hair and a new straw hat and red plaid dress. She sat stiff as a statue with tears streaming down her face. Her dread was almost unbearable, but she had a new phrase with which to beat back the tears. *"Tomcat stinks, I will not cry; Tomcat stinks, I will not cry."* Miss Cunningham heard her mumbling but couldn't make out the words.

It was Mrs. Tompkins who came to the door of the pretty yellow and white house. She was the saddest looking woman Carla had ever seen. Her dark brown hair was combed back smoothly from her pale face. Her large gray eyes looked questioningly at them.

"Oh yes," she responded to Miss Cunningham's introduction. "I was expecting you." Her face remained immobile while the social worker brought the suitcase in and gave the usual farewell admonitions to Carla.

Mrs. Tompkins led the girl upstairs to a large dimly lit bedroom with dark heavy furniture and cloudy blue curtains. There were two single beds with matching blue spreads and dark headboards sharply outlined against the white wall. "This will be your bed," Mrs. Tompkins indicated the one nearer the window.

Somehow the day passed. Finally Mr. Tompkins came home. He was no longer a fish peddler in a greasy felt hat, but a milkman in white overalls, jumper and cap. However the dough-colored face had not changed, nor the droopy moustache, nor the eyes that looked at Carla as if she were something to eat. Carla ran at once to the kitchen where Mrs. Tompkins was preparing dinner.

"Why are you running away from me?" he asked in a whiny voice.

She hesitated. "Because—"

He sat down at the kitchen table. "Come and sit on my knee," he slapped his knee invitingly. "I want to talk to you."

"I'm listening, Mr. Tompkins."

"Don't call me that. Call me Father."

"You are not my father."

"I will be. I plan to adopt you."

Carla pressed her lips hard together and held back the tears. Her impulse was to stamp her foot and scream, but she fought that back. Coldly and calmly she said, "I hate you, Tomcat."

He had been prepared to deal with tears or a temper tantrum, but this cold contempt took him by surprise. "We'll see, we'll see," he said. His hands grew clammy and he wiped them on his trousers. He clenched and unclenched his fists; he stared at the child. What lovely rosy cheeks, what a captivating mouth! But he'd have to go easy, what with her temper and his wife's everlasting plotting against him.

The woman worked at the stove, silent save for an occasional sigh, but there was no plot, only a prayer and little faith. *Dear God*, she prayed silently, *help us, in the name of Thy merciful Son, help us. Spare this one, oh dear God, spare this one.*

Carla the mouse had roared, but a nameless fear remained, for the Tomcat continued to stalk her and the house was small. He was a palpable presence in the long dark night when Carla lay in the bed by the window and Mrs.

Tompkins lay sobbing in the one by the door. In the morning when she came down to breakfast, he was already gone. Outside in the bright spring day under the pink and white blossoming trees, with a pretty lunch basket in one hand and a streetcar ticket book in the other, she stood waiting, for that one moment without fear. Two girls came from the next door house, and shyly she turned her eyes toward them.

They introduced themselves, Lily and Rose Tompkins. Yes, *he* was their uncle. The streetcar, big and brownish yellow, with a pole on top like a tremendous fishing rod, rattled over the steel rails, propelled by power which it fished from the overhead wire. Rose, sturdy and quick, led the way. Lily, who was several years older and quite sedate, pushed Carla ahead of her. Three other children, two girls and a boy, came running and jumped in behind them, and the streetcar moved on.

Rose began eagerly telling about their candy machine, a home business with which their mother supplemented the family income. Carla had seen one of the machines through the window. It was stirring something in a giant kettle and reeling it around the bars on a wheel. Fancy having a candy machine in your house!

"So your name is Wingate." Lily mused. "That sounds like a word, but I can't think what it means."

"Ever since Lily got her glasses," Rose put in, "she's been the big scholar, particularly words."

Lily's pale face flushed. "It wasn't the glasses, it was a teacher I had. And words are fun. Do you like crossword puzzles?"

"I never saw one," Carla admitted.

"I'll show you. And there are lots of other word games. Tell me, does your mother say soda or saleratus, and does she say cinnamon or cassia? I mean," Lily noted the bewilderment on Carla's face, "you do have a mother?"

"Oh yes," and suddenly she was telling Lily she wanted to write to her mother and had no stamp and didn't know where to mail a letter.

Lily took it gravely. "You *must* write," she said. "My uncle—" she hesitated. "I'd better come right out with it. We aren't allowed to visit him. There's a reason."

Carla stared at her.

"She means—" Rose began, but did not continue.

"I'll get you paper and stamps," said Lily. "You'd better use our address."

Abruptly the streetcar stopped, and the children crowded off, with Lily and Carla at the end of the line. Out on the sidewalk children were streaming from every direction. The building was two-storied and extended ever so far and was painted a tan color with dark brown trim, strictly no-nonsense. The playground was hard-packed dirt, surrounded by a sturdy wire fence, next to which shrubs were sparsely scattered.

There was a room for every grade! Carla would not be with Rose who was in the fourth nor Lily who was in the eighth. She'd be all alone at recess and there would be games and she wouldn't be able to run and they would laugh at her. She wouldn't go out; she couldn't, and all morning she agonized over it. She was rescued by Lily, who led her out to the end of the playground where Rose was resolutely hanging onto the chains of two swings.

Rose and Carla started swinging, standing up on the boards and pumping vigorously, Carla going even higher than Rose. She was higher than the houses along the street, as high as the trees, as high as the sky. Down below a voice was calling her name, but she would not slow down, she would keep on swinging. But the voice kept calling, and she slowed down and came to a stop.

"Carla," the fifth grade teacher said, "your father is here. He brought you some milk." There just outside the yard stood a milkwagon and inside the gate stood Mr. Tompkins.

Carla started to pump herself up. Soon she was flying high again. The bell signaled the end of recess. She came down slowly. Tomcat was gone. There stood the fifth grade teacher.

"Carla," she said, "that was not nice."

Carla scowled sullenly and kicked at the dirt. She resolved never to speak again to the fifth grade teacher and adhered to the resolution throughout that long first day. Her one consolation was that Lily had kept her promise and at noon provided her with a stamped envelope. Quickly Carla wrote urging that her mother do something. "Get me away from here. Oh Mama, you must!"

"You should hear in a week," Lily was sure.

And indeed exactly one week later, Lily came running out of her house calling to Carla that the letter had come.

Her heart beating furiously, Carla took the letter and tore it open. "Be patient," Abigail wrote. "For now you must remain there. Be a good girl." Be patient! Fat lot of good that would do! Angrily Carla crumpled the letter and threw it on the ground. Lily picked it up, smoothed it out, read it, and shook her head sadly.

Each day Carla went to school, and each day at recess Tomcat drove up in his milk wagon, stopped and called through the chain link fence to her, and each time she ignored him, and he never again came into the yard. Day after day at the house he continued to make his advances, never too fast, and her very innocence worked against him. It was not that Tomcat respected the innocence, but rather that he feared it. She was so abysmally ignorant that he knew she wouldn't know enough to cower, to blush, to be silenced by shame. He would never be able to make of her an unwilling co-conspirator. She would always be ready to cry out. And what lungs she had, a regular calliope. He must move slowly, subtly. Even the slightest physical touch, which he kept trying, was met with suspicion and anger. He tried gifts. He gave her a profusely illustrated book, which she disfigured with crayons; he gave her an expensive red sweater which she refused to wear. He promised her a dog, any kind she wanted, and she said she'd bite it. One day he showed her a dark red automobile of imposing appearance which stood in the garage raised on blocks. "We'll get it fixed," he promised, "and go for long rides."

"I won't go."

We'll see about that, my pretty, he thought. He went into the house, to wait for dinner.

Carla wandered down the road and noted the wild iris, the flag lilies, fragile blossoms in the midst of slender green leaves. It occurred to her to pick some for Mrs. Tompkins. Soon she was joined by the three children from across the street, the boy about her age and the twin girls, somewhat younger. "See," Carla cried. "There are lots of them." She looked at the deep blue flowers, some actually blue, others purple, at the delicate complex pattern, like the garden iris but much more dainty. She joyed in the delicate pattern, the light line on the petal, the dark center of the light line, the long grasslike leaves. They wandered from the road deeper in among the shrubs. The little girls grew tired and trotted home with their bouquets, but Carla and the boy Andrew went on. There was a bird singing, a whippoorwill like the whippoorwills at Amsterburg. She and Andrew went deeper into the brush to get a glimpse of the bird. She glanced at the boy Andrew. He wasn't at all like Roger, nor like Howard, but he was nice, and he'd gone with her to help her find the bird.

A man called harshly. It was Tomcat. "Going off to play in the woods with that nasty boy," he yelled.

"We went to find a bird," she answered, startled into something like courtesy.

"I know what you did, I know what it means." He reached out to seize her but she evaded him and started to scream.

Andrew took to his heels, back to the road, shouting, "Daddy, Daddy," and running toward his home. Close behind him stumped Carla, even in this emergency unable to run, evading Tompkins with sudden sidewise maneuvers. He was close upon her when Andrew's father came out to the road. He was tall and broad and lithe, and his black eyebrows met in a scowl.

"What are you up to?" he cried, advancing toward Tompkins.

"Came to call her to dinner." Tompkins was all smiles, all oil and smoothness.

The man turned to his son. "What are you making such a tarnation noise about?" he asked. The boy felt rather foolish and silently followed his father into the house.

"Carla," said Tompkins in a fierce low voice, "don't you ever let me catch you again with that boy."

She looked up at him and saw saliva slowly sliding from the corner of his mouth.

"If I do, I'll, I'll, I'll—" he struggled for words, he choked, he coughed, his pasty face grew red, purple.

Carla watched hopefully, but he recovered. Still he seemed shaken and walked very slowly. Carla went into the house and offered the tattered remnants of the bouquet to Mrs. Tompkins, who sighed and put it in water.

After dinner Carla went out onto the front lawn as usual and lay there doing her homework. The sky grew dark, and the air cool and damp, but she stayed there shivering long after Tompkins had called her many times. At last he came out and walked toward her. She started to scream, louder and louder. Oh someone hear! When he was a pace away, she jumped up and ran into the house, straight to her bedroom where Mrs. Tompkins was preparing for the night.

The next evening shortly before dark Carla was in front of the garage trying to chop some wood, not because they needed it since they cooked and heated with gas and never used the fireplace, but just because the wood was there and it reminded her of Amsterburg. Tompkins approached her. "Come, come," he said, "let me do that."

"I like to chop wood," she answered, resisting his efforts to take the axe. She swung at the big block of wood, swung clumsily for the axe was heavy and she'd never chopped wood before. At home, oh at home, Howard had been the one to chop wood. She sliced off a narrow slab, swung again and did a little better.

Tompkins stood behind her watching. What a big girl she was, almost a woman, he thought. The muscles of her bare legs tightened as she braced herself for the next swing of the axe. He was pleased to note that the girl found the axe too heavy to handle properly. He straightened his necktie, an unconscious gesture, and stepped around in front of Carla.

"You should let me do that," he said in a low voice.

She stared at him. He reached out his hand for the axe. She swung it again. She brought it down on the block of wood, splitting off another section. She's strong, thought the man. And then he saw that the axe had slipped. There was a gash in her leg, and blood streamed down to her pink and white socks. He took the axe from her, and she jumped back as if he had threatened her. Frightened by the blood, the child began to cry, and when the man moved closer, she became hysterical, ran from him, ran into the street. The sister-in-law next door dashed out of her house.

"What now?" she cried. "Oh she's bleeding! You, you—your family has covered up for you long enough."

"Don't be a fool," the man admonished her. "Carla cut her leg splitting wood. Which she had been told not to do."

"Yes," said a soft voice. Mrs. Tompkins came out in her bathrobe with a big white towel around her head. "Yes, I saw it. I got to the window just as she brought down the axe."

"You saw it? You wouldn't say it if it weren't so?"

"Am I in the habit of lying?"

"Not unless keeping silent is lying." The sister-in-law inspected the cut, then went back to her house. Carla threw herself face down on the lawn and lay there crying, unmindful of the bleeding cut on her leg. Gently Mrs. Tompkins went to her, took her into the house and bandaged the wound.

Since it was still early, Carla went back out to the lawn, but even when it became dark, she did not go into the house. At last Mr. Tompkins approached her. "You must come in, Carla," he said.

"I won't! I won't!" she screamed. She lay there and screamed defiance.

Tompkins glanced at his brother's house. There was someone in the window. He shook his fist angrily in that direction. "Stinking busybodies!" he growled. "I've been accused of many things, but never of chopping them up with an axe."

Carla continued to scream. "Come, this won't do," he said. "I'll have to carry you in."

He glanced at the window of his brother's house and hesitated. Carla scrambled to her feet and ran into the kitchen, where Mrs. Tompkins stood at the stove preparing warm milk. Tompkins went into the living room and sat moodily reading his magazine. He'd had a bellyful of screaming. He'd had more than a bellyful of that wretch his brother was married to.

The night passed, the day came, Mrs. Tompkins dressed the cut, said it was healing. Carla said nothing. Mrs. Tompkins looked even sadder than usual if that were possible. A dense fog of evil lay over the household. *I can't stand it any longer, I can't,* thought Carla.

It was Tompkins who had reached the end of his endurance. One more night of this, he swore, and he'd be ready to throttle the little wench. He'd give his sister-in-law something real to report! No, no, that wouldn't do. That harpy would report all right, who knows, maybe already had. He left his milk-wagon in charge of the knowledgeable old horse, ducked into a phone booth and succeeded in talking to Miss Cunningham. "Take her away," he cried,

"Take her away. What has she done? Why? Don't ask, don't ask, just take her away, today, today!"

He was not at home that afternoon when Miss Cunningham came. "I don't see why it wouldn't work out," she said to Mrs. Tompkins. "Do you think you could persuade him to reconsider?"

Mrs. Tompkins looked at her in horror. "He phoned and told me that you must take the child away. He said today."

"You seem to want her to go."

"You're a little late to be asking what I want," said Mrs. Tompkins.

Carla entered the room dragging her suitcase and stood waiting. Mrs. Tompkins drew the girl to her and did what she had never done before; she embraced her and kissed her. "It's better that you go, my dear," she said, "but I shall miss you."

Carla kissed her tenderly, then threw her arm around the woman's neck and clung until Miss Cunningham had to interrupt. So the child can be affectionate, she thought.

Carla took her seat in the car.

Miss Cunningham was silent at first. Then looking straight ahead she asked, "What really happened?"

"Nothing."

"Did he hurt you?"

Carla hesitated but finally said, "No."

"Well, what then?"

"He looked at me."

"Looked at you?"

Carla was silent, pulling at a loose thread in her skirt. They rode on. Then Carla asked, "Why doesn't Mama come for me?"

"I don't know."

Carla resumed pulling threads from the loosely woven cotton of her skirt.

"Don't you want to know where we are going?"

Carla gave her one fleeting glance, shook her head, and continued tearing at the dress until Miss Cunningham told her to stop.

FOUR

They were headed in the direction of Hambledon West. Carla sat straight and felt something like hope as they rolled past familiar landmarks—a tumbledown barn, the house where her teacher lived, a tremendous oak growing by itself in the middle of a field. A half mile away along the dirt road she could see dust rising, out of which materialized a sulky drawn by the Thorfinnson horse Dickens, the one Roger was allowed to drive. The driver was Roger's father, who shouted something at the horse, and didn't see Carla. Why should he? She wasn't a horse. Aunt Beulah would see her, maybe hug her, Uncle Mark would take his pipe out of his mouth and tell her she'd grown.

The car pulled to a stop. Aunt Beulah was standing near the driveway, her arms folded, her face set and angry. The heat, thought Carla, or Woodie. "A bad penny always turns up," said Beulah. "Go put your things in your room."

In the living room Uncle Mark was playing checkers with Woodie. Neither paid any attention to Carla. After stowing her belongings, she took off her new dress and put on the old green plaid, by now so outgrown that it reached only halfway to her knees. When she entered the kitchen, Aunt Beulah snorted angrily, "You shameless hussy! What do you mean running around in such a short skirt?"

Carla ran back upstairs, changed hurriedly and returned. She paused, hoping Aunt Beulah would now hug her, but Aunt Beulah intentionally ignored her and busied herself at the sink. So Carla escaped out the back door. She had been near evil, and Aunt Beulah with her sensitive nose could smell it on her. There must be something bad about me, or he wouldn't have taken me, thought Carla. Roger would understand and help her; he'd know she'd fought the evil. She would not be able to explain, but he'd understand, maybe help her to understand.

She was soon at the brook, her shoes and socks left neatly on the bank, her hands busy with the clay, her feet soothed by the coolness of the water, her eyes taking in the green and gold beauty of early summer. There was the green of the rushes, of the slender flag lily leaves, of the wide heart-shaped pads floating on the water. The cow lilies glowed golden among the pads, heavy flowers, the cow of lilies. The buttercups on the bank were in full bloom; the grass along the stream was long and sharp and bright green. The pink and blue of spring had been replaced by the gold and green of summer, the delicate shapes by the fullblown. The gray clay was cool in her hands.

"My, my," she heard a voice. "Look who's here. I see you've got a new style haircut."

She glanced up at Millicent, bold and beautiful. "I like it," Millicent said. "Makes you look more grownup."

Carla stared at her, half afraid, but not knowing why.

Millicent came nearer and leaned over, careful not to get in the wet. "I'm glad to see you back," she said. "Tell me all about it."

Carla hesitated, not knowing how to answer. She smiled happily, for Millicent seemed truly to welcome her.

Millicent moved a step closer. "Tell me all about it," she said, her eyes glowing with excitement. Then hearing the loud call of Aunt Beulah, she added in a whisper, "You'll tell me tonight."

❧❦

Carla went to her room before her bedtime and sat reading the Sermon on the Mount as Mama had told her to do. She wondered what it meant. Aunt Beulah came and took away the lamp, and Carla lay in the dark, sobbing until she fell asleep.

Sometime in the night she was awakened. Millicent was shaking her gently. "Wake up, it's me." She pushed the half-awakened Carla closer to the wall, insinuated herself into the bed, and lay there under the thin blanket softly caressing Carla's head.

"Now," said Millicent, "you can tell me all about it."

"Oh it was a lovely house and a big school and a woman who cried."

"No, no, no! Stop stalling, tell me about *it*."

"About what?"

"Did he get to you, did he really?"

Carla was honestly puzzled.

"What a stupid brat you are!" Millicent suddenly lost her temper.

She slithered out of the bed and left the room. Carla lay very still, and the night was without sound. She felt totally confused. "There is something wrong with me," she thought. "Something bad, but I don't know what it is." She buried her face in the pillow too ashamed to cry.

She escaped from the house as often as she could, going usually to the brook. Once Woodie came there and got fresh and she pounded him. Carla felt ashamed, but she didn't know why, and there was no one to talk to. Woodie ran away, minded his manners thereafter and bore no ill-will. Millicent was hateful to Carla or ignored her.

It was some time before she saw Roger. She was walking aimlessly along the road when two boys came running towards her. The first was Roger, dressed in T-shirt and shorts, and running, actually running, in a smooth rhythmic stride so unlike his former ungainly capering that at first she doubted it was he. He paused, stood running in place, waited for her to speak.

"You can run!" she gasped.

"God answered my prayers," he said easily and continued running in place in full command of every movement.

His companion came up, slowed down, slapped Roger on the shoulder, then continued. Roger hesitated, then hurried after his friend. Carla watched Roger gaining on the other boy, watched the ease with which his legs kept up the pace, watched the swing of his arms. God had answered his prayers!

Carla tried to run. Her feet were weighted down as if with mud, her knees trembled, she moved a dozen paces, tripped over a rock, and fell. *God does not like me,* she concluded. She picked herself up, brushed off the dirt and went to the barn, past the old horse to the very back and hid her tears.

※❦※

The school year began, and Carla sat alone at her desk. Roger had a seat at the back of the room where the desks were larger. Once in a while he spoke to her, and she answered. Her birthday came and Christmas came and the snow melted and Carla did her lessons and showed off how clever she was, but she had no friends. Roger was a stranger, a wonderful stranger.

The school year ended, and one day in June, Aunt Beulah received a letter saying that Carla should be prepared to move. It's for the best, thought the woman. Carla accepted the news without comment, without hope.

"Where do you suppose?" asked Aunt Beulah.

Carla shrugged her shoulders. "When shall I pack?" she asked.

In a way this lack of interest was for the best, inasmuch as Aunt Beulah had not been told where Carla was to be taken. She never was told; the social workers said it wouldn't do for foster parents to have any future concern, but she always thought about the children's fate. She wondered about Carla, would have liked to know where she was being taken, in a way felt sorry for her, felt sorry for even this sullen piece of soiled goods. But what would be, would be and heaven only knew what they'd send her next. "You pack on Monday," she said.

❦

"Ticket to Megunnaway for this child," Miss Cunningham spoke sharply to the stationmaster.

"Megunnaway!" Carla, startled out of her mournful silence, repeated the name aloud. It was a strange sounding name to be sure, but to a Maine-bred child such names are not all that strange, though admired for the way they trip off the tongue.

"How old's the kid?" The stationmaster pointed his pen accusingly at Miss Cunningham.

"Ten."

"Looks thirteen."

"Ten. Well, ten and a half but still half-fare. Now you know," she went on archly, "I wouldn't deceive you."

"Hmmph!" said the man, who detested artful females. But who ever heard of a state bureaucrat trying to keep down costs? "Okay, okay!" Anything to be rid of her.

Carla sat staring at the ticket which Miss Cunningham thrust in her hand before hurrying off in a swish of gray skirt. Megunnaway! Carla got up and went outside. The resonant whistle came floating across the open space, the black giant train whooshed into the station. Hissing steam poured its fog from underneath, passengers looked out the windows of the first car, several Bangor and Aroostook freight cars moved slowly by. The blue-coated conductor was beckoning her, and when she stood stock-still, he came over and looked at her ticket. "Your train, Miss," he said. He hurried back to the passenger car, and Carla followed. He stopped, and the hills of all the Hambledons reverberated with his mighty shout, "Alll Aboaaard!"

"Wait, wait," came a shrill boyish cry. Roger jumped out of a racing sulky drawn by a skittish horse, threw the reins over a post, and came running toward Carla, who stood upon the step.

"You going on this train?" the conductor asked.

"No, no, just—"

"Then I don't see no cause to wait. All aboooard, up with you, Miss."

"Carla, Carla," Roger cried. "I've come to say good-bye!"

"Hey kid," shouted the stationmaster, "you'd better get that horse before it says good-bye to you."

Roger turned, ran, caught the reins, tied the horse more securely. The train had started, slowly at first, then gathering speed. Roger ran alongside. Carla had found a seat by the window, she saw him, she was waving. "Forgive me," he shouted. "I've been wrong. Don't forget me!" But he knew she hadn't heard a word he said. Dispiritedly he went back to the horse.

Carla sat close to the window. Megunnaway! The town from which Mama had been writing of late. Oh it couldn't be. "Mama, Mama," she said softly to herself. She hadn't seen her mother for almost two years. She closed her eyes and pictured her mother as she had looked that last day, a little woman with her hair carefully piled high, an elegant lady in a lavender dress with long skirt and puffed sleeves. A worried woman too. Carla opened her eyes and watched the land roll by. They rode alongside swift-moving rivers, through towns, through a dark forest of pine. There flashed by a field of white daisies in bloom, a tremendous field, and beyond it a house and big red barn and in the foreground those daisies waving in the slow moving breeze. How fresh and clean they were. Once she and Roger had picked daisies; if she were in the field she'd pick one. There was a silly counting game, he loves me, he loves me not. Roger, yes, Roger had come to say good-bye. Good-bye forever.

Hardly daring to breathe she sat there for hours. Finally the conductor's voice rang through the coach. "Megunnaway, change for Dover. This train for Sagamore, Reheboth, and Dedham Falls. Megunnaway, coming into Megunnaway, change for Dover."

They were slowing down. They slid past a two-storied, many-windowed gray building with a big sign "Megunnaway Cotton Mills." Then they were alongside a river which flashed cool in the hot summer sun. They rumbled over a trestle, they crossed a street guarded with a black and white gate. They pulled into the station. Carla came down the high step and stood on the platform looking for her mother, but Abigail was not there. A woman was coming toward her; maybe her mother had sent her. The woman was short and heavyset; she was wearing a faded blue cotton dress given shape by a white canvas apron tied about her waist. Her hair was drawn up to the top of her head in an untidy knot. She paused and wiped her face on her apron, then came closer.

"Carla, Carla!" the woman cried. "I'm here, don't you know me?"

Carla stood still and waited as Abigail embraced her eagerly. Carla shuddered in fear and distaste.

"Merciful heavens!" cried Abigail. "Don't you know it's me, your mother?"

The child relaxed her muscles, but deep inside the tension remained. She saw her mother with a stranger's eyes, worse, with the eyes of a disappointed dreamer. Abigail picked up the suitcase. Silently they walked along. At the end of the street, up a hill, not far away, Carla could see an imposing brick building with wide steps, big white door, and a clock tower. "What's that?" she asked.

"The library," Abigail answered proudly. "We're living in town now, not out in the country twenty miles from nowhere. We turn here, down this street." She led the way along a narrow street past a couple of small shops.

"I'm so grateful, I've so many things to be thankful for," the woman went on. "That library with more books than I can ever read, and the hills, see them there, and the church, oh we've the nicest church, and a school for you, and you here at last. Oh my heart sings a song of praise! Oh how I thank God. And I have a job, a place to stay."

Yes, it was her mother, thought Carla, her talkative mother. "Where are we going?" she asked.

"To the boarding house where I work. I'm a dishwasher there, the lowest of the low," she said, "but you mustn't mind. I don't." And indeed her tone was cheerful enough.

They came to the Pine Tree Inn, an old three-story building to which several additions had been made. The pine tree in the yard was exactly as tall as the house, the lawn was neatly clipped, and low evergreens grew around the base of the building. There were no flowers. There was a broad porch and a big front door, but Abigail went around to the back.

They went up a dark stairway, Abigail dragging the suitcase, bumpety bump up the stairs. The hall at the top with doors every few feet reminded Carla of the jail where she'd spent her last night with her mother. Abigail took a key from her pocket and let them into one of the rooms which was hardly as big as that in the jail. But they were not locked in, and the window had brightly striped drapes which matched the bedspreads, and on the walls were three old friends, the pictures Faith and Hope and El Greco's "Toledo." On a table near one of the beds was the work basket.

"See," Abigail exulted. "Faith, Hope, and Charity. It's home, my darling."

Carla stood looking around. A tall chest of drawers, a straight chair beside each bed, a table some two feet by four and a small easy chair covered with the same striped material as the bedspreads completed the room's furniture. Abigail looked at a battered alarm clock on the table. "Oh, it's time to go. Tonight," she went on to explain, "we're eating with the boarders. Mrs. Hembonny, she's the boss lady here, said we might. Usually we eat in the kitchen a little before. But come, follow me. No, wait, here's the bathroom. You must wash, your towel is there on the bed, and I will comb my hair."

When at last Abigail led her daughter into the dining room, the boarders had already assembled, some twenty of them, around a long table. A stout, tightly corseted woman in a loose pongee dress with colorful embroidered flowers came to meet them. "I'm Mrs. Hembonny," she introduced herself. "Little Carla, Abbie, you two sit here. Now Louise—"

A younger woman of majestic build, about six feet tall and broad of shoulder, stood up, tossed her wavy dark hair back from her face, raised her hands, and led them in a song.

"For she's a jolly good fellow,
Which nobody can deny."

Lest there be any misunderstanding they sang it twice over, once for Abigail and once for Carla.

There was a great clapping of hands and a demand that Abigail speak. The little woman brushed back a strand of hair and a tear and said, "If you don't mind, I'll just lead us in grace. For Your many blessings, Lord, we offer psalms of thanksgiving. We thank Thee, Lord, for bringing Carla here, and for the beautiful welcome. Bless the food we eat, bless the fellowship of this table. Hear us, God, and grant us Thy protection. Amen."

Whispers of admiration ran up and down the table. They had known all along that there was something special about Abbie, the dishwasher. The twenty boarders were ten men and ten woman, none related to any of the others, but most of them employed at one or the other of the two textile mills. Louise was a weaver at the Megunnaway Mill.

Though it was her special night, Abigail had her work to do, and it was past nine when she joined Carla in their room. The child lay on the bed half asleep, but Abigail was too excited to feel fatigue.

"Oh my darling," she cried, "in no time we'll have a place, a house, an old one no doubt, but oh we will. As soon as I get a better job. And then we can send for Howard."

"Howard," the child repeated thoughtfully. "Yes, Howard."

"And you'll go to school, and when you're through high school, you'll go to college. I don't know how we'll manage, but you will, and you'll get work in some profession, and in time you'll marry well. Oh this is just the first step."

Overwhelmed by her dream, she grew silent. Oh she had ambition for Carla, not for money, not for power, but certainly for status. And that meant education, a profession, preferably teaching. Medicine was not for the fastidious, preaching was not for girls, though a missionary to far countries living in danger and on the ragged side of nothing—oh she would take pride in that. To other professions she gave no thought. Certainly if she could have heard of Carla's announced intention of some day becoming governor, she would have thought that impossible and as unladlylike as a female wrestler. Miss Abbott's profession was dignified, she could see that, but it didn't seem right for Carla.

Carla lay there and listened, hardly able to take it all in. Had you asked her was she happy, she would have said yes, of course, happy to be back with Mama, happy at having escaped Tomcat and Miss Cunningham and the Hubbards. But Mama was a stranger.

Early in the morning Abigail went down to her work and somewhat later Carla followed. As she entered the kitchen, she heard a harsh voice. Her mother was being chewed out by Mrs. Hembonny for some dereliction. Carla saw Abigail hang her head and promise to do better, and she learned what a very humble position they occupied.

After breakfast she got permission to go for a walk and went out to the main street where men and women and children were moving briskly along the sidewalk. In front of the feed store platform stood a one-horse wagon into which a stout woman in overalls was throwing sacks of grain. Next to it was a grocery store with glistening red paint and gleaming glass and two young women in light summer dresses going in. Beyond the grocery store was the Bijou Theatre where a young man was examining the billboard in front of the door. Maybe she could go to the movies some time. Up one street she saw the library. She could go there, but she'd wait until her mother could go with her. She saw stores, the railroad station, houses. She saw two churches, the Methodist Episcopal, a white frame building wth a neat steeple, and the Catholic Church made of red brick and surmounted by several towers, each decorated with a golden cross. Mama would take her to the white church. How peaceful it looked.

She went back to the library, peeked in, and was awed by the vast number of books. She ran down the steps and resumed her walk. On a side street she found Blodgett Shoddy Mill, a square three-story building throbbing with power-driven machinery. Suddenly the air was rent by a shrill whistle. Men and women came rushing out of the building, for it was the noon hour. It was scary, out there with strangers, men and women who seemed not to see her and a little girl who ran away when Carla spoke to her. It was like being invisible.

But she was not invisible. The Methodist minister, peering out of his window, had known at once who she was. He would have gone out to greet her, but he'd had a bit of a headache that morning and was still in his robe. He'd see her on Sunday, or if he dressed hurriedly, he might meet her somewhere in the street. His warm heart was filled with the deepest sympathy for the mother. Poor woman, trying to raise a child in that boarding house. He had to go to the drugstore anyway. He hurried into his clothes, then went out, but Carla had disappeared.

Having used the drugstore as an excuse for meeting the child, he felt it only honest to go there. He was a tall, rawboned young man, with strong, square features, and sandy hair somewhat in need of a haircut, which he didn't have time for that particular day; he never had time for all the things he had to do. He was an excitable man and most conscientious. He felt the deepest pity for all his parishioners, even those who were happy. He had been in this mill town a couple of years now and had several millworkers in his congregation. He considered a job in a factory a sad fate and busied himself with studies of labor laws, laws which he longed to improve. So far he had found no such opportunity. There was no trade union in the town. And he had little communion with others of the cloth, for the only other minister of Christ was the Catholic priest, an amiable old man who left mundane problems to God, was said to hear confessions with compassion, but who merely sighed whenever the younger minister sought to discuss with him the social problems of the day. He wasn't even concerned about the horribly lax enforcement of the prohibition laws. Yet he was a good man, was Father Shaughnessy, and the young minister was delighted when he saw the priest coming toward him.

"Good morning, Mr. Acheson," puffed the old man, who was portly and easily grew short of breath.

"A fine morning, Father Shaughnessy, a fine day."

The two men stopped at the street corner. "You look as if you bore upon your shoulders all the cares of the world," said the priest.

Rev. Acheson laughed. "The cares of this one town would be enough," he said.

"It's not that bad, not that bad."

"My dear people!" the minister went on. "Their hearts are so good. And such faith, such abiding faith. They work so hard but have so little."

"If they worked less and had more, would they be better people?"

"They'd be better educated, they'd find more interesting jobs, they'd have better homes."

"Come, come, you must not succumb to worldly ambitions."

"As for myself, I'm content to live in poverty, to be a humble soldier of the Cross."

"I believe you, my son. Be not ambitious for them. They have their daily bread. Again I ask, if they worked less and had more, would they be better people?"

"I doubt it."

Yet because the priest was an honest and humble man, he added, "Yet I confess it grieves me that we have no Christian school here for the children."

Rev. Acheson went on, "Right now I'm worried about one of my people."

"And why are you worried, if you wouldn't be violating any confidence?"

"It's Mrs. Wingate. She's brought her daughter, a child of maybe twelve or so, to live with her. She's the dishwasher at the Twin Pines, you know. I doubt it's a wholesome environment."

It so happened that Louise had been that morning to confession, and as always she talked not only of her sins, of which she always repented, but also of all her concerns, and she had spoken of Carla.

"That little girl is guarded," said the priest, "and guarded well by one who knows both good and evil."

"Her mother?"

"She knows good, I have no doubt of that. But I spoke of one of the boarders. I think I violate no confidence when I ask if you know Louise Vigue?"

"Yes," said Mr. Acheson. "And I'm not reassured."

"I am. She's trying to find a mill job that the woman, who's not very strong you know, a job that she could do."

"That hardly seems the answer. I'm sure she has ambitions above the deadening routine of a textile mill."

The priest looked hard at him. "Were you planning to take up nudism?" he asked.

"Certainly not." Acheson tried to turn it into a joke. "Certainly not in this climate."

"Then you'd do well to be grateful for textile mills."

The priest was silent for a minute. "I wonder," he said changing his tone, "if you know anything about roses? Several of mine are nothing but dead sticks."

"I've never studied flowers. I don't have time for a hobby."

"I'll try at the library. Good day, my brother in Christ." The old man stretched out his hand. There was a warm pressing of the flesh and they parted. *That young man could use a hobby,* thought the old priest as he walked toward the library. *His father, he told me once, was a college professor; while mine, dear man, was a digger of ditches, a construction laborer. So naturally I'm more conservative than he. It's too bad he'll soon be moving on, those Methodists always are. Though for one so restless, perhaps it's better.* The priest's mind went back to his own parishioners, particularly Louise, whom he'd dearly love to help in her battle with sin, for he hated the sin and loved the sinner. He hoped the library had a book on roses.

As for the Rev. Acheson, he kept thinking about Abigail and the girl, even into the Sunday School meeting that afternoon. They were deep in discussion of plans not only for the summer but for the fall as well—what books to order, what other supplies, what did he think of cards to mail to absentees, were pins for attendance in accord with the will of God, and where on earth were they going to find enough teachers for all the classes.

"There's one possibility we've, er, perhaps overlooked," the minister began.

"Yes?" The speaker was Mrs. Pomeroy, the Sunday School Superintendent. She was a dignified middle-aged woman, with a rather loud voice which she tried, when she remembered, to modulate. She was the Principal at the Elementary School and the wife of the owner of the local hardware store.

"I'm thinking of Abigail Wingate," said the minister.

"The dishwasher at the Pine Tree Inn?"

"Er, yes, at present. But she's had teacher training, has actually taught."

"It wouldn't do, I assure you, simply wouldn't do."

"I don't know," said a young woman, new in Megunnaway, having married into the town.

"Let us be realistic," said Mrs. Pomeroy. "What would our parents think? And quite frankly, what kind of rapport could she establish with the children? I mean, you've all seen her."

"What if she is a dishwasher?" Again the new young lady spoke.

"I think Mrs. Pomeroy is using good judgment," said another of the teachers.

"If you'd only give her a chance," insisted the young lady. "Why in the church where I was before—"

"That," said Mrs. Pomeroy, "was out West."

On Sunday, no one could have been kinder or more gracious to Abigail and her daughter than Mrs. Pomeroy. She even invited them to her house for tea, an invitation which Abigail, to Carla's great relief, declined. It was a wonderful church service, thought Carla, such joyful singing, and the responses, and the minister's deep voice, but next week she hoped they could skip Sunday School. She'd ask her mother, not now but when she knew her better.

FIVE

Abigail stood over the big tub, poured in more soap, whipped it to a suds, continued washing the cups, her hands moving in patient rhythm. She fought back the dizziness of fatigue, finished the luncheon dishes and began the baking pans. She started to hum "Let the Lower Lights Be Burning," but neither work nor song could distract her from thoughts about Carla. November had set in, and Carla had, Abigail hoped, fitted into her niche at Megunnaway Grammar School.

"I'm somewhat concerned," Mrs. Pomeroy had said earlier. "Oh she whizzes through the tests, but she doesn't do her homework." But if she whizzes through the tests, thought Abigail, perhaps the homework is mere busywork. Mrs. Pomeroy had gone on. "And she talks too much in class, oh not rudely, she's always polite and obedient, but the other students—" She had paused and Abigail felt again her own questioning silence. "She doesn't make friends." Mrs. Pomeroy had sounded accusing. "Oh I realize she has no place for the girls to come to play, but when they invite her, she never accepts. She goes mooning about town, they tell me, and out into the country. She needs a more normal social life."

Abigail had promised to talk to Carla. *I could talk to a brick wall,* she thought. *Sure she needs a more normal social life; I need a million dollars.* She seized the soup pot and banged it into the sink, then glanced at the clock. Carla was long overdue. She felt her knees tremble. What might she be up to now?

She stepped outside and looked up and down the street. Indian summer was over, the sky was gray, the wind foretold a storm. What could be worse than rain in November! She went back to the kitchen, finished the dishes, took up her task of potato peeling. What on earth had become of Carla? What had she done? Where had she gone? So high-spirited, so daring! She'd always been, even as a child—that time under the horse's hoofs, the many days in the brook jumping from slippery stone to slippery stone in water over her head, that game of seeing how many times she could run back and forth before an approaching car. Luckily the traffic had been light. And Howard had restrained her. He'd been the cautious one. Another potato done, the cook grabbed them, she must work faster.

Carla had left the schoolyard at the usual time, but she did not go directly home. She was quite aware that she was being disobedient, but it caused her neither fear nor remorse. She'd grown used to her mother, guessed she loved her. She walked sedately along the sidewalk and sought a favorite knoll overlooking the river. Below she could see whitecaps rippling on the usually placid ribbon of water. Carla ran down a narrow path to the rocky riverbank. It was warmer there than on the ridge and she threw off her coat. Finding a flat rock she skipped it over the water, then another, but the second sank, and a third did little better. She took off her shoes and waded in the shoal, skipping flat rocks, throwing big round ones with a splash. "I could swim the river," she thought.

Abigail grew more and more uneasy as Carla failed to appear. Bob Nelson the kitchen helper came running in shouting excitedly. "She's in the river," he cried. "Carla! Help!"

Abigail dropped her knife and ran out. Louise and Matt Jellico were just returning from work. "Where? Where?" cried Louise, but she didn't ask who, for she'd seen Abigail's distraught face.

Bob, a lanky brown youth, dashed off. Louise and Matt were close behind and Abigail came laboring after. A half mile up the river in the midst of the whitecaps and headed for the opposite shore was the swimmer, tossed about and struggling. Abigail ran fully clothed to the river and would have jumped in had not Louise caught her round the waist and held her. "Get a boat," the big woman shouted. "Where on earth are all the boats?"

Matt and Bob had found a battered rowboat and were furiously propelling it toward Carla, who saw it, waved in a gesture which no one could interpret, and swam on. Suddenly she was caught by an eddy and swept downstream. The rowers were gaining on her but the river was broad. She turned as if to swim back toward the boat, and Abigail shivering with the cold and still squirming to free herself from Louise's grip, saw the girl turn and she shouted, "No, no, the shore is nearer, the shore is nearer."

"She can't hear you," said Louise.

Abigail gave up the tussle and hid her face in Louise's bosom. When she looked up, she saw Carla standing in the water by the shore, her wet dress clinging to her body and her hair plastered close to her head. She was dancing up and down and laughing! It was starting to rain, great heavy drops. Carla got into the boat, allowed herself to be wrapped in Jellico's coat, and sat close to him as he rowed.

The boat returned safely, and Carla was in great spirits. "I did it!" she cried. "I could have swum back."

Even the scolding she got from Louise—only Louise for Abigail had no spirit left for anger—made no impression.

The months passed, and Carla did nothing even approaching the outrageous. She did her homework, and she kept their room neat, and she read. And Saturdays she'd go out with the little Mills children and go sliding down the steep hill, coming home singing, healthy and happy. Abigail was almost relaxed with her. She began to think about Howard, her neglected child whom she hadn't seen for years. He'd be a big boy by now, quite tall, no doubt. He said so little in his letters, and they came so seldom. They must visit him. Carla was nonchalant about it.

It was not until the following August that they set out on the trip. Abigail's natural optimism took over, and she hoped great vague things from this encounter. They rode on, each with her nose in a book. Abigail had suggested reading aloud, but Carla had demurred, saying, "People will look at us!" After dark the conductor dimmed the lights, helped them tilt back their seats, advised them to try to catch a wink. And indeed they did catch a wink.

Before the sun had risen, they were climbing down the steps at an isolated flagstop where a small tousle-headed boy stood, undoubtedly Howard. He took charge of them like a bantie rooster in a flock of big hens.

"We have to go to the school for a while," he said, "because there ain't no one up at the house this early." The eastern horizon was faintly tinged with pink and blue, the crescent of the moon was white in the distant sky, stars lingered. Far away they heard the crow of a rooster and then the lowing of a cow. They came to a small white building set in a grove of oak trees. Howard proudly drew the doorkey from his pocket and let them in. "I have a job cleaning up here, and I'm already supposed to be getting ready for the school's opening." The room was cold and damp and so dark they could see nothing. The flick of a switch gave them light.

"This is my desk." Howard led them to one in the middle of the room. "See, the lid raises. Some of them don't. I'm going into the sixth grade."

"I'll be in the eighth," said Carla.

"Okay, so you're a brain."

He could have forgotten about not being a brain if only he had had a little more body. Yes, his sister was bigger and taller than he, but softer. He flexed his muscle for her, and she didn't even try to compete. From his desk he produced a brown paper bag and drew out some crackers. "They're not expecting you for another hour," he said. "We can eat these."

A fine thing, thought Abigail. They could have gotten up an hour early to welcome their guests. However what mattered was Howard. True he'd grown hardly at all, but he was so capable for a young boy. Impulsively she swept him into her arms. The hug at the railroad landing had been perfunctory; this was warm and real, and he clung to her. At last they both drew back.

"I brought some oranges," she said.

He scored the oranges with his jackknife. Carla thought she'd never before had oranges with such a fine aroma, nor crackers quite so crisp. They ate together and grew closer and were one family.

"Mama," said Howard with a sudden show of determination, "why can't I be with Papa?"

Abigail was silent. She had started something she could no longer control, now that the State had control of her children. "Aren't you happy here?" she asked.

Howard's pale face flushed. "Why did you do it?" he cried. "Why aren't we on the farm where we belong?"

Abigail bent her head upon the desk and wept, while Carla just sat there.

"Now I've done it," the boy said disgustedly. "Well, I may as well do my work."

The three worked industriously, and by midmorning the room was swept and mopped, the windows polished, the woodstove blacked, the woodwork washed, and even the desks had had the thickest of the dirt scrubbed off.

"It ain't never been so clean," exulted Howard.

"We'd better go to where you live," said Abigail. "They'll miss you."

"No, they won't."

"Why of course they will," said Abigail, but Carla understood and felt close to her brother.

Mrs. Staples, the bustling lady of the house, greeted them cordially but without surprise at their delay. They had cookies and tea, with milk for the children. Back and forth the women batted the small talk, while Carla and Howard sat quietly at the table. The talk advanced, the two women getting along famously. Soon they were discussing the topics current in the newspapers, and Abigail had a copy of the latest Bangor paper. Big news was a threatened coal strike.

"President Coolidge will know what to do," said Mrs. Staples. "He's a man you can trust. Much more so than that Harding."

"Oh yes, I'm sure," agreed Abigail. "Do you think Harding knew about that graft, do you really think he did?"

"Of course he must have," and Mrs. Staples went on to develop her views.

How wonderful it was, thought Abigail, to be talking like this, talking politics. Why she hadn't talked a word of politics since she had left the farm, and oh how she and Josiah had gone over the daily paper, what decided ideas they'd had. Agreeing or arguing, she wasn't sure which had been the best. That was in the irretrievable past, yet not completely in the past, for here she was talking the same way with this woman.

"You children are no doubt bored stiff," said Mrs. Staples.

Abigail agreed. "Why don't you children run out and play?"

She looked after the children as they left. In a minute she and Mrs. Staples were happily discussing the details being unearthed by the Senate Committee which was investigating certain scandals having to do with oil fields. They leaned over the table, spoke in hushed tones, poured more tea, reaffirmed their belief that President Coolidge was clean as a hound's tooth, repeated their doubts about his predecessor, heaped scorn on sundry cabinet members, drank more tea, and thoroughly enjoyed themselves.

Howard and Carla wandered across the field and into the woods. Birds were chirping softly, the birch trees glistened white, their green leaves at motion even in the quiet air. The few pine trees appeared almost black by contrast. Carla saw a flash of water and hurried toward the brook, but Howard was there ahead of her. She could no longer run faster than he; indeed she hadn't run at all, had just quickened her walking pace. They skipped rocks on the water where it formed a pool, and they took off their shoes and socks to wade in the shallows. The sun filtered through the branches of the closely crowded trees and made a pattern on the water. They heard a splash and saw a long-legged green frog diving into a pool.

"Do you still have that green bottle?" Howard asked.

"Oh I've always kept that, at Aunt Beulah's and even when they took me to Tomcat's."

"Tomcat's?"

She could not tell him. "Once I dropped it, nicked it a little at the top."

"If anything ever happens to it, I'll find you another," he said, and it was the greatest promise he could have made.

They splashed in the water and climbed trees and lay down on the damp ground to rest. "I hope Mama gets you back with us," said Carla.

"And I'll tell you what," said Howard, "once I'm there, we'll go to see Papa."

"How can we?"

"We'll hitchhike. I've a map. I've figured it out. I could go from here, but Megunnaway is nearer. Besides, there'd be two of us."

"Mama wouldn't let us."

"Of course not, silly. Don't you say one word about it."

They returned to the house. Carla's dress was muddy and Howard's clothing in no better condition. They took the expected scolding with fortitude, for their real wickedness, which was the plan to go to Papa, remained concealed.

The next day the little family went again to the school, not so much because they had to work there as from a desire to be alone together. However the work was a welcome shield. The desks got another going over. The grass around the building got clipped right down to the ground and was just finished when a burst of rain drove them indoors.

Great black clouds blew across the sky so that although it was two o'clock in the afternoon, the room became dark. A fierce wind lashed the trees, the sky grew darker, the rain increased. It pelted the roof, it flattened the grass, it dripped off the eaves, and the family in the schoolhouse looked out the window in awe. Then there came a giant flash, chain lightning in jagged path across the sky. Almost immediately the thunder crashed above them.

"That was close," murmured Abigail. "Get away from the window."

She tried to interest them in playing games on the blackboard but with no success. She wasn't even interested herself. They were at the window again, jumping back at the flash of lightning, cowering at a desk during the crash of thunder, but back at the window almost immediately. It was tremendous, a demonstration of the might of God. There was another flash of lightning, and Abigail stood there, no longer frightened, only excited. Never before had she seen such brilliant light, such deep purple sky.

"See, see!" cried Howard. A ball of fire rolled along the road, not far from the oak tree. "Ball lightning."

Abigail had never seen it before. Fear had been dissolved by the glory of the storm, which lasted in all its fury for some twenty minutes, though there were no more balls of lightning in the road, only the long jagged chains which ripped across the sky and the tremendous crash of the thunder. The storm ended as abruptly as it had started, and the sun shone out upon a dazzling world of iridescent raindrops.

"It's a good omen," said Abigail. "Oh it means something special, I know it does."

"Does it mean you'll get me back?" asked Howard.

"I've no place."

"I can sleep on the floor. I can work. I'm small but I'm strong. I'm dumb but I know lots of things."

Abigail drew him close to her. "My dear, dear son," she said and the tears steamed her glasses.

Dark was just settling over the road when they set out for the train. They waited at the flagstop, in the midst of nowhere.

"What if he doesn't stop?" said Howard. "Then you couldn't leave."

But the engineer high in his cab waved knowingly at Howard and braked his train to a dead standstill. Abigail hugged Howard and climbed the steps. "Come, come, Carla," she called.

Carla hugged her brother, kissed him, and clung to him.

"You have to go," the boy said firmly. As she left, he whispered to her, "I get awful lonesome, Carla. Don't forget me."

The conductor dragged her up the steps, pushed her into the coach, not roughly but with due concern for the train's schedule. By the time they had found their seats and looked out the window to see Howard, he was a very small figure standing there by the railroad track, waving gently and sadly.

"Will we really get him back with us, Mama?" asked Carla.

Abigail burst into tears. She could only hope and pray.

❧❦

The change in their fortunes would come, Abigail firmly believed, through Carla. Perhaps this is it, she said to herself as one winter day Carla went crunching through the snow to the City Hall for the annual grand competition of the Central Maine Learning League. The Learning League was the brainchild of Mrs. Pomeroy. Using her persuasive powers on the local School Board, she had succeeded in setting up an annual scholastic competition, which had become quite an event in Megunnaway. Megunnaway won the first year, but in the eight years since it had been forced to settle for second or worse.

Finally the School Board began shuffling its feet, wondering if the contest should be discontinued, but two things had happened to strengthen Mrs. Pomeroy's hand. It was Megunnaway's turn to be host, and Carla Wingate had come to town. It was Eva Wilmont who recognized the difference Carla made. Eva Wilmont was that young lady from the West who saw no reason why a dishwasher couldn't be a Sunday School teacher. She was also the latest addition to Mrs. Pomeroy's staff and, by default, the coach for the Megunnaway Learning League team. She assured Mrs. Pomeroy that Carla would give Megunnaway the edge.

"I hope you're not letting your fondness for her influence your judgment," said Mrs. Pomeroy.

"I'm not fond of her. She's an obnoxious smarty pants."

"Mrs. Wilmont, your expressions are unprofessional."

"She needs to be challenged," said the younger woman, ignoring the rebuke.

Obnoxious smarty pantses don't need to be challenged, thought Mrs. Pomeroy, they need to be spanked, but she abruptly censored her thoughts. "Can she win?" she asked. "Will she be calm under pressure? Will she care enough to try?"

Eva Wilmont hesitated, then leaned forward. "If she's on the team, she'll pull it through, and she'll win the individual prize." To herself she vowed to make it come true.

It took some doing on the teacher's part to even get Carla to enter the contest. If she wins, thought Mrs. Wilmont, it'll be through native brilliance, certainly not hard work. But at home Carla *was* working, studying all the things the teacher gave her, practicing the spelling, the math, and the grammar lessons, reading history and geography books until she was swollen with names and dates and longitudes and latitudes.

She went alone to the City Hall that frosty morning. Abigail could have gotten leave, but Carla had made it clear she didn't want her to.

There were six members on each of the eight teams. The first two hours were spent eliminating the duds. By then it was clear that there were two outstanding individual contenders, Carla and a stout boy named Henry from Dover. At every opportunity Eva Wilmont whispered advice to Carla. Carla ignored her. Still all went well until the middle of the History Rapid Quiz. "Who was the first European child born in America?" asked the Master of Ceremonies, a Professor of History from a nearby college. He stifled a yawn and waited.

Carla looked at him, knowing she was supposed to say "Virginia Dare." For a moment she thought she would, but some indwelling imp got the upper hand, and she cried in a distinct and arrogant voice, "It was Snorri Thorfinnson!"

She glanced around and could see Mrs. Wilmont hiding her face in her hands, could see the scowl on Mrs. Pomeroy's face, and she felt both righteous and deliciously wicked. Roger's grandfather had told her about Snorri Thorfinnson, and he knew, but of course it wasn't what they wanted. The three judges exchanged glances. What on earth! Before they could render their thumbs down signal they heard the Master of Ceremony's hearty laugh. They thought he'd never stop. "She's right, you know!" he cried. "Who'd have thought a child from Megunnaway would be possessed of that bit of esoteric historical lore?"

"And why not a child from Megunnaway?" Mrs. Pomeroy was on her feet, shouting and gesticulating in a manner neither professional nor ladylike.

The contest continued, Dover and Megunnaway neck and neck, Henry and Carla eyeing each other like boxers. It was tied, and there was the final essay which the six surviving students had to write. "I tried to get that one out," whispered Mrs. Pomeroy to Mrs. Wilmont. "How can they really judge?"

The remaining contestants were told, a last minute announcement, to write on the subject "Art." There was no explanation, just that broad-as-the-ocean subject. "I know something about that Henry boy," Mrs. Wilmont confided. "Last summer his folks took him to Europe."

That clinched it, the two teachers were sure. But lo and behold, Carla won. And Megunnaway won! Though they were sure there was some mistake, Mrs. Pomeroy and Mrs. Wilmont cheered wildly. Megunnaway had won, exulted Mrs. Pomeroy. "I told you so," said the irrepressible young lady from the West.

Soon Carla was on the platform having her picture taken with Henry the runner-up, and with her team, with all the teachers at Megunnaway Grammar and half a dozen other town notables. Mrs. Pomeroy and Mrs. Wilmont were sidelined for a moment, and they'd been entrusted with Carla's essay. They huddled in a corner to read it. "'Storm over Toledo,' by El Greco," Mrs. Pomeroy read. "Now where could she have seen such a painting?"

Together they scanned it, picking up phrases, "The dark melancholy of that painting, the winding road, the gray stone buildings, their Gothic towers, the light behind the blue-black clouds, and in the foreground the yellow-green of the grass. The mood of the scene, both terrifying and exhilirating, the dark spots of life."

"I didn't realize," said Mrs. Pomeroy, "how academically gifted she really is. And so poor. Some way must be found for her to go to college."

"It's a long time," said Eva. "A way will open."

"Ways don't just open. And what if the child when the time comes doesn't want to go on? It's by no means sure. Why my son absolutely refused, went and became a lumberjack."

Eva knew enough not to ask if he were academically gifted.

"My daughter did get her degree in music," Mrs. Pomeroy added, "but married a tone-deaf minister."

"Girls are more tractable," suggested Eva.

"Is this one?"

"Well, no, I guess not," Eva admitted.

"For starters, she needs a better home environment. We have to help."

Eva Wilmont knew exactly what Mrs. Pomeroy meant. Eva must nudge her husband, Brad Wilmont, Personnel Manager for Blodgett Shoddy Mill, must nudge him, nag him, do whatever it took, until he found Abigail Wingate some kind of job. And it had better be a good one. Eva sighed. Brad wouldn't like it.

A few days later Abigail came plowing through the snow, in her right hand fear, in her left hand resolve, moving slowly toward the Blodgett Shoddy Mill. Horrible name, she thought, but accurate. It would be no disgrace to work there; the name didn't mean the product was inferior, just that the mill used not only new woolen and cotton thread but also reclaimed wool. Still she couldn't abide the word shoddy. Old Mr. Blodgett, Brad Wilmont's uncle and owner of the mill, was a stickler for truth, too much so, an old curmudgeon. She hoped she wouldn't have to talk to him. Half a block from the building, a square, four-storied structure which seemed at some time past to have been painted brown, she could hear the rumble of the machinery, she could see the narrow door through which she would have to pass.

She tried to think of an inspirational verse to help her, but her unruly mind dredged up only: "And was Jerusalem builded here Among these dark Satanic mills?" This dark Satanic mill. There was something about "my chariot of fire," but she had no chariot of fire, only a terrible need which pushed her on. Every day saw a widening gulf between her and Carla. If they had a home, it would be different. What was the wildness within that girl, what was the loneliness? For herself she'd settled into the life at Twin Pines, her body was equal to the task, she'd come to see even the worst of the boarders as God's struggling children, she'd learned to shrug off Mrs. Hembonny's insulting reprimands. But she had to make a home for Carla, and she had to get Howard back. She sighed, squeezed through the heavy entrance, kicked the snow from her overshoes, then hesitantly shuffled through an open door. There behind a cluttered desk sat Brad Wilmont. He was a big, round-faced fellow with a smiling mouth and watchful eyes.

"Oh," he said gruffly, "you did come."

"I hope I'm not late."

"Oh no." He was silent for a moment summing her up, noting the worn coat, the graying hair, the weary face, the eagerness in the brown eyes behind the old-fashioned wire-rimmed glasses. "You know I didn't promise anything," he said. Oh yes, she knew.

He turned her over to a gloomy old man who led her into the mill proper. The noise billowed over her, and for a moment she could hear nothing the man was saying. Frightened right down to the soles of her old-fashioned shoes, she held fast to her purpose, and her prayers for strength and courage were answered. With head held high she followed the man's brown shoulders past the banging looms, which seemed about to burst from their moorings to take after her like dragons. What tremendous machines to be restrained by mere men and women, large women to be sure, and muscular men, tending those swiftly moving machines with an amazing nonchalance.

Past the looms she went and down a flight of stairs, up which floated the sickening smell of old rags. They went into the sorting room where two women were busily picking over what seemed like tons of old clothes and blankets, separating them, the man explained, according to the type of fiber from which they were made. She could feel the vibration of the machines above; surely they would at any minute come crashing through the ceiling. But she had set her feet on the path, and she would not retreat. Yes, she could do the work, yes she could start in a week.

"Think it over and let me know," he said, and she could see that he expected her to back off. "I have thought it over," she replied. Mrs. Hembonny gave them permission to remain in the room and eat in the kitchen for two weeks after Abigail stopped washing dishes. Abigail was profoundly grateful. She went each day to work in the stuffy sorting room with the other women, sorting the rags, as she had been instructed, which, though they had been laundered, had strange smells of dyes and unidentifiable substances. Above, the giant machines crashed and thundered.

Every morning the sudden shriek of the whistle, a warning whistle first, and then the deadline whistle, called Abigail to her task. What a bad-tempered sound that whistle had! In the late afternoon when it dismissed the workers it had such a different sound! By then Abigail was so exhausted that before going home, even to the nearby Twin Pines, she had to sit on the factory steps for five or ten minutes. Once Brad saw her there and asked if she were ill, whereupon she assured him that she was fine, had just sat down to tie her shoelace, then got up and hurried away lest some bad fortune follow her having been caught resting.

SIX

Bone weary after a week at the mill, Abigail was not discouraged. She had been paid; Brad Wilmont had written a "To Whom it May Concern," stating that she was on Blodgett's payroll. Mrs. Pomeroy had lent her money, which she'd solemnly vowed to repay, come hail or high water. Ah yes, she had resources. They could find a house. She would tramp through the snowy streets, she would inquire at the post office, the library, she'd search until she dropped. For once Carla was working with her. Just as they were about to set out, Louise came bursting into their room. She'd prevailed upon a current friend to drive them house hunting, and he knew a place a bit out of town that might do. It proved to be a decrepit cabin with one room downstairs and two upstairs. There was a ramshackle shed in the rear, and in the kitchen they found a wood stove and kerosene lamps.

"We've used those before, haven't we, Carla?" said Abigail.

"Yes, yes," cried Carla, to whom even the inconveniences had a charm. And her mother! Why, in her excitement she looked almost pretty!

Water they could get from the well of the house next door or from the brook an eighth of a mile back through the woods. The downstairs had been papered by some unskilled hand using brown wrapping paper. In the upper rooms the barebone rafters of rough lumber were neither decorated nor insulated. It was partially furnished, with a rickety bed in each of the upper rooms and downstairs the rusty cookstove, a wooden sink, a pockmarked table with three chairs and, looking austere against one wall, a black horsehair sofa.

"A house, a real house!" Carla exclaimed. "Look at all the room outside."

They went out and walked around the house. The unfinished wood was weathered a deep brown. The bushes and weeds, indistinguishable with their snowy covering, grew close around the building, and Abigail was sure that all of them were flowering shrubs. The snow-covered fields glistened in the sun.

In back were tall trees, ice-coated deciduous trees forming a crystal filagree against the dark green of the snow-tipped evergreens. Abigail gave a sigh of deep contentment. A home, thank God, at last a home.

With the help of Louise and Alfred they moved in at once and by four o'clock were quite at home. The house was warmed by the wood fire, their clothing stored in boxes, and the pictures "Faith" and "Hope" graced the walls downstairs. Abigail placed the workbasket "Charity" on the table. The "Storm over Toledo" hung upstairs in Carla's room. She set the green bottle on an apple crate under it.

Abigail rejoiced as Carla went singing and dancing about the house, and cheerfully made countless trips to the next-door neighbors' to draw water from the well. The family were not complete strangers, for Mrs. Putnam and the daughter Elsa, two years younger than Carla, were occasional worshipers at the Methodist Church. The mother, Margaret, a tall angular woman, her fair hair tinged with gray, sincerity evidenced in every line of her freckled face, assured them that they were most welcome to water at her well. Barclay Putnam, dark and dour, was embarrassed by Abigail's profusive thanks. Elsa, dark, slender, and frolicsome, was turning cartwheels in the snow when first they went to the well. Delighted at having an audience, she continued till out of breath, then ran over and said gaily, "We'll be friends, oh I know we will." The son Ray was not at home.

Carla looked at Elsa and said nothing, emotion too deep for words welling up within her breast. Friends? She stared at Elsa and said nothing, only smiled wistfully. The house was located just beyond the built-up section of town and was a mile from the Blodgett Shoddy Mill. On Monday the wind whipped the snow in a veritable blizzard, and Abigail was sure she'd faint on the way, but bravely she set out. Sheer determination saw her through that day and those that followed. As she became used to the walk, it seemed to grow shorter, the fair days more frequent. By the time the last patch of snow had melted, she knew that this walk in the fresh air gave her the strength to work in the staleness of the sorting room and was essential to her well-being.

The Wingates and the Putnams were together enough to permit understanding and not enough to cause weariness. Margaret was an impassioned gardener and between times she tended four hives of bees, a score of chickens, and a cow. Barclay was working in another town where he stayed during the week, coming home only for the weekend. He was silent and withdrawn, often easing his pain with alcohol. Elsa was light of step, lithe of body, always running or climbing or turning cartwheels. One of her favorite pastimes was walking across the ridgepole of their barn, for she was absolutely without fear of heights. Carla was entranced. In a vague way Elsa admired Carla for winning the Learning League contest, but she wasn't overwhelmed by it, since she really didn't care that much about studies. But she admired Carla for more substantial reasons—the clever way she talked, her rosy cheeks, the dignity with which she moved, the graceful curves of her long legs.

Then there was the son Ray. At fifteen he was nearly six feet tall, broad-shouldered and muscular. With his wavy golden hair, his bright blue eyes, his regular features, and his pink cheeks, he was saved from prettiness by a strong jaw and the axle grease which never failed to streak his face and hands and clothing. He spent his spare time working on motors, mainly motorcycles. The barn was littered with parts, bits of a dozen bikes and so scattered that one could not say whether he had there the makings of one whole motorcycle or ten or maybe none. And in the midst moved Ray, whistling a tune, twisting the pieces about, assembling, filing, bolting and unbolting, pushing back his hair with his greasy hand, determined that he would get at least one complete, roaring, speeding motorcycle.

"He's the only boy I know," his mother said once to Abigail, "who can roll in the snow and come up smudged with axlegrease. I swear he sweats the blasted stuff." She laughed a big, loving laugh.

When he paid attention to his sister and to Carla, his favorite role was that of good-natured tease, cracking jokes, making up whoppers to see if they would bite, calling names. "Monkey-Face" was his favorite for Elsa, and he quickly dubbed Carla "Little Owl." To him she was a strange, eggheady kid. To Carla, he was the eighth wonder of the world and a disconcerting presence.

"Elsa has a brother," said Carla to her mother one day some time in April. Yes, Ray was Elsa's brother, nothing else. "Mama," she went on, "will I ever have one too?"

"Soon, God willing," answered Abigail. "I've written Miss Abbott."

"What does she have to do with it?"

"The department she represents is still Howard's legal guardian."

"Oh."

"Yours too, for that matter," Abigail sighed.

"I don't like that. You support me."

"Mostly. But how do you get those caps on your teeth renewed as you grow? And what about the teeth you had filled?"

"I wasn't sure."

"Anyway I don't want to change it, don't want any hearings." She didn't want to run the risk of any confrontation with Josiah.

"You said soon? Howard will be with us soon? When?"

"Be patient," Abigail spoke calmly, confidently.

Patience finally had its day of fulfillment. Howard was scheduled to arrive at Megunnaway a week after the closing of the school year. Carla went to meet the train, tugging a little red wagon which she'd borrowed from the Putnams to haul whatever luggage her brother might have. It was embarrassing for such a big girl to be hauling a kid's wagon, and she hurried to get past the houses. She arrived a few minutes early and stood in the cool shade of the overhanging roof, close to the building, as inconspicuous as possible. Finally the train moved into the station, letting out hot steam and making a tremendous noise, speaking loudly of travel and adventure. Forgetting the childish wagon, Carla rushed forward. There he was, Howard, but so much taller than a year ago. He was standing on the steps, walking down, tugging at a suitcase, looking about. Glory be! He spotted her, dropped the suitcase, ran to her, shouting, "Carla! Sister! I'm here, I really am!"

Joyfully they started on the walk home with Howard pulling the wagon, which didn't embarrass him in the least.

"Do you remember what we said last year?" he asked.

"About going to see Papa?"

"We'll hitchhike. The map is in my suitcase."

"Mama will never let us."

"I know, but afterwards she'll be glad."

"Not likely. But we're going, we're really going!" She did an absurd little dance while Howard paused, glad to rest.

They continued trudging along under the hot sun. "Don't you blab," he said.

"I won't," she promised, and indeed there was no danger of that, for she was not used to confiding in Abigail, or for that matter anyone else. "They think I've settled down to being such a good and proper child, no one will ever guess." She threw back her head and laughed.

By the time Howard had examined the house, been shown the brook, had lunch, and taken possession of the shed, which he announced would be his room, Howard was thoroughly exhausted. There was a narrow cot in the shed, and he threw himself upon it, and turning his face to the wall went promptly to sleep. In late afternoon Abigail came and saw him, and looked tenderly upon him, and wondered why he was in the shed. They'd planned to help him fix a place in the downstairs room.

She found Carla by the stove, sweating over a steaming kettle. Abigail sighed. Her poor dear children. She took up a paper and fanned herself. They decided to take the dinner to the shed, or as they had already begun to call it, Howard's room, and eat there. And so it was that the boy's first glimpse of his mother was when she came in with a plate of macaroni and cheese in one hand and a bowl of green salad in the other and looked helplessly about for a place to set them down. He jumped up at once to assist her. He set them upon a block of wood, and in no time had improvised quite a comfortable eating area with three chairs from the house and three blocks of wood. True the little tables were too low, particularly his, but this picnic-style meal helped them relax. And when the boy sat down on the floor and pretended to lap his food from the dish like a dog, Carla laughed heartily and Abigail smiling indulgently said, "Get along with your nonsense."

When Carla came downstairs the following morning, she found Howard alone at the table poring over a dilapidated road map. "See," he said, "here's where I was," pointing to a spot to the south and not far from the New Hampshire border. "And here is Megunnaway. We can hitch rides to get us pretty close to home."

"Home?"

"The farm."

Howard moved over to the horsehair sofa and opened a small khaki knapsack. "I've got a change of socks and underwear and a tee shirt. We'd better put in some things for you."

Carla hesitated, and Howard felt irritated. He should have just gone off by himself, not saddled himself with an excitable girl. He eyed her critically. She was wearing a blue-checked dress, too short for her, the skirt well above the knees. "You'd better put on that skirt and blouse you wore last night," he said. He was wearing fairly new blue jeans and a red plaid shirt. His light brown hair was neatly combed, and he stood straight and proud, though still not quite so tall as Carla. He was very much in charge. His whole face, broad at the forehead and narrow at the chin, was alert and crafty as that of the proverbial fox. There was determination in the gray eyes. No setback in his plans would deter him from his goal. Since he had to take Carla along, he'd have to see she acted sensibly. "The gray skirt," he ordered.

It was still cool from the night, and they were fresh as the morning. They reached the Bangor highway without having met anyone whom Carla knew. Not even the Putnams had seen them leave.

"Elsa would have asked questions," said Carla.

"Does she really walk on the ridgepole of their barn?"

"Loves to."

He gave a low whistle. But there was no time to think about girls who weren't afraid to walk on ridgepoles. "Here, we'll stand by the intersection and thumb a ride."

An old Ford touring car with flapping curtains and somewhat wobbly wheels pulled up beside them. A middle-aged man in overalls peered out at them. "Where you kids think you're going?" he asked.

"To see our dad," replied Howard.

"Where's he at?"

"Amsterburg," replied the boy. "First we go to Bangor and then—"

"You seem to know where you're headed. Guess it's okay. Hop in back, don't want to disturb the Chief."

The Chief, an obese little black dog, looked up from his post in the front seat and yawned. This ride, pursued in silence, took them twenty miles on their way, and the man let them out on the highway at the intersection where he was turning off to go to his farm.

"I'm thirsty," Carla said after the man was gone.

"I'll be a monkey's uncle!" Howard exclaimed. "We never thought to bring water."

"We could ask at a house."

"No, the fewer people we talk to the better. Someone might do us a favor and send us back."

Yes, they were still children, and as they both very well knew, children had no business out on the highway thumbing rides. But there they were, and Carla was thirsty. The highway led past broad fields, bright green with stringbeans on the left and yellow-green with corn on the right. In the distance they could see a row of trees at an oblique angle from the road. "Maybe there's a brook there," said Carla.

They soon reached the spot. The cars, of which there were several, had ignored their signals, every one. The trees did indeed mark a stream which wound almost to the road, then turned abruptly and flowed alongside of it. By clambering down a steep bank, they stood beside the water, which in spite of the slowness of its current, seemed clear and clean. Pure water in the heat of a July day! They made their way back to the highway, somewhat dirtier and with their hands scratched. For an hour they walked along the highway, and no one stopped.

A huge truck came barreling down the road so close to them that they felt its drag and jumped back lest they be sucked into its wake. The driver slammed on his brakes and pulled to a stop. They ran toward him, hoping against hope. Yes, he was stopping for them. He was a young man, fair-haired and sunburned. Just like the farmer, he questioned them, and he too was satisfied with Howard's answers. With Howard going first and pulling Carla after him they climbed into the truck and were on their way. A wonderful perch it was, high above the road, high above the cars. They got to talking, Howard lowered his guard somewhat, and told not only where they were going, but also some of the circumstances—parents separated, hadn't seen their father for four years—and also that they had never been to Bangor. The truckdriver, just recently become a father, was sympathetic. He'd have to leave them off in Bangor, but he explained to them exactly where to go in Bangor, where to cross the river, and how to get onto the Bucksport road, which would take them to Amsterburg. When they stopped, he drew a crumpled paper from his pocket and drew them a map. "Good luck," he said. "Just follow this and you can't no way get lost."

Even with this briefing the city was overwhelming. Bangor, which to a city-bred person would have appeared merely a tree-lined overgrown village, was to these children a bustling metropolis where everyone was in a hard-hearted hurry, both pedestrians and vehicles, and where the multiplicity of streets offered many opportunities for losing their way. However, the map and directions given them by the truckdriver were both clear and accurate, and they did actually succeed in finding the road to Bucksport.

It was late afternoon when a bright red roadster driven by a handsome youth pulled up beside them. "Going my way?" he asked gaily. "Then hop in."

Howard did as he was bade, Carla followed him, and Howard pushed the knapsack down by her feet. "We're going to Amsterburg," said Howard. "You going by there?"

"Just before Bucksport, isn't it?"

"Yes."

"We'll have you there in a jiffy," said the cheerful young man. "What you going to do there?"

"Visit our father."

"Visit your father? What's his name?"

"Wingate, Josiah Wingate, has a farm three miles out of town."

"I've heard of a Wingate. But this must be a different one, not the one I've heard of, who's a crazy old fellow, sort of a hermit."

"I guess," said Howard.

"Of course that old hermit wouldn't be your dad. Wish I hadn't mentioned him. They say he drinks too."

When they reached the little town of Amsterburg, the young man discovered that their ways separated. He let them out and sped off toward Bucksport. "Weird kids," he thought. "Maybe the old hermit is their dad." He'd visited his uncle's summer place three years running, but he still couldn't figure out the natives.

"Could it be Papa?" Carla asked in alarm.

"Not likely," answered Howard.

They trudged along through town, met a woman whom they thought they recognized but who didn't even look at them. On past the end of the sidewalk, along the pavement, and onto the dirt road they walked, their feet growing heavier and heavier, but Howard insisted that they not thumb a ride.

Several cars passed, and again they saw someone they thought they knew but who took no notice of them. The excitement and spirit of adventure of the morning had turned to a dogged determination and on they plodded. The western sky was tinged with the orange of sunset, but the air retained the heat of the day, and the dry dust parched their mouths. Mosquitos stung their faces and arms, bits of gravel in their shoes irritated their feet, hunger gnawed at their bellies.

At last they saw it, the giant elm, the barn, the house. Breaking into a run, they drew closer. It was just as they had remembered. Well, almost. There had been a stack of cordwood the day they left, but that was gone; the hens formerly kept in a pen were running about in the yard; somewhere in back of the barn a cow was mooing. They hurried into the house. A couple of hens were complacently scratching the floor in the living room.

"Papa!" cried Carla. "Oh dear, he's not home."

"I guess not," agreed Howard. "Can't be. The place stinks."

"Get out, get out," Carla shooed the hens.

"Who's that yelling?" called a man's voice from the bedroom.

"Papa, Papa!" cried Howard and together the children ran to find the voice.

Yes, it was Papa, lying on top of the quilt, dragging himself up to a sitting position. He turned to face them, his face blank, no sign of recognition.

"He's drunk," said Howard. There was no mistaking that blank stare, that alcohol smell, the awkwardness with which he moved. The children retreated from the room.

"Come back, you hear, come back!" the man shouted, his voice thick and mumbling. The children froze, and soon he was silent.

Carla sat down in a chair and began to cry.

"He'll be sober tomorrow," Howard tried to comfort her.

They made themselves a dinner of milk, eggs, and bread which they found in the kitchen. The eggs in fact were in a nest which a hen had made in one of the lower cupboards, and the bread was fresh. There being no fire, they prepared the eggs by beating them in milk with sugar, sugar carefully separated from the ants which had overrun the bowl. Then they went outside and found some raspberries. At least the berries were every bit as juicy as they remembered.

"I'd better take the cow in, poor thing," said Howard, "and milk it."

"I'll clean up inside," his sister responded.

They went about their tasks, his far more easily completed than hers. "I haven't gotten rid of half the hen dirt," she wailed when Howard came in with the milk.

They looked in upon their father several times. How gray his hair had gotten, and how dirty his clothes were! Sick with disappointment and fear, they went upstairs to their old rooms, which were much as they had left them, with sheets and quilts turned back and pillows in place. Ignoring in their weariness the mustiness, they went to bed and almost immediately fell asleep.

Josiah Wingate woke early the next morning, sat for a while on the edge of his bed pondering his strange dream, then went to the kitchen for his breakfast. He clung to the sink for support. Someone had been there. Oh no, he thought, they couldn't have come and found me, no, not that. If so, he didn't want to see them, he couldn't face them. He would disappear deep into the woods. At that moment he heard a voice.

"Papa," Howard said gravely. "We've come back."

"We?" Oh not Abigail, that he couldn't stand.

"Carla and me," said Howard and felt himself in the strong embrace of the man. But Papa still smelled of unwashed clothing and stale whiskey. The boy drew back.

"I don't blame you," said Papa. "Stay right here. I'll get some clean clothes, go down to the brook, wash. Don't go away."

Howard, having at last returned to his father, would not for a moment let him out of his sight, but followed him into the bedroom, went with him to the brook, where Papa gave himself somewhat of a bath, back to the bedroom where the man brushed his beard and tangled hair and then into the kitchen. Carla came down and found them there, Papa starting a fire, Howard sitting at the kitchen table watching. The two of them were in a heated argument as to whether or not pigs were unclean, an argument precipitated by Howard who had said he hoped there'd be bacon for breakfast and continued by his father who stoutly defended himself for not raising a porker.

"My little girl, my little girl," the man cried. "Why you're almost a young lady."

Her heart singing, for the morning was so much better than the night before, Carla got a bowl and ran out to pick raspberries and stood there in the cool morning air, plucking the red jewels from the canes until she had filled the bowl to overflowing, even as her heart overflowed with love for this strange man. She had a sense of being back in her proper place and a sense of being needed there. Papa needed them; they'd straighten things out. Oh it would take a few days. She'd noticed the night before that not only were the hens making free use of the living room, but also it was half full of other kinds of trash. Stacks of old newspapers, piles of rags, windows dark with dirt, the place called out for the hand of a tidy woman, and this tidy woman Carla resolved to be. Papa was an old man; he just wasn't strong enough to do all that work, and he was lonely; that was the trouble.

They sat down to eat, and all went well until a hen came in and the girl got up to shoo it out. Papa interposed a sharp command to let the chicken be, said it was his pet, was free to come and go as it pleased and as he pleased.

It was at that moment that Sheriff Kingsbury walked in through the open door. "Good morning, good morning," he said, trying to be jovial. "I see I'm just in time for breakfast." He brushed aside Josiah's polite invitation to join them and got at once to the business end of his visit. "I'm sure, Mr. Wingate, that you know why I'm here."

"Sheriff Kingsbury, I wouldn't know."

"Come, come, these children. What do you have to say for yourself?"

Howard rose quickly and went to stand behind his father's chair, the hen scooted out the door, and Carla sat back down. The children waited expectantly for their father to speak, but for some time he simply sat there, his head bowed, his shoulders slumped, all the starch gone from him.

"I'll not answer a question like that," he said at last, trying to rally, but he knew that once again, he'd let the children down.

"That's more like the Josiah I know," said the Sheriff sitting down. He would do what he had to, but he entertained no desire to see Wingate crawl.

Howard cleared his throat. "I can explain," he said. "It wasn't Papa, it was us. We just come."

"Then I trust it's agreeable to everyone if I just take you on back."

Carla was silent, her momentary optimism dampened. Josiah was silent because he knew the futility of a struggle. But Howard answered, "I come home to stay."

"Josiah," said the Sheriff. "Explain to the boy. Custody and all. Miss Abbott's in a tizzy. You know I can't let them stay." The hen, or one of her sisters, had returned and was pecking under the table, and he kicked her away with his heavy shoe.

Josiah watched the hen scurry for the door. Sure, the place was a mess, he knew it, but neatness would not have helped. Custody was custody, a court order was a court order, and this worried-looking man was the Sheriff. "I guess I don't have much claim," he admitted.

"I'm staying," said Howard.

"No," said the Sheriff. "You are not staying."

"Going to handcuff him?" asked Josiah.

"If I have to."

"You must go," Josiah said to the boy. "Might as well face it."

"I'll come back."

"In a few years, yes, in a few years."

"If I go, will you write to me?"

"I'm not sure where he'll be," said the Sheriff answering for Josiah. "He'll have to let you know."

"Go upstairs, son," Josiah quietly ordered, "get your knapsack and things."

"I want him in my sight," said the Sheriff. "Let the girl go."

She soon returned with the knapsack, which she handed to Howard. Throwing her arms around her father, she burst into tears. "Oh Papa, we can't stay, I know we can't. But we love you, we do, we do! Come to Megunnaway and be with us. We'll manage, I know we will."

Josiah laughed bitterly. "What do you take me for?" he asked. "Get on back to your mother, baby girl, don't keep the man waiting."

And so the children left. Josiah could no longer restrain his sobs. Sheriff Kingsbury heard the sound and turned back, horrified at a man's weeping. "Pull yourself together," he said. "Don't blubber."

"Things will go from bad to worse," Wingate answered. "No matter what I do."

"I told you no good would come from taking to drink."

"I wasn't divorced for drunkenness," Wingate reminded him. "And if you think I'm going to face my wretched life cold sober, you've got another think coming."

"I could do with a shot myself," said the Sheriff and left.

Miss Abbott met them in town by the post office. She looked very much the same, a tall, long-faced woman with a no-nonsense air, clothed as before in russet brown. Her suit, being of lighter weight material seemed somewhat more flexible, but her hat of straw made up for that with its rigidity.

"Get in back, Howard," she said as they approached her russet brown Buick. "Carla in front. I suppose you know you've caused your mother no end of worry. And I'm taking time I can ill spare just to drive you back to Megunnaway."

"No need to," said Howard, pausing on the runningboard. "We can go back the way we come."

"Don't be impertinent. Besides—"

"I'd take my sister back, I'd promise."

"And then?"

"I'd return to Papa," Howard said.

"You wouldn't promise to stay with your mother?"

Howard made no answer, but he got into the car.

"Carla," said Miss Abbott as they drove along. "I want you to remember that I am your mother's friend and your friend."

"Yes, ma'm."

"And what I do, I do for her sake and for your benefit."

"Yes, ma'm."

When they arrived at the house in Megunnaway in early afternoon, Abigail was already there. She came running out to meet them. "Oh my babies, my babies," she cried, hugging first Carla and then Howard. "Thank God you're safe."

They went inside, and she gave them lemonade to drink. The two women sat at the table, the children together on the sofa. "I'm so worried," Abigail began.

"But we're home," said Carla.

"I know, thank God, but, oh Miss Abbott, the burden's so heavy, my back so weak."

Jennifer Abbott sipped her drink. Why had it turned out the way it had? Everything had seemed to be working out fine, until that miserable boy—she turned to Howard and asked sharply, "Why did you pull this crazy stunt? Whatever made you want to leave?"

The boy kicked sullenly at the floor. "I had to go home," he said at last.

"What's the matter with you, child?" demanded Miss Abbott. "You have a home here. You have a house and food and clothing, and as you get older you'll have a chance to get on in life, you and Carla both. We'll find a way for her to go on to college. With her fine record I'm sure we'll be able to. And you'll be provided for, maybe learn some trade, whatever seems right."

"I'm going back to the farm."

"Can't you see how you're upsetting all your mother's plans for you?"

"To think he wants to leave," wailed Abigail. "It breaks my heart. I thought he'd be happy, that we'd be happy together."

"Take me back to Mrs. Staples," said Howard. "I've caused trouble enough here."

Quick as a flash Miss Abbott responded, "Howard, go pack your suitcase. I'll do what you asked."

"Please don't take him away," begged Carla. "I promise not to do it again."

"Let him stay," pleaded Abigail.

"Will you promise, Howard, not to pull such a caper again?" Miss Abbott asked.

The boy was silent.

"Mama," Carla pleaded, "don't let him go."

Abigail took off her glasses, laid them carefully on the table, bowed her head upon her arms. "I can't help it," she mumbled. "I'm not his guardian." The children went to the shed and started packing Howard's things.

Miss Abbott glanced nervously at her wristwatch. In a few minutes the children returned. "I put my suitcase in your car," said Howard.

"Good. I'll wait outside while you say good-bye."

"I'm glad I came," said Howard as he felt the warmth of Abigail's embrace. He guessed she was doing what she had to do.

"Oh Howard," Carla entreated. "Go out and promise Miss Abbott you'll stay here. Do promise, then I'm sure—"

"Yes, do," said Abigail.

"Nope," said Howard.

They went out and Howard started to get into the back seat, but Miss Abbott told him to sit in front. "Well, Howard," she said, "we're taking you back to Mrs. Staples' boarding home."

"Yes, ma'm," said Howard. *For right now she'll take me there,* he thought.

Abigail and Carla went into the house, and Abigail sat down at the table, bowed her head upon her arms and sobbed audibly. Carla sat upon the horsehair sofa and refused to cry. She felt a stray horsehair, pulled on it until it lay wriggling in her hand. It was not true, she thought, that it could turn into a snake. She found another, pulled on it, found another, sat there aimlessly destroying the fabric until at last her mother looked up and growled at her to stop. Then remorseful at the harshness of her tone, she ran to the girl and held her close. "Oh my baby, my baby," she sobbed. But Carla drew away, went out to the shed where two nights ago they had had the family picnic. Her heart was filled with hate, but for the moment she was too dejected to plan rebellion. She just sat there, eyes dry, shoulders slumped forward, her body limp as an empty sack. Nothing in the whole world was right or would ever be right.

SEVEN

The seasons moved on. Carla grew to be five-foot-seven and Abigail grew weary, and they struggled and survived, but mere survival was not enough for either. Each in her own way sought the answer to the riddle, the meaning of life. To Abigail the answer was partly clear, respectability and faith in God, but—oh, there ought to be some pleasure too! Sometimes coming from the smells of the sorting room, itching all over but too ladylike to scratch, she would almost give up and lie down in the ditch to die. But it was always too hot or too cold for that. On arriving home she would jump at Carla for not having cleaned the house better or because dinner was overcooked or for nothing at all, later to apologize, weep and moan, "I have committed three crimes, I am poor, and I am a woman, and I am old."

The answer to the riddle, the meaning of life, sought by Carla even more intensely than by her mother, continued to evade the girl. It had to do, she was sure, with courage: the courage that Elsa displayed when she climbed high on flimsy structures; the courage of Jesus, not only when He faced the cross but also earlier when He faced the sneering "Can any good come out of Nazareth?"; the courage of Ray riding at breakneck speed in his shirtsleeves on his motorcycle. When she looked at Ray, she found herself thinking of Roger until they seemed to meld into one: dark-haired Roger and golden-haired Ray; clumsy Roger and athletic Ray; considerate Roger and teasing Ray. How could two such disparate personalities be one in her thoughts? Well, her thoughts weren't exactly the same, for the physical thoughts were of Ray alone. But of course he didn't know. For her classmates at school she cared not at all.

Her thoughts went swooping like swallows, floating from Roger to Ray to Christ. Perhaps the meaning of life lay in Christ, and she talked to the minister about it. Rev. Mr. Acheson had been replaced by Mr. Cameron, who was older and more literal-minded. The voice on Mt. Sinai, the Virgin birth, Lazarus raised from the dead, the Second Coming, the life hereafter were graphic realities to him, and he described them over and over in great detail, but what was clear to him was hidden in mist for Carla. She greatly disturbed him.

"This is sad," he said. "I fear for you, my child, I pray for you. Do try to have faith."

Living or not living the life taught by Jesus, that could be a choice, but faith, thought Carla, was a gift from God, and she had not been blessed with it. She felt keenly her need for some guide, for she believed herself to be desperately wicked. Not only did she have lustful thoughts, she also harbored within her a vicious meanness. One day she cut up her mother's clothes brush, which was the one bit of luxury left from Abigail's early life. It had a polished mahogany base with the initials A.J. in silver and bristles softly brown and firmly efficient after years of use, an elegant expensive brush highly prized by Abigail. Carla took it and cut angry gashes with the scissors, deep into the bristles, right to the base. Why? Because she was jealous of her mother's more prosperous youth, jealous of the clothes her mother had had, envious that she had lived in a big house, had been sent to school to be trained as a teacher, had lived at home with her sister and brothers and both parents, and no one in town had ever thought her poor. And she had had this elegant brush. When first the scissors bit into the bristles, Carla hated her mother, but the sight of the poor mutilated thing made her hate herself. Poor Abigail had so little. How terrible to begrudge her this brush!

Carla, fully repentant, showed her mother the ruined brush, and when she saw the sad bewildered look on Abigail's face, she burst into tears. Abigail wept too but not for the brush.

In silence they prepared the dinner. Abigail bowed her head for grace. "Help us God," she said. "Bring us Thy peace, and oh, a little bit of love."

"Mama," said Carla, "I want to be baptized."

After seven sessions with Mr. Cameron, Carla was adjudged ready to bear public witness to the faith. There were two other candidates for baptism, Ray and Elsa Putnam. It was a Sunday in the middle of May, when the birds were singing, the fruit trees were in bloom, and Megunnaway lay resting from the week. Then the Putnams, with Abigail and Carla, filed into the church and took their seat in a pew halfway down, all of them very much aware of the many eyes fixed upon them. Three young people were to be baptized, and Mr. Putnam had come to church! A great day for the Lord!

After the ceremony, the congregation was inclined to be noisy in its congratulations and the Putnams and Wingates subdued. Carla and Abigail had barely entered their cottage when Carla took her mother by the hand and said earnestly, "Mother, I know what we must do!"

Abigail looked up in surprise. "What now?"

"We must go back to Papa," the girl said.

The surprise turned to dismay. "Never!" the woman cried. "Have you forgotten? Forgotten the drunkenness and the filth?"

"Mama, that's why we have to go. He needs us."

Abigail slumped into a chair. "I can't" she said, and her voice quivered. "Dear God, I can't."

When the school year ended and Carla had more free time, she became even more insistent that they must go to Papa. Since it was part of her religious wakening, so long prayed for by Abigail, she was hard put to argue against it. The girl had an idea that somehow their going to Papa would in the end result in their getting Howard back. Poor dear Howard, thought Abigail. She'd been told by Miss Abbott that he'd disappeared, run away. "Mama," the girl said, "if we get back to the farm and have a place for him, we can find him. Maybe through the Salvation Army or the power of prayer or perhaps he's already at the farm, lying low."

"My poor dear baby," said Abigail. "He's gone, so young, who knows what has happened? And if he *is* found—"

"Oh Mama, let's just go."

The new life of spring opened into the fullness of summer and Abigail kept hearing that "Let's go," both in her mind and in her ears, for Carla continued to nag her. How Abigail longed to give in, to go; oh they wouldn't have to stay; she'd see how things went. Then Miss Abbott came to call. No, she had no news about Howard. She'd come to take Carla to a dentist in Bangor. The caps on her front teeth should be checked, possibly replaced. Carla went out and the two women sat down to talk. Abigail found herself telling about the clothes brush, pleading for some word of wisdom that would help her cope with this strange daughter. And she told about Carla's desire, one might say determination, to return to the farm. Miss Abbott's brow furrowed and she pursed her mouth and was obviously displeased. She didn't have to say a word.

It was clear, thought Abigail, they couldn't go. They relied too much on Miss Abbott. There'd been a layoff at the mill; she'd lost a week's work. No, they couldn't risk it. By September she was able to persuade herself that Carla had given up on it. The autumn passed, gold and scarlet, then gray November, and the snows fell in December. Abigail shivered and worried. She'd been off work day after day.

"Come the first of the year it should pick up," said Abigail bravely, and Carla accepted the assurance.

Early one evening a little less than a week before Christmas, the Wingates, in company with Mrs. Putnam, Ray and Elsa, walked the snowy road, not yet plowed after the latest storm, to the church program. The big social hall had been transformed with green branches, red and white paper streamers, and a tinseled tree decked with candy canes, and shiny globes of many colors. Underneath the tree were mounds of presents, all gaily wrapped.

Children were running about, parents and grandparents were beaming with special Christmas love, and worldly adolescents were children once again, but big children who helped attain some degree of order. After the musical program was over, a corpulent red-suited Santa Claus with a bushy white beard came ho-ho-hoing through the back door. The beard identified him as Mr. Bates, well known to even the smallest child as Megunnaway's perennial Santa Claus. But no one let on.

Santa Claus beamed upon them all. "Candy canes!" he cried. "You big kids hand them out to the little ones." Satisfied when this had been done he ho-hoed once more and cried in his deeper than normal Santa Claus voice, "Now for the presents!"

The very first to be called was Carla, which embarrassed her; this sort of thing was for the younger kids. The present was a set of pencils with Carla Wingate embossed in tiny gold letters on each one. How nice! From her Sunday School teacher, she guessed. She must remember not to chew these, a nervous tic she was striving to control.

Other names were called. It was the custom for every family to bring to this tree one present for each child, retaining the others for the home festivity. Sometimes children brought a present for their parents. Thus the giving was, without any formal rules, quite limited, and nobody expected or received more than two or three gifts. Much to Carla's surprise, her name was being called again. Someone had given her a pair of warm woolen gloves. The card did not contain the name of the giver. Could it be Mama? Or Mrs. Putnam? Santa went on calling names one after another, and the room was filled with squeals of delight. Carla watched eagerly as Elsa opened the little package containing a bracelet. Mrs. Putnam had shown it to Carla, had asked did she think Elsa would like it.

"Oh," cried Elsa, "it's darling."

"Carla Wingate," boomed Santa once more. She was amazed. No one else was being called so much. One more summons, and her face grew crimson. Her mother had to push her forward, tell her it would be rude not to go. Before the evening was over, she had received thirteen presents. No one else had received more than three. When Santa began distributing the traditional bags of goodies among the children, Carla hurried out and started toward home.

She hadn't gone far before Ray came running after her. "Wait for the ladies and Monkey Face," he said.

Carla carried only two of the packages, the pencils and a small white box of candy. "I have your things in this sack," said Abigail as she and the others came up. Carla groaned.

The two women walked briskly, happy with the evening and eager to get out of the cold. Carla dragged behind, and Ray stayed with her. Elsa was here, there, and everywhere. She was fancying all sorts of shapes in the snow, there a cradle, here a Madonna, elsewhere a cow. She would run up to Carla and point out her fancy, then she would run ahead to tell her mother and Abigail. After a while she settled down to walking by her mother's side.

The cold air bit the nostrils, stars were frozen spots of light, the snow gleamed with a bluish tone that turned to violet in the shadows. A slight breeze rattled the ice upon the bare limbs of the trees. The snow crunched under foot. Carla plodded along and was silent.

"What's wrong, Little Owl?" asked Ray.

She held up the small white box of candy. "Did you give me this?" she asked.

He saw that she was crying; oh no, she mustn't in the cold. "No," he said. "I didn't. I didn't give you anything."

"At least I'm glad of that." She walked on, kicking at the snow.

"It was kind of much," he said.

Someone understood at least. He put his arm around her and drew her close, and they walked on, and the arm was still there when they came up with the others.

The next morning before her mother was up, Carla neatly rewrapped the presents, put them in the sack and stamped through the snow into town. Resolutely she knocked on the parsonage door.

"Why Carla!" Mr. Cameron greeted her. "This is a pleasant surprise." He led her into his study.

She refused to sit down, so he stood beside her. "I brought these back," said the girl, emptying the big brown paper bag onto his desk.

"Your presents?"

"Who made me a charity project?" she demanded.

He was silent for a moment. "Carla," he said at last. "The truth is, I do not know. I could guess, but I don't know."

"It wasn't you?"

"No. But I am sure that the person who did it, I mean, all who gave you presents, meant only love and kindness. Wanted to make you happy."

"They didn't care about my happiness or they wouldn't have done something to make me look ridiculous. How do you know what they meant?" She was too upset to notice how rude she was being.

"Really I don't know," he confessed. "God looks down and sees into their hearts. Only He knows for sure."

"God looks down?" she repeated. "Like a person?"

"Not exactly and yet, yes, He sees."

"I wish I could believe that."

He looked at her earnest, intelligent face. "I had supposed you did."

"I don't know what to believe."

"What, then, does church mean to you?"

"It meant a place where there was peace and I was as good as anyone else," she replied. "At least until last night."

"I will find out where these came from and give them back. It will not happen again. I hope you can feel once more about the church as you did prior to last night."

He held out his hand and shook hands with her, one adult to another.

Later that day he reported the matter to Helen Clark, Carla's Sunday School teacher, who as he surmised had arranged it. "What an ungrateful girl!" she sniffed.

"I wouldn't call it that."

"Her mother is such a nice little woman, works her fingers to the bone for that girl."

"The girl is her source of joy. There's strength there, my friend, real strength of character."

"She doesn't make friends with other girls."

"She and Elsa Putnam—"

"They giggle in church, great grown girls though they are," said the woman, closing the conversation.

Elsa was standing in the Putnam driveway when Carla returned. She listened as Carla told what she had done. And this Elsa, who used to walk on ridgepoles and who still giggled in church, said, "Oh Carla, did you really take them back? I wouldn't have dared."

Ray came and kissed her, right there in front of Elsa, and there only remained, to close the incident, the need to tell Abigail. Carla found her mother busy warming up last night's baked beans for breakfast. It took but a few words for Carla to tell of her visit to the parsonage.

"My poor baby!" said Abigail. "You did right! I didn't realize. I should have. Come! I have an orange to share with you."

"From last night?"

"No, I bought it yesterday, special for us."

Oh the rare fragrance of that orange! It smelled exactly like those they'd eaten years ago in Howard's schoolroom. There were tears of joy in Abigail's eyes as they finished, but Carla hid her joy deep in her heart, for Ray was part of it and that she could not talk about.

❧❦

A girl may be the same day after day and month after month, and then some incident causes her to take a giant developmental leap, and some character strand, which no doubt lay hidden all along, suddenly stands out in sharp relief. The incident of the presents was such a jump for Carla. She sensed it as did Abigail.

She was consumed with a sharp new ambition to rise from her lowly position to one of prestige and, she was quite clear about this, one of wealth. Abigail, who loved to preach the equality of man and the sinful nature of materialism, egged her on. Abigail assured herself that the girl's ambition was not evil, but rather a natural desire to take her rightful position in the world, a position to which she was entitled by reason of her intelligence, her family background, and her beauty. Carla's road, they agreed, lay through education to some profession, neither knew what. There must be a scholarship, thought Abigail, and once when doing housecleaning for Mrs. Pomeroy during a slack time at the mill, she asked that authority for information. Yes, there was a scholarship which would cover the first year's expenses, the income from an endowment fund set up by the original Blodgett years ago. Scholastic standing was one criterion but not the only one, and the recipient was usually a boy, since he would be more likely to make good use of an education, but there wasn't any rule.

Carla resolved to win that scholarship. It was not hard for her to establish herself as Megunnaway High's outstanding student. She was the school brain, unchallenged. Then she heard something about the "well-rounded" student, and she resolved to be that too. However her efforts at sports led only to frustration. So she went out for debating; she made the team, indeed she was the team. Although she proved a dud as a cheerleader, when it came to football rallies no one could rev up the student body quite like Carla Wingate! Abigail followed her daughter's progress with the greatest pride. Carla would never go into a mill as she had done, would never clean other women's houses. No, not Carla. True Abigail had come to terms with her life, felt that she had found a certain niche. She witnessed constantly her love of the Lord to her fellow workers and fancied she'd made some progress because they no longer swore in her presence. Well aware that it is more blessed to give than to receive, she'd worked out a unique giving project for herself. She solicited worn out sweaters, unraveled them, and used the yarn to knit mittens for children she knew needed them. It had started with the Mills children; now there were others. And Blodgett Mill had given her permission to salvage sweaters from their rags. Oh she was busy every evening, knitting and dreaming of Carla's future.

Abigail was sustained in the roughest times by this glowing vision, but simultaneously she had her worries about Carla. For one thing the girl, who had had that wonderful religious awakening, had lost her faith. Yes, Abigail had to admit it, she'd given up on God and the Methodist Church. However, Abigail comforted herself, she hadn't given up on her sense of justice and duty. What a good girl she'd become! No more wild escapades, no running away, no temper tantrums. But was she happy? She had no friends except Elsa, who was after all two years younger. She refused to go to socials at either school or church and refused invitations to parties until they were no longer extended. Still she seemed happy enough, but of course Abigail had no way of knowing.

Carla's ambition to get that scholarship by no means consumed all her energy. She felt within her something of the compassion Elsa showered on maimed animals, but for Carla it was directed toward people. She hadn't forgotten Papa, and she was touched with deep pity for Abigail, but in both cases the pity was tinged with scorn. What kind of a father had Papa been, she would ask herself. Then compassion would drive out such selfish thoughts, and she would be once more committed to going back and rescuing him. Some day. And Mama! How hard she worked, but how ineffectual she was. Poor dear Mama! Carla took over most of the household chores, help which Abigail greatly needed. She also painted the woodwork white, how it freshened the rooms! And she dug up a patch of ground which she filled with starts from Mrs. Putnam's plants and another patch where each year she grew beans and tomatoes and squash.

And she had that secret which she hardly dared entertain. It was foolish she knew, hopeless. Ray Putnam was the star athlete, the handsome golden youth, and he was going steady with Nettie Newman, which the entire school considered most appropriate. Even Carla had to admit the rightness of it. Nettie with her light brown curls and her rosy cheeks, Nettie who could unerringly shoot the ball through the basketball hoop, who could run like the wind, who could dance and sing and tell the funniest jokes. Who could match the charms of Nettie Newman? Certainly not Carla, the kid sister's friend, the Little Owl.

One day a few weeks after Ray's graduation from Megunnaway High, when Carla was at the Putnam's getting a bucket of water, Ray came thundering into the yard on a newly acquired motorcycle, a big red Indian, solid, powerful, a tremendous machine. He jumped off, set it on the kickstand and stood back to admire. His tightfitting denim shirt and pants outlined his long lean muscles. His golden hair gleamed in the sun. His face, no longer boyishly

pretty, looked fierce and strong. He was the very incarnation of young man-
hood and life and motion. He was a young Nordic god controlling vast ener-
gies, riding on the wind.

He turned to Elsa. "Want a ride, Monkey Face?" he asked.

Elsa hung back, she wasn't sure. Usually fearless, the one thing about
which she had reservations was a motorcycle.

Ray laughed. "You're scared," he said. "How about you, Little Owl?"
He turned his grown-up face with the boyish, teasing eyes to Carla. She had
never been on a motorcycle before, but she climbed onto the seat in back,
and as he took his place, she clung to him as he instructed. They were off in
a whir of sound, a cloud of dust. The wind blew her hair back from her face,
then whipped it into her eyes. Frightened by the speed, she bent forward and
tightened her arms around his body. They were flying now on a paved road
so that it was less dusty; they were going faster; they wheeled once and she
screamed; then they were back on two wheels and flying smoothly at terrific
speed. Gradually the fear left her and she felt only exhilaration. Her body
leaned against his back, and the cold wind blew through her thin slacks and
shirt, and the warmth of body touching body was the warmth of young blood.
At last they stopped far out on a country road. She hid her face from him,
but he turned her gently toward him. She was no longer the kid sister's play-
mate—she was Carla.

He got a job in a summer resort but returned in the fall. He was living
at home and working as a mechanic in Pete's Garage. Some day, he said, he'd
have his own business, something small, maybe him and one other man. He
was seeing much of Carla now, but the parents might never have noticed it
had it not been for Elsa. Elsa, who was with them on most of their excursions,
lived in a glow of vicarious romance and eventually confided in her mother.

"Do they really have to wait until Carla is through high school?" she
asked. "Why can't they get married now?"

"You're talking nonsense," said Margaret.

That night the Putnams, man and wife, huddled head to head in earnest
conference. Although they agreed that Carla was beautiful and certainly smart
as a whip, they did not share Elsa's quite impractical view. Carla was too
bookish, too arrogant, she'd nag Ray and boss him, her kind always did. And
what sort of a family did she come from? Abigail had told them a little; the
father was living in filth on some neglected farm. Oh Abigail was good in her
way, but there was no denying that she at times had an odd way.

Abigail too was alerted by a chance remark of Elsa's about her brother
and Carla. She had no one with whom to talk it over, but she resolved to keep
her eyes open and upon doing so decided that it wasn't just Elsa's romantic
notion. Oh dear! She liked Ray, she was very fond of him; he had such a

good-natured way of noticing everyone, even an old woman like her. Yes, she liked him. But that was no reason for her to want Carla to marry him or worse become involved in some other kind of entanglement. For one thing he had no ambition. He'd be content to be an auto mechanic all the days of his life. And what kind of intellectual companionship could Carla find with him? No, it didn't promise at all. Furthermore it wouldn't make him happy. They hadn't enough in common. She felt helpless; she must trust in Carla's good judgment; if she said anything, it would only make matters worse. She must concentrate on Carla's plan, on the hoped-for scholarship, keep ever before Carla the long-term goal.

Carla made the debating team a winner. She edited the *Megunnaway Clarion* like an old pro. She led her class in scholarship by such a margin that from the time she entered her junior year there was no doubt that she would be the class valedictorian. Abigail had no fears. She could hardly wait for Carla's graduation. Soon the junior year passed and the senior year was going fast; it was already February and nothing definite about scholarships had been settled. Abigail wrote to Miss Abbott, who had once said she might help, and reminded her that applications had to go in. But Miss Abbott was not her main hope. Her main hope was the Blodgett Scholarship. She spoke once or twice to Mrs. Pomeroy about it, and that lady smiled encouragingly but declined to be pinned down.

One windy afternoon in March, Carla looked out the window and saw a russet brown Buick driving, at slow speed and considerable churning of snow, up the highway. Inside the house it was cold as Alaska. Carla hurried to the stove with paper and kindling and small pieces of wood. She set a match to it and the crackling began at once. She heard the car stop in front. Oh dear, she hoped it wouldn't get stuck. She gave a poke to the fire and put the lid to one side to give it more air. The knock at the door was a brisk summons.

There in her heavy cloth coat of the usual russet brown, her brown felt hat pulled down over her graying hair, stood Miss Abbott. Except for the graying of her hair she had changed little over the years. She was the same energetic, long-faced woman with the same matter-of-fact manner. "Go on fixing the fire," she said. "I'll just take a chair."

She deposited her briefcase on the floor, took off her gloves, loosened her scarf and was ready to talk. "Your mother wrote me about helping you go to college," she said. "That's why I am here."

The fire was blazing, the room growing less cold, and Carla stood there staring at the briefcase as if expecting to see a cap and gown hop out. She moved up the kettle to heat water for tea. "Mother won't be home until six," she said.

"Good. I want to see you alone."

"Oh?"

"I take a great interest in you. I suppose you know our agency is still your legal guardian?"

Carla nodded.

"We have followed your progress in school. We congratulate you. And we have explored several avenues trying to find funds for further education."

"I'm beginning to give up hope."

"There is always hope; there are always new opportunities, new beginnings."

"Yes, ma'm."

"I could not help noticing that on occasion you and your mother do not understand each other."

Oh that clothes brush, thought Carla and felt her face grow warm.

"Perhaps I should say she does not fully understand your emotional needs, the turmoil of youth, the frustrations of—if you will pardon the word—the frustrations of poverty."

"She tries her level best."

"Yet she cannot give you the opportunities she would like and which you deserve."

"She does what she can."

"I am sure of that, but she would be the first to admit that it isn't what you would both like." She allowed her eyes to wander around the room, still papered with brown paper, the furniture as it had been from the first except for a crude desk which Carla had made from orange crates. Her eyes paused briefly at the wooden sink and at the shiny black stove which was making such a futile effort to warm the room. "Carla, my dear," she said at last, "something has opened up for you."

Carla sat down and drew her chair near.

"There is a family," Miss Abbott spoke slowly and distinctly as if each word were of the utmost importance, "a family who would like to do all these things for you."

Carla jumped up. Shades of Tomcat! Aloud she said, "The water should be hot. I'll make tea."

"Never mind the tea. I haven't time. But thank you, my dear. Nice to see good manners in a young girl." She sat very straight and continued, "There is in Augusta a family who know about you, have seen your picture, have even been to Megunnaway and seen you at school when you didn't know about it. They want to take you into their home as their adopted daughter."

Carla stood in the middle of the floor staring at the woman. What was she saying? It didn't make sense.

"They would send you to college, the very best too. You could start on whatever career you select. There's no telling how high you might rise."

Carla sat back down. It was incredible, fantastic. She could visualize herself entering a beautiful living room with soft carpet and blue and rose furniture and a great brick fireplace and a tall handsome woman helping her carry a couple of suitcases. And then she could see her mother's face with tears streaming under her glasses. Her mother would tell her to go to her new magnificence, saying she didn't mind being left alone.

"No!" the girl cried vehemently. "I wouldn't do such a thing to my mother, never."

Miss Abbott started buttoning up. "She'd give her consent. Think about it carefully," she advised, "and let me know."

"I don't want to think about it. My mother has nothing left in life but me."

"In the normal course of events you will be leaving home."

"I'll never do it in a way that would be a slap in her face."

Miss Abbott straightened her hat. Carla stood tall and defiant. Miss Abbott looked at her with admiration and compassion. "I wish we could help you in some other way," she said as she left.

Carla sat down and drank the hot tea. She must not tell Mama about this. Abigail would say—who knew of what sacrifice she might not be capable? Carla glanced up at the pictures on the wall, the snowstorm and the wave-tossed woman. Poor Mama had known so much stormy weather.

That night after she'd washed the dishes Carla sat late at the table doing her homework, then just sitting there, reliving the afternoon and becoming more and more angry with Miss Abbott. Her anger carried back to all the visits the woman had made, back to the very first time she had come to the farm. No, no, she mustn't blame Miss Abbott for that. She'd only come because she'd been summoned. But today she certainly hadn't been summoned. Well, in a way maybe she had. How very clever of her to hold out that particular bait!

Still nursing her anger, she went to bed and fell asleep. Some time in the night she started dreaming. She was a small girl, and yet she was also sixteen. She was lying face down upon the grass, and she heard a voice, a man's voice, soft and entreating. She sprang up, and suddenly she was no longer a little girl but her sixteen-year-old self. She was standing in front of the yellow house in Hambledon Hill and before her, speaking in a soft wheedling voice, was Tomcat, the Tomcat she'd feared in her childhood without knowing what she feared. He came closer. She tried to scream, but no sound resulted. She tried to run, but her feet were cemented to the ground. In another moment he would touch her; she felt the touch; she continued frozen in horror. His hand was upon her bare arm; she shivered. "Go away! Go away!" she screamed and Tomcat disappeared. Now Ray was standing before her. She felt a hand on her shoulder. She awakened abruptly. Abigail was there in her nightgown, her hair in a braid, a flashlight in one hand, while with the other she was vigorously shaking Carla by the shoulder.

"Wake up! Wake up!" the mother cried. "Why are you screaming so? You're having a nightmare."

Carla sat up in bed, too dazed at first to speak. At last she was able to say simply, "I must have been."

"Would it help if you told me about it?"

"Oh no, no."

Abigail went downstairs and brought back a glass of water which she insisted Carla drink. If only she'd talk to me, she thought.

Carla had never talked to anyone about Tomcat. It was years since she had even thought about him, yet now he came back to haunt her dreams! How would she ever escape from him and from Miss Abbott? It was inextricably mixed with making good and getting on in the world. Her hopes of the Blodgett scholarship were weak at night, strong in the morning. The college was some forty miles from Megunnaway, and she'd live on campus. She'd sleep in the comfortable dormitory and go to her classes in ivy-covered halls and quite distinguish herself with her quickness to learn. But what about Ray? She'd miss Ray, how much she wasn't sure.

EIGHT

It happened the very next week that Miss Castleton, the English teacher, requested her to stay after school, and she approached the classroom with trepidation. Miss Castleton stood beside her desk and smiled as the girl entered the room. Oh, she's going to be sarcastic, thought Carla. Miss Castleton was much given to sarcasm, and she stood now with a slight smile playing around her lips, her little eyes sharp and lively, a woman of medium height and enormous girth. She might have served as the model for the cylinder drawing seen in geometry books, so perfectly round was her build. She was dressed neatly in a long gray garment, an exact match for the color of her thick gray hair. Gray-rimmed spectacles occupied a small portion of her smooth gray face, and those little eyes just flashed and twinkled and found whoever she looked upon amusing. "Miss Wingate, my dear," she said. "I may have some good news for you. Let's sit down."

Miss Castleton eased her body into the chair behind the desk while Carla slid into the chair beside it, hardly daring to hope.

"Mr. Blaisdell, our Principal, has talked to me about you, my dear, and about your further education. He and Mrs. Pomeroy."

"My further education?" Carla could hardly speak.

"Yes, my dear. I have told you of the difficulties we have in arranging scholarships. There are just more needy students than there are funds available. But there is a possibility."

"Oh Miss Castleton!" Carla spoke breathlessly.

"Yes, a scholarship for one year covering tuition and board. You'd have to take care of books and clothing."

"Oh I can, I can wear the clothes I have; I can get some work, I know I can."

"Wait. It isn't settled. It's for Winthrop College, not Smith or Wellesley or even Radcliffe, but a good solid liberal arts college."

"The Blodgett Scholarship?"

"To be sure. I said it isn't settled." The teacher thoroughly enjoyed the suspense. "There remains a question."

"What question?"

"There are two students here at Megunnaway High who need the scholarship and who have the ability to do honor to it."

"I'd do my very best."

"You are the more academically gifted. The other is Judd Tewksbury, who is, how shall I say—perhaps the more dependable, a plodder, but a good plodder. It's between you two."

Why does it have to be between us two, Carla moaned inwardly. *I have no desire to push anybody aside, least of all hardworking Judd Tewksbury. Still, heavens! How I want it!*

"We have decided to talk frankly with you," Miss Castleton went on. "Just what are your intentions as to Ray Putnam?"

Carla blushed. The question came so abruptly. Usually, she thought, the question was what are *his* intentions and that she did not know. "We're not engaged," she managed to answer.

"That may not be good," mused the teacher. "If you were, we could have him in here and the three of us could lay the cards on the table and have it out."

"Please, don't say anything to him."

"He never was one to value education," Miss Castleton mused. "As it is, it would be improper for me to talk to him."

Carla sighed in relief for Miss Castleton would never do anything improper.

"I have to say quite frankly to you, my dear, we don't want to give the scholarship to someone who isn't going to stay the course and use the education afterwards."

"Oh Miss Castleton, I'd stay, I'd finish," said Carla earnestly.

"Hmm. Maybe. But how could you do well if you were spending your time traveling back and forth to be with your sweetheart?"

"He could do the traveling. Motorcycles travel fast."

"I know and it's only forty miles. Frankly, the greater danger is that you would take a notion to get married. I really have to know which means more to you, the chance to go to college or your relationship with this boy? I do not call it an affair for that would be unjust." It would be easier to manage, she thought, but this she naturally did not say. "I must ask, which means more?"

"They both mean a lot to me."

"I sense a conflict. If I could go to Mr. Blaisdell and say you and Putnam had agreed to, well, sort of forget about each other for the next year, I think I could promise you the grant."

"I couldn't talk to him about it."

Miss Castleton looked at the handsome intelligent face, into the clear gray eyes, at the strong healthy body, the strength that in this case might be a source of weakness. "I understand," she said. "If you will give me some assurance that you will stop seeing him, I will leave the details to your ingenuity."

Carla hesitated. How easily she could have agreed! But what right did they have to tell her what to do about seeing Ray? Why should that be a condition of the scholarship? It wasn't fair and she rebelled against it.

"No, Miss Castleton," she said at last. "I don't know what will happen between Ray and me, but I won't give any promise I can't keep, and I won't say anything that would make you think I'd see him less."

"Not even for a chance to go to college?"

"Not for anything."

That was that. Carla was curtly dismissed by the teacher. She walked down the hall and into the snowy street. How clean and pure it was, and for the moment she was clean and pure. She'd been tempted to say anything Miss Castleton wanted, but she had not yielded. As for planning to have a serious talk about it with Ray, that she had not even considered. This was as bad as Miss Abbott. It was ironic. Out of loyalty to Mama she had refused what was Abigail's dearest dream for her daughter, and out of loyalty to Ray she had refused Miss Castleton's offer when she didn't even know if Ray wanted that kind of loyalty.

March was cold and windy and April dripping rain. Abigail talked no more of Carla's going to college. Nothing had worked out; she didn't know why. Carla would have to find a job. The gentleness of May was followed by the sudden heat of June. On a day shortly before Carla would graduate from Megunnaway High, Abigail and Margaret, Elsa, Carla, and Ray were all in the Putnams' front yard. Carla stood close to where Ray was lovingly checking out his motorcycle. Elsa pretended to be busy transplanting a rosebush but actually was there to watch Carla and Ray. Margaret Putnam noted her daughter's way of handling a trowel and sighed. There was no use correcting her; she just didn't have the knack.

Margaret turned to Abigail. "Did I tell you Ray's only working part-time?" she asked.

"Times are hard," said Abigail.

"Of course," Margaret went on, "Ray is the best mechanic for miles around. I know his boss won't let him go unless he has to, but this part-time schedule doesn't give him much money."

Ray laughed. "So far I'm paying my keep," he said, glancing up at his mother. "Maybe I should move to Boston. Last week I cased it, and the cars were so thick you couldn't cross the street."

"Don't catch me up so quick," Margaret said hastily. "You know I don't want you to move to Boston. A crowded city isn't healthy."

"I don't know," rejoined Ray. "The people there were so many you could hardly walk."

For a while the women were silent, just standing there, basking in the warm sun, glad to be near their children. Oh dear, thought Abigail, don't let her go and marry a man who's not even earning a living, not that. She comforted herself that there'd been no talk of marriage. Carla moved close to the cycle to be near Ray as he worked. She was dressed in casual blue slacks and blouse, her hair tied back with a yellow headband, her body outlined by the close-fitting garments. Abigail almost cried, she was so beautiful.

Ray stepped back to look at the big red Indian. "She's ready," he said. "Come, Carla, we'll test her." And they took their places on the cycle.

They're like two young pioneers, thought Margaret, a man so rugged and adventuresome and a woman of strength and daring. They could pose for a statue of the opening up of the West, but the West had long been settled.

Ray guided the cycle onto the highway with Carla clinging to him. They gathered speed, and Carla felt the throb of the machine, the bounce when they hit a rock. She held tightly to Ray. How she loved the feel of his rough denim jacket! They gathered speed and flew faster than the swiftest racehorse. The sun was bright, the sky clear, and the wind rushed against them. Soft green trees and trees white with blossoms and dark green pines flashed by. A rabbit scurried out of their way, an occasional car appeared on the road ahead to be passed as if it were standing still. After a half hour they turned onto a rough dirt road and their speed slackened.

"Hang on," Ray yelled at her.

"I am."

"Tighter, hold tighter."

They slid into a clearing where a small brown building stood by the side of the water. Lake Maranakeag was perhaps two miles long and a mile wide. All around it the trees, hardwood mixed with evergreens, grew close to the water except for the one clearing and a sliver of sandy beach on the other side. The water threw back the picture of the trees by its banks. Soon the young couple were gliding in a canoe into the middle of the lake, with Ray in the stern dipping his paddle deep in the water and Carla in the bow using quick surface strokes. Ray glowed with admiration. How straight she sat and how vigorously she paddled. He couldn't stand the dolls who just sat letting him do the work; he could forgive those who tried and were duds at it, but oh Carla with the beautiful back and strong arms!

They landed at the beach, secured the canoe, stripped for swimming and dashed into the water. Soon they were racing. Of course he won. Then they were surface diving, were splashing each other, were floating calmly side by side, were lying in the sun yearning for each other and struggling, he no less than she, to control the surge of passion propelling them toward what would be for them the point of no return. Lunch, which they had purchased at the store by the boat landing, was a temporary diversion, as were getting dressed and hiking through the dappled woods. The finding of flowers, the arguing over the flower names, the walking until every muscle was weary—these were all diversions. At last they lay down on the pine needles in a secluded grove and drew close to each other. His desire was sharp and specific, and so was hers, and they clung to each other. But when he put his hand upon her knee she suddenly pushed him away and started crying.

"Why Carla," he protested. "You know I'll never do anything you don't want. Don't you love me? Don't you want me?"

"There's so much you don't know about me. I've never talked to anyone about it."

Thoroughly alarmed he sat up straight and helped her to sit by his side. "What on earth are you talking about?" he demanded.

"I can't tell you."

"You must. It's come between us and I've a right to know."

"Let me lie down so you can't see my face."

At last she began, in a voice muffled with tears, her face still pressed against the pine needles. She told him about Tomcat and then she lay there unable to control her sobs.

"Is that all?" he said with great relief. "You're talking about something which never really happened."

"It did happen! All the fear and repulsion I felt—all the shame—they were real. They *are* real. And even though I never let him touch me, what did he see in me that encouraged him? Why did he think—"

"He was just a dirty old man."

"There had to be something, Ray," she wailed. "Something that made me different—evil. Something he sensed."

"Garbage, absolutely wrong! All he sensed was that you were alone, no one to protect you. How could you possibly blame yourself? You were a child; he was a grown man!"

"But Aunt Beulah, the others, they treated me like I had leprosy when I came back."

"That proves my point!" Ray's eyes gleamed in fury. "They knew him, knew what he was like, so they just assumed he got to you cause you were just a kid. I'd like to horsewhip the lot of them!"

"I don't know—"

"You were a child, Carla! Just a kid. Forget it!"

"You forgive me?"

"There's nothing to forgive," he said. "And Carla, I'll never touch you in such a way nor push you nor anything until we're married. I swear it."

"Married?"

"My little wife!" He kissed her tenderly, then led the way back to the canoe.

❦

They were married on the Fourth of July. It was a quiet wedding party with only the immediate family and half a dozen friends. Josiah had not answered the letter Carla wrote him and they hadn't heard from Howard, so Abigail had to give the bride in marriage, though she knew it wasn't proper. Then she broke down and cried as was expected. She complained bitterly because Howard hadn't been there to perform his duty, but she made no mention of Josiah. After the simple ceremony the little party stood on the steps of the church.

"Well, Mother Wingate," said Ray, "it's honeymoon time. We're taking off."

"God bless you, my children," Abigail said through her tears.

And then, to the despair of the staid old Reverend Cameron, the young couple departed with a flurry of dust and tremendous engine roar gaily riding the big red motorcycle. Carla's skirt flapped around her legs, her hair blew in the wind, her arms circled her husband's waist and she leaned close to his sturdy back, then looked up for a moment and smiled happily at her mother.

It's done, thought Abigail, *not my will, dear God but Thine.* Bravely but in vain she fought the tears. *But is it God's will? I'm not even sure about the legality of it. Carla is too young to marry without her guardian's permission. I signed the paper, but did I have the right?*

"There, there," said Margaret. "Don't cry."

"Silly me!" said Abigail.

They walked together, the Putnams and Abigail, to the car. "What'll they live on?" grumbled Barclay. "Times are hard, going to get worse."

"Now, now," replied Margaret, "we'll manage somehow. We'll share."

No one can share my grief, thought Abigail, for she could voice it to no one. *Is the marriage legal? No, I suppose not. The law says a bride under eighteen must have her guardian's written consent and Carla didn't have that. I should have called Miss Abbott. Merciful heavens! It's come to this that I can't sign for my baby to get married!* It was no sin, they'd been wed in church and Mr. Cameron had said he understood about the father not coming to give away the bride. That part of it was valid enough. It was a mere legalism, this other. True enough, but what would happen when Miss Abbott *did* find out?

At the lake Ray and Carla paddled gently about in the canoe; they lay together under the pine trees; they walked arm in arm, talking of the wondrous thing that had come to pass quite as if they had invented the way of a man with a maid and the way of a maid with a man, and they forgot to get hungry. For a while they were unaware of the mosquitos which buzzed about them in increasing numbers, but the stings grew more numerous and could not be ignored.

At last they rode back to Megunnaway on the big red Indian, drove it right by the Putnam house, across the field, along the path between the trees to the clearing where Ray had pitched the big blue tent which was to be their temporary, oh very temporary, home. At the entrance he bent and picked her up and carried her through the opening, over the threshold as it were. Once inside he straightened up and set her down. "Well," he said, "you're sure a lot of woman. Like to broke my back."

"I'm sorry," she said.

"No, no, no," he cried, then whispered in her ear, "You see, I'm a lot of man."

When they awakened in the morning, they lay side by side and watched the sun shine on the blue canvas, which got lighter and lighter as the sun rose higher, until it was like the sky. The wind began to blow, filling here and billowing there, and the canvas became the sails of a magic ship, their ship as they set sail upon the sea of wedded life.

✻❀✻

"We'll have to go somewhere to find work, won't we?" she said.

"I'm afraid so. I've heard of something in Dover. Jack's driving over some time today and I'm going with him."

He held her close. "What a weird class prophecy they had for you," he said. The graduation's light touch with a venomous sting, the class prophecy, had predicted that Carla would be an old maid school teacher living in Boston and in her spare time writing history books. "Anyway I've rescued you from being an old maid."

"I liked the other part."

"Writing books?"

"Yes."

For Carla, he thought, for Carla, wonderful Carla, nothing was impossible. He began to sing, not thinking about the song or why he chanced upon it, "Just Mollie and me, and baby makes three, And we're happy in my blue heaven."

"Oh Ray, no, not yet."

"I hope not yet," he said soberly. "But it could be. Are you afraid?"

"No," she said. "But let's not yet."

Cheerfully switching to "It ain't agonna rain no more, no more, How the heck can I wash my neck? If it ain't agonna rain no more," he hurried into his clothes and interrupted the song when he saw that she had finished dressing. "You're beautiful," he said.

"This old dress," she scoffed.

"Yeah, ratty old dress, take it off."

But she was hungry, and together they went through the woods and the field and into the Putnam house for breakfast, and then next door just in time to say a word or two to Abigail before she left for work. Jack drove up in his old Ford and Ray went away with him.

Feeling quite sure that both Ray and Jack would be hired, Carla went humming about the house. They'd find a place to rent in Dover, she'd better get her clothes packed, they might have to move right away. Then there were the other things, the treasures made dear by association, not so many either; it wouldn't take long to pack them neatly into boxes. But when one sits mooning over each item for fifteen minutes, even a half hour, the time is considerably stretched out. Abigail, coming home in the middle of the afternoon, found Carla in her bedroom, with a box full of clothing packed and another box standing ready to be filled. Carla's Bible was in it and a couple of other books, and Carla was sitting on the floor gazing dreamily at an old green bottle, that old green bottle that she'd taken with her from Amsterburg.

Abigail sat down on the bed. "Do you remember the farm?" she asked.

"Oh yes," the girl answered. "That's half of why I kept the bottle, but mostly it meant faraway places, exciting, romantic places."

"Oh do tell me your plans," cried Abigail.

"We'll go where Ray can find work. He and Jack went to Dover. They heard about a construction labor job."

"Oh," said Abigail dejectedly. Was it for this she'd left Josiah? "I don't suppose you have a picture of your father?"

"No, where would I have gotten one? I do have this snapshot of Howard."

Abigail took the snapshot. "Poor little tyke," she said.

"He's no longer a poor little tyke," said Carla. "I wonder where he is."

She found another souvenir, a handmade valentine, red and white paper with lacy edging and a drawing of a boy and girl hand in hand. "And I wonder where he is." She handed it to Abigail.

"He?" she queried. "I see it's signed 'Roger.'"

"Yes, Roger."

"Who on earth is Roger?" How could this schoolgirl have a past?

"Didn't I tell you about him? Boy I went to school with when I was at Aunt Beulah's."

"Your age?"

"A couple of years older." Carefully she placed the valentine in the book and laid the book in the box.

"Carla," said Abigail gravely. "Either you tell Ray about that, or you destroy it."

"Oh? It's no secret. I'll tell him."

"Maybe—"

"Of course I'll tell him." She kissed her mother. "I'll tell him about both the valentine and the bottle."

"The sooner the better." Abigail stood up. "I'm going downstairs, I hear a car." Carla followed her.

Ray stood by the sink, taking an inordinately long time to drink a glass of water. "We didn't get any job," he said at last.

The young couple went upstairs to be alone. "What's with the bottle?" he asked. "Anything in it?"

"No, no," she said. "It's something I fished out of a brook on my father's farm. It's my good luck piece."

"Pagan superstition," he scoffed. "But I see you also have a Bible. So you fished it out of a brook on your father's farm?"

"Yes, we didn't always live in a hovel like this."

"Don't talk that way about your home. Look at it this way, if it were a hunting lodge or a summer cabin, you'd say it was first-rate."

"I want something more."

"Sure, Baby, and we'll have it."

"I want more than just to live, just to get by," she said earnestly. "It isn't really the house."

"I saw Judd Tewksbury today," he told her. "He says you could have had the scholarship instead of him if you'd agreed to give up seeing me. Is that true?"

"How on earth did he know?"

"He says old Castle laid it all out before him."

"I wish she hadn't."

"So it is true. I'll make it up to you, I swear I will. No matter where I have to go or what I have to do."

"Maybe going away is right for us. Forget I complained about this house. Any kind of place with you—"

"It beats the old blue tent."

"The tent is prettier."

"Wait till November."

It was a pleasant dinner, with Abigail bustling about trying hard to be a good hostess but burning the biscuits. Something always seemed to go wrong when she wanted it most to be perfect. They joked about the "burnt offering"; Ray had such an easy, teasing, joking manner that every mishap seemed but an excuse for laughter. Abigail grew thoughtful and was far away, herself a bride, standing at an altar in her elegant gown, and after the ceremony glowing with love and pride at the reception at her parents' home, the big living room and the dining room and even the kitchen filled with friends and relatives, oh cousins by the dozens. How she wished she could have given Carla half as good! But it would work out better; Ray was younger than Josiah had been, he was more flexible, more adaptable. She sighed. As Ray put his arm around Carla, she felt the strong man arm of Josiah around her own shoulders, around her waist, drawing her close. Ray was fun, but you never really could have a serious conversation with him, not at all like Josiah. Still, if that was what Carla wanted— She hoped he wouldn't let Carla boss him around. She flashed back to the present and realized that Ray was telling her that Carla and he would do the dishes.

They left as soon as it was dark and after a brief visit at the Putnams' snuggled together on the mattress in the tent.

❧

The amount of work Ray could find lessened. However, the short working week did not mean that Ray was home with Carla, for all through the hot days of August and the more comfortable time of September and October he went far and wide, walking or on his cycle, looking for work, going to other towns, visiting friends who might have heard of something, putting in applications at garages and mills and stores and every conceivable place, looking for work as a mechanic, willing to take anything he could get. He got a few days splitting wood, he got a few days cutting weeds, but nothing more and even the days at Pete's Garage grew widely spaced. Carla too went looking for work, but only in Megunnaway. Margaret warned Carla that if she found steady work and Ray didn't, things would be bad indeed. An occasional odd job wouldn't hurt, she said, but a man's pride is a fragile thing.

More and more there was talk in the air about "the times." Yes, they were bad. There were various explanations: high wages, low wages; the President, the Congress; speculation or failure to speculate; departing from tradition; sun spots and sin. No one doubted that times were bad, but no one knew what he personally could do about the times. There were various ways of coping. Suffering most of all were those who believed that if times were bad for them, it was because of their own shortcomings.

At times Ray was sure that if he couldn't get a job it was his own fault, but the next day he was sure to blame the government or low wages or high wages. At last he came to the conclusion that it was because he hadn't been venturesome enough, and in this he found his mother and his mother-in-law pulling in opposite directions. Abigail agreed that yes, he ought to strike out, try some other place, while Margaret urged patience. Barclay Putnam, at first reluctant to express an opinion, began to talk of the opportunities he heard about in the big cities. Carla trembled and feared, thanking God that at least she wasn't with child. How cruel that she must give thanks for this!

One cool October day as she was scrubbing the potatoes before putting them into the oven to bake, she heard the sound of an unfamiliar motor. Ray burst in, in a strange excited mood.

"Model T Fords," he said, "aren't all black."

Carla and Abigail stared at him, puzzled.

"Some are the color of mud—maybe from back roads, maybe fresh off the assembly line."

"Did you work on one today?" asked Carla.

"Yeah," he said. "And guess what? We've got one of those mud models. I think it's the paint, not quite sure."

Carla dropped the potato and ran out. There stood a weary old car, a sedan, a drab and mud-colored car.

"I traded the Indian for it," he said. "Been working on it, it runs now."

He had traded his motorcycle, his beautiful mechanical mountain goat; traded the motorcycle on which they had ridden to romance, the wonderful, purring, whirring, roaring Indian that of all the motorcycles he had ever worked on was the prize. And here was this clumsy, oafish, ox of a car.

"Gets good mileage," he said. "Could take us to Boston."

Carla and Ray were quiet at dinner. It was Abigail who bubbled with excitement. Surely now with a way of traveling, they'd find work. The car was big enough to carry clothing, blankets, cooking utensils, sleeping bags, and groceries which they could cook in state campgrounds on their way. By the time she got through, she had quite convinced herself that it was practically a home on wheels. And they'd caught some of her optimism.

When Ray went out to work on the car, Carla drew close to her mother, embraced her. "I've been such a brat," she said. "Can you ever forgive me?"

"Good heavens, for what?"

"The clothes brush and the awful things I've said over the years."

"Oh Carla!" Abigail's eyes filled with tears.

When the chill of November made sleeping in the tent no longer feasible, Ray and Carla packed the car, and one Saturday morning they drove off down the highway. Abigail went back into her little house and stood in a daze. She couldn't even pick up the dishes; she was drained, exhausted. She sat down by the table, cluttered as it was, took up her knitting, and wasn't even able to do that. Her life was over, she could neither think nor feel. After a while the dirty dishes prodded her into action, and the physical movement set her mind in motion. It was good that they were going to Boston. There were great opportunities in the city. She'd never been there, but she knew. And for Carla, Carla the beautiful, Carla the brilliant, there'd be a new and shining life. She'd always liked to write, had talent too, maybe she'd get a job on a newspaper. Abigail stopped just short of her becoming editor-in-chief. This is nonsense, she chided herself. What will happen is that Ray will find a job as a mechanic, and they'll rent some place to live, and they'll have a family and live a respectable life. What more should one ask? She thought of herself as a bride. Oh, but that was different. She and Josiah were such good companions, both such intellectuals, and no matter how poor they were, they'd never been common. Oh the wonderful hours they'd spent sharing ideas! Is there anything more beautiful than the sharing of ideas?

Well, there was faith in God, but sometimes even that seemed far away. She sat down to finish an urgently needed mitten and to read. The Good Book lay at hand. She tried a couple of passages, but they didn't speak to her condition. She continued her search. Micah, the book opened there of its own accord. Micah 6:8, "He hath showed thee, O man, what is good; and what doth the Lord require of thee, but to do justly, and to love mercy, and to walk humbly with thy God." She read it silently, she read it aloud. How often we, in the old days, read that together, and thought we'd learned to live it. Josiah, Siah! I left because of the children, but now the children are grown. "And what doth the Lord require of thee—" It frightened her, and the fear had a fascination. With contrite heart she confessed to herself and to God that she had not actually lived as that scripture commanded. Maybe if she read it a thousand times. Yes, she must read that verse a thousand times.

NINE

It took Abigail a long time to read Micah 6:8 a thousand times, for often she was too tired and occasionally she forgot. She kept the tally on the envelope of a letter from Carla, laughing at herself as she did so. It was superstition, a device for delaying what she had vowed to do. She had vowed to go and visit Josiah, but on the summer night when the last little mark was made, she faced up to a lack of funds so absolute that she didn't have the train fare even if she were to spend her last penny. By December she had the money. She wrote Carla and Ray of her plans and then sat down to pack.

She would use Carla's old knapsack, she thought. It would look ridiculous, but she didn't care, at least not much. What should she take? Toilet articles and a change of clothing, of course. A pair of woolen stockings for Josiah. One of Carla's graduation pictures. And certainly the letters from Carla, at least the most interesting ones. There were some which she never tired of rereading. There was one about the enormous library and others about the museum and the tremendous statue of Victory at the entrance. In another Carla told how she and Ray had walked along the Esplanade and looked across the Charles River at the white buildings of MIT. "I wish I could go there to study architecture," Carla had written. Maybe sometime she will, thought Abigail. They seemed to be doing so well, though it wasn't clear why Ray was working in restaurants. They had no children and both were young enough to wait, and they had obviously learned how to postpone their family. Abigail sighed. Young people knew so much these days; she wasn't sure if it was good. It worried Abigail that there was nothing about churchgoing in the letters. Well, there had been one thing. Yes, she'd show the letters to Josiah, but she'd never talk about the troubles she'd had with Carla. And she certainly wouldn't share her anxiety about the legality of the marriage. Josiah was so straight-laced! She finished packing, rejoicing in Carla's happy life and hoping some day to visit her and absorb into her own being some of the excitement of the city.

An hour later she stood on the station platform with Barclay by her side, for she had yielded to his insistence on giving her a ride and carrying the knapsack. He was silent and glum as always, but she sensed his sympathy and was engrossed in her own running account of Amsterburg. Oh, such a farm, she enthused, and the house. Four bedrooms, and a fifth if you counted the half finished room upstairs. And the orchard, you never saw such an orchard, MacIntosh and Duchess and Bellflowers. Oh it would be good to get back! Barclay took it with a grain of salt and grunted every once in a while.

Abigail gazed up the street at the library, red brick, two story, imposing against the white. Smoke whirled from the red brick chimneys of the adjacent houses; the snow had slid from some of the gabled roofs leaving dark gray geometrical shapes outlined against the general whiteness. Further up the hill huge evergreens towered fifty feet in the air, and everything reflected the sparkling sun. A beautiful town, a rugged scene. She watched the people scurrying along the snowy sidewalk. She should have said good-bye to Louise, she thought, and to the Mills family. Beyond the station lay the river, frozen solid and a solitary boy skated in wild circles. Icicles along the roof reflected the sun, hung like crystal pendants, a few in the center were beginning to melt and she watched the slow drip. A flock of chickadees pecked along the edge of the tracks where the snow had been brushed away. What lively little birds with their black caps and gray-brown backs, beautiful in their softly colored way, thought the little woman in the new black hat and not so new gray coat, as she stood waiting for the magic carpet.

The train was as always on time to the very second, and she was on her way. She'd really done it. She sat beside the window and watched the town recede, looked eagerly at the Megunnaway Mill, saw the waste water from it flow into an open spot in the river, knew that some of its people were working, Louise probably. She lifted her eyes again to the hill and could just make out a man and a boy carrying a small tree between them. They would have a Christmas, yes they would, and so would she, for she would be home, back on the farm, back with Josiah. Even after the years and the bitterness that she knew he had felt, his arms would welcome her, of this she felt sure. She wished now that she had questioned Howard and Carla more about their visit to the farm. Carla had said so little. Well, that was Carla, she never talked. Oh she used a lot of words but what was inside was buried deep, at least buried from her mother. *Carla, Carla,* she thought, *my beautiful baby, so much of her father in her. Maybe she and Ray will come to the farm.* They'd bring new energy, and she herself would work.

Oh she realized she hadn't done her full share before, but she'd learned to toil. She'd cook and she'd sew and she'd milk the cow and she'd pick potato bugs and she'd can a hundred quarts of wild berries. She'd waste no time. The very next day she'd roast a chicken; surely Josiah would be willing to kill one—she couldn't do that. And she'd bake apples, with cinnamon and nutmeg and a beautiful glaze. He'd always said her baked apples were superb. They'd joked about it, said they were all she knew how to cook, then after a while it wasn't a joke. She sighed. She really wasn't a good cook, hadn't the knack for it. Carla, however, was much more practical—cooking, sewing, handy with hammer and nails. Yes, much more practical. She herself had been more of a dreamer, more romantic, she thought rather smugly. No, no, that was wrong. She'd been wrong. But now she knew better.

She took up her Bible, and it opened of its own volition to Revelation, the sixth chapter. She read a few verses, then closed it firmly. She didn't want to read about the four horsemen or the shattered universe or anything about the end times. She wanted the world to go on, at least to last out this her new life. Only miserable old women hoped for the end to be near. She closed the book and sat gazing out the window. The train passed miles of hills green with trees, and many of the trees had snow upon their branches, soft and white and warm upon the dark green branches. Here and there she saw farmhouses, saw the smoke rising from the red brick chimneys, saw horses trotting along pulling loaded sleighs. They sometimes came so close that she could see the rosy cheeks of the children and their bright red mittens. She saw the stations; some were brown and some were green and one was white. The one at Amsterburg used to be gray, but they'd been talking of painting it. She wondered if they had and if they'd used the same color, which she rather hoped they had. She wanted nothing to have changed, nothing at all, for she was going home.

The trees along the approach to Amsterburg were mainly hardwoods and stood bare and gray against the white snow and the blue sky, their branches forming a delicate, intricate pattern. In the fall they'd be crimson again, and green in spring, and the elm tree in the yard would be gray now, green in the spring and golden bright in the fall. She supposed Josiah would have piled pine and fir branches around the base of the house, and if he'd painted it, it would be gleaming white, and the shutters would be dark green against the white. If she'd let him know, he'd have been at the station to meet her, but there might be people around; there would at least be the stationmaster, and she wanted to be alone when first she met him.

She was the only passenger getting off at Amsterburg. They hadn't painted the station or if they had, they had used the same gray and it had already weathered, for it was just as she had remembered. There was a different stationmaster, a middle-aged man she'd never seen before, and she was glad of this, for she wanted to see no acquaintance until she was actually at the farm. She wondered if she'd changed and went and looked in the mirror on the gum vending machine. No, she hadn't changed that much, hardly at all.

She set out upon her way, the clumsy pack upon her shoulders, her hat pulled down over her face as far as it would go. The road had been plowed, but it was rough going and there were few vehicles about. Snow was banked at the sides but packed enough in the roadway to provide some kind of footing. It was already dark when she came to the neighbor farm just before the Wingate place. Though she was weary now, her feet cold, her nose so chilled she feared it might be frostbitten, yet her heart still sang and she quickened her pace. A scant quarter of a mile and she'd be there. She could see the tall dark frame of the elm, but she couldn't see the barn, which was strange. First there should be the barn and then the house. She could see a dark patch, but it seemed close to the ground, whereas the barn was a big building and the house two stories tall. Had she forgotten what the place looked like?

When she stood leaning against the elm, she had to admit the awful truth. Both house and barn had burned to the ground, and all that was left was rubble and dead charcoal and the smell of smouldering wood. There was a crunch upon the snow, and she turned to the man who approached her. It was the neighbor from the next house beyond, the big house upon the hill.

"Abigail!" he exclaimed.

"Yes, Bill," she said. "I've come home. Where's Josiah? He at your place?"

"No," said the man. "But you'd better come. Ma'll tell you."

"It's burned!" She was still aghast.

"Yes, it's burned. Let's hurry now, it's freezing cold."

All the strength of her high resolve seeped from her; she was near to collapse, but she managed to walk close behind the man, who held his lantern carefully to light her path. He didn't say another word until they were inside the warm house, and his wife was greeting them. "Ain't told her nothing," he muttered. "You'll have to." And he disappeared.

Mrs. Bill Starbuck was a stout middle-aged woman with a gentle face. Abigail had many times turned to her for comfort, many times those long years ago, and now she stood looking to Mrs. Bill for the answer to her question. And Mrs. Bill, Bessie, hesitated, unable to find words.

"Sit down, sit down," she urged. "I'll get you a cup of tea."

"Where is he?" cried Abigail. "Was he hurt? Where is he?"

There was no evading it. Bessie had no choice. She must say the dreadful words. "He's gone," she said. "He's dead. They done their best, but—"

Abigail bowed her head upon the table and sobbed. Finally she let Bessie take off her hat and coat, and give her a cup of tea, then lead her into a warm bedroom. "We'll talk more in the morning," said Bessie. "Try to rest."

"Tell me about it, just how it happened," pleaded Abigail.

"In the morning," said Bessie.

Abigail knew she wouldn't sleep, but she blew out the lamp and lay down upon the bed. Toward morning she dozed off and when she awoke heard voices in the next room. Now they would have to tell her; she couldn't stand it any longer.

Going into the kitchen she found the Starbucks drinking coffee and with them sat Sheriff Kingsbury. "Sheriff!" she cried. "What happened? Where is he?"

The Starbucks edged out of the room. "You'd better have a cup of coffee," said the Sheriff.

"No," she said. "Not one drop or one crumb. I'm putting on my hat and coat, and we're walking over to the place."

"Okay. Put on your duds," he said. "We'll go there."

He offered to take her in the car, but she insisted on walking. At last they stood by the ashes, and Kingsbury had talked nothing but drivel about the weather. "Any fool can see the place burned down," Abigail said acidly. "But Josiah? Where is he?"

"Abigail, you're a woman with a lot of gumption."

"Where is he?"

"I guess you know by now he's dead."

"Bessie said, but I didn't believe it."

"They done their best."

She leaned against the tree. "Don't torture me," she cried. "Talk!"

"Well, ma'm, we don't know just how the fire was set," the Sheriff said. "I'd seen him that afternoon, and he was pretty upset."

"Upset?"

"Place had been foreclosed, and he'd been given notice to vacate, had no idea where he'd go. I made an appointment to come out next day and help him figure out what to do. But that night Bill Starbuck called me, said the place was in flames, said he'd round up what men he could. Bill hurried down, but he couldn't get into the place, flames everywhere. Josiah wasn't nowhere around."

"Then maybe he wasn't —"

"We found him next day. Know'd it must've been him."

"Could he have left already, could it have been some tramp careless with fire? You know Josiah was always so careful."

Hope dies hard, he thought. And the coroner, who should have known better, had given him a bad time about identification. As if there could be any doubt! Kingsbury drew from his pocket a bronze belt-buckle ornamented with a grinning Teddy Roosevelt. "You recognize this?" he asked.

She seized it and pressed it to her lips. "I gave it to him, the first present I ever gave him," she sobbed.

The Sheriff looked on compassionately. This ought to settle any question of identification, yet he almost wished he hadn't shown it to her. He himself had removed it from the body, kept it for the next of kin, had hoped that boy would show up, had planned to write to Abigail whose address he'd gotten from Miss Abbott. That Abbott woman had said no one knew where the boy was, Abigail had no phone, and the girl wasn't around. Now he almost wished he'd kept the buckle hidden in his pocket.

"When was it?" she asked at last. "And the funeral?"

He shifted uneasily from foot to foot. "Fire was a week ago Friday. We had the funeral Sunday. Had to, there was a thaw and a hard freeze on its way."

"Where is he?"

"In the graveyard by the meetinghouse."

"Take me there."

They went back up the hill to the Starbucks' and she got in the car. Silently they drove to the meetinghouse, past the houses she remembered well, past the place where they used to have honking geese, past two more farms, and came to the meetinghouse, dark and deserted in the snowy waste. The burial ground was ringed with a rusty fence as she remembered well. In summer weeds grew there, seemed like no one ever got time to clean them out, but now they were covered with snow. There was a path where the snow had been trampled, and in one corner a dark plot of earth lay exposed.

"Was there a preacher?" she asked.

"I said the prayer," he answered, "and some of the ladies sang the hymns. Sang 'Abide with Me.'"

She stood there in silence. "'Abide with me, Fast falls the eventide,'" she said. She turned to Kingsbury and shot out the words, "Was it my fault?"

"Maybe he'd already given up before you left and you sensed it and had to take the kids," he answered. "No, I don't place no blame on you." Now, at last, he didn't. "Maybe it was the foreclosure that finally did it."

"Did they have to do that? Kick him out in the midst of winter?"

"He got the notice months before; then they let him pick his apples and dig his potatoes. He kept hoping he'd sell them, get a grubstake, but mostly they just rotted."

"I'd come back to stay," she said.

"Maybe he knows that," said the man. "I don't understand such things."

"If he knows, he knows I came too late. And he knows I never should have left. I sinned and I'm being punished." There was a fierce comfort in this punishment; she was paying her debt; she'd always been one to pay her debts.

They heard the sound of boots upon the snow and turned around. A young man in a red plaid mackinaw with a bedroll flung over his shoulder was picking his way across the yard.

"Howard!" she cried. "Is it really you?"

Still a scrawny runt, thought the Sheriff, but wiry strong. "I wouldn't have known you," he said to Howard

"Oh Howard," cried Abigail. "I'd given up all hopes. At least I've found you!"

"I've been following the crops," he said. "But now there's no crops to follow, so I'm holed up in Portsmouth, in a sort of mission place."

"How come you're here?" the Sheriff asked.

"Nothing to do but read the papers, so I read them all. Saw an item in the Bangor paper about the fire. Looks like I got here too late for the funeral."

"If you'd been here then, you'd have missed your mother."

"Maybe I can build some kind of shack on the place."

"Son, it isn't ours, it's been foreclosed."

"Then I'd better be drifting along."

"You'n your mother better put your heads together and do some planning," said the Sheriff.

Howard had learned to make quick decisions, pick up and leave in the flash of an eye at any rumor of work, hole up somewhere when that was what he had to do, catch a freight or hitch a ride when the weather turned warm, move fast and free, travel light. It didn't take him long to decide he'd better get Abigail back to Megunnaway where at least she had friends and, he hoped, a job. Abigail leaned on him and followed him. He had money enough to pay her fare, well yes, his too, but that wasn't necessary, he'd just see her onto the train. On this one point she refused to give in. He must go with her; there was no one at home now that Carla was gone. When they got off the train in Megunnaway, he yielded the lead to her, for this was her turf, but she would not accept the responsibility. She sat down upon the bench, bowed her head into her hands and refused to move.

"You'd better go to the Putnams," he said.

"There's no point."

"Then let's go to your house. You've got to go somewhere," he insisted. "Say, do you know what day this is?"

"What day?"

"Why, it's Christmas Eve."

She consented at last to go home. She unlocked the door, saw her things still in place. How strange! She sat listlessly while Howard built a fire. Her son, a scruffy young man who traveled with a bedroll following the crops. A stranger. She sighed. But a kind stranger. Had she done justly by him, had she shown him mercy? She found her Bible, turned to the 6th chapter of Micah and with her eyes closed recited the 8th verse, with tears running down her cheeks.

When Margaret came over, it was Howard who had to give her information. Abigail sat there with her head bowed, her eyes closed. She saw plain as day Josiah's face surrounded by bright orange flames; she saw him writhing in pain. Her body quivered and trembled.

Margaret came and put her arms around her. "There, there, dearie," she said. "Have your cry out."

"Have it out?" Abigail sat suddenly erect, her eyes behind the glasses flashing. "My cry can never end. Don't you understand, he killed himself, killed himself." There, she'd put it into words, admitted it to someone. "What will happen to him?"

"God is good and merciful," said Margaret. "He'll understand."

"If he goes to hell, I should too, that's my place."

"You did what you thought was best at the time; no one can see into the future. Come spend the night with me," urged Margaret.

"No, I'll stay here tonight. Maybe in a couple of days I'll take to the road with Howard."

Howard groaned. "Hush," whispered Margaret. "Of course she doesn't mean it."

Two days later he left. He picked up his bedroll and said, as casually as if he were just going out for ten minutes, "I guess I'll be drifting along, back to Portsmouth for a while. Write me General Delivery."

Thus he left, a wiry little man in a red mackinaw with a bedroll slung over his back, just drifting along. Abigail felt in her bones that she might never see him again.

Just then Margaret came in and started talking cheerful nothings. Everything would work out, it always did, it surely would.

"Nonsense," scoffed Abigail. "Nothing has ever worked out. Just look at Howard, bumming his way here there and nowhere without even an extra pair of pants."

"Things aren't going well," agreed Margaret. "But times will get better, maybe after the election."

"That's not till November."

Abigail pulled herself together and went to the mill. There was no work, maybe in a month. She returned home, and Margaret told her that Mrs. Hembonny had phoned for her to come to work at the Twin Pines boarding house, a couple of weeks, maybe permanent, the dishwasher just hadn't shown up. She could have her old room. So there she was right back where she'd started in Megunnaway. Yes, she'd go and resume her high and exalted duties as dishwasher at the Twin Pines. She walked through the snow to the old familiar building. She went directly to her sinks, filled one with hot soapy water and started work on the dishes which had already accumulated. Mrs. Hembonny came in and said it was nice to have her back, to which Abigail made no reply at all. The cook grumbled at her for missing a burned-on spot on one of the pans, and even to this Abigail made no response. If only she could get through that one night without breaking down and bawling; that was her one goal and she had no strength for peripherals. Doggedly she worked, carefully she watched and gave the cook no further cause for complaint. The sweat was running down her face, and she took time only to lift her apron and wipe it away. She toiled on until at last the task was done and she was free to climb the steep stairs to her room. Now at last she could weep.

Now she could weep, but her eyes were dry. There was a terrible numbness, and she wondered if she would ever feel anything again. Ah, better to feel the most agonizing sorrow than to be emotionally paralyzed. She closed her eyes and lines from a poem she once had known in its entirety came to her:

※❦※

"The night, in silence, under many a star;
The ocean shore, and the husky whispering wave, whose voice I know;
And the soul turning to thee, O vast and well-veiled Death,
And the body gratefully nestling close to thee."

※❦※

What was the next line? Something about floating this carol to thee, O Death. And now the tears flowed, and after a while she was able to pray, silently but with definite words. She prayed that the days through which she must struggle might be few, oh fewer than that, not one more. *Take me home, Father,* she prayed, *take me this very night. Have I not walked humbly long enough?* And with eyes closed she once again saw Josiah's face in the midst of flames. *Take me to him, Father,* she prayed. *No matter where, only make it soon, soon, soon. Or give me courage to take myself the fatal step. But if he be forgiven, forgive me too, that we may be in death united.* She ended her appeal to God with a formal Amen and hoped to sleep, but her mind was sadly awake. What if God answered her prayer and took her to Josiah, and Josiah turned on her in anger and hatred? She moaned aloud, "Don't hate me, Josiah, oh I deserve it, but don't, don't. Have mercy on me, believe my repentance, believe my love, and even in the flames of hell let me hold your hand. Help me, help me."

Whether God had forgiven her she knew not. She could not forgive herself since her repentance had come too late for reparation. Josiah had died, she was sure, thinking bitterly of her, had perished in the flames heaping curses on her name, and every curse had been deserved. Or could it be that at some last moment he had realized the hard life she'd led and had compassion and had at the end dwelt on those days of happiness they'd known at first? She'd never know, not in this life, and maybe not even in the life to come. She fell into a fitful and troubled sleep and waking at dawn dragged herself out of bed and into her clothes and upon the weary round of daily toil. It was some consolation that Carla and Ray were doing so well in Boston, working full-time she hoped.

TEN

Unknown to Abigail, both Carla and Ray were unemployed, not in despair, but plenty worried it must be admitted.

"Come, Little Owl," said Ray. "Let's go out."

"I ought to finish this letter to Mama." She sat upon the bed using a book as a prop for her paper.

"If you'd level with her it wouldn't take so long," he said. "Or if you can't do that, cut it short."

She laughed. "You've got something there. But I have to write enough to get her to answer. You know what she said about going to see Papa."

"You're getting nowhere. Come, Little Gray-eyed Owl, let's go out." He put his hand gently on hers.

"If Mama were here, she'd wonder if owls ever do have gray eyes."

"Dear little Mama!" he said. His own mother was Mom, Abigail was Mama. "The most learned mill worker I've ever seen. And she can knit a mitten the fastest."

Carla's eyes filled with tears. "I had to go away to really appreciate her. And now I want to spare her. Don't urge me to level with her. Maybe Mom could stand it, Mama couldn't."

She had no idea of all that Abigail had had to stand, not the slightest. She put aside the paper and dressed for the outdoors. Wandering aimlessly, they came to snow-covered Boston Common, the central park which lay just below the gilded dome of the State Capitol Building. Orderly paths, the snow crunched down by the passage of many feet, crisscrossed the park; green benches were neatly arranged by the paths; to one side a bandstand was surrounded by an amphitheater of benches; frequent thirty-gallon trash cans encouraged neatness, and there was no stray debris anywhere in evidence, unless one placed in that category the ragged men who moved slowly about or huddled on the benches. One such group stood in a circle not far from the bandstand.

"Wonder what gives," said Ray.

They discovered that the men were warming their hands at a fire blazing in a trashcan and were engaged in a lively discussion. Carla pressed in close to hear. The men looked wonderingly at the fresh-faced young woman and continued their argument. One grizzled fellow in a khaki overcoat maintained that the six days in which the world was created was a literal six days while his companion, shivering in a ragged sweater, stoutly defended the thesis that this was quite naive and that the days should be taken figuratively. "A thousand days are but one in His sight," he quoted. "And geology teaches—"

"Geology, smeology," said the other. "I go by the Bible, the literal word by word interpretation of the Bible."

"Ridiculous talk like yours places the Bible in disrepute."

"When you get to hell—" the old man countered, but he was interrupted by the surprising advent of a newcomer to the group.

"Nothing," cried Carla, "can be interpreted literally. Not even the phone book."

"Carla!" cried Ray, horrified by her boldness. He pulled her out of the circle and she let him do so. "Bunch of nuts," he said.

"You always call anyone who thinks a nut," she retorted. She would have said more, for she was never at a loss for words, but at that moment her attention was arrested by an old man walking along an adjacent path at some distance.

"Look! Look!" she cried.

"I don't see nothing."

She pointed to the man. "It's, oh I think it's Papa. The face, the bushy beard, and even the old bearskin coat and the way he walks."

After some hesitation on Ray's part, they hurried after the man, but he had left the park and disappeared down some street or alley or maybe into some building. "If you'd gotten a move on," she chided.

"You're imagining things. What would he be doing here?"

"You've nerve contradicting me. You've never even seen him."

"Okay, Know-it-all."

In this unamiable mood they returned to their room, where Carla busied herself with her Bible. "See here, Ray," she cried. "The young man was right, you can't really tell the exact time."

"Aaah, what difference does it make?"

"I wish Mama were here, she'd find it interesting. Those men did too."

"Those men," he snorted. He sat upon the bed idly reaching down and picking up pieces of lint, a scrap of paper, whatever he could see upon the threadbare carpet and placing them carefully on the bedside table.

Carla scowled. She found it intolerably annoying. Picking up dirt and putting it on the table, and a wastebasket not two feet away.

"Speaking of Mama," he said, "do you suppose she really went to see your father?" He'd found a tiny feather and added that to his cache of debris.

"Of course. She said she was going." Carla scowled fiercely at the clutter on the table, then reached over and brushed the trash back onto the floor.

Anger flared in Ray's eyes, his face flushed. "What'd you brush that onto the floor for?" he cried.

"If you want to clean up the floor, you could at least put the trash in the wastebasket," she said.

There they were glaring at each other over this senseless little thing. She returned to her Bible, and he carefully picked up the debris and just as carefully placed it once more on the table. This was not to be borne by Carla, who swept it once more onto the floor.

"What's with you?" he yelled.

"Put it in the wastebasket, dummy," she retorted.

"That does it," he cried and, grabbing his hat and coat, headed for the door.

She said nothing. He reached the door in one stride, for the room was small. She said nothing.

He walked out and gently closed the door. Carla stared blankly at the door, heard the latch click. What had she done, what had her tongue done? She heard his step in the hall, she heard him at the stairway. She ran to the door, leaned against it to hear better, but all was silent. Ray had stopped. But he hadn't come back. What if he never came back? She hesitated, uncertain whether to remain there leaning against the door or to run out after him. Then she heard voices, one clearly that of her landlady, the other indistinct.

Ray had stopped when he saw the street door blocked by the landlady, a little old woman dressed now as always in red and probably as usual not making much sense.

"Go away," she was saying. "Go away. We don't want any tramps here." She looked with distaste at the slender young man in a none-too-clean red mackinaw with a bedroll slung across his back. He removed his battered hat as an act of courtesy, an act which revealed his straggly brown hair in need of combing and his thin face covered with two days growth of beard.

"I've come to see my sister," the young man said. "Carla Putnam."

"Ridiculous! How could she be your sister? You must have the wrong address."

"I do not have the wrong address," he insisted. "I gave you her name."

"Do I have to call the police?"

As calmly as if he were wishing her good day, he said, "You must let me see my sister. If you don't, I'll call the police and tell them you've made soup of her."

"Don't be ridiculous, I haven't a pot big enough, I mean, oh dear!"

At this point, Ray came tramping down the stairs, and begging the land-lady's pardon, proceeded out the door. Howard moved aside to let him by, then stared after him, and said tentatively, "Ray! You *are* Ray?"

"He didn't even know you," scoffed the landlady.

Ray turned and glanced at the man standing there but could not place him. "Ray," cried Howard. "Don't you recognize me?" He straightened his shoulders and looked into the taller man's face.

Those eyes, those gray eyes. "Howard!" he cried. The undersized boy had grown into an undersized man.

They found Carla sitting on the bed intent on her book.

"Hi, Carla," said Howard. "Look what the cat dragged in."

She jumped up at once. "Oh it can't be! It is!" she cried, forgetting even the wonder of Ray's return in her realization that it was indeed her brother. "Howard! Where are you coming from?"

He laid the bedroll down, took off the mackinaw and placed it neatly on top. "From Amsterburg and Megunnaway," he said.

"Oh. And Papa? And Mama?"

"I saw her safe back to Megunnaway."

"I'd half expected," said Ray, "that she'd stay a while."

"I think she meant to." Slowly, staring at his shoes, not daring to look into anyone's face, Howard told of the fire, of their father's death, Mama's grief. "He done it on purpose," Howard said. "That's the worst."

"Oh no!" Carla was silent a moment. "No," she said, "I don't believe it." She leaned toward her brother. "I think we saw him on the Common today. In a bearskin coat. You remember that old coat?"

"Holy cow!"

They sat in silence for some time, then Ray and Howard began to talk again, avoiding the tragedy, talking of everything else, but mainly of the efforts they'd made to find work and of the pitifully few dollars they'd earned.

"I'm about ready to give up," said Ray.

"How do you go about giving up?" asked Howard. "Just lie down and starve?"

Yes, how does one give up? And how does one keep going? They sat pondering until they were finally roused by a knock at the door. Carla went to answer and found the landlady there. "That brother of yours," she said, "can't stay the night. Can't have it."

Howard came and answered quickly, "No such intention, ma'm. Got a room elsewhere."

"Hmmpph," said the landlady and disappeared, but was back again in a minute. "And you know the rules about no food in your room."

They assured her that they did. As soon as she was gone, Carla whispered to Howard, "We smuggle things in. Like raisin bread and canned spinach and baked beans. They're not bad cold."

Howard nodded sympathetically, but Ray was embarrassed. "We'll do better soon," he said and then asked Howard, "Do you really have a room?"

"No, but I'll find some corner."

"You can't sleep outdoors in this weather," said Ray. "I don't care what she says you'll sleep on the floor here."

"I'll hit the road in the morning. I'd better go out now and get back in later when old Hawkeye isn't looking," said Howard.

"We'll go with you," said Ray. Each of the three, though not wanting to mention it, was intent on going back to see if they could find the man in the bearskin coat. Outside in the crisp sunny air of late afternoon they headed toward the Common. "We'll ask around," said Ray. "Surely some one—"

They reached the Common. As before there were men hanging about, and here and there a woman, and by the trashcan near the bandstand a group deeply absorbed in discussion. It was as before an elderly man and a younger one but not the same two. "I tell you," the gray-haired man declared, "we have entered into the final decline of capitalism, and the one and only thing that can give hope to the starving people is socialism. That's it, my friends, that's it in a nutshell." He closed his jaw with a snap and looked about daring anyone to challenge him.

"Talk, talk, talk!" cried a sturdy young fellow in a ragged sweater. "Talk is cheap. What we need is direct action. Get everybody on this Common, get everybody out of the holes in the wall that they call rooms, get together, march on the biggest grocery store in Boston, march on the clothing stores."

The older man continued his line of thought as if he had not heard this proposal. "Fat cats everywhere," he said. "With the world facing the final crisis their idea of atrocity is a dog wetting the carpet."

A sardonic voice interrupted. "They are not fat," he said. "The rich are not fat, they're elegantly slender. They eat up everything, us included, yet are nothing but skeletons."

The speaker was a tall dark-haired man in his thirties, dressed in a handsome black woolen coat with beaver collar and wearing a neat brown felt hat. He had pushed his way into the circle. "Now you two," he chided. "Why are you always at each other?"

"Professor Zero!" cried the younger of the two debaters. "What'd you do? Rob a bank?" He reached over to finger the cloth of the handsome coat.

"I'll tell you what I did," the man replied. "I refuse to go in rags when there, on that hill, people crowd dozens of overcoats into their closets. I go to them—"

"I'm not down to begging." The young man clutched his sweater tightly about him. "I'd rather freeze."

Professor Zero looked haughtily at him. "I do not beg," he said. "I go to the house. I rap briskly on the door. I say to the woman who answers—it usually is a woman—I say, I need an overcoat."

"Then what happens?" asked another of the men.

"One called me a bum, and I cursed her house and left. Another brought out a pitiful summer coat, not half big enough, for which I said thanks but no thanks, and then I left. She begged me to stay, to accept money, but I refused. It does the soul good to refuse money once in a while."

"But this coat," the man insisted. "Where did you get it?"

"At last I found one which I could accept," said Professor Zero. "But I did not beg. I demanded."

Carla had edged her way right up to Professor Zero without difficulty for the men gave way before her. "Have you seen an old man," she asked breathlessly, "in a bearskin coat? A tall old man with stringy hair and a bushy beard?"

"What have we here?" he cried. "A young lady." He doffed his hat with a sweeping bow. "I regret, my dear, that I have seen no bearskin coat. And the beards I know are not bushy; they're scraggly, pitiful, underfed beards."

"Come, Carla," said Ray. "Let's go."

"And her handsome swain," said Professor Zero, bowing now to Ray.

"You know how to find coats," said Howard. "Except bearskin. How about jobs?"

"Sometimes I find jobs too, but not often the kind I'm seeking.

"You find jobs by going around to houses?" Carla asked.

"I go only to the rich. Who else hires?"

"Did you find a job where you got that coat?"

"It so happens, young lady, that I did. Not in my line, though I'd half a mind to try it. But I think I'll have to back off."

"What's the job?" cried half a dozen voices.

"My friends," asked Professor Zero, "is there an auto mechanic in the house?"

Hardly believing his ears, Ray seized the Professor's hand. "Yes, yes," he cried.

"Come," said Professor Zero, with no sign of surprise, "Let us find a seat. I'll give you the details."

"Bring us back something sometime," cried one of the men. "I could use a coat."

"The houses," said Professor Zero with a sweeping wave of his hand, "are there. You have only to knock." With that he left the group and led Ray and Carla and Howard to a bench, which he carefully cleared of snow before inviting them to be seated, his guests as it were.

Yes, he did know of an auto mechanic's job, but it was twenty miles away, and the mechanic was expected to have tools, the usual for a mechanic he supposed. "The tools," he mused. "No way I could fake that."

"You don't look like a mechanic," said Ray.

"Thank you."

"No compliment intended."

Professor Zero laughed. "I see you're down but not out," he said. "Those men over there, completely beaten, demoralized, reduced to a mere animal existence." He took a notebook from his pocket, scribbled an address and phone number on it. Ray took it in a daze.

"The way those men talk, the ideas they express," said Carla. "That's not mere animal existence. Religion, philosophy, politics!"

"The religion is pure regression to childhood superstition," said the Professor. "And the politics mere letting off steam. They should be organizing to do something about their wretched condition."

"After the election things will be better," said Ray.

"You should be thinking beyond the old treadmill of bourgeois politics," said Professor Zero.

"What do you mean?" asked Carla.

"Aha, young lady, I see in you a questioning mind."

"I go to the library, I read."

"Pap! Mere pap! Come here, some Sunday afternoon, go to that section of the Common," and he pointed, "and you will find a wisdom far exceeding what you on your own are likely to pick up. You'll learn what to look for in that great pile of desiccated learning; you'll find the living, breathing word." He got up abruptly. "I have to leave," he said and walked briskly away.

"We didn't find Papa," said Howard. "I never thought we would."

"I haven't given up," said Carla.

"I'd better find a booth and phone this number, see if there really is a job," Ray sounded anxious.

"I'm sure there's a job," Carla kept repeating.

"I hope so," he answered.

"Sunday we must go to that place on the Common that the Professor told us about." Carla said.

"Can't see why."

She now had a new refrain and kept repeating that they must go, until finally he grew impatient and told her to shut up about it. "I'll make you a bet," she said. "If there really is a job, then we'll go there, and if not, I'll hold my tongue."

"Done," he said.

They found a phone booth, and he went in to make his call. Carla paced back and forth to keep her feet warm; she kept peering through the frosty glass to see the expression on Ray's face, but it was not until the very end that it varied from deadpan. Then he was grinning from ear to ear. "I'm to come to work Monday morning; he says he'll try me out," he reported. "He says he likes Maine boys. Maybe he thinks we're dumb enough to work for peanuts."

"Or hungry enough." Carla suggested.

"Yeah. Which reminds me, now we have to survive till Monday, maybe longer, till payday." He groaned. "Five days. How can I work if I don't eat for five days?"

"I'll pay my night's rent," said Howard. He dug three rumpled bills from his Mackinaw pocket.

"Where did you get it?" asked Carla.

"Honestly, you'd better believe!" he cried angrily. "What do you take me for?"

"This will keep us from starving," said Carla, "and we'll go on Sunday to the Common."

"Yeah, you win," Ray admitted. "Strange man, that Professor."

Howard left the next day. On Sunday afternoon Carla and Ray headed for the Common. "Maybe Professor Zero's got a job for me," said Carla. "Or maybe we'll find Papa."

Professor Zero was nowhere in sight, nor was the old man in the bearskin. The speakers, however, were vociferously present, lined up in a row along one end of the Common, eight or nine men and a couple of women, each standing raised upon something, one a kitchen chair, another a wooden box, another a small table. First in the row was an old man dressed in white, with long white hair and straggling beard, preaching the end of the world. He stood upon a box, and a helper at his side held a carefully lettered banner which proclaimed, "Joy to the World; The End Approacheth." The man seemed confident of his own place in the coming cataclysm.

Carla stopped in the group which had gathered. "No," she said at last to Ray. "I don't want it to end yet."

They moved on. "Workers of the World Unite!" said the banner at the next stand. They meandered on. "Recognize the Soviet Union," read the next sign.

"Bunch of foreigners," said Ray.

The man on the platform gave no indication of foreign birth, but certainly his message centered on a foreign land, and he was sure that this foreign land held the clue to America's problems, and to him it wasn't foreign at all but "Our one and only fatherland."

"I've heard that story before," said Ray, and started off to the next speaker, a woman who was shouting for the impeachment of the President.

They went on down the line. There were Socialists, Communists, someone from what was called the Proletarian Party talking in a professorial manner about surplus value, and a vegetarian man who, whether by vegetables or otherwise, had managed to put on more weight than he needed, and a very young man urging that the unemployed organize.

"What's his trade?" Ray asked a man standing near the speaker.

"He's a Harvard student," the man answered. "Smart kid, I guess."

The next orator had worked himself up to an almost hysterical pitch. "Revolution, revolution, revolution!" he cried.

"Bunch of radicals like I warned you," said Ray. "I'm getting out of here."

He couldn't leave, however, because Carla had gone back to the "Proletarian Party" and was standing open-mouthed listening to the speaker. She fished in her purse, found pencil and paper, started taking notes. A woman came over and handed her a pamphlet entitled, "Value, Price and Profit." "You got a dime?" the woman asked.

"Not to spare."

"Well, take it anyway."

"Oh thanks!"

"Come, Carla," said Ray now at her elbow. "Time to go."

Reluctantly she followed him. "It's exciting!" she exclaimed. "So many ideas!"

"Bunch of hot air artists," said Ray.

Ray pointed to a big red apple sign on a restaurant. "Think we could swing a coffee and baked apple?" he asked.

"Come on," she said. "Maybe a hamburger instead. But no more."

They sat side by side eating their meal. Tomorrow was Ray's big day. Oh it had to be for real! Carla examined the pamphlet which the woman had given her and turning it over found a list of books on the back. "I'll look them up in the library," she said eagerly.

"You'd do better to chuck that radical tripe in the trash," growled Ray.

Carefully she put the pamphlet in her purse. "I certainly won't chuck it in the trash," she said. "I'll read it. I've got a mind, I'll use it. I refuse to be a mere animal."

"What good's a mind without common sense?"

"Common sense!" she scoffed. "Stick in the mud."

"What are we really fighting about?" he asked.

"Oh I don't know, I don't know. It's been such a day, there's so much for me to learn. And we didn't find Papa."

"Little Gray-eyed Owl," he said tenderly.

She leaned her head upon his shoulder, happy to be reconciled. Suddenly she leaped forward. "Come, come!" she cried. "It's him, the bearskin coat!"

They followed him down the block, caught up with him as he turned the corner. Ray touched his arm, started to speak.

"No, no," Carla cried. "It isn't, oh no. Sorry sir, a mistake."

"Crazy kids," he muttered.

❧❦❧

Monday morning Ray pulled on his sheepskin jacket. He had already put on his boots and his old gray knitted cap. Carla stood looking appraisingly at him. The outer cotton shell of the coat was hopelessly stained, and though she'd mended several tears there was one on the sleeve that she'd overlooked. He refused to wait for her to find needle and thread to fix it. "I'm not going for no silly office job," he said.

"And that cap. You look like such a hayseed."

"Don't forget I am a hayseed. Besides it's twice as cold as zero. These duds are warm."

Knowing he needed her support to go off to a new job, she said, "Anyway, you're a handsome hayseed." How true it was!

He picked up his toolbox and clumped down the hall, down the stairs, out into the snowy street and seated himself in the car which responded to the turn of the key with surprising dispatch.

A capricious wind blew flurries of snow, but it wasn't too bad the first five miles. Then he came to streets where the snow had not been broken by traffic, and the Ford began to grumble and rebel. Suddenly the car hit glare ice and swerved, heading straight for a pickup truck coming in the opposite direction. Ray held his breath, turned into the slide, twisted the wheel, knew that he was safe. The truck driver yelled angrily at him in some foreign language. *He should have been able to see I was doing my best,* thought Ray. *I wish I knew what it was he said. Makes me feel stupid to be yelled at like that. Well, I suppose I am stupid. Why else am I out here in the cold on the mere say-so of that Professor Zero? Headed for a place with the unlikely name of the "Olavin Garage"? It could be a practical joke. Back home I'd know a practical joke fast enough, but here I've lost my bearings.* In time he'd get back to Megunnaway where he belonged. Here nobody knew you; in the stores they looked at your clothes, turned up their noses. And just now he'd been yelled at when he was in trouble and doing his best which actually was good enough, and he hadn't even understood what was yelled. The guy should have waved and smiled, given an okay sign; that's what would have happened at home. Of course he couldn't go back broke.

He struggled to overcome the persistent feeling that the drive would at the end be for nothing. He had to get this job. How else could he take care of Carla? And oh how she needed care! Why she'd been practically hysterical ever since Howard came, laughing, crying, talking stuff that just didn't make sense. How quickly her grief over her father's death had been swallowed up in her joy at Howard's presence. Or was it her joy at this job prospect? She hardly knew what she was doing these last few days, and that was why she listened to that Communist rot. "Poor kid!" he said aloud.

He'd land this job, and they'd rent a real apartment with a kitchen, and they'd have kids and be a family. People did have kids in the city, he'd seen kids. Maybe they'd even have a dog. And finally they'd go back to Megunnaway. *There I go,* he thought, *counting my chickens before they are hatched. This Professor Zero might be just that, Zero, some kind of actor who has had his joke and disappeared. Carla is sold on him, but I don't know.* Then just beyond a restaurant and past a vacant lot there sure enough was the "Olavin Garage," looking not too different from Pete's Garage. The big doors were open, and there were cars inside and parked to one side a couple of other cars, one a battered wreck, one glistening white and obviously new. So people even brought new cars here to be fixed. He pulled in next to the wreck and went looking for Mr. Olavin. What kind of a name—oh well, what did it matter? In a tiny office to one side of the garage he found a man busily pouring coal into a small stove. The man set the scuttle down, carefully closed the door of the stove, and turned to see who had come in. *He doesn't look like a practical joker,* thought Ray, *more like an undertaker.*

He greeted Ray with a sad good morning, then more briskly as befitted a businessman went on, "And what can I do for you, sir?"

"I came about the mechanic's job," said Ray. Mr. Olavin seemed sunk in sad and distant thoughts, and Ray didn't know if he should interrupt with a catalog of his skills or should wait in respectful silence, and because he was not by nature a talkative man, he waited silently. Mr. Olavin busied himself setting a battered aluminum percolator upon the top of the stove. He turned and saw that Ray, though he had taken off his cap, was still standing there.

"Coffee'll soon be done," said Mr. Olavin. "Care for a cup?"

"Yes, sure. Thanks." Sure, coffee, but what about the job?

It wasn't until the room grew quite warm and the coffee perked to Mr. Olavin's taste that he spoke again. "Got a brake job first thing this morning," he said. "I'll put you on that."

Holy cow! I really do have a job! A brake job! The boss hadn't even asked if he knew brakes. Well, he should say he did.

"You'll work with Archie," said the garage owner, still speaking in a sad, controlled voice.

The mechanic Archie was as jovial as his boss was melancholy. He was in his early thirties, sandy-haired, of medium height, on the pudgy side, talkative as all get-out, yet an efficient worker. "You'll do," he said after about an hour. "You know your stuff and you don't back off from work."

"I hope the boss thinks so," said Ray with a glance at Mr. Olavin, who was intently studying something under the hood of another car.

"Don't worry, he's watching," replied Archie.

What a joy to get those brakes relined, all four wheels! Grease on his hands, grease in his golden hair, grease on his old sweater! It was pure unadulterated happiness. When lunchtime came, Archie said casually, "There's a place in back we can sit and eat."

"Er, I didn't bring lunch, I'll go find something. There's a restaurant—"

"Who ya kidding?" asked Archie. "You got no money to spare for restaurants. And you didn't bring no lunch because—" Here even Archie, the original fool who rushes in, paused.

"Maybe."

"Okay, feller, I brought extra just in case, and Olavin furnishes the coffee. You'll treat me when you get settled."

There was real beef in the sandwiches, and dill pickles, and cake with chocolate frosting, all washed down with big mugs of hot coffee which they got from the office.

Carla had spent the morning making her usual round of employment agencies and heard the repeated "nothing in your line today." Around eleven she headed for the big main library, intent on finding those books which were listed in the pamphlet from the Common. She walked quickly toward the library. Soon she could see the building clearly, a magnificent structure, and for a moment she hesitated. There it stood a massive block, dark against the snowy white of the street. There was a quiet dignity to the broad facade, the wide steps, the multiple-arched windows, the mellow gray of the stone. It was a veritable temple of learning, a symbol of the intellectual glory that had been Boston. Was there hidden in that great rectangle the answer to the real mysteries? And if so, could she find the treasure? She took the pamphlet with its list of books from her purse. One of them had been checkmarked in pencil. *I'll get that,* she thought, *if they let me take out books.*

She paused inside the door in awe at the magnificent murals. As she stood there several shabbily dressed men came out of a reading room, and she found their appearance reassuring. She walked into the room they had left and up to the desk. With the help of the young lady attendant she learned how to look up the books she sought. Several were listed in the big card catalog, and two of them were available. She waited for them to be brought, then eagerly scooped them up and found a seat at one of the big tables. She selected the larger of the two books, and her hands trembled as she opened it. It was big enough to contain most anything. There were six chairs around the table, and one of them was occupied by an elderly man. She noted that he was watching her with the greatest attention. Carla smiled; he continued to stare at her, pursing his lips thoughtfully, then got up and came around and took the chair next to her.

"Pardon me, young lady," he said, and his voice was deep as one would have expected from his appearance. "I've been puzzling over what you're reading."

"Oh?"

He picked up one of the books. "*Capital* by Karl Marx," he said, then laid it back upon the table. He put his hands to his temples and shook his head sorrowfully. "Have you read Adam Smith?" he asked.

"No."

"Then what are you doing reading Marx?" he asked.

"One has to start somewhere."

"That's it. You have no plan, no schedule, no system. Are you a student or what?"

"I'm not a student," she said. "I just like to read. I have time, I'm looking for work."

"Just because you're not in a university doesn't mean you can't be a student, but you must have some idea what you're looking for."

"Maybe if I read enough I'll find out."

"Not in a million years," he insisted. "Take this other book, this *End of the American Dream*. It's trash."

"Have you read it?"

"Don't have to to know it's trash. I'll give you a list from which to begin."

His voice had risen, indeed he had spoken loudly from the start. The young lady attendant came over, placed a pad and pencil on the table between them. "Could you be more quiet?" she said. "Write your messages. Someone is being disturbed."

The old man pushed the paper aside. "You start with Adam Smith for economics," he said, and Carla seized the paper and began to write. "And a basic history of America, maybe Bancroft, and then Aristotle and the Bible."

"The Bible?"

"Yes, of course. 'The Federalist Papers,' and—"

The young lady attendant was back. "Do be more quiet," she pleaded.

"I've said my say," the old man boomed, then stood up and headed toward the door. Halfway across the room he turned. "Good luck, young lady," he cried. "You just keep on trying."

Carla wanted to run after the man and thank him, maybe talk more with him, but she didn't. She reviewed all his words. Funny he'd mentioned the Bible. She kept the list he'd given her, but the books she took home were the two she'd originally chosen.

Ray found her later that day sitting on the bed propped up with pillows struggling with *Capital*. Let her have her books, he thought, he had his wrenches and axle grease. Later that evening he picked up the book, *The End of the American Dream*. "Trash!" he jeered, then awaited her angry retort. However, she made no reply whatever. She was amazed that he had used the same word as the scholarly old gentleman.

"Let's not quarrel over some silly book," he said. "Everything's coming up roses for us."

She sat silently, and he noticed there were tears in her eyes. "Oh darling," he cried. "Read what you want. Whatever it is, you'll understand it better than I could. Oh Carla, I wouldn't hurt you for the world. Little Owl, Little Gray-eyed Owl."

Mollified, she smiled through her tears. "You're a better mechanic than I," she reminded him.

"For you I'll be the best mechanic in the whole wide world."

At the moment she was happy to settle for that.

ELEVEN

Each morning that cold and blustery January Ray got up early, treated himself to a real breakfast in the cheapest place he knew, then drove through the snow-packed streets to work, holding his breath every inch of the way, fearful that the old car would splutter and cough and stop, but his determination communicated itself to this mechanical contraption and enabled it to put forth an effort far beyond its natural capacity.

Carla continued her haphazard search for work, haphazard because she had so little hope; and her despairing search for wisdom, despairing because she felt so keenly the need of a guide. She took the advice of the old man who'd startled her so at the library. She put *Capital* aside, she plunged into Adam Smith, she read the "Federalist Papers," and she was getting exactly nowhere. What was it Professor Zero had said about the books in the library? Desiccated something or other. If she could find him, surely he could help. She went looking first for the old man, through all the rooms in the library and up and down the neighboring streets, but she never found him. Then she went looking for Professor Zero on Boston Common and Beacon Hill. He too had disappeared, and she had no guide in her search for wisdom. She felt like a chip tossed on the waves, like a piece of paper blown about, yet she remained determined to find her way in this metropolis which had so much, could she but grasp it. She walked with long strides through the snow from one end of the city to the other. She saw MIT's shining white buildings across the Charles River, and she knew that that other temple of knowledge, Harvard University, lay also across that river though she couldn't see it, nor even dream of either one for herself. Just to know that they were there was something. She wondered, how does one get to be a part of the life of the city? Must one be born here, grow up here?

She felt herself akin to those urgent crying voices she'd heard that Sunday on Boston Common. On Sunday not only did Ray refuse to go himself, he told her to stay strictly away, and she did as he said. She went to the Common on other days but always came away dissatisfied. She investigated the more fashionable streets, where elegantly dressed women went to shop. They seemed so self-assured, filled with a kind of knowledge, but it was not the cold smartness of these women that she sought for herself. She didn't envy their furs and delicate spike-heeled shoes. Nor did she want the hard competence of the employment agency managers, many of them women. Nor did she seek the street smarts you could see in the faces of certain loudspoken women she met every once in a while in restaurants and employment agencies.

On the Common she felt more at home. How sorry she felt for the homeless, ragged men, both those who seemed always to have been there with no likelihood of leaving and the wanderers who came and went, wanderers like Howard. She wouldn't have been surprised had he suddenly put in an appearance, but he never did. There were women among the derelicts too, dejected and silent; and children, much as she and Howard had been, she supposed, lost somewhere between their fathers' despair and their mothers' impotent discontent. Oh the injustices of the world! Injustice was a swollen robber giant. Oh where was the sword with which to slay him? It would take not one sword but myriad swords, wielded by a million awakened people, the victims of the world aroused to mighty deeds, and she in the very front ranks! She felt great power within herself, if only she knew how to direct it. Where was the lantern to guide her?

She thought of the tragedies of her own family, particularly that of her mother, and worried when for weeks no letter came. Then one day she came home from a day out in the cold that had left her rosy-cheeked but tired and found a letter from her mother lying white upon the red bedcover.

"Dear Carla," Abigail wrote. "Forgive me for not writing before. I've been through a deep valley, and from here on out the hills don't get any higher, but the valleys get deeper and deeper. I rest my soul in the love of God. How can one survive without God? I'm back at that miserable boarding house, back in the dish-tub. I go on Wednesday to prayer meeting. We bear each other's burdens, we share each other's joys. And we talk such deep talk. I'm sure God has a mission for each of us. What mine is, I do not know. To walk humbly with my God, that I know. And oh from now on I will, I will! And was it my mission to bear two children for whom I've done so little? Where oh where is Howard? I pray for you, dear Carla, for you my brilliant child, my morning star.

"But enough, I must get to work on mittens for the Mills children. It's still cold, and theirs are worn right down to the wrists, and even those are raveled. Mrs. Hembonny gave me a sweater to render back into yarn, and I have that, enough for three pair. I wish it weren't black. But it's good wool and not too worn, it'll be fine. Love to Ray, Mama."

Yes, Mama was resigned, though it was clear she hated her job. She would never take such a step as Papa had. Neither would she be one of that million Carla was going to lead to slay the robber giant. At this point Ray came in, bounding up the steps with considerably more vigor than usual. Yes, Ray was happy; he'd never understand her inner restlessness; he'd never carry the burdens of the oppressed on his shoulders.

"Pretty soon we'll be able to go house hunting," he said.

Her head came out of the clouds, her feet hit the floor and the most important thing in the world was to find a place to live, a place to cook, to eat, a place to invite people. In due time the needed funds accumulated, the day came, and house hunting they went. Not exactly house hunting either, for an apartment was all they could hope for. Archie had told Ray about a place not far from his own. The apartment was on the second floor of a building which housed sixteen such cubicles, each of which consisted of a living room, a bedroom, a kitchen, and a bathroom. "Everything we need!" cried Carla.

"Except," said Ray, "a yard."

The manager, a tall handsome woman in her sixties, went ahead extolling the accommodations. "Shades on all the windows," she said. "And the stove and refrigerator are both in good condition. You don't always find that, but I see to it things are kept up." She waited for them to exchange glances, then went on, "And Fenway Park is just a few blocks away."

Carla and Ray hesitated, afraid to ask the rent. The landlady hastened to inform them.

"We can swing that," cried Ray eagerly.

At last an apartment! A kitchen! Their own bath! There was central heating and a kitchen range and refrigerator. Otherwise walls and floor but no furniture. They moved in with a few dishes bought in a secondhand store, a mattress and bedding from the same place, and a table and two chairs dug out of the storeroom where the manager kept odds and ends left by departing tenants.

"Are you glad you married me?" Ray asked eagerly as soon as they had put everything in place.

"What a question!"

"Now I'm a man again and can talk about it. I've been so ashamed not to be able to give you a home."

"We managed," Carla insisted, "apartment or no apartment."

The weeks passed. The bed was raised upon a frame, and the cardboard boxes in which they had kept their clothes were replaced with a chest of drawers. Then there was a new dress for Carla, soft blue, cut princess-style following the lines of her body and flaring to give ample room for her stride. And a suit for Ray, dark blue, not expensive, but showed off to its best advantage by his broad shoulders and slender hips. They stood side by side in front of the mirror in the clothing store. The salesman, a wiry little man, stood back and evaluated.

"A perfect fit," he announced. "What a handsome couple."

They stood there and admired themselves, the tall, graceful, dark-haired Carla and the even taller, golden-haired, strong-featured Ray. "Our kids," said Ray, "will sure be good-looking." Carla blushed furiously, which made her even more beautiful.

"You shouldn't have said that about our kids," Carla chided afterwards.

"Why not?"

"I'm still looking for a job, we need to save some money."

"You don't need to work, you can stay home and raise the kids."

"How can anyone raise a family in an apartment?" Carla demanded.

"I dunno. Arch and Maisie are doing it."

"But we have to make something of ourselves first."

"Make something of ourselves!" he snorted angrily.

"We can't even afford a new car."

It wasn't really the car. As a matter of fact, Ray was the one who really wanted the new car. Carla wasn't sure what she wanted, only that something was lacking. Maybe he was right, maybe it was a baby.

❧❦

In time Carla developed an acquaintance with Archie's wife, Maisie. Indeed it could hardly be avoided since Maisie, who lived two doors down the street, was a most insistent visitor, fond of sitting by the hour sipping coffee and eating as many rolls as were offered her, often bringing some of her own baking to share, and talking endlessly of her most personal problems.

"I can't have any more children," she confided one day, not too sadly either. "After Johnnie, I had an operation, I forget the name, but—" and here she went into great clinical detail, which Carla found offensive. Thus Carla learned something from Maisie, but certainly not how one raises children in an apartment. However the acquaintance had to continue because the men worked together and because Carla in any case could not have been rude to the woman. And the boys were delightful. Ray particularly enjoyed them, and many Sundays took them to the park where they spent most of the time with baseball and bat. Usually Carla went along to watch and more often than not to join in. Sometimes all four adults went and had a picnic lunch, and on those occasions Maisie was more cheerful and less confidential.

Maisie kept coming to call, and Carla shortened the visits as much as she could and resolved to never, never go to Maisie's apartment, though urgently invited time after time. However, the day came when she was really on the spot. Archie had invited Ray to come with Carla for dinner the next Saturday, and as they sat and ate, she'd found all sorts of reasons not to go. It was still unresolved after they'd finished and she'd clattered off to do the dishes and he had settled down to read the paper.

Of course we'll go, decided Ray, *I'll see to that.* But there was so much more to it. *I am sick and tired of being nagged about advancing myself. I hope some day to have a home and family, long for it, but I could do that as a mechanic. No way am I going to sign up at night school to learn something fancier. No, nor to become a more skilled mechanic. I see no sense in it and that is that.* Sure, he admired her flair for the frills of life, a woman should have that, that's where Maisie fell down and Carla shone. He never tried to interfere with her in that, but he was not about to learn to like books. He'd read the paper, sports first, the comics next, enough politics to decide how to vote. *Arch and Maisie are good enough for me. Too bad they aren't good enough for her. I guess I didn't understand the driving force of that egghead nonsense Carla was brought up in. Abigail always had hoity toity ideas, still she was capable of accepting reality when it knocked her on the head. But Carla!*

Next morning long after he'd left, Carla lingered over her coffee priming herself to go tell Maisie they'd come to dinner Saturday, thank her for the invitation and all that guff. She sat there thinking about Arch and Maisie, particularly Maisie. Carla had almost gotten herself to the point of going when Maisie arrived with her invitation. With hypocritical graciousness Carla thanked her and accepted. For a change Maisie couldn't stop to chat. Carla rejoiced. His and her friends!

Carla took a streetcar to town and walked through Boston Gardens. Beds of crimson tulips and golden daffodils sparkled in the sunlight, children ran about on the walks, men and women sat on the benches. The ridiculous swan-boats, little flatboats with seats for passengers, floated about on the calm water of the lake. Carla wandered past the lake, along the walk and across the street to Boston Common.

What a different scene! In the Gardens all peace and charm, on the Common a frenzied mass of humanity, jostling, excited, shouting. Policemen on horseback rode among the crowd, herding them about. "What on earth?" cried Carla.

"Sacco-Vanzetti Day," answered a stranger. Her face flushed, fully sharing the excitement of the crowd, Carla too began to shout, not in English but like the others in Italian.

Carla, no longer a greenhorn, knew who Sacco and Vanzetti were, two men who had been executed some five or six years before on a murder charge. There'd been some question at the time about their guilt, claims had been made that it was political and that they were prosecuted because they were anarchists. The courts had found for the State, attempts to stay the execution failed, the men died in the electric chair. Terrible thing to think about, still if the men had committed the murder, cold-blooded murder, then that was a terrible thing too. The amazing aspect to Carla was that this huge demonstration was taking place so long after the event. Carla looked around; this would be the kind of scene one might expect that strange Professor Zero to take an interest in. Or the old man from the library. But she didn't see them though they would have been easy to spot for they were tall men and this crowd was mostly short and stocky. The Italian community of Boston! In Megunnaway she had never known that there was an Italian community in Boston! The crowd was pressing close together as the numbers swelled and the police kept them off the street. The shouting grew louder, was hushed when a band played, music unfamiliar to Carla, though apparently not to the crowd who hummed along with it. Then the shouting resumed. Now Carla was sure the men had been innocent. She was sure because this crowd was sure and she had become part of it. Gradually the numbers decreased, open spaces began to appear, there was no longer danger that the horses hooves would step on someone's foot.

Exhausted by the emotions she'd experienced, Carla sat on a bench. A woman, red-haired, snub-nosed, still young, sat down beside Carla. "Do you remember me?" she asked. It was the woman who had given her the pamphlet that day of speeches on the Common.

"Oh yes," cried Carla. "And I did read the pamphlet. I'm really surprised you recognized me," she added. "You must meet so many people."

The woman laughed. "Not many as country fresh as you."

Carla blushed.

"I'm Katy O'Connor of the Proletarian Party," the woman explained.

"Well Katy," said a shrill woman's voice. "What are you doing corrupting this young woman with your sectarian teachings?" A stout, gray-haired woman with good-humored coarse features stood before them.

"Better me than you, Sarah," Katy responded.

Without waiting for an invitation, Sarah sat down beside Carla. "Will you introduce me, or do I have to introduce myself?" asked Sarah.

Katy did the honors. The woman was Sarah Friedman, a member of the loyalist Communist groups. How amazing, thought Carla. Everyone belongs to some group or other. The two women on the end seats were soon engaged in a fierce debate, shouting at each other across the more or less silent Carla. They were both what they called Marxists, which seemed to mean Socialist or Communist, but each vehemently accused the other of heresy.

"You know the socialist fatherland is under attack, yet you undermine the unity of the masses," screamed Sarah.

"Not at all. There is no true socialist country, not yet. The Soviet Union is just another dictatorship," Katy screamed back.

"No, no, no," cried Sarah. "The dictatorship is directed against the enemies of the people, the enemies of the State, against them and them only. Surely you agree that the answer is socialism?"

"You know I do. But—"

"It's not a tea party, my dear, by no means. And in this country—"

Carla managed to get a word in. "Things will be better when we get rid of this Hoover," she said.

"What you have to understand," said Sarah, "is that this is the final crisis of capitalism and neither the Republicans nor the Democrats can make a bit of difference."

"Well, there we agree," said Katy. "And I have to be going. Maybe now's a good time to leave. Carla, dear, do give me your address."

Before she could reply, Sarah asked, "Carla, where do you work?"

"I'm looking—"

"Isn't that the story all over? So many looking. I'm a stitcher in shoes. Maybe my place could take you on. I'll give you the directions. Or better, I'll inquire and you can call me Saturday at my house to find out what the score is."

"You win, Sarah," mumbled Katy and walked away.

"I've never made shoes," said Carla.

"So who's born with a sewing machine in her hand? Here's the number. I know they'll hire you." She got up and hurried after Katy.

"I don't know—" Carla began.

❧❧

In any event when Carla called Sarah the following Saturday, Sarah said, "Nothing doing right away, but don't you worry. We'll get you on. Give me a number I can call."

Carla stayed much about the house, endlessly waiting for a phone call, but she had a gut feeling that in time Sarah would call. Eventually she told Ray of her adventure.

"Bunch of reds," he spluttered. "Whatever possessed you to go there?"

"I just want to get out of the apartment."

"You should know enough to steer clear of reds."

"There were two women there who called themselves socialists, and they got into such a dispute. They're not all alike. One is helping me find a job."

"They're all poison."

She said no more, just sat quietly at the table. Idly she took up a book of snapshots which Abigail had sent not too long before as a birthday gift for Ray. He came and sat beside her, and eagerly he turned the pages. "Did you see, here's the school, in color yet? And the hill and the river and our house!" There was also a group picture of Abigail and the Putnams grinning cheerfully at the camera. Carla, tired of this pastime, found work in the kitchen, but Ray sat there for an hour turning the pages, over and over.

"Carla," he said at last. "We must go back, we must." And tears stood in his eyes.

Carla hesitated. What could she say? "If it's fated to be," she said, "it will be."

"Fated? What kind of talk is that?"

"Do you want to go right now?" she demanded.

"We can't, you know that, not right this minute."

"If I get work, we can save for it. Surely Sarah will call."

"A man should support his wife," said Ray. "But yes, we could save. Maybe get back sooner."

How could she tell him how she really felt about going back? Boston had something for her, she didn't know what. She was determined to find out, but there was no use provoking an untimely rumpus over it.

"I'll make us some hot chocolate," she said.

"Good," he said and continued to warm his heart in the light of the Megunnaway pictures.

TWELVE

Not long after on a temperate day in June Ray and Carla headed north in their car and entered the State of Maine at Kittery. There had been a thunderstorm the day before, and winds blew constantly from over the sea. They were going to Elsa's wedding.

"One lousy week," he griped. "But you could stay longer."

"No! No!" she cried. She had to get back. Sarah had called, said to stand by; some time in June there'd be a break.

They came to an isolated stretch. To the right they could see a dirt road which wound along the top of the rocky cliff. Ray left the highway and after several hundred feet, pulled into a grassy spot under an oak tree. They got out of the car, and Ray came quickly to her side. Carla let him draw her close to him; she shared the passion of a kiss, then pulled away.

"Let's go swimming," she said.

They changed to their swimsuits and crossed a narrow strip of soft earth and proceeded to traverse the rocky barrier. Ray sought to give her a hand, but it was soon apparent that she was as sure-footed as he and that they made best progress by each one leaping independently from rock to rock. They sighted a sandy beach and headed toward it. The rocky coast, she thought, was very like the one where she and her brother had wandered that day with Miss Abbott. They waded the creek which bubbled down the rocks and just beyond they reached the beach and dashed, now hand in hand, into the surf.

The water washed over them, tumbling Carla's hair into her face. Letting go of his hand she threw herself upon the wave. Ray dashed after her. Her sea-green, slender figure, tossed by the gigantic waves, was so fragile that he was sure she needed his help to escape disaster. But she'd ridden the wave, had not been thrown by it, had emerged laughing and triumphant. They continued swimming, sometimes side by side, sometimes with him outstripping her, going further out, then turning and coming back in with her. At last they tired of the sport and returned to their car.

"Oh Ray," she cried. "I feel like a new person."

"I liked the old one," he said. "I love the old one." And he sang softly, " 'I've got my girl, Who could ask for anything more?' " They were no longer athletes contesting the sea, but man and woman face to face.

After spending the night in a roadside cabin, they continued their journey. Megunnaway lay pleasantly cool between the river and the hills, and it was home to Ray. Carla wasn't sure what it was to her, for she was a new person.

They found the Putnam household in happy turmoil. "All this fuss just to marry off Monkeyface?" teased Ray.

They hastened through the few tasks which Margaret set them, then drove over to the Twin Pines, getting there in time for five minutes with Abigail before she had to go to the kitchen. She was looking well, thought Carla, and in good spirits, though perhaps she'd lost a little weight. After the first greeting she asked at once about Howard, and when Carla said they had heard nothing, she shook her head sadly.

Ray and Carla arrived back at the Putnams' as a carload of relatives from New Hampshire were climbing out of a big Buick. They were cousins on Barclay's side, even Ray was a bit mixed up as to the identity of a couple of them. "Just park us any old place," said the jovial middle-aged man who was clearly their leading spirit. "In the attic, in the bathtub, the cow's stall."

"The cow's stall we have," laughed Margaret, "but I don't think it'll come to that."

They also had the old blue tent, and that was Ray and Carla's chamber for the night. There was a bright moon, and it shone upon the canvas and filtered through so that they lay there in a soft blue diffusion of light. "It's a second honeymoon," breathed Carla.

They lay awake far into the night, just talking. Mostly it was Ray who talked. He told her what that farm had meant to his family—pioneered by his great-grandfather, held onto for dear life by his grandfather who had had to combine farming with millwork to make ends meet, and finally used as a resource by his father who rather early gave up on farming, became a full-time spinner, and had gotten out of tight places by selling parcels of the land. That's how they'd got their car, Ray recalled, and the tent too, for Barclay had insisted on going even deeper into the woods each summer for as long a vacation as he could manage. Now there was barely land enough left for the orchard, for a cow, for a garden. "And," he added, "when we come back to Megunnaway, I guess we'll build our place where old Bossie pastures now."

Carla was silent.

The wedding went off very well. After the reception and the departure of the bridal couple, Margaret lay upon the sofa in the living room, her feet raised. "What a day!" she said. "I was so busy I forgot to cry."

"Any jobs around here?" Ray asked.

"If we hear of anything—" Margaret had no need to finish the sentence.

Carla said nothing. They'd go back to Boston and stay there, which was what she wanted.

Two days later they pulled up in front of the apartment house. Their landlady came running out. "I thought you'd never get here," she cried. "Some woman named Sarah's been trying like mad to reach you."

"I'll call her this minute," Carla rushed to the phone.

Ten minutes later she went to the apartment and found Ray deep in the evening paper. "There's a job!" she said excitedly. "In a factory in Laurel where Sarah works."

"Oh." Ray was absorbed in his paper. "The Braves won," he began.

"Is that all you care?"

He put the paper down, carefully and slowly. "Mixed feelings, I guess," he said. "A man should be able to support his wife. And family."

"What family?"

"Who on earth is Sarah?"

"Didn't I tell you about her? Woman I met on the Commons."

"Oh." He intensified his study of the paper.

He didn't have to be so negative, thought Carla.

Next morning Carla went to Laurel, and the trip proved longer than she had anticipated so that it was already eight o'clock when she arrived. "Can you direct me to the shoe factory?" she asked the bus driver.

"There's seventeen of 'em."

"Caldwell."

"Two more stops. Don't reckon they're hiring."

He might not reckon, but Sarah had said to come. The town was larger than Carla had expected and older. The stores, the apartment houses which she had seen from the bus, and the big square building with the sign "Caldwell Shoe" were all of red brick, varied only by the paint on the wooden trim. Perhaps the driver was right, and she was on a wild goose chase. But Sarah had said to come. Carla continued on her way into the office of the Caldwell Shoe Company, and as directed, back into the hallway, up the stairs to the stitching room. Three long rows of machines with workers seated on either side ran the length of the room; the strong smell of leather filled the air; the whir of the power shaft, the uneven counterpoint of the individual machines, the sound of many voices made a combined noise which overwhelmed Carla, who stood just inside the door, vainly trying to locate Sarah. The foreman, a tall, balding, middle-aged man in shirtsleeves and vest, came rushing over, shouting excitedly. Carla could not distinguish his words, wasn't sure in what language he spoke, was much too frightened to open her mouth. He repeated what from his inflection was obviously a question.

"Excuse me," she said at last. "I don't understand. I only speak English."

He tore his hair, he stamped his feet, he exploded in a torrent of words.

The women at the nearest machines were laughing, and Carla's face had turned a bright crimson. Into this madness came sanity in the person of Sarah Friedman.

"Shut up, Jake," she said. "You don't have to make a federal case of it." She turned to Carla. "He was speaking English," she explained, "or at least what passes by him for English. As for what he's saying now in Yiddish, better I shouldn't translate."

"Oh dear," wailed Carla. "Shall I go away?"

"Of course not." Sarah turned her calm countenance on Jake. "This is the young woman I told you about. You hire her and you'll see she does a good job."

"If I hire that greenhorn, *you'd* better see she does a good job," he retorted.

"Okay, it's a deal," replied Sarah. "The machine next to me is vacant."

"You said she already knows running a sewing machine?"

"Yes," answered Sarah, hoping it was true.

Jake pulled a note pad from his pocket. "What's her name? Address?"

The conversation continued with Jake addressing every inquiry to Sarah, while Carla stood by feeling angry and foolish and grateful and excited. Finally Jake put his pad away. "Okay," he said, his voice rising once more. "Get her a bundle of work, show her what to do, you want to waste your time on her, okay by me. But don't you let her spoil no leather."

"Alright already," said Sarah and led Carla down one of the aisles to the machine. "We'll start you off on linings."

How grateful Carla was to her and how grateful to Margaret Putnam who had somehow found time to teach her to operate a sewing machine. Different as the factory machine was from the home version, the basic principle was recognizable. Carla, with her natural quickness, had by the end of the day elicited from Jake a grunt that might be interpreted as approval of the work she had done and certainly as permission to return the following day.

As the weeks went by, the confusion sorted itself out, and Carla settled in. The jangle of noise became separate sounds, the work flowed smoothly and no longer required the intense concentration of the first day. Carla knew more and more of the workers in the room by name; they became individual personalities. Sarah held a special position among the stitchers, for the work was paid by the piece, and she settled the prices to be paid for each new style. She hadn't been elected to do it, nor yet chosen by Jake, but simply did it because she and everyone else knew she should. She was shrewd and unafraid, and she had known Jake for many years. This ancient tie was, however, counterbalanced by her self-appointed role as defender of the rights of the workers, as well as by her own desire to take home a fat paycheck. Not that she was suffering, she said. No, her husband had a job, a tailor doing alterations now for Filene's in Boston, and her oldest was married to a dentist, not doing too good just now; people neglect their teeth, it's a shame.

"What does it matter?" scoffed one of the women. "Who's got meat to chew?"

Sarah, who brought meat sandwiches in her lunch every day, ignored the remark. Someone else had a cute story, another a sad tale, and so the day went. Carla sat and mostly listened. The factory was a veritable League of Nations, and this intrigued her. There were the Jews, Sarah and Tanya and a few others; and the dark-haired Italians, many of whom conversed together in their native tongue. And there were the Germans and the Poles and the Greeks. Most of the stitchers were women, but there were also a few men, sitting together at the far end of the third row. As Carla got better acquainted and moved about the premises at lunchtime, accompanied by the universally known Sarah, she found even more exotic peoples: Arabs in the lasting-room, and a bevy of Syrians among the treers and packers. Then there were the Irish edgemakers, lasters, and some among the cutters, jovial men who loved to laugh and talk nonsense. The cutters were all men, many of them middle-aged or older. Among them Jews and Yankees were well represented. How fascinating, thought Carla, these people from so many far away places. If only she could know their stories without having to ask, for in this strange community she was really very shy. Only her friendship with Sarah and with Tanya, a recently hired employee who sat at the machine opposite Carla, kept her from being considered standoffish.

Tanya, though like Sarah an American Jew, was quite a different being. She was much younger, and where Sarah was steady and down-to-earth, Tanya was light-hearted and gay. Sarah could be counted on to get the best possible prices, Tanya to lead in song. There was something puzzling in the relationship between the two. Sarah had introduced the younger woman to Jake, that was certain. At times it seemed as if they were old acquaintances, relatives perhaps. But then Tanya by chance remarks showed herself quite ignorant of Sarah's personal life, yet to see them with their heads together in earnest and confidential talk, one could only conclude that there must have been some strong tie in existence before Tanya's arrival at Caldwell Shoe. Carla couldn't decipher the riddle. It was obvious that both took a more than casual interest in the girl from the New England frontier, as Tanya once described Carla. Carla was grateful to them for they helped her become part of the life of the factory. In a few days she no longer trembled whenever Jake came near her. Soon he seldom had to correct the way she did her work and though he never apologized for his outburst on the first day, he spoke to Carla thereafter with somewhat less brusqueness than he was accustomed to use with others. Why? Sarah had told him to. And why did she tell him to? Jake never asked that question, and Sarah couldn't have answered.

Carla arrived home thoroughly tired each night, but it was a point of pride with her nonetheless to fix a hearty supper. Ray, bless him, helped with the cleanup. He kept writing urgent letters, he who was ordinarily no great correspondent, reminding his parents of their promise to let him know of any job in Megunnaway or nearby. The answers were not encouraging. Throughout the country hard times continued. There was a general opinion, among those who had jobs as well as among those who did not, that things were getting worse. Certainly things were worse for the garage where Ray was employed. First his hours were shortened, and then one day in August he was placed on indefinite layoff. Oh sure, he did good work, sure the boss would rehire him if things picked up, maybe even with the same amount of business if all the outstanding bills got paid, but as things were—

It wasn't easy telling Carla, and he waited until after dinner when they were doing the dishes. "You'll find something soon, I know," she reassured him.

"Wish I knew how you know." He paused, then went on. "If you hadn't gotten a job, maybe I wouldn't have lost mine. Maybe the boss would've shared the work between Arch and me. As it is, he knows I won't starve."

"Archie does have seniority."

"But I'm the better mechanic. Anyway, why do you have to stick up for him?"

"I didn't mean it that way."

He was at once contrite. "You're only saying what I've already thought," he admitted.

"You only got laid off today."

He took small comfort from her words, and as the months rolled on, the events bore out his pessimism. Beyond an occasional odd day's work here and there, he found no employment the rest of that year.

There was a name after a while for the hard times. The Depression, they called it. It saddened a woman and took the heart from a man, particularly when the woman had a job and the man did not. It made good sense, after a while, for the Putnams to move from the apartment in Boston to one in Laurel, and so they moved. And it was only fair that with Carla coming home tired from a day of working against time to turn out as high a pile of work as possible, Ray should be the one to cook and later to wash the dishes. It made good sense and it rankled.

Late one rainy afternoon not quite a year after she first started working at Caldwell Shoe, Carla left the factory and walked with long strides down the brick-paved sidewalk, past the brick-faced apartment houses and stores. At some distance she could see one of the few buildings not of brick. It was the public library, a gray stone building which looked like a chapel and had actually been built as a church many years before when the town of Laurel was still the unincorporated area of Caldwell Corners and the ancestors of the present owners of Caldwell Shoe had been prosperous wholesale merchants. *I'll go get me a book or two after dinner if I'm not too tired,* she thought.

She turned down Genoa Street and continued past more brick apartment houses. A couple of elm trees on a vacant lot were just bursting into soft green leaves, elm trees like the one in the yard at the farm of her childhood, tall, magnificent trees. Not even the gray of a rain-soaked dusk could obscure the resurrection quality of their beauty. Carla threw back the hood of her jacket. The freshness cleaned her lungs of the leather-laden air from the stitching room. She walked past a couple more brick apartment houses and entered the shabby wooden door of a third such house and climbed the stairs to their apartment. Ray was there before her, as she had expected. The blare of the radio filled the room. Ray sat hunched before it intent upon the ball game.

"Been looking for work all day, just got in a few minutes ago," he apologized. "Didn't have time to fix dinner."

"It doesn't matter," she said.

They were painfully aware of the lies, both his and hers. The air was filled with cigarette smoke, he was dressed in rumpled shirt and torn pants, his beard was two days growth. He made no move to get up but slumped on the sofa and lit another cigarette. She opened the window to let air into the room, then went to the kitchen area. The other end of the room served as living-dining room and was furnished with a table, four unrelated straight chairs and a faded brown sofa with sagging cushions on which Ray now sat. On the wall were a couple of Van Gogh prints carefully mounted on white cardboard, one of sunflowers, the other an old peasant in blue smock. The kitchen end had modern conveniences which, though not in the best of condition, nonetheless functioned and would in the little Megunnaway house have been greeted as luxurious by Carla. Now she muttered angrily at the gas stove because it did not light as quickly as she desired. But it was soon burning with a hot blue flame under the frying pan while a can of string beans was being heated on another burner.

Ray got up and set the table, moving heavily about the room. Carla looked at him with compassion. How terrible that now she looked at him with compassion! Lithe, athletic Ray was developing a flabby stomach. Ray with a flabby stomach and so soon! Or perhaps it only seemed that way because of the stoop to his shoulders. Ah, but he was still handsome, he was still strong. Just let him get a job, and he would be his own self in an hour's time. At least with her working they wouldn't starve. If only he weren't so sensitive about her being the one to support them. It wasn't his fault and it wasn't hers that she had been the one to continue on the job. He had seemed happiest, most like his old self, on the few occasions when she was laid off and they worried about the rent and went to bed hungry. Now they ate in silence. "I heard about a job," he told her as she was clearing up the debris. "For an auto mechanic. Harrison down at the drugstore told me when I went for cigarettes. I hope I still remember how a car is put together."

She wondered why he hadn't mentioned the job when she first came in. Perhaps he just couldn't believe he had a chance. "You've had a lot of practice on the old Ford," she reminded him.

"Yeah," he said. "That old Ford has been a concentrated course in obsolete auto mechanics."

"Obsolete?"

"She's a Model T, you know."

"Anyway it's running, it can get you there."

"Yeah."

"Where is the job?"

"In Quincy, way the other side of Boston. I'll have to get up at the crack of dawn. Harrison told me who to see. I'm not going to lose this one by being the second man in line. No sirree, I'm going to be the first."

The ebullience proved, however, to be but a sudden bubbling up, subsiding almost as soon as it started. He went to the couch and sat slumped and despondent. Carla saw that she would have to forget about going to the library. Under her prodding he shaved and washed his hair so that it shone with its old golden luster, and she trimmed it as best she could. Oh he was a fine-looking man, surely the man they would want to hire, if only he remembered to stand straight. The sadness in his eyes didn't matter. She laid out clean cotton pants and a clean shirt and his tweed jacket, worn shiny around the sleeves, but who cared about that in a mechanic? She inspected the clothing again, sewed on a couple of missing buttons.

"Where's your toolbox?" she asked.

"Locked in the car, Mom," he answered.

She laughed at the sarcasm, laughed happily knowing from it that his spirit was not broken. Surely he'd stand straight tomorrow; he was so competent-looking when he didn't slouch.

He woke while it was still dark, reached for the clock and lit a match to see the time. "Holy cow!" he yelled. "This blasted thing didn't go off. I'm late. Oh Carla, I'm late!"

Hurriedly he dressed while she made coffee, toast, and bacon. In his haste he spilled coffee on his jacket. She wiped it off and said it hardly showed since it was the right shade of brown. Still jittery he gave his hair a last comb and clattered down the stairs. She could hear the car wheeze. It started, thank goodness, and he was off. She looked out the window. Day was beginning to dawn. She could see the rain in his headlights, a slow, steady drizzle.

It was still raining when Carla walked to work. She pushed open the heavy door to the stitching room and went to her machine. Other workers were coming, some were already at their machines, large heavy sewing machines on metal stands shaped to allow the free handling of the small pieces of leather. Carla selected a brown bobbin from the drawer and put it in place under the presser foot. Her bundle of work was already in place. Jake threw the switch at the end of the room near the door, and the power shafts began to whir. Carla was now a back seam stitcher, promoted from her original job on linings. She slid one seam after another quickly through the machine, braking with her knee lever, sliding another, another, another, never anything but that one seam, faster and faster and faster. The workers got in the swing. They began to talk, pitching their voices to be heard above the loud hum of the power shaft and the uneven whir of the machines.

Tanya, sitting across from Carla, began to sing a song she had introduced to the shop and which was now an old favorite, "Michael, Row the Boat Ashore," and several voices joined, including Carla. They missed the firm contralto of Sarah who was for some reason absent today. Jake came down the aisle, silently, not humming along with them as he usually did. He hesitated as he came to Carla, stopped completely at the empty chair where Sarah should have been, then sighed and retraced his steps. A few minutes later he was walking down the next aisle. He went to Tanya and tapped her on the shoulder. She broke off the song and stopped her work to listen to what he had to say. He spoke softly, leaning over close to Tanya. Tanya looked up at him, and her dark eyes filled with anxiety. She rose quickly and followed him into the office. No one took up the song, the work continued. In a few minutes Tanya was back, but instead of going to her own machine she slid down the aisle in back of Carla. She put her arm around Carla's shoulder.

"Come, dear," she said. "Come with me. We have to go to the office."

Startled, Carla pushed back her chair and stood up. "Is it Sarah?" she asked.

"No, no," cried Tanya. "No, she took the day off to go to the dentist. No, no, Sarah's okay."

Then, thought Carla, we're being laid off. Why else should Tanya seem so upset? Work must be getting slow, but why single out the two of them? It wouldn't matter if Ray were working, as well he might be. She tried to express something of this to Tanya, but Tanya moved quickly and didn't listen. Inside the office Jake and Tanya and Gracie the bookkeeper looked at her with strange, sad looks. The bookkeeper sat her down gently, compassionately. A policeman who was standing by the door shifted his weight from one foot to the other.

"What has happened?" Carla cried. "Why are you all so gloomy. I'm not made of china, I won't break. Tell me."

Gently Tanya began to explain, but break it gently as she could, lead up to it as considerately as she might, the content of her talk fell on Carla like a crashing tree, fell on her and numbed her and quite literally threw her to the floor. When she came to, she was lying face down where she had fallen. Tanya knelt beside her, smoothing her hair, softly singing a lullaby in a tongue which Carla did not understand. Carla pulled herself back into the chair and drank the water which Gracie brought her. Jake shook his head sadly. The policeman had gone.

"It can't be," moaned Carla. "Not Ray. He's such a careful driver. There must be some mistake."

"The policeman said he swerved," Tanya told her, "to avoid another car. The pavement was slick. It wasn't anything anyone could have avoided."

Jake brought their coats from the rack.

"Could it be a mistake?" asked Tanya. "Somebody else?"

Jake shook his head sadly. "No, Tanya, there's no mistake."

Gently the slender little woman guided her tall workmate through the street and to the apartment. Once there Carla threw herself upon the bed. "This Depression caused the crash," she cried. "He was late, he wanted to be there first, he was hurrying or he never would have, oh he's such a good driver!" It hadn't happened, it couldn't have happened.

"Yes it was the Depression," Tanya agreed. "Be angry, you've every right to be angry. And every need."

"Take me to him," Carla demanded.

"Yes, in good time," Tanya answered, choking on her words. She had been told that Carla must come to identify. She left Carla on the bed and went into the other room. Although she had known Carla for months, Tanya had never been in the apartment before, and now she realized how shallow their acquaintance had been. She noted the Van Gogh prints on the wall and went over to them. "Mmm," she mused. "This is interesting. She never spoke about Van Gogh or any other painter. Who would have expected to find these here?"

There was a small bookcase which held a dozen books, and this came as less of a surprise to her. Carla often talked of what she read, but Tanya would not have expected to find there a copy of *Leaves of Grass* nor one of Francis Parkman's *History of the French and English in America*. This was new to her, and she opened it and examined it. A hasty perusal showed her that it was a serious, even scholarly, history book. "This tells me something," Tanya murmured. "I'll have to get more intimate with our country miss."

Tanya set to work scrubbing, partly to be helpful and somewhat to postpone that awful visit she had yet to make with Carla. At noon she found a can of soup, a thin broth with noodles, and she warmed it for Carla. Carla came out and sat by the table but would eat nothing, would only drink a little tea, not more than half a cup. Tanya ate the soup, found two hotdogs and some lettuce and ate them, and drank her tea. And she talked.

Carefully she propounded the concept that everything which had happened had its place in a system. Nothing happened by accident. Everything could be understood in the light of the teachings of a philosophy which she identified by name as dialectical materialism. It was quite involved, and Carla wasn't listening. "This happened," Tanya summarized, "because of the vicious contradictions in the economic system. That was the ultimate cause. The failure of the shoe workers and others like them to organize and win higher wages was the cause."

"It would have been worse if I'd been getting higher wages," moaned Carla. "It was partly because I was earning and Ray wasn't that he was so desperate."

"The policeman said the accident was the fault of the other driver," said Tanya.

"Ray was in too much of a hurry," Carla insisted. "Maybe even speeding."

"If the shoe workers had more money," Tanya went back to her premise, "they would buy more cars, and there wouldn't be unemployment among mechanics."

"The kind of cars shoe workers could ever buy would certainly need mechanics," said Carla wryly. She stopped. How horrible that she could still think and make remarks like that when Ray was lying somewhere dead. Or was he? Where was he? She must go to him. Yes, she believed he was dead, she almost believed.

"Where is he?" she demanded. "Where is he?"

"I have the address," Tanya replied. "Jake says I'm to go there with you."

"Right this minute." Carla was putting on her coat.

Tanya saw that it could not be postponed and made haste to go with her. *Yes*, thought Tanya, *there's more to this girl than I ever realized. She's a real live one and so calm to look at. But what bitterness is surfacing. This bitterness will open her eyes, make her see that under this thieving capitalist system the workers will never get new cars, will always be miserably exploited. She will see the need for struggle, eventually revolution.*

It was still raining when they went out. Carla kept the hood of her raincoat well down to hide her tear-filled eyes. Tanya guided her, paid the bus fares, led her off the bus, down the street, a street in Boston. Carla was sure she'd been there before but couldn't quite get her bearings.

In a daze she went into the big white building and felt suddenly chilled as she realized their destination was not a hospital but a mortuary. They followed a black-coated young man into a dimly lighted room. Could she identify? Yes, there was no doubt, it was Ray, his face the white of death, his head bandaged, his eyes closed, his hand so cold to her kiss, oh so cold. Yes, it was Ray. She knelt beside him, and the minutes flowed over her and were filled with all their life together. Back she went to the time when Ray was simply the boy next door. And then they were flying on the motorcycle. Oh if it had only happened to them together, flying together to meet death. And then they were paddling the canoe across the lake, and there was the blue tent, the honeymoon tent. And they were in Boston together, huddled in the little room, and they were exploring the city, the city rich with the tradition of the past and humming with the vigorous present, the sad city and the beautiful city. And it was cold white winter, and they were in a theater warm and out of the cold and holding hands and listening to an Irish tenor singing "The Hills of Home."

The young man put an envelope in her hand and suggested she read the letter at once. "He swerved to avoid hitting us," the letter said. "There were four of us in the car, and we could have been killed. Our car had stalled in the middle of the road, we tried to get it started. His courage saved our lives."

His courage saved their lives? *And my life*, thought Carla, *is gone. My brave, brave husband.* She was with him once more clambering over the rocks, leaping in the waves. At last Tanya led her back out, and they walked quietly to the bus stop. They passed a movie house, and Carla cried out and stood there in the midst of the foot traffic, unmindful of the passersby. Yes, it was the one. "The Hills of Home," she said aloud. Back in the apartment Carla sank upon the couch and sat staring before her. Late at night she was still sitting there like a frozen body. Tanya, desperate for sleep, dared not leave her but finally went in and lay down on the bed. Twice in the night she got up and looked. She spoke to Carla, but Carla merely glanced at her as if she'd never seen her before. A third time Tanya went to her, and Carla looked kindly at her and told her to go back to bed. Tanya hesitated.

Where are the tears, she thought, *where oh where are the tears?*

THIRTEEN

The tears came when Margaret Putnam arrived.

"My darling girl," she said gently. "My poor dear girl."

She sat down at the table, placed on it a small black suitcase and from it took a long black stocking stuffed with something. It reminded Carla of the long black stockings her father had made her wear, the ones he had brought to the courthouse so long ago. Margaret carefully emptied the stocking on the table. Dollar bills and fives and a few tens fell in a gray-green heap.

"I've been saving this for years," she said. How much Ray had resembled her! "I hid it to keep Barc from drinking it. Help me count it. Now he's glad we have it." The self-possessed surface cracked, and she buried her face on the table, her tears wetting the hoard of money. Together they wept.

"It's my fault he died," sobbed Carla. "If he hadn't married me, he wouldn't have come to Boston. If I hadn't been the one with a job—"

Margaret became calm at once. "My dear daughter," she said. "Nothing is your fault. The world doesn't revolve around any one person."

"If I hadn't nagged him about getting ahead—"

"I nagged Barc about the drink. All women nag their husbands. Have to. And remember Ray died a hero."

I wonder, thought Carla.

"Your mother is terribly upset," Margaret went on. "The poor dear! I left her at the house with Barc and Elsa. But she's strong. She insisted she'll go back to work tonight."

"She loved Ray," sobbed Carla.

"She's had a visitor."

"A visitor?"

"Didn't your mother write about Howard?"

"Howard was there?"

"I wonder she didn't write. No, really, I don't wonder. They did nothing but fight. He'd hitchhiked to get there, and he didn't have a job, and he was ragged and dirty, poor boy."

"It's so long since I saw him. Has he changed?"

"Well, he's still a scrawny little fellow, needs fattening, could stand a haircut, eyes like yours. He's got a little wooden flute that he plays all day long, not too good, but he's getting better. They let him stay at the hotel a few days, and that flute got on your mother's nerves."

"Where did he go?"

"Who knows? I don't suppose he himself knew where he'd wind up. He was just wandering, trying to find a job, had worked a few days setting out strawberries before he came to your mother."

"My drifting, wandering brother!"

"He came to say good-bye to me. Barc was away at work. I think years ago he kind of fell in love with Elsa, but of course—" Margaret stopped herself. How tactless could one get?

"Howard never had a chance."

"Mostly we make our own chances," the older woman replied. "And you and I, my daughter, have a funeral to arrange."

The service in Boston was very simple, held in a white-painted chapel; the only music was one unfamiliar hymn played on a small organ by a member of the mortuary staff. The minister, who had been recruited from a nearby church, read the scripture, followed the ritual for burial of the dead, tried to say a few comforting words.

"You'll be going to Maine?" Sarah asked Carla as they left.

"For a week or so."

"Jake says to tell you he'll hold the job."

"I hope she'll come home with me to stay," said Margaret.

"Better he should hold the job a while, just in case," said Sarah, and Margaret could not argue with that.

"Do come back," urged Tanya.

"What will be, will be," Sarah said, feeling the impropriety of this urging.

Tanya persisted. "We have plans—don't hush me, Sarah, you know we do. I can't talk about it now."

"Since you can't talk about it," said Sarah, "better you should hush."

"Plans?" queried Margaret as she and Carla walked along. "What did she mean?"

"I don't know," replied Carla.

The second funeral service was held two days later in the sanctuary of the Megunnaway church where Carla and Elsa and Ray had been baptized, the church where Carla and Elsa had giggled during service, where Ray and Carla were married. The dark casket lay closed upon the trestle, the pews filled silently and solemnly. Miss Castleton was there in her impressive mass as the official representative of the High School, and Louise, who had taken time off from work, and Pete of Pete's Garage. "We grieve," said the minister, "but not as those without hope."

"Lord, Thou hast been our dwelling place in all generations," he read the scripture, "Before the mountains were brought forth, Or ever Thou hadst formed the earth and the world, Even from everlasting to everlasting, Thou art God. For a thousand years in Thy sight are but as yesterday when it is past, and as a watch in the night. Thou carriest them away as with a flood; and they are as asleep: In the morning they are like grass which groweth up; In the evening it is cut down, and withereth. So teach us to number our days, that we may apply our hearts unto wisdom. Let Thy work appear unto Thy servants, and Thy glory unto their children. And let the beauty of the Lord our God be upon us: And establish Thou the work of our hands upon us. Yea, the work of our hands establish Thou it."

He stepped back and folded his hands, white against the black of his robe, and the church choir stood in their place to sing: "Alleluia! Alleluia! Alleluia!"

How can they sing Alleluia, thought Carla, oh how can they? Yet she made no protest for this was a favorite hymn of Ray's. "The strife is o'er, the battle done; The victory of life is won; The song of triumph has begun."

Oh grant, she prayed silently, that it be so.

"Lord, by the stripes which wounded Thee, From death's dread sting Thy servants free, That we may live and sing to Thee. Alleluia!"

The story of Ray's tragic death was told by the minister, told calmly, without flourish, but giving due credit. Yes, he'd swerved that he might not hit the other car.

At the graveside, in a clearing in the woods, on a rise where to the right a glimpse of the lake shimmered through the birch trees, the dark coffin was lowered into the earth, and the minister again had words of comfort.

The family rode home, Barclay driving very slowly. "Take me back to the Twin Pines," said Abigail. "Carla, will you stay with me tonight?"

"Go in for a few minutes," said Margaret. "Then come home with us."

Though it sounded like a contradiction of Abigail's request, it wasn't meant so, and there was no strain; they felt at ease with one another, and it was only a making of arrangements, and Carla did as Margaret suggested.

When they approached the Putnams', they saw a car in the driveway, Miss Castleton's old Pontiac. Laboriously she hoisted herself down from the seat, a tremendous mountain of black cloth. At last she stood upright upon her stocky legs and faced the family. "I won't take up much of your time," she said.

"We're glad to see you," replied Margaret quite insincerely.

Miss Castleton turned to Carla. "Once not too long ago," she said. "We talked about college for you."

"It was very long ago."

"Maybe I said some things I shouldn't."

The Putnams were silent. Only Carla knew what had been said.

"I didn't come to rehash that," the big woman continued. "I came to tell you, Carla, that you have but to say the word, and I'll use my little influence, my little influence," she repeated the words plainly, implying it wasn't all that little, "to start anew and help you get that education, to which I know you'll do credit."

"I'll think about it," said Carla.

Carla went at once to the room that was to be hers for the night and sat there upon the bed, glad to be alone. After a while Margaret knocked and came in and sat down beside her. "Carla, my dear," she said, "call Miss Castleton, tell her you want to go to college. Maybe it'd mean a full scholarship."

"It's too late."

"Then stay here with us."

"Ray wouldn't sponge off his folks, and I'm not about to."

"Carla, Carla, how can you talk like that? Don't you know how my heart aches and how having you here would help?"

"I have to go back."

"Carla, tell me, is there a child?"

"No, Mother," Carla used the endearing address. "No, Mother darling. I wish there were, but there isn't."

"Promise me one thing. If you find there is a child, promise you'll come home to us."

It was easy enough to promise.

"Carla," said Margaret, "don't let your heart die with Ray. Something of mine must die with him for he is my son. But you are young and you must live; you have most of your life before you."

Carla kissed the dear freckled face over and over and clung to the mother of her dead love. If there had been a new life within her, oh if only there had been, she would have stayed, and she and Margaret and Barclay would have devoted themselves to the child, and she would make up to the child for all the ways she'd failed her husband Ray. But there was no child.

"That was a strange young woman in Boston," Margaret abruptly changed the subject. "The foreign woman, at least she looks foreign. Tanya. What did she mean when she said they, whoever they is, had plans?"

"I really don't know."

"You're curious?"

"Yes, I suppose I am."

"So am I, curious and leery."

Carla stayed three days, and during that time she had one good talk with Abigail. "I was hard on Ray," she said. "I told myself it was for his own good."

"Hard on him? In what way?"

"Urging him to read more, to go to school and learn more. Criticizing his friends and him too toward the end when he seemed to kind of give up."

"Men need to be built up; it's so easy to tear them down, even when you don't mean to."

They were in the room at Twin Pines, sitting side by side on the bed. Carla put her arms around Abigail, laid her head on her mother's shoulder. "Oh yes," she sobbed.

"Ray was understanding. No doubt he knew whatever you did was from love."

Carla was silent. Had it been love or pride, vanity, dissatisfaction? She had more than once wondered what her life would be like if she were free once more. Yes, she'd thought of it as free. How shameful that she had had such thoughts!

"The days ahead will be hard," said Abigail. "Full of temptation."

Carla turned wondering eyes toward her mother.

"Though you've forgotten God, He's still mindful of you. I pray, oh so earnestly, morning and night, for you."

"Keep praying, Mama, keep praying."

"Do you think I could ever stop? And oh Carla, listen to me. I know I amount to nothing, but from my mistakes I've learned. Some day you'll marry again."

"No, no, I won't." Old women, she thought, were all alike, Margaret and Mama, marrying her off, the one who'd stayed with it and the one who had not.

"You've a passionate nature. Don't be surprised at my saying that. You're very young. You'll marry again, and it's right you should. But Carla, think long and carefully."

"I can promise that."

"Think long and carefully because the next time it must be for the rest of your life."

Having said what was in her heart and somewhat embarrassed, Abigail pulled herself up as quickly as her weariness allowed and sat down at her table facing the little row of neatly arranged books. "What shall I read?" she asked.

"Something from the Bible," Carla said.

Nothing could have pleased Abigail more. She opened the book at random and sat dumbfounded before its riches. She turned the pages, pausing here, pausing there, till she found a familiar passage from which she read two verses: "'Jesus said unto him, If thou canst believe, all things are possible to him that believeth. And straightway the father of the child cried out, and said with tears, Lord, I believe; help thou my unbelief.'"

"'I believe; Lord, help thou my unbelief,'" Carla repeated, then turning, buried her face in the pillow.

Abigail went and touched her gently. "My child, my child," she said. "My baby girl!" And then she left, it being time for her to work.

As she walked slowly through the hall, she held Carla in her mind as it were in her arms. Boston was so far away, so strange. And Carla there alone! Ardently she prayed that God would guide and guard her dear, good daughter. And she too repeated, "'Lord, I believe; help Thou my unbelief.'"

❦

Back in her apartment in Laurel, Carla moved about in a state of numbness, going through motions from force of habit. There was no question of belief or unbelief. Then one day there came a troubled awareness. *I'm dead,* she thought, *dead as a doornail.* The very fact that she thought herself dead was proof of her being alive, but she had no sense of that. She recalled how Abigail had once spent a half hour speculating on the origin of the phrase. "Why a doornail?" she'd asked. "Certainly that's no deader than any other metal object." She'd looked in the dictionary and in a book on quaint sayings and been no wiser. How typical of Mama to care about such trivia, thought Carla. Abigail could never be dead till her heart, the physical organ, ceased its beat. But that was Mama. For Carla nothing, big or small, mattered any more. Her ambitions, her enthusiasm for causes were faded flowers. Ray had been wiser than she and better, for she had scorned his wisdom. Perhaps she'd scorned him; it must have seemed that way to him. Even the desires of her body, which from the time of too early awakening had fought against her fierce control until given full rein in his arms, even these had died. It was hardly worth bothering to eat.

Abigail had written a letter full of remembering, life and love, and she had ended, "Come home, dear Carla, come home."

Mama would cry, she thought, *if I should die.* The childish rubric came back to her. She must go through the motions and pretend to be alive.

She went to work, she wrote to Mama, she cleaned the apartment, she swallowed food. Eventually she went about packing Ray's clothing to give to the Salvation Army. That was what one did with the clothing of the dead, the fortunate dead who lay in graves. Feeling something hard in one of the pants pockets she fished out six ball bearings. She rolled them about in her hand, and they were more precious than jewels. Carefully she laid them on the table, beside the green bottle. The light now struck through the bottle making a pattern, a still life, but one she'd never seen painted. The perfect little spheres spoke to her of Ray, and yet they were such a small part of him. Something in him had responded not only to the precision ground metallic parts of an engine but equally to the whippoorwill singing deep in the woods. She hadn't loved him half enough.

And she didn't love her mother half enough. Mama had written that she had a new nickname, Mrs. Mittens, because of the many pairs of mittens she'd knitted for the neighbor children. Abigail was rather proud of the title. It was part of the pattern of her life, not her life as she'd planned it, but her life as God had helped her live it. But Carla found the nickname vaguely embarrassing, God help her, she did.

Carla picked up a book, the old book of poems from the Amsterburg school. From its pages a paper fluttered and fell to the floor, a childish valentine, the hand-drawn figures of a boy and girl inside a red paper heart. And above the figures, "To my Valentine CARLA from Roger." What a cheerful, yet serious boy he'd been, and how graciously he'd helped her at that Hambledon School. She supposed his life had a pattern, that he'd found it easily enough. Gone into some profession no doubt, probably married.

She went to the kitchen and sitting down at the table with a big pad of paper started writing. She'd always been fascinated by little-known stories from the history of America, Snorri Thorfinnson, for instance. Roger's grandfather had claimed that the first European child born in America was sired by one Thorfinn Karlsefni, a Greenland trader who some time before 1100 had founded a colony on the coast. After two years, during which time a son Snorri was born to Thorfinn and his wife Freyda, the colonists retreated from the attacks of the local natives and returned to Greenland. Carla was seized with a desire to write it into a story, a story a child might read. What a good old man that grandfather had been! He'd let her, a little waif, handle his books; he'd talked to her about them; he'd delighted in her childish interest. Yes, he'd told her, his name was indeed Thorfinnson, meaning son of Thorfinn. He didn't claim to be descended from that Snorri; he might or might not be, he'd never been able to trace it, and his son cared only for the pedigrees of horses. And Roger only for mechanical gadgets. She sat a long time but didn't know how to start.

※❦※

From force of habit she went to work at the factory. Her hands of their own volition pushed the leather under the needle. The other women talked, Jake went about shouting and tearing his hair, Sarah still settled prices, and Tanya sang.

"No, no, no," she heard Jake one morning, unusually vehement even for him. "Sarah, if I add one penny to the price, this shoe won't sell, I tell you it won't sell!"

"The cutters and lasters make more than us stitchers."

"Their jobs are harder, takes longer to learn, they're harder to replace. Listen Sarah, I could show you all the prices for every stupid operation, but you wouldn't know any more than you do now. Believe me, trust me."

"But this adds up to less than we were paid for Style 987."

"No. Six percent more."

She persisted. Jake threw up his hands in disgust. "See," he cried, "there on paper, add up those figures, the price for every operation in this room, lining, back seam, everything, add it up."

"I did. It's six percent less."

Jake snorted angrily. "Try to talk sense to her," he said. "Whether it's politics or religion or prices, once she gets an idea. Oy vey! Go ask one of the girls to help you add those figures, go!"

"No."

"Do me a favor, go."

"When did I ever refuse to do you a favor?" said Sarah and went down the aisle, looking right and left as if trying to decide whom to approach. At last she stopped by Carla, handed her the paper with the figures for both Style 987 and 988. "Add," she said. "He'll see."

"Why not?" said Carla. She added up and she added down; she figured percentages. Jake was right. At last Sarah admitted it. "Just couldn't read my own writing, thought that seven was a one."

She would have gone back in good humor to see if she could do a little better had not one of the other women interrupted. "You just try to make trouble," cried Angela, a stout middle-aged woman. "Make him mad, we won't get nothing."

"We must get more," interposed Tanya. "Even if it means strike."

"Strike and we really do starve," retorted Angela.

Both strike talk and political arguments increased and took on a new intensity. Franklin Roosevelt was nominated for President by the Democratic Party, and support for him was fervent but not unanimous. "He's talking liberal," cried Tanya, "but it's only a pose to demoralize the working class in the face of the ceaseless offensive of socialism on all fronts. He and Hoover alike will rule for the capitalist class."

"In other words," Sarah interpreted, "he knows workers are fed up, and he's trying to head it off. But it won't make a smidgen of difference which one wins. Both are for the bosses."

Carla began to wonder, just like a living person. Maybe socialism was the wave of the future, though few people believed it. When Carla heard Roosevelt on the radio, heard the beautiful, strong voice proposing new approaches, voicing sympathy for the suffering of his country, talking about national defense, unemployment and old-age insurance, better financing of farm mortgages—what indeed did he not touch upon—she was deeply moved. "The future," he said, "is ours to conquer and to hold. The time has come. The hour has struck." She forgot about socialism, just a pipe dream. Roosevelt was for real!

Once while they were having lunch, she championed him in an argument with Tanya. "Roosevelt is a patrician snob," was Tanya's scornful answer. "He'll only bind your chains the tighter."

Carla got up and started back to the workroom but was intercepted by one of the men, Gilbert Strong. He was an edgetrimmer, somewhat older than she, perhaps in his forties, and he'd been pointed in his attentions to her, but there was something about him which repelled her. She thought it was his eyes. Tall and well-favored, with wavy black hair and rugged features, he would have been handsome had it not been for the strangeness of his eyes, the lids of which sagged so that the eyes were half hidden. The effect was that of a constant leer. Bedroom eyes, some of the women called them. "Carla," he said softly, "why do you run from me?"

"I don't, believe me, I don't." As she looked up at him now, the eyes no longer seemed sinister.

"I want to get better acquainted."

She stood awkwardly like a schoolgirl.

"Will you go bowling with me Saturday?" Gilbert asked.

The bowling alley, she thought, was much too expensive. "I'll do you a favor," she said, "and refuse."

"Then to lunch, or even to the park, just so that we can talk."

She ended by going to lunch and then for a walk in the park. To her surprise she found him an interesting companion. He'd moved to Laurel from a farm in western Massachusetts, he shared her love of books, they'd read many of the same authors, and that look of unuttered devotion which he fixed on her was like warm sunshine. It was mid-afternoon when he walked back to her apartment with her. She started to invite him in for coffee, but the intensity of his gaze as they stood there at the door brought back her old apprehensions about him, and she bade him good-bye, a definite, get-lost good-bye.

"Carla," Gilbert said. "We can't part like this. I must come in."

"There's no must about it."

"Don't you realize how much I care for you?"

"You hardly know me."

"Well enough to know how I feel." Gilbert lowered his face suddenly and kissed her cheek. "No, no," he cried. "Give me your lips."

"My teeth, if you come too close," she retorted drawing back from him.

He straightened up, released her hand which he had been holding, and said quite gravely, "I'm not one to force myself on you."

"Good."

"Maybe in time."

"Never."

"Will this prevent us from being friends?" Gilbert asked.

"I, I don't know."

"I'd better haul in my sails for a while. But Carla, there is something I had in mind to talk to you about and didn't get to. Will you listen?"

"Okay, so long as we stay on the sidewalk and you behave."

He laughed. "You're not afraid of me?"

"No. I'm not particularly timid."

"Good. I want to talk to you about organizing the stitchers into the union."

It was such a sudden change that she found it ludicrous and laughed. "We already have two red-hot unionists among us," she said.

"Only two? We have much more than that among the cutters, the lasters, and the making room. Who are the two?"

"Sarah and Tanya. Talk to them."

"Those Communists! They're only out for power," Gilbert scoffed.

"And you?"

He looked solemnly at her, then hurried away.

Monday morning Tanya sought out Carla. "So you did date Gilbert Strong," she said.

"Who told you?"

"A little bird. Was it supposed to be a secret?"

"No, of course not."

"Did you know he's married?"

"Oh, I think you're mistaken."

"My little bird says he is. Ask Sarah."

"Why should I?"

The power had not yet gone on, and they were talking quietly, heads close together. "I can understand you're wanting to go out with a man," said Tanya.

"We just had lunch together and went for a walk."

"It'll lead to other things if I know that one. Maybe it's what you need. Sure, get yourself a man, but not Gilbert Strong."

"I will never remarry."

"Who's talking about remarriage?"

The power came on, and they turned to their work, and they spoke more loudly. "He talked union to me, Tanya," said Carla after a while. "Maybe strike. But it seems to me we'd get a few dollars more and maybe lose whole weeks of work."

"The point isn't the few dollars." Tanya's eyes were glowing, her voice filled with excitement. "Oh that's *his* point. He's just a porkchop unionist."

"If not the few dollars, what then?"

"Oh, my dear infant! The point is that through struggle the workers learn, through struggle they become radicalized, and through radicalization they become revolutionary. We build a whole new world."

Carla stared at her. "Oh!" she said.

"But what does he know? What does he know of freedom, why, he's nothing but a social-fascist. Oh Carla! Think of the day when there'll be no more oppression, no more poverty, no more bosses, no more war!"

"No more boils on the neck," scoffed Angela. "Strawberries and cream every day for breakfast!"

"It's nonsense anyway," said Carla. "How can we have a union when even you and Gilbert Strong hate each other so?"

Jake loomed in the aisle. "Hush," said Sarah. "Don't get us fired before we've so much as begun."

Jake was there in the aisle shouting and tearing his hair. The words poured forth in an angry torrent, a mixture of English and Yiddish and Italian and who knows what else. "He says," translated Sarah, "better we should shut up and get the work out."

The machines whirred, the women's hands moved faster and faster, and the tongues for now were silenced, but the fever remained. *I'll bet*, thought Carla, *that this is the exciting thing Sarah and Tanya talked about after Ray died. How far ahead they were looking! To strike or not to strike? Gilbert and Sarah and Tanya are all convinced that the pay raise they seek will never be granted otherwise.* Carla found herself wondering and caring, just like a living person.

FOURTEEN

A few weeks later she went home with Tanya and learned from the young radical's parents that she had a degree and a teacher's credential as well. The parents, who eked out a living in a mom-and-pop grocery store, were quite disgusted that their daughter was working in a factory.

"Tanya," cried Carla, "since you have that kind of education, why *are* you working in a factory?"

"I had a job teaching," said Tanya. "But what good was that? Filling innocent minds with falsehood."

"You talk like that schlemiel Leonard," scoffed her mother.

"Thank you, Mom," Tanya retorted. "If it'll do you any good to know it, I haven't seen him for a year."

"There, there," the father tried to calm them, "it'll all work out. Don't worry, Mama, she'll get married and have her children like other girls and come back to the fold. Just give her time, give her time. So Leonard wasn't the one. We never thought he was. It'll work out."

Tanya tossed her head, her eyes flashed. "I wouldn't bring a child into this horrible world," she cried. "Not for anything."

Carla sat transfixed. It was like something out of a Russian novel, the educated young woman going to the people. "Why Tanya," she said softly, "it's as if you had a mission."

"Mission schmission," snorted the mother.

One Friday soon after that Tanya went home with Carla and they talked incessantly, but there was a wall between them. *She gives too much advice,* thought Carla, *though I'm not sure the advice is bad. Maybe Tanya is right. Maybe I should yield to my desires. Not marriage, Tanya says, just a good old romp in bed. And maybe there is no God. And maybe it is the final crisis of capitalism.* She wasn't sure about any of these, but one thing she had no doubt about; she didn't like Tanya's air of superiority; she was too much the authority, dispensing knowledge, and sometimes hinting at knowledge she had but couldn't trust Carla with. Carla, with an ornery streak of independence, resolved not to be drawn into the orbit of the flaming star Tanya. And yet, there was the pull. If only they could be truly friends! Not comrades, just friends.

At work Tanya talked more and more of union and strike, and so did many others. What was once a whisper became open speculation and open advocacy. And there was a counter move, for there were those who feared it. It was not something to reason about; it was a gut feeling one way or the other. When will we start marching, thought Carla? And how will I know what I must do?

One evening when this was much on her mind, she was interrupted by the sound of the outside door opening. She looked out the window to see if there was a car, but there was none. The snow, which by day was dimmed by the gray of coal ash, in the moonlight glistened as if new-fallen. The slush on the sidewalk had been trodden down so that two people could walk abreast. Someone had come up the stairs, several people, several men, walking quietly up the stairs. They knocked at her door, and she stood frozen by the window.

"Carla," she heard. It was Gilbert. "Don't be afraid."

He and three others from Caldwell Shoe filed into the room, a union delegation she knew at once, entering her cloistered chamber. First came Gilbert, those eyes gazing at her; there was the quiet, middle-aged Frank from the cutting room; there was Arthur Moses, tall, lean, darkly handsome; and Mike McGuigan, a heel fitter by trade and known throughout the factory for his jovial manner and his slightly overdone gallantry toward the women. Carla felt his eyes upon her and blushed. "Don't you be frightened, Carla," he said.

"Oh I'm not," she retorted. "I wouldn't be even if you were alone."

Arthur Moses burst into a loud guffaw and even the cutter, Frank Dawson, chuckled. Mike was taken aback for a moment but recovered quickly. "See," he said, "I told you she had spunk."

There was light talk as they found places at the table and Carla made them tea. Yes, they'd come to talk union; she must organize the stitching room. Oh yes they knew about Sarah and Tanya, but they were Communists, how could you trust them? "We're having an organizing committee meeting next Wednesday," Frank said. "And we want you to represent the stitchers."

"The stitchers haven't chosen me to be on any committee," Carla replied.

"They will in time," said Mike, smiling down at her and patting her on the shoulder.

Something electric came from his touch, and she drew away and looked into her cup of tea. Oh no, she thought, and him married, a family man.

"I want you at that meeting," she heard Frank's dry, solemn voice. "Things are moving fast."

"We've others to visit," said Arthur. "Thanks for the tea."

Left alone, Carla was in a turmoil. Why had McGuigan laid his hand on her? She neither rejoiced nor repined, she simply wondered at it. But she wasn't about to lose her head.

She supposed she'd go Wednesday; they were right, something big was in the making. Tanya had seen it for so long, seen it as a crusade. Eventually the different factions must come to an understanding, but for now she'd say nothing about the meeting to Sarah and Tanya. It was coming, the strike was coming; you could feel it in the air just as you could feel an approaching storm. It would do good, and it would do harm, even as the storm, and who knew how the balance would swing. But at least she knew her next step, that meeting, yes, that was her next inevitable step.

At the meeting, open to a select group made up of the men who had called on her, two very silent women from the packing room and a couple of men she didn't know, Carla felt elated at being in the inner circle. Of course she hadn't earned the right to be there, but that didn't prevent her from boldly saying the entire Caldwell stitching room would walk out, not one would scab. Yes, she said the word, it sounded indecent, which was quite appropriate considering the vile treachery it denoted.

She was walking toward work a week later, determined to talk directly to Frank and find out just when they'd hit the bricks. She had to find out, she simply had to. If Frank wouldn't tell her, then Mike McGuigan. She hurried on, she was sitting on top of the world, she was humming "Solidarity," she met a couple of young men whom she didn't know, and they looked beautiful to her, and from their glances she was aware that she looked beautiful to them. Springtime! And, yes, the springtime of life.

She turned to glance after the young men, hastily that they might not notice, and then there was McGuigan coming down the street, with the sun giving a golden glint to his light brown hair, a red scarf flashing under his unbuttoned coat. He came running toward her, and singing in a musical tenor the very thing she'd been humming, "Solidarity forever, the union makes us strong!"

"The Shawmut workers are out," he cried. "They jumped the gun, but can Laurel be far behind?"

Carla stopped, uncertain what to do. "Go into the stitching room," he shouted. "Wait there."

She reached the stitching room just as the power was being turned on and hurried past Jake, who gave her what she interpreted as a dirty look. No one was working; they were gathered in little groups, arguing furiously. "Strike, Shawmut workers on strike, can Laurel be far behind? And who should lead Laurel? Why Caldwell Shoe of course. No! No! No! We'll starve, what'll we feed the kids? If they can, we can. We ought to leave this minute. Caused by a bunch of trouble-making outsiders!" Faces were flushed, eyes flashing, hands gesticulating.

"Where on earth is Sarah?" Tanya threw out the question despairingly.

"She's gone somewhere to take care of a sick grandbaby," said Jake who was just then going through the aisle. He went on, mumbling to himself, "Thank God for small blessings. That's all I need, that one here, talking Industrial Union."

"From a boss's point of view you're right, Jake," cried Tanya, and he stopped to listen. "You know the difference between a no-good, phony, all-for-the-bosses outfit like the American Shoe Workers Union, the difference between that and the militant Industrial Union.

"Okay, Miss Smarty-pants," cried Angela. "I know the difference too. The American will cost us maybe three weeks wages and with the Industrial we'd never get back to work. They're not even a union, they're a Commie front."

"They're for the workers."

"They're for Russia," retorted Angela.

A shrill voice far down the room shouted, "They're splitters, dual unionists."

"Yes, we will split from sell-out artists like American Shoe Workers Union, you'd better believe we will!" Tanya shouted back.

Jake waved his arms in the air and shouted, "You want to argue, rent a hall. This is a factory, we make shoes. Remember?"

The women leaned over their machines, and Jake continued on his way. Carla heard him shouting, "Strike, shmike! Let's get these bundles out. Howya going to get paid if you don't get the work out?"

Tanya's songs that morning were love ballads of sorts, she was singing "Barbry Allen," and "Darling Clementine," then something in a foreign tongue which had the moaning sound of hopeless love. Angela was un-wontedly voluble but seemed to have forgotten English and talked only in Italian. Jake went running up and down the aisles, urging patience, urging caution, predicting dire failure for the strikers in Shawmut, raising his hands in exultation as the women became quiet and concentrated on their work. Then a couple of the men sat down and Jake went over to praise them, but they wouldn't look at him. "Oy vey!" he shouted. "What a bunch of crazies."

Carla was running the leather under the needle very slowly. *Oh Mike,* she thought, *come and tell me what to do.*

As if on cue, Mike McGuigan and Frank Dawson burst into the room and headed for the power switch. Jake ran toward them. "No, no!" he shouted. "Get out, go back to your own departments, leave the stitchers alone."

Frank Dawson moved resolutely toward the switch, waving his right arm as he walked and from his hand there came the gleam of polished metal, just a small piece of metal, the curved blade of the wooden-handled knife which was the tool of his trade. Jake, near enough now to intercept him, paused. "Threatening, huh?" he said angrily.

"Nope," said Frank. "When cutters are on strike, they carry their knives around."

Jake hesitated for a moment, not so much out of fear, for he did not really think that Frank would use the sharp knife as a weapon, but rather because he had mixed feelings about the union. God knows the workers made little enough, and there were days when he was sick to death of bargaining and driving, caught in the middle, pushed from both sides, and never able to forget the days when he himself had sat at a machine. Frank reached the switch and with a quick movement pulled it down. There was a whir, the sound of the power shaft slackening speed; there was a hubbub of voices and above it all the thrilling voice of Mike McGuigan, "On strike! On strike! Out on the picket line."

How handsome he looked, thought Carla, with his tall, muscular body, his rumpled hair, his ruddy skin, his wild excitement. A shrill sound coming through the windows reverberated off the walls, came nearer and nearer, beat upon her eardrums. Carla hurried toward the door, shouted for the others to follow, dashed past Mike, saw Tanya at her side and others grabbing coats. She scurried down the stairs and outdoors.

Promenading down the street was a bagpiper, his pipes draped in red and gold tartan, a matching cap atop his head. That the rest of his costume was plain brown jacket and blue denim pants didn't matter. He blew with the vigor of an impassioned Scot leading his warriors through the rocky gorges of some mountain pass. Straight down the middle of the street he came, the sound echoing off the brick buildings. And behind him came a loud procession, wildly shouting.

"Come out," they shouted. "On strike, on strike, shut it down, on strike!"

The workers from Caldwell Shoe flowed into the street and became part of the stream. It was a good-natured crowd, shouting greetings to friends, yelling, whooping. It was like an unexpected holiday from school. Walking down the street was an adventure, the weight of the day's work was lifted. It was freedom, sweet freedom, and at the same time a battle for freedom. True a few of the women were grumbling and predicting failure, and there were men whose faces were tight-lipped and grim, but these were the exception.

One young woman was crying, and an older woman told her to hustle her bustle on home and look after her kids. After one scared look around, the young woman left the procession and ran down a side street. Others quietly dropped out at street corners, but the main contingent followed the bagpiper down the street.

They turned right on Second Street and came to the Bijou Theater, closed for a year or so due to lack of business. Glory be, the doors were open. The bagpiper was now standing silently in front of the theater. Several men under the marquee were directing the marching crowd into the building. The bagpiper approached a waiting car, placed his instrument carefully on the back seat, then climbed in after it, closed the door, waved gaily, and was driven away. The advancing crowd pushed against Carla, and she found herself entering the theater auditorium. The dim lights shone kindly on the faded red upholstery and dingy carpet. Carla continued down the aisle. In front of the movie screen was a long narrow stage, on which about a dozen men and a couple of women had gathered, some seated and some walking about. A fair-haired man of middle age dressed in a neat gray business suit got up from his seat on stage and stepped to the center front. Carla could see his lips move; as the hubbub grew less, they could hear his voice. He persisted and at last the audience was quiet.

Tanya was at Carla's elbow. "That's Eli Stanton from Shawmut," she whispered. "An old-timer, slick as they come. I don't trust him."

Carla moved toward a seat near the back, but Tanya cried, "No, no, don't sit there. We must be up front to take control." Carla was confused, but together they edged further front.

The man was speaking, slowly and distinctly. First he wanted to set a few facts straight. It was true that the workers of Shawmut were on strike, all but a couple of shops. The bagpiper was from Shawmut, a laster. He had gone back to join his shop on the picket line. It was not true that the workers were out in Boston. Laurel could rightly claim the honor of being the first to follow the courageous workers of Shawmut. He was proud to say he was from the American Shoe Workers Union, now leading the strike in Shawmut. He had been making contacts in the shops in Laurel for a long time, and there was already a committee—wild cheering and some boos, among them the soprano wail of Tanya. *Oh,* thought Carla, *so it isn't quite as local as I supposed.* She noticed that Frank Dawson had taken a seat upon the stage.

"A roll call," Stanton continued, "would show that half the shops of Laurel are out, or at least represented. Biltrite Shoe?" He paused to give the crowd time to cheer as workers from that shop stood up. "Stylerite, Matawamkeag, New England." The crowd went wild and he stood there smiling. "Harlan, Caldwell!" Each was given an accolade.

Stanton went on. "Massachusetts Shoe, do we have anyone here from Massachusetts Shoe?"

For a moment there was silence, then the rustle of looking around. Somewhere in the middle of the theater a big blonde woman struggled to her feet. "I'm here," she said. "Big Hannah Bixby."

Across the room a woman's voice shouted, "I thought you quit work to take care of your kids."

"I did, but they're at school now."

"When did you go back to work?"

"I didn't. I heard the row and came a-running. And if you're worried about whether I'm really from Mass Shoe, just let me tell you I worked there for five years, and I'm here to represent them since no one else is. What's more, I'll show you. I'll go get those people out." She pushed her way through the aisle and out the door, and the crowd roared approval long after she was gone.

Stanton stood applauding until the crowd was silent. "With spirit like that, how can we lose?" he cried.

Complacently he waited for the new round of cheers to subside. "I have to get back to Shawmut," he told them. "I've asked Frank Dawson from Caldwell to act as temporary chairman until you can elect whoever you want."

There were shouts of "Dawson, Dawson, we want Dawson!" The Frank Dawson standing there was a new Frank Dawson, his back straight, his eyes glowing. It took something like this, thought Carla, to bring out the real person. The shouts continued, Carla adding her voice, too excited to notice how well it carried, even in this medley of voices. Suddenly she noticed that Tanya was screaming something quite different.

"No railroading, no railroading," Tanya shouted, and she began to shove and push her way through the crowd in the aisle.

While she was still some distance from the platform, a slender young man named Gus grasped the edge of the stage and leaped up beside Stanton. "Wait a minute," he cried. "Let's not railroad this thing. There's more than one union. I'm from the Industrial. We've been organizing in Laurel for two years now, and we're not about to be pushed aside."

There was an angry hum interspersed with a few scattered cheers. Carla saw Arthur Moses come on stage, scowling angrily, his body tense, ready for action. Stanton just laughed. "Organizing for two years? And what have you to show for it?" he scoffed. He turned halfway and motioned Moses back. Then calmly facing the young man he went on. "We've just started this campaign within the last few weeks, and we don't intend to take two years to get results. But in a larger sense we've been organizing for two generations. Our name has changed, but we are the lineal descendants of all the former unions of Shawmut and Laurel and the whole North shore. We're what got Shawmut to strike, don't forget that!"

"We demand the right to be heard!" Gus shouted angrily.

"So you demand the right to be heard?" Stanton stepped back and looked at him, his coolness a studied contrast to the excitement of the younger man.

"We refuse to be beaten down, to be deprived of our rights, to be pushed around," Gus yelled.

"Don't blame you," said Stanton. "None of us want to be pushed around. But I don't recognize you as having done much of an organizing job here, and I suspect you have lots of *political* demands too."

"Of course," Gus said. "We always seek to broaden and deepen the struggle."

"We want to be fair," Stanton went on, glancing ostentatiously at his watch, "so we'll put it to a vote."

"Right now?" Gus looked anxious.

"Yup, right now."

Gus hesitated. Tanya cupped her hands to make a megaphone. "Tomorrow," she yelled. "Give us time."

"Oh I reckon all your people are out of the shops," Stanton said calmly.

"Of course!" Tanya shouted.

Stanton smiled. "You didn't expect me to be willing to vote on it, did you? But we don't run as tight a ship as you Communists do."

Tanya was clenching and unclenching her fists. "Why the social fascist fink," she cried and was promptly shushed by Carla and others.

Without waiting for anyone to phrase a motion, Stanton put the question. "Everybody for the Industrial Union raise your *left* hand," he cried sarcastically, and the crowd roared with laughter.

"Why the dirty back-stabber!" spluttered Tanya. "Left hand indeed!"

"I object," cried Gus. "Brothers and sisters, fellow workers, comrades, yes, *comrades!* Have we sunk so low as to tolerate these gutter tactics, this redbaiting?"

"Okay," Stanton interrupted. "I'll call for a voice vote. All those for the Industrial Union say aye."

"Aye, aye, aye," shrieked Tanya. She turned to Carla. "Vote Aye," she said as if giving an order. "We'll get real organizers in here."

Carla responded with an angry scowl. She was watching the transformed Frank Dawson; she would follow his lead. He was standing quietly beside Stanton, a faint smile on his lips.

It was he who spoke next. "All those in favor of affiliation with the American Shoe Workers Union, which I represent," he began, then paused.

Shouts of approbation came from every section of the hall. On the podium Arthur Moses was jumping up and down like a cheerleader, shouting wildly and waving his arms. "Aye, aye, yes yes, hurray, all the way," he cried. "Yes, yes, hurray, all the way," the crowd echoed.

Gus was still in there trying. "We want at least to be represented on the Strike Steering Committee," he said.

"Poor Gus," Tanya murmured. "That's not the way to do it. If only Sarah were here!"

"It wouldn't matter," said Carla.

"If she'd known, she'd have come."

"But her grandchild?"

"She'd have arranged it. She'd have been here. But I can't leave now to phone her."

Eli Stanton had handed Frank the gavel, a symbolic gesture certainly since there was no rostrum nor even a table. He hurried to the exit waving farewell. Arthur Moses was escorting the still expostulating Gus off the platform, and Frank was shouting for silence. Carla was amazed at how commanding he was. "Each shop," he instructed, "must get together somewhere."

Somehow they managed to get sorted out into shops, with Caldwell Shoe at the front of the theater. Out of the three hundred Caldwell workers about half were present.

"Where's Angela Rossoni from stitchers?" Dawson asked. "I wouldn't have expected her to go home. Nor Sarah Friedman."

"Sarah's not at work," Tanya explained quickly. "I didn't see Angela come out."

Carla turned around and satisfied herself that indeed Angela was not there. "I'll go into that shop and get her," she cried. "Right this minute."

"Will you come back out?" shouted one of the men, Carla wasn't sure who.

"How can you ask?" she cried, so loudly and clearly that workers in other shop meetings turned to stare. "Brothers and sisters, how could anyone once out, go back? We've passed the point of no return, what we've started we must finish. For too long we've been silent. Now we're making ourselves heard! For too long we've let ourselves be ground down and down and down, but now we're standing tall. We must get those slowpokes. As for coming back? How could you ask!"

She stood there, tall and slender, her face suffused with color, her voice that had been the pride of the Megunnaway debating team ringing out in that vast auditorium, and not only did Caldwell Shoe applaud her, so too did the workers in the other shop meetings.

Frank was ecstatic. "Good girl!" he said. "But you can't go till we get the committees set up."

Frank Dawson was elected Chairman, and he and McGuigan were elected delegates to the Laurel Strike Committee, sometimes referred to as the Strike Steering Committee. Carla found herself the stitchers' representative on the Caldwell Committee, but the best Tanya could do was picket captain, of which there were four, and this she owed largely to Carla. Dawson and McGuigan were so obviously determined to freeze her out that Carla resented it and became for the moment her champion. Carla riding high, elated with this turbulent world in which she had suddenly and to her surprise found recognition, nay honor, looked patronizingly at her erstwhile mentor. "I wouldn't want you to get mad and go home," she joked.

"A militant class-conscious worker doesn't get mad and go home," retorted Tanya.

Quickly the delegates to the Laurel Strike committee met and elected Frank Chairman. He called the whole room to order and pronounced the meeting adjourned. "But I want every last living one of you back here by one," he said firmly.

"I'll go to Caldwell and get Angela," Carla shouted, eager to play some role.

"I'll go with you," said Tanya.

"No," said Frank. "Only Carla. You'd get Angela's back up."

Carla left the theater alone and walked from the dim light into the bright outdoors. The sunlight reflected brilliantly off the melting snow, and the street seemed unusually busy, more cars than normal, more pedestrians, even more children. But of course, Carla reminded herself, it was the luncheon hour. Luncheon hour? Why yes, the business of living went on as usual, even on this day of days, the day the workers marched, the day of the bagpipes, the day of the crowded theater, the day Carla found a new excitement, a new sense of purpose, the day she had almost forgotten how lonely she was. She hurried up the stairs at Caldwell Shoe and could hear the hum of power; they'd be shutting down for lunch any minute. She hesitated for a moment. Should she walk into the stitching room or go to the lunchroom? Angela might choose to eat her lunch right at the machine; the outside entrance to the lunchroom might be locked so that the only access would be through the shop. She opened the door to the stitching room and saw that about half the workers were there, and sure enough there was Angela Rossoni, her head bowed over her work, her hands moving with their usual dexterity, working against time.

Jake came running toward Carla, shouting, waving his arms. "Get out, you can't come in," and in the next breath, "Go sit at your machine, I'll bring your work."

Carla ignored him, for after all she could hardly obey both commands.

She walked calmly towards Angela, who put aside her work. Carla started to give her a pep talk, but Angela interrupted her. "Who's running the show?" she asked.

"The American Shoe Workers Union. Eli Stanton from Shawmut was here, and Frank Dawson is Chairman for Caldwell. He and Mike McGuigan represent Caldwell on the Laurel Committee and Frank chairs that."

Angela listened carefully, thought for a moment, then asked, "And what about Sarah Friedman and Tanya whatsername?"

"You know Sarah isn't here today. Tanya will be one of the Caldwell picket captains."

"That's all she'll be?"

"Yes."

"You wouldn't lie to me?"

"Okay, be a scab if you want," cried Carla suddenly angry and using this ultimate insult.

It was Angela's turn to be angry. "Nobody calls Angela Rossoni scab," she cried.

"Break it up, break it up, girls." Jake was there, anguish in his voice.

"Get lost," Angela advised him, and he spluttered incoherently as he walked away. She turned to Carla. "You go on back," she advised. "You said meeting at one?"

"Yes."

"I'll be there, and not just me."

Carla left and started back to the theater. *I did it! I did it! I did it!* she thought exultantly. In her haste to report she fairly ran. She found Frank seated in the front of the auditorium, doing figures on a paper attached to a clipboard.

"She's coming out," Carla cried. "She promised. And with others."

Frank glanced up. "Could be she'll keep her promise," he said. That air of confidence which Carla had earlier remarked in him seemed to have evaporated. He went back to his figures, and he had a worried look.

"Oh she will," cried Carla. "I know she will." How could it be otherwise, thought Carla? Angela had to come out; they all must come; it was inconceivable that it should be otherwise.

Once more Frank glanced up and now, if there was no longer exaltation, there was at least a calm and steady determination in his countenance. "I'll go with the Caldwell picket at one," he said. "Want to be there to greet them. Maybe prod them."

"You seem worried."

Frank laughed. "Oh! Well I mustn't let it show. But Carla, little girl, I've got real worries. It's a big responsibility being Chairman of the Laurel Strike Committee, the committee for the whole city."

"Didn't you want it?"

"I accepted," he said gravely, "but when you've got a crowd of workers already on the ragged edge of starvation and you talk them into hitting the bricks, an honest man can't help worrying."

"We'll make it," she cried. "With so many off the job the manufacturers will have to settle. Oh I know they will!"

He threw aside the clipboard, stood up and gave her a fatherly hug. "With kids like you," he said, "we can't lose."

She bridled at the term "kid." "Before it's over, I hope to show everybody I'm no mere kid," she said.

He drew back and looked speculatively at her. "I expect you will," he said. "I'm rather counting on it."

FIFTEEN

Carla went out and wandered about till she found Tanya, toward whom she felt a sudden warmth in which there was just a hint of patronage. Tanya didn't notice the change in their respective positions, and as they went back into the theater, she rattled on, something about a food kitchen, getting help from outside, maybe the Industrial Union would still use their contacts. Carla guessed it was important, but her gut feeling was that what really mattered was Angela Rossoni's promise to bring out the Caldwell stitchers. The theater was half full, there was a subdued mutter, and Carla found herself actually biting her nails. Frank had told her to wait until twenty to one and then bring the Caldwell people to meet him on the picket line. Five more minutes, four, three. And then it happened. Into the hall they marched, Angela Rossoni at their head, Frank bringing up the rear. The crowd came to life, and Carla was on her feet clapping and cheering and stamping her feet. To her surprise she herself was being cheered for her part in bringing them out. Some day she'd really deserve those cheers, she resolved, indeed she would.

The hours and the days that followed were a kaleidoscopic whirl of events: Big Hannah Bixby with the workers from Mass Shoe, Frank Dawson erupting in wild cowboy yells, the picket lines each morning marching around the hold-out plants singing "Solidarity," singing "The Walls of Jericho," singing "The Union Girl," shouting till the very clouds threw back the echo, "On Strike, shut it down, On Strike, shut it down!" And there was Mike McGuigan rushing from the front of the line to the back, his voice roaring above the others, and Mike McGuigan coming to Carla as he dashed about lining up talent for the pep rally. "A poem, a song, whatever you can do," he said breathlessly. And somehow without willing it, there she was back at the theater being pushed onto the stage by Mike, facing a blur of faces, dizzy, almost in a faint, for the first time in her life knowing stage fright. Then the room stopped whirling; she opened her mouth, hoping something would come out.

A newsboy, some twelve years old and brash as became a newsboy, came running down the aisle: "Read all about it, get your paper, read all about the Shawmut strike! Strike spreads to Laurel! Read all about it!" McGuigan seized a paper, thrust it into Carla's hands. "Read it, read it to them!" he urged. Ah yes, what they were doing had its validation; it was front page news.

As she read in her clear, youthful, enthusiastic voice, applause rolled back at her, and the more she read the more they clapped, and the more they clapped the more excited she became. "The Highland Laddie of Shawmut," she read the headline. "Remember what he played—'Do ye hear that surging billow, wave on wave follow battle's distant sound?'"

"Yes, yes, it's battle," she declared, "and you the valiant soldiers." Her eyes moved across the audience and she saw their faces all alight. A man with a camera, a reporter, had come in; he drew close, the lens was focused on the stage. And Carla was thrilling them with that poem she'd learned so long ago.

> "Behind him lay the gray Azores,
> Behind the Gates of Hercules;
> Before him not the ghost of shores;"

The crowd sat in silent expectation, her voice rang clearer and clearer:
"Sail on! Sail on! Sail on! and on!"

She was leading them in a mighty shout. "Solidarity! The union makes us strong!" They were one invincible body and she their voice.

The headline next day featured—she could hardly believe it—featured her, Carla. A picture stared out at her, her picture captioned "The Joan of Arc of the Shoe Workers." She sobbed as she read it. Joan of Arc was a military leader and led some to triumph, some to death.

"You're on every day," said McGuigan, and she turned frightened eyes toward him.

❧✳❧

The pace of events continued like a runaway team down a steep hill. The picket lines grew louder and fiercer, the rallies more enthusiastic. By the second day Hannah Bixby had a food kitchen running, and food came pouring in from Laurel stores, from anonymous sources, and three carloads of students from Boston and Cambridge arrived one morning, staggering under great bundles of meat and vegetables and bread. They were eager to help, and Hannah shooed them out with instructions to go beg more food. No, they couldn't go on the picket line, they must stay away from the picket line, no they weren't needed in the kitchen. But if they could round up a lawyer—

Quietly they walked out to their cars, but two young strangers who had seemed to be with them remained, talking earnestly to each other. One was a man of somewhat less than medium height, dressed in faded blue jeans and a red and black mackinaw out at the elbows. His sandy brown hair straggled over his collar, and at his feet there lay a disreputable bedroll. The other man was in marked contrast, a tall, lanky, broad-shouldered fellow, his dark hair cut short. He wore a beaver-collared brown overcoat beneath which could be seen the crease of his trousers and the buckles of his sturdy overshoes. Each young man had a copy of some folded newspaper, and they seemed to be comparing notes.

Not far from them stood Gilbert Young. At last he went over to investigate. As he approached, he saw that they were studying the Joan of Arc story. "Well, well," he said, his eyelids drooping even more than usual. "Stage door Johnnies!"

"No, no!" cried the small ragged fellow indignantly.

"Why yes, sort of," the other said. His eyes met Gilbert's directly, and an amused smile swept over his face.

For Carla it was one more astounding turn of events. "Howard!" she cried. "Can it really be?"

The tall dark young man in the beaver collar stood amiably watching, until at last Howard remembered him. "This here's Roger something," he said. "Says he knows you."

She turned to face him. It couldn't be, not the Roger of her childhood, who had helped her survive the bitter days of long ago, had trotted alongside the train waving his farewell. Yes, yes, the same gentle brown eyes, the same square jaw, the same generous mouth. "Roger Thorfinnson!" she cried.

"In person."

"But your friends are leaving."

"I'm not with them."

"Then what *are* you doing here?"

He slapped the newspaper with his glove. "I came to find you," he said. "And what, if I may ask, are *you* doing here?"

She looked at him, trembled and started to answer but could find no words, for she saw judgment in his eyes. "I'm here because I'm here," she was finally able to retort.

"Driftwood cast here by the waves?"

"That's enough philosophy," said Howard.

Roger laughed and his eyes twinkled. "I'm really not such a serious chap," he said. "And hot diggety dog, I'm glad to have found you, no matter where. As for now, maybe you're right. I'd better catch up with those students." Roger hurried out just in time to catch the student leader, who had paused for a few words with Frank.

Well, thought Carla, that was short and sweet.

Roger, on the other hand, had formed what he considered an astute plan. He would help Carla, poor girl, pouring out her heart at those rallies, and at the same time he could draw near to her in a casual sort of way, but he was in Boston to study electrical engineering and nothing must interfere with that. *And what really is Carla?* he asked himself. *She is even more beautiful than I'd expected. Easy, boy!* he warned himself. He resolved to become part of the student group, which would give him a chance to see her on neutral ground in that big barn they called a kitchen.

He remained a somewhat alien part of the group, but one who talked strike relief to whoever would listen and proved remarkably successful in his solicitations. He found his new student companions rather amusing. They were nice kids, too youthfully idealistic to be dismissed as mere crackpots, too childishly naive to be taken at their own evaluation. He had fun with them and enjoyed his self-assigned status as an older, wiser man than they, though he was roughly the age of the others. He laughed as he played the role of the windmill at which these Quixotes tilted. He smiled smugly as the sinner whom they would reclaim. The students accepted the challenge eagerly for seldom did they have such a fine prospect on whom to hone their argumentative skills. They were Socialists, every one, and he was a dedicated free enterprise man. Too much government interference was ruining the country, he assured them. Sometimes they'd even listen to his talk about electrical engineering, which none of them cared about. Still he was a find; they had no other contacts in engineering, and contacts in engineering certainly were much to be desired. At times they grew angry and accused him of laughing at them and jeered that nothing more could be expected from a technocrat. Then he smiled with perfect good-nature and begged them to be patient with him.

Two of the girls fell in love with him and grieved together at his indifference, the cause of which they soon identified. He kept seeing Carla at the strike headquarters, and once he kissed her gently on the cheek and was saddened by her startled, frightened look. When he and she had been childhood friends, he'd seen that frightened look, poor waif. Howard, who also came regularly to the strike hall, had told him about her husband and his heroic death. Quite recently really, thought Roger. Poor kid!

The days passed and the second week began. In the dusk of early morning, as the first blush of day appeared and while the air was frosty, Carla would come to the union kitchen, welcoming the warmth. There was excitement too, as was to be expected, and also a sense of comradeship which gave the union terms "brother" and "sister" warm life. Carla had worked for almost two years at Caldwell Shoe without really getting to know even the other women in the stitching room. Take Rita, who'd sat just three machines away.

Carla had certainly never realized the fierce determination that lay under Rita's quiet manner. They emerged as friends, as sisters. They walked hand in hand; they shared the tense moments on early morning picket lines which patrolled to keep out the hated "scabs." Together they yelled indecencies at the workers who crossed the line. Together Carla and Rita had stood in front of the door one morning and faced a group of five women who were attempting to enter the factory, and together they had triumphed for the women had turned back. They had shared the hours of boredom at the union hall, and Carla's standing up in front with her pep talks did not alienate her from Rita nor from the others. They shared the kitchen work, Sarah and Rita proving extremely competent and Tanya something of a fish out of water.

Hannah Bixby, big, bossy, and in her element, found energy to be everywhere. In the morning she was the first at the kitchen, then she was out on the picket line, then back in the kitchen making beef stew or whatever they had supplies for, then on the picket line again, returning to sit in at meetings where she had no official position but where she usually, as she said, "Put in my two cents worth." What a woman! The Joan of Arc of the Shoe Workers said the title should have gone to Hannah Bixby!

Sarah, though she caught cold and suffered a stuffed nose and croaking voice, was there early and late. One day she brought in some bandages, salves, aspirin and coughdrops in a cardboard box which she had labeled "First Aid," and she became the official bandager of wounds as well as a ready source of practical wisdom on subjects as diverse as ways of cooking legumes and the settling of family disputes. It was she who worried when pickets didn't wear their overshoes and who set the students to rounding up sturdy footgear when she discovered that many had only broken shoes.

Tanya seemed to have forgotten her compulsive dedication to the defense of the USSR and spent her time defending the union. The women forgot their hostility to her, though Frank Dawson and Mike McGuigan still viewed her with suspicion. "She's worth a million," the women said. And, "We understand how she feels about Russia, her people came from there, and haven't some of us soft spots in our hearts for the old country, Italy, or Poland, or Ireland?" Tanya was at her best on the picket line, leading in song or shouting slogans. Her voice quivered with rage as she howled her hate at the "scabs"! Boldly she took the lead in getting the whole group to shout slogans. "On strike, shut it down! One, two, three, four, who are we for, the union, the union forever. This is a union town!" What spirit she gave to the picket line! At the long meetings held each day to keep the strikers occupied and to maintain morale, she became a regular feature with an inexhaustible repertoire of songs. Frank and McGuigan kept her from speechifying.

McGuigan and O'Brien from Mass Shoe worked tirelessly and with considerable tact at lining up talent for those meetings. From among the strikers they discovered a cutter who danced a jig. "My brains are all in my feet," he used to say in a lovely brogue. He knew a pianist who could play the piano for him. They found a cornetist, a barbershop quartet, and a tenor who crooned love songs. From among the students they recruited an a cappella choir (which sang a strange mix) and turned down three student pianists in order not to set up competition with their local talent.

Howard, too, was pressed into service to play his recorder. He had stayed a couple of days at first, then drifted off, found a day's work, then had come back. He kept coming and going like that. Sometimes he had money when he returned, sometimes he didn't. Big Hannah insisted that he eat at the union kitchen, and he did so willingly enough, and when he had money he gave generously. He was delighted to contribute his musical talent, such as it was, to the union meetings. Sometimes he played alone, sometimes he was the accompaniment for a singer, often Tanya. At first his stage appearance embarrassed Carla; he was so ragged, and he didn't really play that well, and he stuttered and stammered when he tried to announce the titles. But gradually she became proud of his contribution and went on stage herself to help him with the talking part. She would introduce him, leading up to it with a funny anecdote or patter, and after his performance McGuigan would shout to her, "Get in there and rouse the old fighting spirit." She would start out soft and easy, standing there tall, good-looking, the country roses still in her cheeks, soft and easy at first, then becoming warm with indignation as she recounted their sufferings, her voice would ring clearly throughout the hall, until they were all shouting and clapping under her leadership and often marching out to the picket line with her coming down from the platform, down the aisle, and leading the march. Sarah worried because those days she didn't wear her overshoes, just those silly loafers. Howard watched her with unbounded admiration and Roger with mixed feelings. *Carla the rabble-rouser*, he mused. *I'll think about it.*

The first week had passed quickly at high pitch. During the second there were murmurs of "Why don't they get it settled?" and even "Let's go back." Strikers complained of hungry kids at home, of landlords pressing for rent. Frank made what he called daily progress reports, but the truth was that so far as negotiations were concerned, there was no progress. The employers had elected to deal through a joint committee representing all the factories. Stanton had come over to participate in the bargaining, but nothing had been agreed to. On the other hand, the number of strikers had grown, very few had gone back, new ones came out every day. Where whole departments were out, other departments had to be laid off due to lack of work. At Caldwell Shoe, where some of the packers remained, all the lasters were on strike so the crafts further on in the process had nothing to do. Mr. Caldwell, staunch foe of unions, was on the companies' negotiating committee.

Brotherly love grew stronger among the determined but did not always prevail among the less dedicated. Tempers grew short and strikers became angry with each other over trifles. Donations of food thinned out except for day-old bread and the poorest grade of coffee, which continued in good supply. But on Wednesday of the third week, new hope came. For one thing, money contributions from other unions began to arrive, not in large amounts but enough to buy the makings of Mulligan stew and enough to give some cash to those with children. Then two shops which had been holdouts hit the bricks, bringing in fresh troops. There were only three factories now where work was being done, and on Friday, that third Friday, they too responded to the picket lines and to the well-organized visits which the strikers had been making to the homes. As the last one, Lexington Shoe, marched that morning into the theater, the cheering filled the big auditorium and bounced off the ceiling, exuberant rejoicing over the sinner who is saved.

"The whole town is out," cried Frank. He threw back his head and gave that long, coyote yell that was always so surprising coming from him. The crowd responded with a medley of shouts and yells and whistles. When the emotion had spent itself, Frank spoke quietly. "This is it," he said. "Eli Stanton is meeting our bosses right now, everything's practically settled, and I have to get over there. Donatelli, will you take the chair and keep things going? Don't anybody leave. I'll be back with details."

Joe Donatelli, short, stocky, shrill-voiced, threw out his chest and stepped to the front of the stage to lead them in one more cheer. He called Tanya to start a song, and she in turn asked the men's quartet to come on stage. Spying Howard she got him up there to play his recorder, and a woman pianist coming in at that moment was persuaded to join them. Soon the whole crowd was singing, singing loudly, rejoicing, stamping their feet, clapping their hands, celebrating already the victory that surely must come. Tanya was leading the "Battle Hymn of the Republic" but with the trade union words "Solidarity, Solidarity Forever, the Union Makes Us Strong," and the second time around the quartet came on loud and strong with the old chorus "Glory, Glory, Hallelujah, Glory, Glory, Hallelujah," but they ended "The union makes us strong!" The strike is won, the strike is won, they were shouting all over the hall. And when they sang "Jericho," you could really believe the walls came tumbling down.

But what if it isn't won, thought Carla. What if they'd gone through this for nothing? The meeting recessed at noon. Many of the workers hung around, drinking coffee, eating bread (the stew wasn't ready yet), talking in small groups, lounging in the chairs, elbows on the tables. Restlessly Carla wandered down the street. The weather had grown warmer, and the snow which had melted to slush seeped through her shoes chilling her feet. She hadn't seen Roger for several days, and she wondered if she'd see him after the strike was over.

She turned back after a while, surprised at how far she had walked. Splash, splash, she went through the slush, and her feet grew wetter and colder while she could feel the sweat on her upper body and had to unbutton her coat. Walking rapidly and out of breath she approached the theater, trembling with hope and fear. She hurried in as Eli Stanton and Frank Dawson stepped onto the stage. Dawson advanced front and center, and the silence was so complete as to be painful. Carla halted just inside the door, hardly daring to breathe. Dawson stood there a moment, and then his face relaxed into a broad smile. "They've settled!" he cried triumphantly.

A sigh of relief passed over the crowd and then a shout of joy burst from their lips. Everyone was hugging his neighbor and laughing and crying and glad and sad for the days would once more be the old monotony, but there'd be food and some day they'd catch up with the rent. Glory be, it was over. Carla looked around for Tanya and saw her cross the hall, withdraw to one side, and begin talking earnestly with Gus. Sarah was not with them.

On the platform Dawson was shouting for order, for quiet, so he could report. Gradually the noise subsided. "We got union recognition," he said. "And we got our ten percent raise. Also no striker will be fired. The settlement had to include that."

No striker would be fired. Yes, they had known that would have to be in the agreement, for they knew that if it weren't, many of the leaders would have lost their jobs, and they didn't know how far down into the ranks the employers considered leadership to extend. Fear had hung over them these three weeks for many were not sure whether they were leaders or not. Carla was proud of her endangered position, and fear had touched her but lightly for she had no family.

"Of course," Dawson went on, "this agreement which we have negotiated has to be approved by the strikers before it can go into effect."

Carla saw Tanya and Gus walking along the outside aisle up to the stage. Tanya skipped lightly up the steps and began talking quietly to Dawson.

"The sister wants to know if there will be discussion," Dawson reported. "Sure, discuss."

Why, thought Carla, *don't we just vote on it? Surely the committee did the best they could.* Tanya advanced to the front of the stage to address the strikers.

"Ten percent is not enough," she cried in an angry voice. "Did we risk our jobs, did we go hungry for weeks, did we pound the bricks until our feet ached, for a lousy ten percent? I say we reject this offer and continue the strike."

A great roar filled the air. "Accept it, settle the strike," men and women were shouting. Tanya kept on talking, but Carla could no longer hear her. The crowd was shouting, "Sit down, sit down!" Gus stood waiting, a scrawny youth, noted for his chronic seriousness which had now deepened into an angry scowl. He raised his hand in signal that he too wished to speak. Near the front, Sarah Friedman sat with head bowed in hands. Later she said her head ached, all of a sudden her head ached.

Dawson was once more speaking, and the crowd quieted to hear him. "We will do it in an orderly manner. Do I hear a call for the question?"

"Question, question, question," they shouted, thus indicating both that they wanted to shut off discussion and that they knew a bit about procedure. Gus gave up and sat down.

"Before the vote, we'll read the contract," said Frank. "I've asked Stanton to present it."

"No more hot air!" a man shouted. "Why do we have to sit here for that?"

"So it can't be challenged later," Dawson gave the answer. "Don't you disappear and leave it to a handful." Carla looked back at the door and saw that Hannah, Arthur Moses and several others, among them Gilbert Young, had stationed themselves in front of the exit.

There followed an anti-climactic half hour during which Stanton and Dawson took turns reading. At the end Arthur Moses, still there at the door, shouted the motion: "I move that we accept the contract as read," and Gilbert standing beside him duly seconded it.

Tanya was for voting on each item separately, but the crowd would have none of it. "No, no," shouts rang out, "we'll vote on the package."

They voted with only a smattering of nays. The contract was accepted. It was over, the strike was settled. They would be going back to work on Monday. They had won. But the first wild exhilaration had been dissipated. As Carla walked out, she heard quiet expressions of rejoicing, but she also heard grumblings that the raise was too small; they had to accept, but it was too small. She heard Arthur Moses say angrily to Tanya, "Trust you to try to louse it up. But it didn't work, did it?"

"A militant committee would have gotten more," she retorted. "We should stay out."

"A committee made up of you and your comrades would have had us out till our belly buttons hit our backbones," he snorted and walked away.

"Oh dear," wailed Carla. "Why do you have to fight now of all times?"

"But I'm right," Tanya cried excitedly. "How can you be so naive?"

Carla grew heated, she grew angry, she and Tanya stood there shouting at each other, until Sarah Friedman came over. "Girls, girls," she admonished them, shaking her head sadly. "So Tanya's right, they settled for too little. But listen, what's the use griping? It's done."

"No, no, Tanya's not right," insisted Carla. "We won the strike."

"Okay, okay," replied Sarah. "So you say we won, we won." And she led Tanya away before more could be said.

Carla felt a strong masculine arm around her shoulders. It was McGuigan, who smiled at her, then was gone. Carla looked around for Howard but didn't see him. Surely he wasn't pulling that disappearing act again.

As a matter of fact that is precisely what he was up to. He'd gone to Carla's apartment to get his bedroll. Time to hit the road. He'd go out West and follow the crops.

Roger came in, caught the excitement, ran to Carla, swung her off her feet, kissed her cheek. She struggled and cried, "Let me go, I must catch Howard."

"Righto, I'll get my car," he said. "Darn thing's a block away."

"I'll run on toward home."

As he approached his car at a dogtrot, he could see Gilbert Young standing beside it. Strange fellow, Roger thought.

"Look here," said Gilbert, " I've been wanting to talk to you."

Roger, expecting a request for a loan or some such thing and anxious to get it over with responded quickly. "Anything I can do," he began.

"No, no, I just want to talk."

"I'm all ears," said Roger, whose ears in truth were not the smallest. Then regretting his flippancy he added, "Mostly I have a reputation for being a good listener, but I'm in sort of a rush."

"It's about Carla," said Gilbert, his hooded eyes intent upon the scuffs on his gloves.

"About Carla?"

"Yes. Did she tell you about me?"

"No, why should she? What is there to tell?"

"Aren't you her cousin?"

"Heavens no. Though I do believe I'm the oldest friend she has in the world."

"Oh." Gilbert was deep in thought for a minute. "Roger," he said at last and turned to face the younger man, his sad old eyes almost open for once. "I'm in love with that girl, but I know it's hopeless."

"Of course," said Roger.

"Of course what?" exclaimed Gilbert. "Of course in love or of course hopeless?"

"Both," said Roger cheerfully. "Naturally you'd be in love with her. But friend, it's hopeless. I can assure you of that."

Gilbert was thoughtful. "You're serious about her?"

"Certainly am."

Gilbert swallowed hard. "May the better man win," he said.

"Of course," said Roger.

Gilbert stared at the self-confident Roger. "Yes," he said finally. "I do believe you are the better man." And he hurried away without a backward glance.

What, thought Roger, *do I mean by serious?* Of course it was the only answer he could have given that fellow. He overtook Carla and they arrived at the apartment just as Howard was coming out, bedroll over his shoulder. "Gotta hit the road," he said.

"You'll come back?" cried Carla as she jumped out of the car.

"I won't promise. Might be tempted to sponge off you. This time I only came because I thought you might need me. I came to protect you."

"From what, for heavens sake?"

"Joan of Arc got burned, I heard tell."

"That silly newspaper!"

"Things are calm now. And there's Roger."

Carla blushed furiously.

"You bet," said Roger and immediately wondered just what he meant by that.

"At least stay for dinner."

"My feet are itching to go." And with one final peck on her cheek and a handshake for Roger he was off, refusing even to let Roger give him a lift to a better location.

They stood there watching his slender figure grow smaller and then disappear around a corner.

"Poor Howard!" said Carla.

"I have a hunch he'll show up again when he's needed," said Roger.

"What if it's he who needs me?"

Their eyes exchanged the answer to that. Howard would never ask for help. And their eyes exchanged another message, but it was unclear, unclear to both of them. There was a tie which bound them, but they didn't know its nature.

SIXTEEN

Later that evening, after dining in a ho-hum restaurant, Roger and Carla stood once more on the sidewalk in front of her apartment house. No, he guessed he hadn't better come in, he'd be in touch. He gave her a brotherly hug and hurried back to his car. I wonder, she thought as she watched the slush spinning from his car's tires. The strike was over, she'd be going back to the old routine. There wouldn't even be Howard, poor awkward Howard. She looked up at the sky full of stars and remembered how she and Howard as children had wished upon the stars half believing when they were very young.

Howard had set out so bravely, walking along the sidewalk, bedroll on his back, head bowed, the wind whipping his faded pants, feet moving quickly along the sidewalk where the red brick showed through the packed snow. Earlier that day he'd said the first chance he'd get he was going to steal a car. She'd reprimanded him, not believing he meant it. What if he had? She wouldn't have been surprised to see a policeman come to make inquiries. How terrible it would be! She turned her eyes again to the stars. How silly! Imagining such things! If she could get a few dollars ahead, she would buy him one, some old jalopie it would have to be, but he wouldn't care so long as it ran. Tears came to her eyes, tears of compassion and tears of loneliness. She chided herself for actually thinking her brother might steal. She was being grossly unjust to him.

A week later she got a letter from Roger. He addressed her as "Little Sister" and asked permission to take her to his church in Medford. She met him downstairs on the sidewalk and went with him to church. He brought her back, and that was that. "Poor dear," she thought. "He's trying to win me back to Christ, to save me from the Communists."

The March thaw was followed by the April rains, the pastel days of May, and then the sunshine of June, and Carla supposed Roger would be going home to Hambledon for the summer vacation. Sunday churchgoing had

—179—

become a regular practice. She was dressing for another trip to church, probably for the last time before fall, when he'd be coming back for more of those strange scientific courses which so enthralled him. She brushed her wavy brown hair until it crackled and gleamed. She buttoned the light blue blouse which made her gray eyes look almost blue. Carefully she put on her suit, a darker blue, not quite navy, first the pleated, straight-hanging skirt, then the trim jacket. She combed her hair again and carefully placed her navy beret at the back of her head and fastened it with bobby pins. She looked in the bedroom mirror. Dear, dear, the mirror was so short, but at least she could see her head and shoulders. She hoped she looked like a student, that people would take her and Roger for two students.

She heard Roger's car and hurried down. It was a new car, a roadster, sporty in that respect, but painted a conservative dark green. He was opening the passenger door. He stooped, picked up a brown basket and carefully stowed it in the space behind the seats, then handed her in and drove smoothly away. He was unusually quiet, and Carla followed his lead. They arrived at the church just in time to be ushered to their place before the service began. The organ was playing soft, dreamy music, and the last hasty confidences were being exchanged. The twittering of voices subsided, and for several minutes there was no sound save for the organ music. Up in Megunnaway Abigail would be attending church at this very moment, Carla thought, sitting quietly and expectantly, bowing her head in earnest prayer. The church was crowded, and Roger was sitting so close to her that she could feel the warmth of his body. She fixed her eyes on the hymnal which he held over for her to share. They stood and joined the singing, "—the silence of eternity interpreted by love." Oh the beautiful words! "Speak through the earthquake, wind and fire, O still small voice of calm."

The minister, a handsome gray-haired man, was leading in prayer. They were singing again, he was preaching. His text was from John: "Beloved let us love one another; for love is of God; and everyone that loveth is born of God, and knoweth God. He that loveth not knoweth not God; for God is love." He was a father talking to his children, giving wise counsel, pleading with them, admonishing them, and at the end blessing them. It was too sweet for Carla's taste. She and Roger walked out with the rest. At the door the minister stood greeting each one. An old man, bony and wrinkled but straight as a ramrod, was just ahead of them.

"That's right, Reverend," he said in a quavering voice. "Love is what the world needs. You've got to beat it into them, it's love."

The minister was taken aback, but he recovered quickly, smiled cheerfully and shook the man's hand.

They went on down the broad steps in the midst of the crowd which was rapidly thinning. "Wait here a minute, Carla," said Roger. "I have to speak to someone." He disappeared through a side door.

When he returned, he saw Carla standing at the top step not far from a half dozen of the young women. How she stood out! Magnificent! Partly it was her clothing for she was dressed in dark blue while the others wore pastels or white. Partly it was her height for she was taller than the others, partly her handsome face with regular strong features, perfect rose complexion. And her loneness. For she stood alone while the others chattered in groups. He hurried toward her.

"It's a perfect day for a picnic," he said as they got into the car. "I brought some food."

They parked just outside a strip of greenery, then walked along a path near a meandering stream, a park much like the beloved Fenway, but it was a place she'd never visited before. It wasn't hers and Ray's, it was special. The banks sloped gently toward the stream, shrubs grew by the water. Near the sidewalk a few sweetbriars were in bloom. Huge trees gave shade, while patches of unencumbered lawn were dotted with groups of people. A half dozen young men and women were gleefully tossing about a tremendous yellow ball, a family with two toddlers were eating their lunch, couples were courting with varying degrees of shyness, an old woman was feeding pigeons. Carla and Roger, very proper in their Sunday clothes, walked to the stream where the air was freshened by the water. She carried the blanket he'd brought and he the picnic basket. In the distance they could see the tall buildings; they heard the hum of distant traffic.

"I wish we were in the genuine country," said Carla.

"I'll be going home next week. You remember what it's like at Hambledon?"

Oh yes, she remembered what it had been like when she first went there, and she remembered her return, and finally she remembered him running along by the railroad track, waving goodbye. *What is Roger,* she thought, *and what am I, and why are we here together today?* Around a curve in the stream they found a secluded spot. Perhaps no one came there because the bank was too steep or because the lawn had not been cut or because the shrubs separated it almost completely so that one might walk fairly close and still not see the clearing. He spread the blanket, and she sat down, while he on his knees kept pulling things out of the basket.

"I'm hungry enough to eat a boiled owl," he said. Sandwiches of rye bread with cheese, salami, lettuce, and mustard; oranges, apples, and a little package of dates; a quart thermos bottle of coffee; a couple of hard-boiled eggs; and finally with a big flourish, a half dozen napkins. "Now that's a neat setup," he said. After lunch he lay upon the blanket looking up at the sky.

He had thrown aside his jacket and his short-sleeved shirt clung to his arms, which had retained something of the muscle of his long years as a farmboy, years of currying horses, cleaning out stables, lugging water. Carla sat near him.

He lay there looking up into the sky, the amazing sky, cobalt blue with clouds softly white. In spite of all that he knew of their actual composition, they appeared warm as woolen fleece. And so it seemed to Carla.

Then he began to get technical. "What impresses our senses as matter," he said, "is really a concentration of energy into a comparatively small space. Did you ever think of it that way?"

She hadn't and she didn't particularly want to, but in order not to appear stupid she tried to understand. "Matter, you say, is energy? Could you explain it to me?"

"It's not quite that simple," he continued, rising on his elbow. "At present we must still assume in our actual theoretical constructions two realities, field and matter. Yes, indeed, in applying the conservation law of mass-energy, we assume the existence of field and matter."

"Field and matter?" What strange picnic talk!

"Yes indeed. You see, homogeneous light is composed of energy grains, that is photons, which are small portions of energy traveling through empty space with the velocity of light. And the energy of a light quantum belonging to a homogeneous color decreases proportionately as the wavelength increases. So there we are back thinking of light as waves." He paused, looking to see if she shared his excitement.

She asked him to repeat, to go more slowly, for she wanted to understand. The request rolled right off of him. "Light quanta differ for every wavelength," he continued as rapidly as before, "whereas the quanta of electricity are always the same. But what is light really? A wave or a shower of photons? What is matter, what is an electron? Is it a particle or a wave? How can we say?" On and on he went, and his eyes glowed with excitement while she struggled like a swimmer fighting a strong wave. At last she cried, "Stop, stop! I feel like Alice in tow by the Red Queen. Go more slowly, explain it to me."

He sat up straight. "Bless you, Carla," he cried. "You asked me to explain it to you? You really did? You didn't just ask me to shut up, not to be a bore, to stop lecturing?"

"No, no. Once I even thought I'd understood a word or two. That bit about quantum jumps. Is that what Tanya means when she talks about a quantitative change turning into a qualitative change?"

"I suppose, in a way," he said thoughtfully, "but what she is saying is quite primitive. She's saying that if you blow enough air into a balloon it will burst, if the temperature gets cold enough ice will form. But what the Communists are really trying to do is to develop a science of human behavior that will agree with their desires." Now she was following him, this made sense. "They deny any relationship between man and his creator and are left trying to force humanity into a channel quite foreign to it. They confuse the pattern they've imagined for the pattern that is. They're arrogant before both God and man."

"I almost understand that. Then science doesn't do away with the need for God?"

"Without belief in the inner harmony of our world, there could be no science."

"God the Creator is real?"

" 'Where wast thou,' " Roger quoted solemnly from Job, " 'when I laid the foundations of the earth? Declare if thou hast understanding. Who hath laid the measures of it, if thou knowest? Or who hath stretched the line upon it? Whereupon are its foundations fastened? Or who laid its cornerstone, when the morning stars sang together, and all the sons of God shouted for joy?' "

"It makes me feel so small."

"It shouldn't. Remember the Psalm: 'When I consider thy heavens, the work of thy fingers, the moon and the stars, which thou has ordained, What is man that thou art mindful of him? And the son of man that thou visitest him? For thou hast made him a little lower than the angels, and hast crowned him with glory and honor.' Never doubt that, my dear female man, crowned with glory and honor." They were silent. There was a passage in Proverbs, he couldn't quite remember, ah, he had it. He said it to himself, not aloud. "There are three things which are too wonderful for me, yea four which I know not; The way of an eagle in the air; the way of a serpent upon a rock; the way of a ship in the midst of the sea; and the way of a man with a maid." The first three did not interest him at the moment, but ah, the way of a man with a maid!

For the first time in her life Carla had met someone before whose brain-power she felt humble, and she wasn't sure she liked the feeling. She looked at Roger, so much at ease as he leaned on his elbow in silence; she wondered what he was thinking and was afraid to ask.

"I never did get to what I brought you here to tell you," he said suddenly.

"You had something to tell me?"

"Yes." He paused a moment before telling her, "I've just learned that I won't be coming back in the fall."

"Just learned?"

"Well, I've had applications in for different grad schools. I've been accepted by Purdue."

"Purdue? Where's that?"

"Why, it's in Indiana."

She was abashed. He'd said it as if everybody knew where Purdue was. Everybody in his world did know, she supposed.

"Tops for Electrical Engineering. You have no idea the strides that are being made."

She noted that his long slender fingers were fairly quivering with excitement. What fascinating hands he had, broad palms, long slender fingers. But Indiana, the end of the world. "Then Purdue is right for you?"

"I'm sure it is."

"Congratulations, both to you and to them."

"Little flatterer. Will you write to me?"

Oh yes, she'd write; he said he'd answer. He'd come to Boston again, he'd make it his business to do that. He said that having found her, he didn't want to lose her again; she knew he'd never had a sister, she was like a sister. She supposed there had been a graduation ceremony at his school, and she wondered why he hadn't invited her. Little sister indeed!

He guessed what she was thinking. He'd intended to invite her, but he hadn't, and he couldn't explain the reason to her. When he'd called home some time in March, he'd said to his mother, "You remember the little girl Carla who used to board with the Hubbards?" Oh yes, she remembered. The frost in his mother's voice carried clearly through the buzzing static, surely another marvel of modern technology. Yes, she remembered Carla. So she was working in a factory? Fine. One never knew how those boarders at Hubbards' would turn out. He had dared say no more, and he certainly hadn't been about to invite Carla to come and be snubbed by his mother. He wasn't sure about his father. His grandfather would accept her, of that he had no doubt. Poor old Granddad! He hadn't been up to coming to the graduation. The future was a long road; it must be traveled step by step.

The last thing Roger said that afternoon as he dropped her at her door was, "You'll surely write?"

"If you send me your address."

Yes, it was his move next. He drew her close to him, kissed her on the forehead, and since she seemed so relaxed, he ventured a kiss upon the lips, not a long passionate kiss, just a bare brushing of the lips. "Good-bye, Roger," she said and ran into the house.

Her heart beat quickly. She supposed he'd write, when he got around to it. Some day he'd write to tell her he was in love, with somebody else. He belonged to a different world, and she'd thrown away any opportunity she might have had to become part of it. Even if she'd gone to college, neither of them would have been able to forget that he'd known her at that awful time. No, she didn't belong to his world. She wasn't about to become a pathetic hanger-on. The summer passed, the leaves began to turn, and she had

had no word from him. When Tanya said they both should go to New York, the most exciting place in the world, Carla, with hardly a moment's thought, replied, "Sure, why not?"

"When shall we go?" Tanya asked.

"I'll have to think about it," Carla replied.

Think about it she did, but could not make up her mind. If Tanya would just get off her high horse and be comradely as she'd been during the strike, she'd be an ideal companion for such a trip. As it was, Carla looked about for other interests.

⚜

As Christmas grew nearer, she determined she'd go home for Christmas, surely she would, even if she had to hitchhike. However, in no time her plans grew vaguer, as if it wasn't this Christmas she meant but some other, far-distant Christmas. Perhaps if Howard were to come, they could go together. And then in December Howard came, late one evening, knocking softly on her door. He stepped hesitantly into the room, clothed in the old mackinaw, dragging his old bedroll. He shook the snow off his cap and sat down at the kitchen table as casually as if he were in the habit of dropping in every day.

"Get me something to put on my face," he said. His left eye was blackened and the cheek scraped raw. "Got in a fight," he explained.

"I noticed," said Carla hiding her horror and also her curiosity as best she could while she brought him ice-cubes wrapped in a towel.

"There's this dude," he said finally. "I run into him everywhere and he keeps riding me."

"Riding you?"

"About any girl I look at, about what I'm wearing, and if I'm drunk about that and if I'm sober about that. I met him first in Portsmouth, one reason I shipped out as fast as I did. And then, wouldn't you know, I'm working in California, and who shows up but this smart-aleck acting worse than ever and concentrating on me."

"Maybe you should have fought him in Portsmouth."

"I'd have got licked."

"Even so."

"With a bully like this you have to win."

"Surely you didn't just come from California?"

"Naah. Him and me was both only temporary and then I hightailed it back East, got a job in a Baltimore restaurant as busboy."

"And then?"

"In he walks, flips my apron over my face, laughs fit to kill, right there in rush hour. I got in one good punch, but he's got arms like an ape. After he was through with my face, they kicked me out the door, and I remembered I had me a sister. Had pretty good luck on the highway. Christmas spirit maybe."

"Let's hope you've seen the last of him."

"I doubt it. He's my fate. I'll see him again and when I do, I'll kill him, knife him in the back if I have to, but surely kill him." His jaw, not a particularly strong jaw to be sure, was set hard. "I might even go looking for him."

He'd stay for Christmas, since she wanted him to, and then he'd hit the road again, maybe back out West. He didn't want to go to Megunnaway, but he wouldn't stand in her way.

"I'm not sure I really want to go," she said. Anyway, she had to stay and calm him down.

They were silent, sharing without words the sadness of their early years. And there was within their hearts a deep resentment of both their parents, but more particularly of Abigail. "She shouldn't 'a left the farm," Howard insisted and Carla silently agreed. Papa had died and Mama was left, so of course they could be angry only with her. Yet life had been hard for her too.

"We'll have to call her," Carla salved her conscience. "The drugstore has a phone booth."

They made the call the day before Christmas, and Abigail came through clearly, excited but not too excited to talk. All was well, she'd have dinner with the Mills family, she saw the Putnams every Sunday, Louise had the flu but not too badly. She kept her hands busy knitting, everyone called her Mrs. Mittens now, had she told Carla about her nickname? It was quite the thing when people met her in the street to hold up their hands, like the praying hands, you know, and greet her thus. Yes, yes, do put Howard on. Before Howard had time to say more than "Merry Christmas," the three minutes for which they'd paid were up. "And Happy New Year," he shouted into the mouthpiece while the operator kept demanding that he deposit more money. "Oh my dears, Happy New—" It was Abigail's voice. The connection was cut. But it didn't matter, they'd talked to her. Mrs. Mittens! thought Carla with embarrassment. Mama, a village character!

"Well, that's done," said Howard. No, he definitely did not mind having so little time to talk.

"Tanya wants me to go to New York with her," Carla changed the subject abruptly.

"Why?"

"She's got a lot of what she calls comrades there, says it's the only place for radicals. Or even for trade unionists."

"How can it be with them fancy Fifth Avenue stores?"

"I don't know. But on May Day the workers all march down the street, blocking traffic, singing 'Solidarity' and 'Hold the Fort' and 'The Internationale.'" Oh Carla remembered well the wonders Tanya had portrayed.

"Big deal."

"And the Statue of Liberty and the skyline rising like mountain peaks, like banked stalagmites and the biggest library in the world and a Russian restaurant where they play the balalaika."

"What's a balalaika?"

"I don't know. And art museums and painters' exhibits in Washington Square and—"

"Highfalutin nonsense."

"Also if Caldwell moves, we can get jobs there, she's sure we can."

"She just wants to get her hooks into you."

"Of course. But I can handle it. I'm not afraid."

"Probably should be. What does Roger think of it?"

"He's at Purdue."

"Oh."

"I get a card once in a while."

"Maybe I was wrong about him."

"Who cares?"

What could a mere brother say?

Carla dreamed that night of Ray. They were lying in a snowbank on which the sun shone, and they felt no cold. The sun disappeared, and the snow felt like lambs' wool, and they clung to each other. When she awakened, she lay there thinking of Tanya and New York. There were all the things she'd told Howard about, but there was more. Tanya had friends there; there was someone special called Leonard, and there were others. Oh New York was the place for romance, the place to meet men, passionate men who weren't mere louts, men of understanding and courage and dreams. Carla shivered with longing and a fear of longing. There was also a renewal of her determination not to be dominated by Tanya. *But I'm a big girl now,* she thought, *I can take care of myself.*

SEVENTEEN

After the holidays and in the coldest part of January when no one wanted to travel, the train company decided to perk up business by scheduling an excursion rate for the run from Boston to New York, conveniently timed as to the evening departure but arriving at one in the morning or thereabouts. What could one expect at such a price? Carla finally agreed to accompany Tanya to New York.

It was a colder-than-cold night, some kind of a record they said on the radio, twenty below in Boston and eight below in New York. Carla plodded through the darkness, took the bus to Boston, and started the short walk to the station. The air was freeze-dried, sharp as needles in her nostrils, and the snow crunched under her feet. Men and women walked with heads bowed to protect their faces, and there were no children about. Carla broke into a run, her small suitcase banging clumsily against her leg. Even in Abigail's warm mittens her hands were aching cold. She lowered her head, fearful that her nose might be frostbitten, but the distance was not great. She pushed the big door open and stepped into the overheated waiting room.

Tanya was already there, sitting on a long bench which was like a church pew, with her coat folded neatly beside her with the gray satin lining outermost. She rose quickly and came to meet Carla. Carla gasped. She'd never seen Tanya like this, so gay and feminine. She wore a small round hat of gray curly fur under which her hair, which she had let grow of late, fell in dark ringlets. Gold earrings with red stones flashed in and out as she shook her head. She wore a black woolen suit which had a bolero-style jacket and full skirt and under it a white silk blouse embroidered with a multi-colored geometric design. Under her skirt twinkled her bright red boots, not the ones she wore to work but a pair with high heels.

"Tanya!" exclaimed Carla. "How beautiful you are! Oh I do hope whatever dream you have will come true."

"I have no special dream," Tanya replied coyly. "But New York! Oh New York! Let's see what you've got on under that coat."

"Nothing special," Carla said as she unbuttoned her nondescript coat to show her dark red slacks, an unusual costume for her, and the lovely matching sweater which Abigail had knit for her.

Tanya stood back and looked at her appraisingly. "For you," she said, "it's just right. You're neat and trim and long-legged. My stars, what a beautiful figure, almost boyish. I hope you brought a skirt."

"Train Number 557, Excursion train to New York," the announcement filled the room. Tanya quickly slipped on her coat, gray like her hat, then picked up her suitcase and led the way to the platform, up the train steps and down the aisle between the green plush seats. Having found two together, they settled their gear and looked about them. Across the aisle was a young mother whose little boy was softly sniffling, in front a gray-haired woman, a young couple in front of her. The train moved slowly out of the station.

It grew colder on the train, and tobacco smoke filled the air. The murmur of voices grew softer and at last dwindled to nothing. Carla snuggled into her coat and fell asleep to dream of her childhood farm home in winter, the banks of snow, the crystal ice, the gray etching of trees against clear blue skies. She dreamed it was night, and she was dragging a sled up a hill looking into the sky where the Northern lights flashed their many colors. The snow under foot had been cut up by horses hooves; she stubbed her toe and was falling, falling, falling; someone was tugging at her shoulder. She opened her eyes, quite disoriented, then recognized her surroundings. Tanya was shaking her. Half asleep she followed Tanya up the aisle and out onto the platform where the sharp cold snapped her back to life.

They walked the width of the waiting room, which seemed about a quarter of a mile, and pushed open the heavy wooden door to stand at the top of a dimly lit flight of steps just outside the building. The air cut like a knife, stung their cheeks, frosted their nostrils, reached through their warm coats to make them shiver. Carla looked down to guide her steps and stopped short. She had almost trod upon a man. He was lying on the step, straight as a corpse, on a spread of newspapers. He wore an old khaki coat and a ragged brown cap. His dark hair fell in greasy strings across a face which was not young nor old but only beat. Thank goodness it wasn't Howard! A bubbly snoring came from his lips. There upon the steps, cold as a tomb, lay about twenty men. "A couple of years ago there were twice as many," said Tanya. "Quick, don't stop!"

They fled down the street. A taxi went by, then another car. They passed an open restaurant, but Tanya insisted on hurrying to her cousin's where they were to stay. On either side buildings rose, ghostly gray in the dimly lit hour.

The world had frozen at midnight and Carla feared that she would freeze at one. They struggled on; faces tingled and fingers, even when the women set down the suitcases and beat their hands together, were numb. Tanya led the way to a side street. They came to smaller buildings, four or five stories high. Tanya walked up to a heavy portal, struggled with it, and succeeded in opening it. At the end of the hall they could see light around the edge of a door. Tanya, fairly running now, pulled open the door and drew Carla in after her. Warmth flowed over them, and there was the smell of fresh-baked bread and the slightly sour smell of wine. The room was filled with men and women, all talking at once. As Tanya entered, they shouted greetings in a mad confusion and surged forward to embrace her. A man in the rear of the room stood up and waited, and the others retreated to make way for him.

"Leonard!" cried Tanya.

He pulled her to him and kissed her gently on the cheek. He was a man in his thirties, of middle height, with dark hair faintly touched with gray, with eyes black as jet. He was not exactly a handsome man, though he would have been had it not been for a striking defect—his mouth was twisted slightly, and only the right side of his face was mobile; the other seemed frozen except for the liveliness of the eye. "Tanya, little comrade," he said, but he was looking straight at Carla, who stood there blushing like a schoolgirl. Having paid his respects to Tanya, he came to Carla. "Welcome," he said. "Let me take your coat." He helped her pull it back from her shoulders. She was intensely aware of those piercing black eyes fixed upon her. So, too, was Tanya.

"Come," he said. "I'll find you a chair."

What with the sudden warmth, the fatigue of the day, and the babel of voices Carla felt faint, but fainting would have been old maidish, so she pulled herself together and took the seat on the sofa to which Leonard directed her.

The room was fairly large and tastefully though not expensively furnished. The sofa was covered with a dark red monks cloth, the windows were draped with gold-colored, flowing material. The small tables scattered in convenient locations were golden brown and shone like mirrors. Several chairs, upholstered like the sofa in monks cloth but in a variety of colors, provided comfortable seating. Everyone was talking except for a couple in their thirties, both on the plump side, who after introductions sat in straight chairs by the kitchen door, every now and then exchanging whispered confidences. They were the host and hostess, Albert and Sadie Hosmer. After a minute or so the woman rose, came over and asked Carla if she would like tea or wine or maybe coffee.

"Tea, thank you, tea would be lovely," answered Carla.

The man was at her side at once. "Let me get it, Sadie," he said solicitously. "You go sit down, you've been overdoing. You must be careful."

The woman laughed and together they went into the kitchen, his arm protectively around her. "Isn't that sweet!" said Tanya. "Albert's so thoughtful."

"Since she's not well, can't I do something to help?" Carla offered.

Tanya laughed. "Cousin Sadie's healthy as a horse. But she's just found out she's pregnant. This is really a party to celebrate it. I'm so happy for them."

Carla stared at her. Tanya, who had not once but many times stated that she considered this no fit world to bring a child into, was happy for them. Albert came back carrying the tea, while Sadie followed with a plate of cookies.

There were a half dozen others in the room, and Carla never did get them sorted out, except that she certainly knew which one was Leonard Engelstein. She also knew which woman was his sister Ellen, who bore a striking resemblance to him insofar as a quite feminine woman can resemble a quite masculine man and except that her face had no disfiguring twist.

An argument raged. Was Roosevelt a social fascist, and if not, what was he? Was or was not the most urgent need of the day to organize against him, to defeat him at all costs, to judge all candidates for Congress that year solely on the basis of electing those opposed to Roosevelt, or were there lurking on the right horizon even greater dangers? Albert grew hysterical. No Roosevelt! Lackey of the capitalist class! Arch enemy of the revolution! Should be hung by his thumbs! Smirking scum!

"It's the beginning of the end, the beginning of the end," said Leonard. He spoke slowly, emphatically, as if there could be no debating what he said, and indeed the others turned toward him as to an oracle.

Carla listened intently, wondering what on earth she had stumbled into. There was something surrealist about this little group of people sitting in their comfortable chairs and as it were disposing of the entire world, talking about political power plays as if they themselves were princes in exile or heads of government, or at least to become heads of government day after tomorrow. They were out to change the world! They had not the slightest doubt that the success of their political movement was indispensable for the salvation of mankind—material and psychological salvation, that is, for more than once they made it clear that they considered all that religious talk about the soul a flagrant con game. Carla thought of the men sleeping on the stairs at the station entry, of Howard beating his way about the country, of her mother faint with the smell of greasy pans, and of her father perishing alone in a fire he may well have set. The mood was reaching her, she breathed deeply of it.

They were talking three at a time except when Leonard spoke, and then the others were silent. They had just about exhausted the Roosevelt subject, and Leonard turned to Tanya saying, "Tell us about your strike."

Highlighted in Tanya's account were the picket lines, the shouting angry picket lines, and the role played by Carla. "Joan of Arc of the Shoe Workers," she cried. "It was on the front page of the Sentinel."

Albert thrust his rotund body into the little clear space in the room. "Oh it's tremendous," he cried, "it's marvelous. And to think that such a country kitten could be such a leader!"

"Country kitten, Carla!" exclaimed Tanya. "That's good, that's perfect. Country kitten."

The others picked it up, applauded the man's wit, and vowed to call Carla forever after by this nickname. She sank into herself, utterly crushed, her reaction quite unnoticed. They went on to plan the execution of the capitalist class, including Roosevelt, who had with his false promises bewitched a proletariat utterly lacking in class consciousness. But all Carla could think of was this horrid nickname. Why should she be wounded by it? It was so utterly ridiculous to call her—tall, gawky, handsome rather than pretty, competent stitcher of shoes, militant trade-unionist, so definitely unkittenish—by such a name. Yet there was a justice to it, for before their great knowledge and their supreme confidence in their own superiority she was indeed an innocent. The tongues vibrated with a thousand certitudes, and Laurel was a million miles away and Megunnaway a century ago. She was whirled through space, and she hung on desperately, dizzied by the speed, lost in a whole new world.

"Good night, Kitten," they were saying, and finally she and Tanya were alone in the living room, and Tanya was making beds for them on the sofa and an army cot.

"There, little Kitten," said Tanya.

"Don't call me that!"

"Well, you don't have to be so snappish about it," said Tanya. And then she went on to tell of their plans for the next day. Carla had made no plans, of course, how could she? The culmination would be a dance, "for a radical cause, of course," said Tanya as if otherwise they couldn't dance.

"I'm not a good dancer," said Carla.

"Oh but you will be, the music will carry you along and when you meet Grove! Oh I know he'll love you! And can he ever dance!" Tanya sighed. "Wait till you see him, six feet tall, straight as an arrow, golden hair, eyes startlingly blue. Face like a movie star, I mean a real matinee idol."

"What," asked Carla, "does one say to a matinee idol?"

"Silly, he's no matinee idol," said Tanya. "If he were, would I be talking him up? No, no, he's a militant class-conscious worker. True he's from a wealthy family, but that's the point, he's left it. Think what he's sacrificed. And his courage! I'll never forget him at that unemployment demonstration. A brute of a cop really cracked his head," Tanya reminisced. "But it didn't faze him, not Grove."

Carla waited to hear more of this Grove, but Tanya had become silent. When she finally did speak, it had nothing to do with Grove.

"Do you think Leonard's handsome?" she asked with disconcerting abruptness, pausing with hands on hips in challenging posture.

Carla felt it to be a no-win proposition and hesitated. That didn't work either, for Tanya stood there tensely waiting an answer.

"Well," Carla said, "no, I guess not exactly." No, he wasn't handsome, she didn't think he was, but fascinating? Ah, that was another matter. And yet frightening.

"He's the most handsome man in the world," responded Tanya and hurried off to the bathroom.

Leonard put in an appearance early the next afternoon, and when he addressed her as "Kitten," Carla blushed and was quite unable to snap at him as she had at Tanya. Yes, that's what she was, the silly country kitten. She'd done everything wrong that day, had flooded the bathroom by leaving the shower-curtain outside of its proper confines, had confessed to never having eaten lox and bagels, had submitted to Sadie looking critically at her costume and adding a touch of color, a pink scarf.

"Too bright," Carla had demurred but what did she know? And then there was the plan to visit some famous paintings by one Ricardo, of whom she'd never heard.

"It's Ellen's idea," said Sadie apologetically. "I tried to talk her out of it, but she's got her friend Lowell enthused and they won't listen."

"It's that Agnes," said Albert sulkily. "Ellen and Leonard's sister. Ellen insists she doesn't care if Agnes is a renegade; she's still their sister, and she knows a thing or two about art."

"Of course I can't go," said Leonard.

"Of course not," Tanya agreed.

Carla listened in bewilderment. What on earth were they talking about? Renegade? Leonard turned to her. "Did my eyes deceive me, or were you looking at that Metropolitan Museum book when I came in?"

"Oh, I was. There is a picture there I'd love to see. My mother had, I mean she still has, a print of it."

"Good. We'll go there and then meet them."

One glance at Tanya told Carla this wouldn't do. "No," she said. "I'd like to see the other paintings."

As soon as Ellen and Lowell arrived, they all, including Leonard, went out together. Cars churned through the snowy streets, the air was cold, though by comparison with the day before not unbearably so, and they walked quickly to keep their feet warm, Tanya's red boots making a gay dance as she hurried along. Apartment buildings, four and five stories high, rose on either side.

Carla wondered who lived in them, particularly if there were any children. How could anyone raise children in such crowded places? She wondered if Sadie and Albert knew how. In the next few blocks were factory lofts and office buildings in various stages of decrepitude. Finally Leonard called them to a halt and announced that he must leave them; Tanya would know where to meet him.

Ellen led them up a dimly lit flight of stairs. A short, tightly corseted woman in a neat black dress and stylish shoes met them at the top landing. "Come on in," the woman said in the crisp clear tone of one used to giving directions. "I suppose you came to see the murals?"

As they stepped out of the dark hall into a large loft, Carla was overwhelmed by the strong light and the bright colors of the mural paintings which covered two fifty-foot walls. These tremendous paintings were of human figures, larger than life, brightly clothed, the faces predominantly round and dark.

The woman led the way, explaining the significance of each panel, identifying individuals and groups. There was Lenin, a benign, saintly Lenin, a tremendous Lenin filling a whole panel. There was J.P. Morgan, a dark-visaged, black-mustached, brutal Morgan. There were sturdy gray-clad troops and workers skirmishing in strike action. There were smokestacks which looked like huge guns, and guns which looked like smokestacks. Everywhere people, people, people frozen in motion, people lying dead, and some just staring out at the viewers with round accusing eyes.

They came back to the door. "And thus you see," their guide summarized in her clear emphatic voice, "the way in which the great Mexican artist Ricardo has painted the cruelty and decadence of the capitalist system. At the same time he has shown developing within the decay of the old, the new world struggling to stretch its limbs in freedom."

A collection basket stood on a table, and into it Ellen dropped a dollar. Carla did likewise, but the others scuttled hurriedly down the stairs.

"Ah," sighed Albert, "that was real proletarian art. What a shame it's in their building, not in ours."

Theirs and ours? I am sure the hostess would have been much at home at last night's gathering. I am sure, but what do I know? Proletarian art? Carla pondered the phrase. *I know what proletarian means, at least I think I do. It refers to the working class people like those of us at the shoe factories. I know what art is, at least I've read Tolstoy's essay. But proletarian art?*

"What was that about you and Leonard going to the Metropolitan?" asked Tanya.

"I do want to go," said Carla.

"I've other things to do. You run along, he'll escort you."

"If you won't go, then I won't either."

"Why not?"

She couldn't very well say because she thought Tanya might be jealous. Maybe Ellen and Lowell? No, no, they were going with Tanya.

Leonard was waiting outside, a block away. It ended by his taking Carla firmly by the elbow and marching her off while the others left in a different direction. "Oh dear," she said. "I don't want to cause any friction."

"Don't be silly," he answered.

There she'd done it again. If she'd had a magic lamp, her one wish would have been to be transported back to her own familiar little shabby apartment where she belonged, but having no such lamp she simply stopped and stood still in confusion.

"Come, Kitten," he said. And then added, "Do I sense that you dislike that name?"

"Oh if you knew how much!"

"Ah, but I do. And you're right. It's not you, not you at all. There's something deep and strong in you that needs to be brought out, to be trained."

He wants to train me like a horse, thought Carla. Humbly she walked along that he might show her the wondrous museum, the great depository of a culture that, as she understood it, he despised. *How kind of him to take me there, the untutored country girl he looks down on from such precipitous heights!*

EIGHTEEN

Carla stood with Leonard before the mighty El Greco painting. "How wonderful!" she breathed. "I'd no idea." The buildings perched on the wild hills stood upright before the threat of an impending storm; dark clouds rolled in, and a luminous electrical force threw a ghastly light over buildings, hills, and even the individual leaves of the tree in the left foreground. Carla stood there half expecting to see jagged lightening streak across the canvas and to hear the crash of thunder.

She could have stood there for hours, but Leonard led her away. He hated to do it, he said, but he'd promised to meet someone. After a short ride in an uncomfortably warm bus and a walk in the cold air, she followed him through a heavy door and was overwhelmed by the smell of cookery. A tumult of voices surrounded her ears. She was dimly conscious of a long steam table and a crowd of people and tables with many chairs. On the two side walls were great murals in which heavily muscled men wielded gigantic shovels; one in blue overalls swung his scythe. Big-busted women toiled at unidentifiable tasks, their faces heroic in size and as expressionless as so many slabs of wood. So this was the restaurant of which Tanya had boasted.

Leonard got her a cup of coffee and excusing himself exited through a back door. At the next table a youngish woman with green eyes set in a flat face like that of a cat was interrogating a dark, hawk-nosed man. She was, Carla could hear, intent on knowing his nationality. And he would only answer indignantly in a marked European accent that he was a truckdriver. All around were earnest conversations, of which she caught fragments. "We'll show those fascist pigs!" "You'll be at the dance?" " We'll strike, I tell you we must." "Come the revolution, we the workers will find all things are possible!"

A young man with flaming hair seated at a table with half a dozen others had uttered the words of the last sentence and then paused, glanced all around, got up and left. Ah yes, thought Carla, come the revolution! What did it all mean, where did she fit in? What was she? A worker? Her grandfathers had been prosperous farmers, one a warrior, but in this arena that wasn't where their greatness lay. It lay in their hard-working nothingness. And her parents, oh how oppressed they'd been! She gloried in it. They were the people on those walls, or rather the people on the walls were what they would have been had they not been destroyed by the system. They'd never known! Mama would never know! But Carla knew, she herself was the real thing. They could keep their petty bourgeois colleges, she had no need of them. She was that last who shall be first. She'd do great things, she and this dark-eyed revolutionary Leonard, this strange and wonderful man. And all the other comrades. She said the word aloud, "Comrades!" and shivered with delight. "Forever comrades." She felt light as air, like a kite which has snapped the slender thread which previously linked it to the humdrum earth.

She jumped at the sound of a voice close to her ear. "Come," said Leonard. "This place smells of cabbage."

Soon they were back at the apartment, talking politics, wild politics and Carla joined in. And they were eating exotic foods and drinking white wine and then preparing for the dance. The dance! Sadie, Tanya, Albert, Ellen, and even Lowell, Ellen's escort, were in a festive mood. Tanya pranced about, devastatingly beautiful in her embroidered peasant blouse and whirling skirt. Carla looked down at her own costume, a tailored, pale-blue blouse over a daytime skirt.

"Take that pink scarf," said Leonard, "and make a cummerbund." After she had done as he bid, he grunted noncommittally and was silent as they walked along to the dance.

The hall had been given a gay appearance with a liberal festooning of red and gold banners and crepe paper. Excitedly Tanya kept introducing Carla, and each introduction varied. This was her dear friend, this was the militant shoe worker, this was Carla Putnam from Boston. The new acquaintances were mere shadows to Carla, some of them dance partners she hoped, and the women, she was relieved to note, were dressed in varied costumes from smart long evening gowns to faded cotton skirts, though everyone had some touch of color, a scarf or necklace or jeweled comb.

"Oh, Grove," cried Tanya, "I knew you'd be here. I want you to meet our dear little Country Kitten, Carla Putnam. Carla, Grosvenor Steele."

That horrid nickname! Mercifully Tanya chattered on. Carla looked up, struggled for self-possession. A tall golden-haired Adonis was smiling down at her. "She looks like a full-grown cat," he said.

The music began with a strong rhythmic beat, and Grosvenor without a word swept her out onto the floor. He was a splendid dancer, light yet strong, with perfect timing. She made a misstep for which she apologized, but he only held her close and smiled. Her face brushed the rough woolen tweed of his jacket, and she drew comfort from the touch. He whirled her on; she caught the feel of the music and surprisingly enough moved light as air, surprisingly because she'd never been a good dancer. But tonight, tonight! All the old inhibitions were gone, her body had no weight, her feet were quick and rhythmic, out she whirled and back she came. The pace quickened—she was an eagle in flight, she was a mountain goat on a cliff, she was a fairy creature with wings of gauze.

⚜

Even enchanted evenings end, however, as do fascinating weekends of discovery in New York. Sunday afternoon found Carla sitting with Tanya on a bench in the railway station, for it was over. But was it really? Carla's eyes sparkled as she relived the whirl of the dance; and there was warmth in her heart, for Leonard had asked her to do him a favor.

"I don't really want to go back to Boston," Tanya sighed. "But Leonard made it quite clear I have to."

Carla remained silent. Yes, Leonard had asked a favor of her, but he had given an order to Tanya.

Tanya sighed again. "He made it clear, made everything clear."

"Except how to do what he asked us to do," said Carla.

A shadow of fear passed over Tanya's expressive face. "At least they got out, poor dears," she mused. "But I wonder are they bad? Really bad?"

"I hope not. Times are bad, that's for sure," responded Carla relieved by the emergence of a subject which she could address. "How on earth does he expect us to find them jobs?"

"Sarah and Meyer should know," replied Tanya. "There shouldn't be any need for me to go back." She paused and glanced at Carla. "Carla, confidentially, wouldn't *you* really prefer to stay in New York?"

"I don't know, I really don't."

Leonard came striding in, his every movement importing boundless energy, determination, and a confidence in his own powers. A man, a woman, and two boys followed humbly in his wake. "Meyer Friedman's cousins," he introduced them. They also were named Friedman, Sam and Pearl, and their sons Max and Willi.

There they stood, four people huddled together, the boys in the center, the parents protectively on either side. With an effort the man moved forward, extended his hand, and speaking very softly said something in German. He was of medium height, slightly stooped, with thin features, hawk-like nose, dark brown restless eyes which darted from one face to another. Pearl Friedman was a slender woman, rather fair of complexion and her gray eyes seemed as restless as the dark eyes of her husband.

Carla smiled at the boys, eager to make friends, but they drew back like frightened deer, as if they would flee if only they could, great dark eyes staring from thin faces. They made no sound, gave no answering smile. The woman was trembling, yet bravely trying to control herself. And the man kept looking about, his eyes darting from one side to another. His face was deadly serious.

"Sam doesn't understand much English," said Leonard and spoke to the man in German or Yiddish, Carla wasn't sure which.

"He used to understood English, he spoke it well," said Pearl. "It'll come back to him. He lost it, how do you say, temporary."

And as they stood there, four well-dressed people with no marks of violence on them, Carla saw that, yes, it was that bad in Europe. Although these people had not been driven raving mad by their ordeal, they had been, while retaining full consciousness of their plight, frightened half out of their wits so that they were completely reliant for direction on those about them. The two boys, said to be thirteen and fourteen, were small and subdued for such ages, as if they had been scared out of at least two years growth.

On board the train Tanya, after having seen to it that her charges were seated, took a place by the window and sat studying the descending night.

Carla sat with Pearl, who was eager to talk. The words flowed softly, for she had no desire to make a scene, but they flowed inexorably for she was determined that this strange young American who wasn't a Jew should understand what was happening in Germany.

"At first," said Pearl, "it was just that people we'd known for years no longer recognized us when we met on the street, that the boys were called names at school, that some customers no longer came to us, though I assure you we had by far the best clothing store in our town, which lay not far from Berlin but far enough that a good shopping place was welcomed. Oh yes, we had a fine store. What we have of that is the clothes we wear."

Carla, who had noted the fine cut and material of their coats, felt ashamed of having noted it. "Things will be better," she tried to be comforting.

"We've left so much behind," said Pearl. "But we've saved the boys."

Saved the boys, thought Carla. What about themselves?

"At first just losing all our friends, for in fact most of our friends were not Jews," Pearl continued. "Losing our friends, was that so bad? Yet I cried over that until after that horrible night. Then I cried no more for those rotten friends."

The story of that night welled up within her, the telling of it continued, her English equal to it, though now and then she had to stop to think of a word or even say "no matter" and use the German expression. On and on she talked, and Carla sat there, not even contributing the usual monosyllables. On and on the story raged, still in low tone, not to make a scene. There had been many fights between political gangs in their community and no one in authority seemed to care, but at first it hadn't affected them, until one night her brother was badly beaten. The next day he left for Palestine—and yes, he'd made it, she didn't know how—there were things that couldn't be written, but they'd heard from him, and he was there safe and on a kibbutz. (What, wondered Carla, is a kibbutz?) It became harder and harder for the boys to go to school; more and more often they came home with bloody faces and torn clothing, and more and more the parents taught them at home. One of the lessons taught was English, at least they'd been smart enough to know they must learn the American language, and with the help of an old woman who'd spent some time in England and with records and with books, they'd learned English. Particularly Pearl and Sam had learned for the boys seemed to have no gift for it. Oh they knew greetings and foods, simple things. But she and Sam had learned, and now Sam had forgotten it—it had been beaten from his head. Yes, beaten on that awful night. A gang of some dozen young ruffians had burst into the store, just as they were closing. Doing what they'd practiced many times before, Max hid himself in one of the big drawers where they kept the shirts and Willi, the younger, in a packing case in the back room.

"At first," said Pearl, "Sam tried to soft-talk those hoodlums. But when they laid hands on him, he fought back. Oh he fought like a tiger! He threw things, and he punched, and he cursed, but at the end he lay on the floor unconscious. And those swine broke every window in the place, they heaped the clothes on the floor, they cuffed me till I fell against the wall, and when they left they hurled a lighted roll of paper onto the heaped-up clothing. I hardly dared move till they left, not even if the place went up in flames. But they had other places to go that night. Some day I'll tell you that too. I got out the boys. Poor kids, they'd heard it, the threats, the insults, the fight, the crashing glass. The clothing had begun to smolder; I couldn't beat it out, but thanks to much of it being made of heavy woolen cloth it burned slow. We got Sam out, and I ran back and got out the cash."

"Couldn't the fire department—" Carla began.

"Them? They wouldn't come," said Pearl. "But a doctor friend of ours came, and we got to his house and Sam's life was saved, though for weeks we had fears. He's never been the same since. All the English gone. Other things he used to know. Why did they have to beat him about the head?"

"Oh it was too too cruel!" cried Carla.

"That gang," said Pearl, "was a Hitler gang. Hitler you know?"

"Yes."

"Let me tell you, young American girl, the horror has just begun."

"Just begun?"

"That beast has vowed by some strange Nordic god that he'll wipe out the Jews, all our people, our great and good and gentle people."

"Wipe out?"

"Like they was smallpox."

"Thank God," said Carla, "you escaped."

"But what I left behind—" Pearl could not continue. She was overcome with grief.

❧

It was not until some two weeks later that Carla discovered what Pearl had left behind. Sarah Friedman had gotten her cousin hired at Caldwell Shoe, and she sat at the machine next to Carla. "We must teach her," said Sarah. "She knows how to sew, she'll try hard, she's smart. You will help?"

Carla welcomed the chance. To help Pearl become a competent stitcher was such a small thing. Yet at times, it didn't seem small. As Pearl sat at the machine, her hands trembled, her arms trembled, even her legs and feet, which she must use on the controls, trembled. And the machine, though mere iron and steel and rubber belts, felt her fear and grew balky as a mule and skittish as a race horse. Belts would break; needles snap and become embedded in the leather; for no discernible reason the knee lever would become frozen in position and refuse to make its necessary moves; or the machine would stop feeding thread so that only needle holes remained where there should have been a neat seam. A dozen times a day Jake came rushing over to get the machine working again, shouting angrily in two or three languages, and before he was done very often his hands were trembling as badly as Pearl's. After the first week, however, some improvement could be seen, and more and more often either Sarah or Carla was able to solve the problem without calling the excitable foreman. Pearl was actually turning out some work, and the breakdowns were occurring less frequently. Still her nervous trembling continued, and all day long she hovered on the verge of crying until Carla half wished she would go ahead and get it over with, without, of course, dropping any tears where they would spot the leather.

Bravely Pearl kept at it. Out of the blue one day at lunch she handed Carla a small photo of a round-faced, white-haired woman. "She doesn't look like a Jew, does she?" she asked eagerly.

"No, I suppose not," answered Carla after due inspection of the photo.

"You suppose not?"

"I'm quite sure."

Now for the first time since she came to work, Pearl actually did shed tears. "My mother," she said. "I left behind my mother. We couldn't get passport."

The news from Germany became more gruesome, and no word came from Pearl's mother. Hardly a day went by when Pearl didn't hand Carla the photo and say eagerly, "She doesn't look like a Jew, does she?"

At the same time rumors of an impending closing of the Laurel plant of Caldwell Shoe were discussed with much foreboding. "You see," said Tanya. "Winning a strike means nothing so long as you have the old system. What good are higher wages if we get thrown out of work?"

Caldwell Shoe suspended operations in Laurel around the middle of April, with the cutters and stitchers being laid off first. Jake, Sarah, and Pearl did indeed find work in Laurel, the three together at Stylerite where they needed a foreman and where Jake agreed to go only on condition that these two women were hired. Carla wound up with a job in Boston, working part, time and making much less than she had done in Laurel. After a week she got a place there for Tanya. She was a subdued Tanya in no mood to sing songs in the stitching room, but a Tanya quite unchanged as to her devotion to the revolution. Carla had moved back into the same building where she had once lived with Ray. But not the same apartment. She'd told the landlady she simply couldn't, and the woman had understood. Tanya refused her invitation to share the apartment, said she'd stay with her parents for the time being and maybe go back to New York. She'd love to go back to New York.

"Even if Leonard is here?" asked Carla, for Leonard was indeed living in Boston.

It was the first open mention of Leonard as someone special to Tanya that Carla had ever hazarded. Tanya wasn't angry, only sad. "Particularly," she said, "since Leonard is here. I'm nothing to him, I never will be. Sometimes I think I never was."

Tanya also explained that she was a soldier under discipline and could not just up and leave for New York, but she had requested it. In due time her request was granted. "Maybe I should go with you," said Carla.

"If I took you away, they'd never forgive me. Don't you know they've got special plans for you here?"

"They've got a colossal nerve!"

"Sometimes you're so childish," said Tanya scornfully.

"I don't want you to be angry with me."

Tanya laughed. "You're too wishy-washy on the revolution," she said. "And I don't like that. I've no other cause to be angry."

Good, thought Carla, she has no other cause. No, she supposed not, really. The special interest Leonard was showing Carla was certainly not the result of any snares she had set. Yet he'd meant so much to Tanya, probably still did. Tanya, dear, vibrant, lovable Tanya! But New York would be better for her, and on second thought she, Carla, would be a fish out of water there, still a country kitten or at least someone cursed with a New England accent and hence suspected of weakness of intellect. A nice kid with strange ideas, who pronounced it idears. How quaint! Well, she'd stay in Boston. Perhaps after all it had something special for her.

It was a relief when in mid-August Tanya left for New York. Carla had gone a few times to the office of "The Lighted Match," the magazine edited by Leonard Engelstein, though she always felt that by so doing she was intruding on an old romance. Romance of course had nothing to do with Carla's interest in the magazine. She'd been drawn by its fiery condemnation of Hitler, the man responsible for Pearl's agony. With Tanya gone she felt free to volunteer more and more time, which she spent typing copy.

By fall she was going on spare evenings just to sit around and talk. She no longer noticed what a stuffy hole in the wall it was but only that it was brightly lit. The dirty tan walls receded into the background, she had mastered the vagaries of the old typewriter, and she had sandpapered the furniture legs so that they no longer snagged her hose. Night after night Leonard and his comrades honed their plots to turn the world upside down, or as they saw it rightside up, until it seemed that in one more day the word from some authority would be given, and there would again be ten days to shake the world. She was fired with their enthusiasm, yet at the beginning she was not really one of them. They all felt that. She was there to avenge the Friedmans, to rescue Pearl's mother, to consign to the deepest dungeon that super-monster Hitler, but beyond that she did not go at first.

One evening Leonard took her home. They went out from the brightly lit hole in the wall to the soft gray of the street at dusk and drove along enjoying the scene. Black taxis were cruising slowly, the traffic was light, the sidewalk crowds sauntered at an evening pace. From a third story window a jazz piano sent its sound out upon the night, and Carla beat time to its rhythm, but Leonard made no response.

"Carla," he said at last, "do you really want to work in a factory?"

"It's a living."

"Something tells me you have other ambitions."

Ah yes, there had been a time! There'd been many times and more than one ambition, but clearest now was the flashback to her days in Hambledon West and the childish dreams she'd poured out to Roger, silly things like being governor to help the poor. And then there'd been a day in the Boston Library when she'd suddenly resolved to write a History of America for children, a resolve still somewhere in the far recesses of her mind. She'd learned new ways of thinking, but the new ways ran against the grain of her. Certainly there was an economic factor at work in the world, but the rest of man's endeavors could not be dismissed. Maybe some day she'd pull it together. She must get back to working on it.

"We've plans for you, my dear. Maybe they'll firm up. A lot depends on our chief angel."

"Angel?"

"You didn't think it was all Moscow gold, did you? I mean Phoenicia Attlebury."

"The writer?"

"Yes." He laughed. "The writer of trashy novels. Which sell."

Several days later Carla was seated at her typewriter when in stalked Phoenicia Attlebury, in person, the famous author of *The Frightened Bride,* and *Augustina's Revenge,* and twenty similar titles. Her spike heels resounded off the wooden floor with a staccato beat and the stale air took on the spicy fragrance of her perfume. She was tall and slender, about the same height indeed as Carla herself, and not too unlike Carla as to the lines of her face and the liveliness of her deep gray eyes. She was, however, considerably older, in her forties or maybe even fifty. Her hair, obviously a wig, was golden blonde and curled untidily around her face.

"Darling Leonard!" she cried. "Here's the check, really two checks, one for 'Light' and one for Mobilization. And here's a story, a new writer, delightful young man, I know you'll want to meet him."

"And I want you to meet my helper, Carla Putnam," said Leonard.

"Oh the young woman from the shoe workers! That perfectly fascinating strike where you made such a splash. In Laurel, wasn't it?"

"Yes," said Carla.

"And you work in a factory? You must tell me all about it some time. Not today, haven't time. But I'll really listen. It's grist for my mill, you know."

"There's not much to tell," said Carla.

"I'm sure you're a most unusual girl. But I really must run, toodle-oo." And she was gone, teetering out of the room on her high heels, the resounding tap of those heels echoing up the stairwell.

Leonard drew a paperback volume from the drawer. "Maybe you'd better read it, just to understand her better."

"Not an enthusiastic review."

Carla took the book, read the first five pages and put it aside. She got acquainted with the writer, however, for Miss Attlebury, when she had time, was quite a talker. Phoenicia was indeed her Christian name, given her by a mother who liked the sound of it and knew and cared nothing at all about the Phoenicians. "Good pen name," Phoenicia confided one day. "Have to have something to sell the ridiculous things I write."

Carla tried to think of something tactful to say, but Phoenicia found nothing awry in the silence. After that Carla had to read the books. Phoenicia was right, they were ridiculous. Their main characters were scheming women who used their beauty for all it was worth, were frightfully cynical, talked with a brittle wit, always got their man though why they cared to was not always clear, and were furthermore raking in the dollars from whatever profession they were in, mostly acting. Carla supposed there was much of Phoenicia in them; certainly Phoenicia was one to use her beauty, even now that it was fading, and certainly she'd raked in the dollars. However she was not cynical, but rather tended to love all mankind in a featherbrained sort of way and to form at short notice very real attachments for quite an assortment of persons, mostly but not exclusively young men. It seemed to Carla that she suffered from a sense of guilt at her undeserved success and that she sought to compensate for this guilt by her role as patroness of causes.

Carla found Phoenicia the most fascinating of all the people who came and went at that office which was such a magnet for strange characters. (She was the most fascinating, that is, except for Leonard.) Phoenicia fairly pulsed with nervous energy. Even her hair was filled with static electricity so that as she walked it stood out from her head, though of course that may have been due to the material from which it was made. Phoenicia was a writer of novels; she was a sought after speaker for numerous occasions; she ran, in conjunction with her brother, an advertising agency; she was always talking about the luncheons, dinners, and parties she'd attended. When, thought Carla, did the woman find time to sleep?

One evening Carla looked up from her typing and caught the older woman intently watching her. "Do you know what I was thinking?" asked Phoenicia.

"No, I guess not."

"Oh you little fox!" cried Phoenicia. "You've such a perfect face for 'Light,' and especially for Mobilization. So earnest, so respectable, even so conservative, while underneath it you're the reddest of the red. But I'm running late." Away she tap-tapped on her high heels.

Carla sat there thinking. She thought of all that she and her family had suffered, the family breakup, her mother at her dishwashing job, her father's despair, her brother undergoing heaven knew what hardships, and she herself working at a factory job which day by day became more odious to her. And the union which had been going to make life so pleasant for the shoe workers, what had it accomplished? Some improvement in wages, a protection against the nasty tempers of individual foremen, even a modicum of job security for it was through the union that she had gotten her job in Boston. But these things were piddling nothings. Caldwell Shoe had snapped its fingers at the union and moved. Old Mr. Caldwell, stiff as a ramrod, heir to the wealth his forefathers had gathered, owner of the means of production of vast stacks of shoes, was the boss, you'd better believe it. If she were the reddest of the red, did she not have reason?

Carla sighed and turned back to her typewriter. She'd finished the work she'd volunteered to do, and now the machine was hers to use. She'd write to Roger. They'd been corresponding regularly and she owed him a letter, but it wasn't only that. If he were there, she could talk to him about the new things she was involving herself in; she knew she could. Perhaps she could write. At least it might get him off his lengthy explanations of the advances in electronics of which he had written far more than she was able to understand. She remembered how the women at Caldwell Shoe had teased her about his attentions, teased her and congratulated her on having such a lover. But Roger wrote of everything save love. Roger was an only child and no doubt was merely adopting her as a sister. She sighed, placed her fingers upon the keys and easily typed a page and a half.

Roger answered her rather more quickly than usual. His letter consisted mostly of questions. "How can your new friends be against both war and fascism? To stop the planned military aggression of fascism will take nothing short of war. Insofar as they weaken United States preparation for war, do they not strengthen fascism?" and "Why is it Mobilization Against *Fascism*, which truly is the Italian name, and not against *National Socialism*, which is the more correct designation for Hitler's bullies?" and a question that at the time seemed quite irrelevant, "How many peasants died in the famine in Russia, and why was there a famine?" And finally, "What shall it profit a man if he gain the whole world and lose his soul?" Carla wasn't sure she had a soul.

Roger, it seemed, had a soul, and Leonard had a cause. Did she not also have that same cause? If Leonard had been in Boston when she first came to this conclusion, she would have gone at once to him as to an altar call and dedicated herself body and soul. He was out of the city visiting a couple of towns where there were attempts to organize local Mobilization clubs and then would go to New York for a conference. He'd be gone for ten days, and Carla must talk to someone at once. One of the frequent visitors at the Mobilization offices was the shoe-worker Gus, who was working in Boston now. He was openly and proudly a radical communist propagandist. What was more natural than that Carla should confide in him? She admired him so, she said, for his forthright stand.

"Coming from you," he said, "that is indeed high praise. You're truly a class-conscious worker." From him this was the highest of accolades.

He went on however to complain that she wasn't making use of her strengths. Gus was a scrawny, quite unprepossessing youth, but at that moment all she could see was the intensity of his fierce blue eyes.

"You must speak for us!" he said. "At our next meeting on Boston Common. We need eloquence like yours. You must do it, you must!"

"Oh I will!" she cried impetuously.

"This coming Saturday then," he said.

"So soon?" she said, startled by the immediacy of it.

"You know the place, there at the end of the Common, the row where the stands are?"

She knew it well! When first she came to Boston how exciting it had been to stand there in the audience, reveling in the boldness of the speakers. She thrilled at being called upon to redeem her promise so soon. It was spring, the perfect time to go to Boston Common. She met Gus at the Mall and went with him to the sign of the United Communist Party. "I'm chairing the meeting," he said. "You'll speak first. Speak as a shoe worker. Speak as a fighter. Give utterance to all their anger! Rev 'em up!"

There she stood on a sunny spring day under the greening trees with a fresh breeze ruffling her hair. "Fellow workers," she began too softly, then repeated it. Ah, she was getting her range, her voice was carrying. Soon she was in full sail, lamenting the exploitation of the working class, celebrating the power of that working class once it awakened from its slumber. She started with war and fascism, went beyond to the real issue, revolution! She glanced from side to side to take in her whole audience. She saw it grow; soon she had the largest group of any speaker there on the Mall, for who could resist the magnetism of this fresh-faced young woman with the clarion call? She stood surrounded by admiring glances, like an actress after a successful performance and felt the same thrill she'd felt in the union hall the very first time she spoke.

The following Wednesday she went to the office of the "Light," expecting Leonard back, eager to hear about his trip and to accept his plaudits for what she had done. As she approached, she heard his voice, loud and full of wrath. To her surprise his fury was directed at Gus. "You had no business doing it," Leonard shouted. "You knew better."

"I thought," Gus began, quite humbly.

"You did not think, you couldn't possibly have thought."

"We can't forever hide the face of the party; we *are* Communists."

"We can act with discipline and you knew what the policy was."

Carla hesitated in the doorway, but Leonard saw her and ordered her to come in. There could be no other word, he ordered. "How explicit do I have to be with you?" he asked.

"What on earth?"

"What on earth indeed, Miss Innocence. Haven't I made it clear to you that you are to stay away from the Party? To on no account identify yourself or give anyone else a chance to identify you with it?"

"You've made no such thing clear. Only that you wouldn't pressure me into the Party."

"Not pressure you *into* it? I was pressuring you to stay clear."

"But I decided otherwise."

"All right, Country Kitten—"

"Oh Leonard!" she cried. "Not that horrid name."

"Okay, I won't use it, but you, my girl, need wising up."

"Wising up?" She knew he hated her repeating his words like that and resolved to restrain herself.

"I suppose I must be imprudently specific. There is, first of all, the United Communist Party."

"To which you and Gus belong?" Carla asked.

"To which Gus belongs. I do not belong—at least not publicly."

"If you're not publicly a party member, what are you?" Carla demanded.

"There are also what are commonly designated as front organizations, where sympathizers can work on some issue more acceptable to the general public than our ultimate program."

"What do you mean our ultimate program?"

"He means the United Communist Party program," Gus was specific.

"It's not easy to explain to an innocent. Okay, here's the truth. Front organizations are controlled by key persons from the Communist Party. Like me. But this has to be concealed for tactical reasons."

"I don't like concealing things," Carla asserted.

"He's right," said Gus humbly. "Carla, Leonard's right. You must follow his instructions. Every group that wants to accomplish something has to have certain masking at times, just the way governments have clandestine agents. Even our Soviet Union has such agents. We must have discipline. I was wrong to let you speak of revolution, of the purpose of the Communist Party. We cannot be that open—not now."

It was hard for her to accept, but in the end she agreed. She still had one question. "Clandestine agents," she repeated the words. "Does that mean that the United Communist Party has some sort of tie with such agents—with spys?"

"Carla, you drive me up the wall with your questions," cried Leonard. "The less you think about it the better. You just concentrate on Mobilization and 'Light.'"

NINETEEN

The summer grew warm; grew hot, magazines were published; meetings were held; Carla typed reams of copy, reports, letters, and a couple of times she spoke, talking about the upheaval caused by National Socialism in Germany. Concentrating on Mobilization and "Light" kept her busy, for there was much to say on the menace posed by Hitler. All political parties had long since been outlawed in the Reich; concentration camps had been established for anyone "suspected of activities inimical to the State"; persecution of the Jews, which had daily increased, was given legal and systematic sanction; Hitler had repudiated the Versailles Treaty. Germany was working night and day re-arming.

Carla continued stitching leather but seldom worked more than thirty hours a week in order to devote more time to the "cause." She continued to write to Roger, and he continued to give conservative answers, always in a professorial, impersonal manner. As for Leonard, he had regained his suavity, his unvarying courtesy, and never again did Carla have even a semblance of an argument with him, nor did she move any closer to him. Was there under that dedicated organizer a flesh and blood man? Perhaps she was better off not to find out.

It was some time in February that Leonard succeeding in scheduling a meeting in Sangerville, a populous industrial city some forty miles west of Boston. He would drive over on Thursday, the night before the meeting, and Phoenicia and Carla, both of them to be speakers, would come Friday. His sister Ellen, who was charged with responsibility for the literature table, would be with them.

The women left Boston around noon in Phoenicia's new sedan. It was a sunny, snow-white day, the roads had been plowed, and looking out from the warm car at the winter scene was akin to sitting cozily in front of a blazing fire while a storm rages outside. They stopped for lunch at what Phoenicia described as "the duckiest little restaurant" and had a delicious clam chowder. After lunch they started back to the car, but on the way Phoenicia insisted on a little fun in the snow, and soon they were up to their thighs in it, tossing snowballs, laughing like schoolgirls, and before they knew it, getting quite cold. Inside the car the snow, which still clung to their garments, melted, and Phoenicia began to complain that she was chilled to the bone, and indeed she was shivering. They found Leonard waiting for them at the motel where he had reserved a suite consisting of two big rooms, each with twin beds, and connected by a bath they'd all use. He and Ellen would share one room, and the others the other room.

"Delightful," cooed Phoenicia. "Just a hint of impropriety."

"There'll be several bit speakers, including you, Carla," Leonard told them and two main addresses which will be given by you, Phoenicia, and by Professor Ditwell from the College here."

"Oh dear, I didn't think of mine as a main address," remonstrated Phoenicia.

"Make it long or short, but since you and the professor are the name speakers, don't be *too* brief. But I'm not worried. He'll take up plenty of time. Have you got it written?"

"Oh yes."

"Good," Leonard opened the outside door. "I'll go check over things at the meeting hall. See you there," he called over his shoulder as he left.

Phoenicia in the excitement of arriving had forgotten her chill, but now it came back upon her with a vengeance. Hastily she took a bottle of brandy from her suitcase. "A drink of this will fix it," she said cheerfully. "And I'll have time to get some sleep."

"Shall I run out and get you a hot drink?" offered Ellen. "No? Then Carla and I will go into the other room and not disturb you till it's time to go."

When they returned two hours later, Phoenicia was sitting in her robe on the bed, her hair disheveled, the brandy bottle by her side quite empty, and she was crying. "I'm so sick," she moaned, and her voice was a whisper.

"What's the matter?" said Ellen. "Do speak up."

But she could not speak up; indeed after a few sentences she could barely whisper.

"Oh no," said Carla. "She's been advertised as a speaker. Leonard's counting on her. Oh dear, what shall we do? Hot coffee maybe?"

Ellen shook her head sadly and said, "She's beyond that."

Carla moaned, "What shall we do, what shall we do?"

Finally Phoenicia, in a hoarse whisper, came up with a plan so daring that the others drew back.

Meanwhile Leonard paced back and forth on the stage of the meeting hall. It was somewhat more cheerful than most such halls, for the walls had been newly painted a soft pale yellow. Leonard looked at his watch. The girls should arrive any minute. Ah, here was the professor and a young student who was to be one of the bit speakers. The audience was trickling in rather well, but where were the girls? He planned to put Carla on first, then Phoenicia. Ah, here was the Women's Club lady who was to preside, a bustling, middle-aged woman with a tightly corseted figure and a rather absent-minded look. But where were the girls? Carla had no business being late. She and Ellen should have been able to get that flibbertigibbet Phoenicia here by now.

The door at the rear pushed open, and Ellen came in followed by a tall woman muffled in black, and the tall woman was vigorously shaking off the snow. Quickly Ellen led her into a side room. Leonard, however, had caught sight of the yellow hair of Phoenicia Attlebury.

"Phoenicia," he cried, running after them. "Miss Attlebury!" He stopped short. They had gone into the Ladies Lounge.

Ellen came running out, her usually pale cheeks rosy from the cold. "Len," she said. "I'm so upset. We just couldn't get her to come. She's in bed with such a cold, actually she has no voice, can only speak in a whisper."

"No need to get upset," Leonard soothed her. "After all, Carla does only what you might call a walk-on."

"But Leonard—"

"I know it goes over real big, she puts it over, those corny jokes of hers. They eat it up. I'm sorry, but the main thing is Phoenicia. She's the one advertised. Get her out here. I want to go over her speech with her."

"But Leonard," wailed Ellen. "It's Phoenicia who's lost her voice, besides being drunk. Carla is here."

"That was Carla! Oh no!"

He stood there wringing his hands, the lines deep on the expression side of his face, while the other side was motionless as always. Carla with curled yellow wig, her slim figure outlined in snug-fitting black dress against which swung a tremendous green medallion, came slowly toward him. She walked with a slight teeter on amazingly high heels. "These despicable heels," she groaned. "I can't get the knack. Besides they're a size too small."

"I could have sworn you were Phoenicia."

"Good," said Carla. "We can put it across."

"You mean?" spluttered Leonard.

"Yup," said Carla, walking back and forth to get the heels under control. "Ellen, go sit somewhere and tell me how I look."

Leonard hurried them both off to an office. Carla took a few steps forward and went into her act. "Ladies and gentlemen, no, that is too formal, dear lovely friends!'' She spoke in a tone somewhat higher pitched than her natural voice and gestured with her long expressive hands.

Ellen giggled and applauded. "You're priceless, it's her, it really is."

Leonard stood there groaning.

"She told us to," said Carla.

"I'm between the devil and the deep blue sea," he moaned.

"Could she be arrested?" queried Ellen.

"Sweet innocent," Leonard teased his sister. "Arrested for impersonating a novelist? If she were, I'd go to jail with her."

"The worst is we'd be embarrassed," said Carla.

"That's much worse than jail," said Leonard. And then with his usual decisiveness he said, "We'll do it, but heaven help you, Carla, if it doesn't go over." He turned to his sister. "Take care of your literature," he ordered. "Carla, you do have her script? Good. And don't you dare deviate from it."

He went out to take charge of the lady chairman. Yes, Miss Attlebury had arrived, but she wanted to wait in the office. He would call her in good time. Unfortunately the young shoe worker couldn't make it. Professor Ditwell was already here. The other speakers were coming in, and he went calmly to greet them: a radical ex-minister who would offer an invocation. A Professor of Psychology.

He led the speakers to the platform with Carla, however, waiting in the wings. He stepped forward and welcomed the audience. He did not need to tell them of the threat to the world now being presented by German fascism. There was a ripple of empathy. He introduced the lady chair, and she in turn introduced the minister, whose invocation was fairly short as such things go, and then Leonard was speaking once more. More about Germany. Now he was lacing it into the United States. "Roosevelt is a stench in the nostrils of all liberty-loving people. We, the people, must insist on action. There is a tremendous reservoir of anti-fascist strength among the American masses. Not only are the black, the foreign-born, and even large segments of the native white American working class courageously anti-fascist, but so too are many of our intellectuals, and many of our writers and artists."

Carla trembled. She would never have the nerve; she must shout to him not to introduce her, to go on to the next speaker.

"We have with us tonight a representative of this class," he went on. "A novelist, a woman who through her artistic insight is able to see clearly, who with great courage and generous heart has come tonight to speak a few words. We regret that another engagement makes it impossible for her to remain for the entire program. You will understand her leaving immediately after speaking. Friends, it gives me great pleasure to introduce Miss Phoenicia Attlebury."

Carla stepped forward, and in spite of the high heels, walked smoothly to center stage. She stood beside the lectern, rested one hand on it, tapping gently with her red-painted nails. She glanced at the literature table, at the dramatic posters behind it, at Ellen's worried face.

"Lovely friends," she began. "Dear lovely friends!" Yes, she was hitting it right. Phoenicia would have said it just that way. She smiled a big smile, and she could feel the lipstick and makeup stretching to accomodate the spreading of her lips. "As we drove over through the soft new-fallen snow, my heart ached within me. Yes, my heart ached to think that in this world where nature provides us with so many facets of beauty, from the rising sun to the falling snow, yet man lifts his hand against man. Hate still reigns in many places, alas in high places."

She had gotten into the swing. She had also lost the prepared script, but she rambled on, which was precisely what the real Phoenicia would have done. She stood there, now tapping the lectern, now toying with the green medallion, now spreading her hands in benevolence toward her audience, now lifting them in horror. At the end she spoke of her books; Phoenicia would have done that. She spoke of the happiness many of her readers had given her by their kind comments.

"All the agony I put into my work," she went on, "is worth it if I can reach one pent-up soul out there." It was a real Attlebury phrase. Now was the time to wind up. She blew them a kiss and ran quickly off the stage. Those silly heels didn't bother when you forgot them. She could hear the applause. Leonard was there smiling a forced smile and saying through his teeth, "Get out of here as fast as you can," and then shaking her hand most cordially. Ellen was right beside him with their wraps, and by the time the chair had finished introducing Professor Ditwell, they had made their escape.

Back at the motel Phoenicia laughed heartily over their account, then turned over in bed and went soundly to sleep. Carla heard Leonard come in, she heard his voice and Ellen's speaking softly in the next room and had half a mind to put on her robe and join them, but she decided against it. She'd learn soon enough what he thought.

She lay back in her bed, but she could not sleep. She found one of Phoenicia's novels, left behind because the jacket bore a photo of the author, and she tried to read, and then she tried to sleep. She looked enviously at Phoenicia. How lightly she took everything. Losing her voice and getting drunk and Carla's taking her place were all part of an hilarious joke. The voices in the next room had long been silenced; Carla could only relive the evening and wonder what Leonard really thought of it. What did it matter? One couldn't quarrel with success, and they'd really pulled it off. She crept out of bed in her pajamas and went into the short hall that joined the two rooms. She meant to get a glass of water in the bathroom, but there in the hall stood Leonard.

"I couldn't sleep," he said. He wore the neatest of navy pajamas, and his hair was not in the least disarrayed. Carla reached up self-consciously to her own tousled head.

He took hold of her hand and moved it from her hair. "On you, mussed hair looks good," he said.

Leonard the impersonal, Leonard the cold? His eyes were glowing just as they had glowed the very first time she'd seen him. "Carla," he said, "tonight for the first time I really believed you were with us all the way, totally dedicated to the Communist cause." He drew her to him and his lips sought hers. "Carla," he said in soft deep voice. "Carla, my comrade! Carla, my love!"

She did not struggle, for she was too deeply thrilled to draw back. She had closed her eyes during the long, passionate kiss, but now she opened them. "Oh, Carla," he said. "If you only knew with what passion I love you!"

⚜

Throughout the ride home Phoenicia chattered incessantly, Ellen made the expected responses, while Carla huddled into her coat, tremulously thinking of Leonard who'd elected to drive home by himself. But he'd phone, she was sure he would.

Several hours after Carla reached her apartment, her landlady called her to the phone. She almost fell headlong in her haste, but it was Phoenicia. Phoenicia had to see her at once. Simply had to.

"What's it about?"

"I really don't want to talk on the phone. My voice, I'm losing it again. And the phone's bugged, you know."

"Not likely." Just more of Phoenicia's dramatics.

"I'm at the office. Do you have the address?"

"Why yes."

"Good," said Phoenicia Attlebury in a stage whisper and hung up.

"Wait, wait," cried Carla. "I just said yes I have the address."

Two hours later Carla stumped up the stairs to the office of Attlebree Advertising. (Phoenicia fancied that by this spelling she kept separate her writing and her hard business world). There was no one in sight. The room was comfortably warm and pleasantly furnished with light wooden furniture of slender twentieth century design. It was a small agency with just three people, Phoenicia who wrote the copy, her brother Francis who did the art work and a secretary who did the rest. Carla heard footsteps from the inner room, soft shuffling steps, and out came Francis, a big, puffy-faced man who must once have been handsome, but who'd definitely gone to seed. "What are you doing here?" he asked. "Her Royal Highness craves words with you at the Brookline Palace."

I wonder what she chewed him out over, thought Carla, *and why wasn't she where she'd said she'd be.* Covering her resentment with a forced smile, she set out for Brookline. *I wonder,* she thought, *if it really is that much of a palace?* It well could be for the Attleburys had, according to Ellen, inherited a considerable fortune.

Carla, very much at home in the big complicated world of the city, located the correct streetcar and was soon in Brookline. After a short walk she came to the Attlebury house. The huge trees in the front yard were steel gray outlines against the white building, a substantial house with lavish ornamentation around the gables and an ample porch shading the front. There was no sign of life, but the snow had been shoveled from the walk and across the porch to the door.

Before she had time to knock, the door opened, and a big woman with a shiny brown face greeted her. "You Miss Carla?" she asked.

"Yes. Miss Attlebury wanted to see me."

"I know. I'm Mollie. She's in bed. She said for you to come up the minute you got here. You just go up them stairs."

Carla hesitated, then followed the woman into the kitchen. The woman looked friendly, maybe she could give some hint. But the woman said nothing, just went back to her ironing board and continued her work. Noting that Carla still stood there, she set the iron on its heel and said, "My goodness, I forgot to invite you to take off your coat and overshoes. You can leave them there in the hall."

Still Carla hesitated. "Do you know anything about why she wants to see me?"

The woman threw back her head and laughed. "Bless my soul," she said, "you look scared."

"Did she get her voice back?"

"She had it real good when Mr. Francis was talking to her," Mollie replied. "And I expect if I don't get a hustle on, she'll have it real good for me. Got to get this ironed." She held up a square of cloth, white as snow. "You know what this is?"

"Can't say I do."

"It's a sheet for Fiddles' bed."

"Fiddles?"

"The dog. Miss Fiddles, I call her. Of all the worst things I ever saw, ironing sheets for a dog! And lamb chops, a lamb chop every day!"

"Where is Miss Fiddles now?" Carla was frankly stalling.

"Running up and down the street looking for garbage pails. You can't keep that dog out of garbage pails."

"Do you try to?"

"Follow me," said Mollie. "I'll show you where the room is."

"Come in, come in," called Phoenicia when Carla knocked.

The room was large, and its colors were gold and gray, gray background with gold accents. The wallpaper was misty gray, the furniture golden oak, and a picture on the wall was a Cubist painting in gold and gray with a dash of magenta. Phoenicia was propped up in bed among the gold and gray striped pillows and soft gray blankets. Her face was carefully made up, eyelashes, lipstick and all, and she wore the blonde wig which Carla had used the night before.

"My poor voice is shot. Come sit here, so I won't have to scream."

Carla took a seat by the bed.

"Oh I wish I could have seen you last night," she said. "Ellen said you did me like a regular actress. Weren't you, oh, just a wee bit nervous?"

"One thing bothered me. Those high heels."

Phoenicia gave a little squeal. "You'll have to get used to high heels," she said. "I can just see you in sophisticated dress. I'll send you to my hairdresser for an upswept hairdo. It would be perfect for you, you're just the type. I wouldn't be. Now don't argue. I know he's expensive but he's worth it. You make an appointment and charge it to me. Not another word."

"I'm not arguing, but I certainly must ask a question."

"A question?"

"What's this all about?"

"Of course, of course, I forgot. I didn't tell you. Our secretary quit. Quit cold, all of a sudden. I'm so mad I could spit. I want you to take her place."

"Oh that's it."

Phoenicia began to cough. "Oh dear, my voice is going again." She went on talking in a whisper. "That Francis, he is impossible. Oh he does the drawings well enough, but he won't leave the secretary alone. I'm glad you're a big girl," Phoenicia continued. "And smart and ladylike. He's afraid of big girls unless they're real dumb. As for petite girls—oh dear! Well, I'm glad that's settled," Phoenicia finished.

"But—"

"Things are pretty well caught up at the office, but I have tons of manuscript for you to type, a story for Leonard and the first chapter of my new novel. Give the story directly to Leonard. I don't need to go over it. Here it is."

Carla took the handful of pages. Of course she'd do this, she thought, for "The Lighted Match," to keep Phoenicia contributing.

"And speaking of Leonard, watch out for him, he's not for you nor you for him."

"We're just friends, comrades."

"Keep it that way. His true love's in New York, girl named Tanya, nothing much, but his choice." She paused, then rattled on, "Now be a good girl and run through the story and see if there are any places you can't decipher."

Carla read it quickly, asked a couple of minor questions, then fitted the papers into a big envelope she found on the dresser.

"And here's that first chapter," Phoenicia added.

Carla took that too. She guessed it wouldn't hurt her to do this much typing. Phoenicia sighed happily and settled back against the pillows. She seemed no longer aware of Carla. Her eyes were fixed straight ahead and far away. Suddenly she looked up. "Run along now," she said. "Oh here's the key to the office." She leaned back on the pillows and resumed the faraway look. Carla had neither accepted nor rejected the job.

She went back downstairs and put on her coat, then went into the kitchen. "Miss Attlebury may not be well," she said to Mollie. "She's in some kind of trance."

"Don't worry," said Mollie. "It's nothing but inspiration."

Eventually Carla got the details ironed out, and, oh yes, she was glad to accept. A month later she wrote Abigail. Abigail responded with excited congratulations; she'd always known Carla would advance in the world; she'd never read any of this Miss Attlebury's books; would Carla send her some? Carla never did get around to doing so, for they weren't exactly Abigail's type of reading matter.

Carla soon felt quite at home with Francis. "You're a good fellow," he said one day in the midst of a dissertation on the Attlebree Agency. It was he who clued her in on her duties, and she in turn covered for his derelictions whenever they might have caused Phoenicia to lash him with her sharp tongue.

She was called often to the house, where Mollie readily accepted her as a fellow worker and filled her ears with rather more complaints about the Attleburys than Carla wanted to hear. And she met "Miss Fiddles," a miniature schnauzer, a stocky little gray dog with square head, a beard, and beetling eyebrows.

Although Leonard was not in general a laughing man, he found Carla's story of the interview at which she was hired hilarious. It was the way she told it, he said. Soon they had advanced from lunches together to evenings walking in the park and every Sunday a trip to the beach, sometimes South Boston, once in a while Nantucket, at each of which there was a broad expanse of sand and always too many people. It was their delight, after having staked out a beachhead, to run hand in hand into the foaming surf and out into the breakers. After that the water was somewhat calmer, but still far more turbulent than the rivers and lakes in which Carla had swum in Maine, though it wasn't as rough as the surf which had beat against the rocks that long gone day when she and Howard had stood waiting for Miss Abbott. Why suddenly did she think of that? There they had stood, two frightened children, and wondered how to find their way home. And here she stood, in so many ways very far from home. And Howard? Months had passed since she last heard from him.

Leonard would lead her out to the calmer water, swim ahead of her, but never forgetting her presence, coming back to help if she seemed to need it and also to coach her, for though she was a fairly strong swimmer, she had no style. Under his tutelage she was soon doing a passable Australian crawl, much to their mutual delight. Ah yes, now she was really swimming, as she'd never done before, for now she swam with Leonard in the vast Atlantic, the lake of world civilization, the highway of the nations, swimming with this sophisticated man of the world. She gloried in the turbulence of the surf but was glad now and then to lie upon the broad, sandy beach and rest under the sun, hand in hand with Len. Yes, she called him Len now, and his nickname for her was Joan, which she didn't like because it wasn't deserved and which she let him use only when no one else could hear.

Then one day there came his soft plea, "Come to me, my dear, I ache with longing, come home to me."

She made no coy pretense of not understanding him, and indeed she couldn't for he was quite explicit. She felt no anger at his importuning, but still she said no. "It simply wouldn't be right," she said.

"There's no right or wrong involved," he assured her. "It would mean so much to me. Don't you know how hard it is for me to be so close to you, to see your sweet fresh face, your long and lovely legs, your enticing arms?"

"I'd better go and put some clothes on them," she laughed.

"Some day, some day."

"Maybe."

Not maybe but certainly, inevitably, he was sure of that. When he was alone in his room, she was still very much with him. She was wrong about its being wrong. He wouldn't desire her if he hadn't the greatest respect and admiration for her. Not everyone could have done what she had done among the shoe workers, nor even that outrageous stunt of impersonating Phoenicia Attlebury. She was a real activist, no parlor liberal. To be sure, sometimes she had strange ideas, her development was far from complete. But even those strange ideas made talking to her fascinating; there was something quaint and smelling of pine trees about the things she said. It wasn't a lack of intelligence, oh no, far from it. And she had strength, courage. He gloried in her strength and found no contradiction in his feeling of tender protectiveness toward her, for he was both a man and more advanced than she. He sat at a desk in his room, which was as austere as a monastic cell, fixed his eyes on the printed pages he must study, and could think of nothing but Carla.

She was the third woman in his life, some episodes one doesn't count, but he prided himself there'd been very few of those. But there had been these three, three including Carla, because he had no doubt of her love. Yes, old twisted face though he was, there had been these three. He had married, while still very young, the daughter of a business associate of his father. She, poor bourgeois soul, had packed her bags and departed when he made the decision to abandon his career as an economist and devote his talents to the world revolution. She was not up to that. Warm, lovable Edith, she was not up to that. After the divorce he had lost track of her.

Then there had been Tanya. What sweet music they had made! He was sure she would have left him had he abandoned the revolution, yet she had drawn back from full commitment. Although they did meet for their moments of love, she had insisted that there would be no setting up housekeeping together without a proper wedding, the works, even the canopy, the rabbi and a fancy reception. She was an only daughter, and she owed this much to her parents. He sighed. It would not have done. Her clinging to hypocritical ceremony proved that she was not radical enough. Soon she would have been making other demands, and she would slowly have turned from comrade to wife, probably nagging wife for she hadn't the slightest bit of tact. They always found excuses, women did, "you must do it because my parents expect it," or "for the children," or for some other woman's reason. To free himself from her, he had engaged in an affair, rather sordid, which had meant nothing, hardly even physical gratification. She had been unable to forgive him that affair, which, stupid child, she did not understand. Then she had fallen for a handsome face, or was that just her way of rousing his jealousy? He saw her infrequently, and when he did, the old magic had evaporated like fog on a sunny day.

Now there was Carla. Oh those lovely long legs, that soft brown hair and rosy country face, an American as he could never be an American. He could never forget his schooldays in Boston and then the school which he had attended in Maybury, Connecticut, where his father had opened a shirt factory. He would never forget the jeers, the parties he was not invited to, the narrow little group he belonged to and outside of which he was always the stranger. New York, where he had fled, was different, but New York was New York. A New Yorker was one thing, an American another. Maybury, of course, was very American; how he hated that stuffy, prejudiced town. And Harvard, the great Harvard, had been no better. Funny that Ellen, though she agreed with him on most things, could never see Maybury the way he did. But then Ellen would be popular anywhere.

He relived the night when he had first seen Carla. He saw her as she entered the apartment that cold winter night, tall and gawky and alive as electricity. He had never failed from that day on to thrill to her presence, but Leonard prided himself on being a rational person. Would it do, he asked himself many times. His appreciation of Carla's capabilities had doubled the night when Carla had stepped forth and impersonated Phoenicia. The girl had nerve and initiative and stage presence. Together what couldn't they do! And how passionate had been her embrace that night! How quickly she'd fallen in with Phoenicia and made herself invaluable to that somewhat flighty angel. And how her appearance had improved under Phoenicia's tutelage. Too bad old Attlebury couldn't do something about her own appearance, but of course that was her act. Carla had grown chic, her hair cut short, heels on her shoes giving just the needed voluptuous sway to her walk. She'd grown sophisticated, playing him the way she did! He couldn't stand it much longer.

Of course he would have to use finesse. There was the possibility that Carla might want those wedding bells just as Tanya had. She too had a mother, quaint old lady he gathered from Carla's description. Fortunately the mother lived at some distance, and they didn't seem too much attached to each other. And there was a brother, some kind of laborer, he believed, who'd disappeared. There was also some fellow she'd known all her life who was studying somewhere to be an electrical engineer and with whom Carla corresponded. He wasn't sure what relation the fellow was; she referred to him as a foster brother and said he'd saved her as a child from being crippled. Horses involved probably, fellow's parents had a horse farm. Oh well, he seemed no threat, not from a romancing nor yet from a family angle. Any kind of legal tie was out, Leonard resolved, for he would not bear the thought of being bound. Leonard, stern devotee of a highly organized political party whose aim was to impose a no-nonsense control upon the world, Leonard clung tenaciously to his own personal liberty when it came to women. It would have to be his way or not at all.

There was, however, no point agitating himself with these thoughts; he'd better finish the reports upon his desk. On the morrow he had to leave for New York. Reading between the lines of current news and the summons he'd received, he had sensed that this conference was no ordinary meeting. Changes were being made, and indeed, thought Leonard, it was high time. This was no revolutionary phase in world history. This was a time for digging in of heels, seeking allies, protecting the radical party and indeed the very motherland of his beliefs, Russia, from the threat of fascist attack. Maybe next Sunday after he'd returned, he and Carla could go swimming again.

The next Sunday, however, was a raw day, and they spent the afternoon working in the office of "Light."

"You've a tedious bus ride home," said Leonard. "Come to my place and we'll fix a bite to eat and then I'll drive you there."

"Okay," she agreed.

They walked along, skirting the Public Garden, and up a hill past several stately old town houses, down a narrow winding street on which the houses from one to the next grew progressively shabbier, to the red brick building where Leonard lived. Originally built as a commodious apartment house for families, the apartments had been subdivided and were now mainly occupied by bachelors, male and female. Up the stairs they went to the third story, where Leonard unlocked the door and ushered her in. It wasn't what she had expected. She'd thought it would be small, as indeed it was, but she'd expected it to be furnished with a sybaritic luxury, and that it certainly was not. The walls, which were an off-white, were badly in need of painting; the furniture consisted of a daybed at the end, one easy chair, a desk with a chair and in the alcove which served as dining area a battered wooden table with two chairs. The drapes on the single window were of an inexpensive cotton cloth, a shade of blue somewhere between navy and royal, a retiring color, but pleasant. Near the window was a birdcage in which a yellow canary hopped from his perch to his feeding dish where he pecked away at his seed and his cuttlebone. A tier of bookshelves with books in brightly colored jackets decorated one wall. Why, he lives in poverty, thought Carla. Dear dedicated soul!

A kitchen of sorts was revealed behind a bank of louvers and a simple dinner soon prepared. "Tell me about your trip," she said after the frugal meal had been cleared away.

He led her to the bed, pulled pillows in place to form a bolster in back of them. He sat there in silence for several minutes, then got up, turned off the overhead light, and swiveled the shade on the gooseneck lamp so that the room was dimly lit. Again he sat beside her, his arm around her shoulder, and she repeated her request that he tell about his trip. The bird began to chirp, and Leonard noted that he had angled the lamp so that the light fell directly on the cage. He went to the desk and turned the light toward the wall, then approached the bird and shaking an admonishing finger said gently, "Behave small self, do you hear? Behave small self," then threw a dark cloth over the cage.

When he sat down beside Carla, he pulled her to him and kissed her passionately as he had that night. She trembled but did not draw away. Indeed it was he who at last moved away, sat bolt upright so that he might release with words some of the emotion that had boiled within him ever since that meeting with the higher echelon of the Party. "Joan, my dearest," he said, "I feel as if I'd been combed and curried and seared and basted. Nothing I'd ever done was right."

Encouraged by what were the merest throat clearings, Leonard talked on and on. "Everything I've ever done in my life was thrown at me. The fact that I'd said we have to stop being so sectarian was cited as a monstrous deviation, and all the time they were saying just what I'd already said. But it wasn't right for me to see it first."

"How do they have this terrible power over you?"

"They're bigwigs. At least they think they are. No, it's more than that, they've been certified. And they do have the power. The assignments I ask for will never be granted. No, I have to be exiled here away from the center of things."

It was strange to Carla to hear of Boston as exile from the center of things. Boston with its museums, library, symphony, theaters, concerts on the Charles River, Harvard, and MIT. Boston with its history.

He was intensely serious. "If they'd sent me to the mines of Appalachia or the giant farms of California or even the factories of Detroit, that I'd have accepted like a disciplined comrade. But to be sent back to Boston. What I really wanted was to be placed in some government office in Washington. I have the training for that, I have the ability. Now's the time to get into the New Deal agencies and use that as a stepping-stone to the old line departments—State, Defense, Justice."

"A communist in government agencies?"

"Of course. In a place where I could work up to being an influence. Others are being sent who aren't half as capable. Of course when they told me no, I acted in a disciplined manner, but it was disheartening to be called unreliable just because I made the request."

"I would have missed you."

"I'd have taken you with me."

She held her breath and waited, but he did not pursue that path.

"They've got an idiot I used to go to school with acting as a secret agent, and he can't even pass a note without being caught. And a fellow who's little better than a con man. They wouldn't even consider me for that kind of work."

"Wouldn't that sort of thing be dangerous?" Also wrong, she thought, but she suppressed that judgment.

"A communist is always on the edge of danger, walks the precipice, is under the threat of death. The individual does not matter."

"Why Len, I do believe you have a martyr complex."

"What I have is dedication and some knowledge of the high stakes. The communists shall rule the earth and if there be other inhabited planets, the universe."

His body had tensed and Carla glanced uneasily at him. It was magnificent, this talk of power here in this shabby room, but it was frightening too. He was incurably unrealistic. She felt ever so much wiser than he, and she longed to comfort his inner pain. "I guess the task now," she said, "is to keep up our work against fascism."

"I accepted that, I told you, but it's hard to accept the reprimands. About everything, big things about seeking allies, and even niggling things like how I dress."

"How you dress? You always look so smart."

"Yes, and this season smart is in. Everybody is being told to get out of those scruffy leather jackets and into suits, but I'm jumped on for already having done it. Oh the snide remarks! They know that my father is in the garment industry and gets me whatever I need for practically nothing. They know even that that fur coat of Tanya's—yes, they even threw that up at me. They know a furrier friend made it for me." He broke off abruptly. "You knew, I suppose, about Tanya and me?"

"I'd guessed."

"It's over, believe me. Even before I saw you. You do believe that?"

"Yes, Leonard, I believe it." She sat quietly beside him, waiting.

"For the underground work they have to have the aristocrats of New England, supposedly enemies of the working class, but actually defectors from their own class. How can they be trustworthy? But maybe they are. It's bred into them, that and their coldness."

"Are you sure they're cold?"

"Of course. But you're not. That's what's so wonderful about you. Oh my darling." He kissed her once again, but the devil within him had not been exorcised. "They reprimand me for paying too much attention to clothes, and then they go ahead and give me fashion advice. They want me to be tweedy, me tweedy! Complete with pipe, I suppose. I'd be ridiculous."

Poor dear, she thought and she ran her fingers through his crisp, wavy hair, and caressed the twisted face and longed to comfort him, and he knew that she was yielding at last. He held her close, but his mind was elsewhere. It would have to wait. "Come Carla," he said, "it's time for me to drive you home."

She knew as well as he, that having bared to her his soul, he must now take time to recover.

TWENTY

Carla spent Labor Day helping Leonard at Mobilization headquarters. Later they went to his apartment, and that night no anger haunted him, and he gave full expression to his passion, and she to hers. There was in her heart only the tiniest residual guilt and a regret that they could not shout their love from the housetop.

The fall air, even in the city, was like the perfume of all the harvests that ever were, and one had only to breathe deeply to be filled with strength. Carla was conscious of the energy which welled up within her like the water rising from the spring on the old farm. She took stairs at a gallop, devoured sidewalks in long strides, typed page after page in nothing flat, did her bookkeeping with swift, unerring hand. She went gracefully from Mobilization to "Light"; from there to Leonard's arms; from the advertising office to the big house in Brookline. At the big house she moved from the demanding instructions of Phoenicia to the confidential moments with Mollie Jackson, at ease with both. She was also on fraternal terms with Francis, who considered her a jolly good fellow. She was in the kitchen with Mollie one day in November when Francis came in and sat at the table, gazing thoughtfully at Mollie as if he intended to make a sketch of her.

Mollie hardly noticed him but continued her story. "My husband been home since April," she said. "But now he's gone with the wild geese."

"Where did he go?"

"I don't know, I never do. Actually he left long before the geese. But what do I know of geese?" She sighed. "Though we used to have 'em."

There came an insistent call from Phoenicia's study. "Gracious," cried Mollie. "I better serve Miss Phoenicia her tea before she has a fit."

"Did you notice?" asked Francis when Mollie had gone.

"Notice what?"

"That girl is pregnant."

"Oh no. She's maybe put on weight."

❧❧

A few weeks later Carla sat in the kitchen over her coffee, and Mollie was busy with the ironing, singing softly, "He's got the whole wide world in his hands." When she came to the words, "He's got the itty-bitty baby in his hands," the tears began to roll down her broad brown cheeks.

"Mollie," said Carla gently, "why do you cry?"

Mollie came and sat at the table, facing Carla. "The poor itty-bitty baby! How'll I take care of him, oh how?"

So Francis was right. "Perhaps Miss Phoenicia—"

"Don't you say nothing to her. She'll fire me, sure as preaching."

"What do you plan to do?"

"Work as long as I can. Maybe nobody'll notice. Promise you won't say nothing to Miss Phoenicia?"

"If you don't want."

The next day when Francis was busy at his drawing board, Carla came and stood beside him. "You were right about Mollie," she said.

"Didn't doubt it."

"It's terrible."

"Don't see why."

"Don't you realize she hasn't anything to live on except what she earns at your sister's?"

"Hadn't thought about it. Know very little about her except she's a rattling good cook, within the limits Phoenicia sets for her, that is."

"She's scared of being fired."

"Phoenicia just might." He lay down his pencil and looked gravely at Carla. "Say, old girl, she ought not, you know."

"Could you talk to her?"

"What good would that do? You're sure Mollie has no other income?"

"Positive."

"Devil of a fix! How long would she have to be gone when her time comes?"

"If Phoenicia doesn't fire her as soon as she knows, she could work pretty close to her confinement and when the baby comes, take maybe a month off and come back, if she could bring the baby to nurse. Or would let her mother give it a bottle. To which, by the way, Mollie objects."

"Mmm. Seems you've been giving some thought to it."

"I have."

"Phoenicia isn't going to want to fend for herself for a couple of months. I don't mind. I can always eat at a restaurant and take my clothes to the laundry. But Phoenicia for one so flighty is set in her ways."

"Isn't there some way we could fill in for her?"

"I say, do you mean things like cooking and cleaning?"

"I do indeed. I can get away from my volunteer job, let things slide a little here."

Francis was coming alive, his eyes were clearer, his face less flabby. "I say, old girl," he cried. "Let's do it. I can cook, I mean you take a book and follow it, don't you?"

Carla laughed. "We'll do it," she agreed. "Now to manage Phoenicia."

"Call in that Leonard fellow of yours if need be," suggested Francis.

The weeks rolled on, and it wasn't until shortly before Christmas that Phoenicia became aware of Mollie's condition. "Oh dear," she wailed as she sat down in the gold and gray bedroom to discuss it with Carla. "What shall I do? My writing is just flowing."

"It isn't for several months," Carla said soothingly. "We'll manage somehow. Francis and I will see to it."

"We could hire a temporary while she's gone." Phoenicia suggested.

"Will you pay Mollie's wages for that period?"

"I really can't. Don't think me hard-hearted, Carla, but there's a cash flow problem."

"She'll need those wages."

"Why must you always talk about money? Oh dear, there's the doorbell. Do go down like a dear and talk to him while I put some finishing touches to my face."

"Mollie's there."

"I know, I know. But you must engage him in conversation; it'll take me at least fifteen minutes."

Carla went down to the big drawing room where Mollie had seated the guest, and there in the softest of velvet chairs near the blazing fire sat an old acquaintance.

"Professor Zero!" she cried.

He leaped to his feet, a cautioning finger on his lips, and quickly went to close the door. "I must beg of you, not that name. Mr. Emil Korvanen, Literary Agent, at your service. Miss Attlebury is expecting me."

"What are you doing here? Is it some kind of a swindle?"

"My, you are direct! Once I did you a favor; now I must ask you to do one for me, really nothing, just a little discretion. Let us say that you and I meet today for the first time."

"Miss Attlebury has also done me favors. Why should I be evasive with her?"

"I swear to you that I do not have designs on her money. I place her books and receive the usual fee."

"That's nice, but no reason for me to conceal our past acquaintance."

"But there is a reason. I've been told you are discreet and fully committed to our cause?"

She neither denied nor assented.

"Because of my appearance and manners I have been entrusted with a most important role. I float among certain important personages whose identity has to be protected, and I carry messages. Need I be more specific? How can I impress on you how essential it is that you be discreet about my past?"

"In plain English, you're a spy." Espionage was something she had no desire to be involved in.

"Not that word, not that word, but well yes. Now do you see the need for discretion?"

"Miss Attlebury would be fascinated."

"Yes, and go babbling all over town about it."

"Do sit down again, Mr. Korvanen," Carla said at last. "I have to think about this."

"Good girl," he approved. "You do understand. I have great hopes for Phoenicia Attlebury. With the right kind of agent, the right kind of promotion I see an ever-expanding sale of her books, I see movie contracts. In short I see money, scads of it, for her, that is. And fame. She likes that too."

"She's already fairly successful, you know."

"Ah yes, my dear, but she is going to be a fantastic celebrity."

"I'd hate to see her taken advantage of."

"How can I convince you? Let me unveil for you my background. I am the son of Jan Korvanen. You may have heard the name?"

"I don't recall."

"He was one of the founders of the American Communist Movement. Dead alas for many years." He looked so solemn that Carla inwardly applauded his histrionic ability.

"Get to the point," she pressed, "why the hush-hush?"

"You don't suppose she knows anything about my history? And there's much you don't know, my dear. Is it so impossible for me to be working for a cause, not out chasing the dollar? I've been a literary agent for a couple of years now. Although I have other income, I need the cover. Not that I'm not a good, aggressive literary agent. Considering what I have to work with, I've done very well for Phoenicia Attlebury. And it's just the beginning."

"And you, what will you get?"

"Ah my dear, just what I said. Believe me, through her I've already met important people essential to my mission and have my eye on others."

"In high places?"

"You'd be surprised." He gave her a broad wink, and at that moment Phoenicia, handsome in a softly flowing dress of palest gold, made her entrance. He leaped to his feet, agile as a dancing master and had soon enveloped her extended hand in his own two palms, telling her how he had looked forward to this pleasure. In the days which followed they saw much of Mr. Emil Korvanen.

"One thing about it," Mollie commented during one of their kitchen chats, "that Mr. Emil do perk up Miss Phoenicia's spirits."

When Carla confided to Leonard her fears that Emil K., previously Professor Zero, might be a con man, Leonard replied that Emil was thoroughly reliable and not to worry her pretty head.

"But why can't he be open with Phoenicia? If he could tell me—"

"You had him in a corner, and even then it may not have been wise. Frankly if I were choosing an undercover agent, I wouldn't pick him. However, I suppose he trusts me to see that you keep your mouth shut."

"You seem to know a lot about it."

"Not a great deal, and what I know is top secret."

Carla sighed and changed the subject. "Did I tell you I'd invited my mother to come for Christmas?"

"I shouldn't think a mother would need an invitation to visit."

Carla was silent. How could she explain poor Mama? She'd tried to edge into it by telling the best of her family tradition, the freedom fighter Grandfather Jensen, only to meet with cynical scoffing. Poor Mama. She'd need an invitation all right and trainfare as well.

"Do you want me to meet her?" Leonard asked.

He paused, but she didn't answer. He continued. "I trust you remember this is the night you're to be introduced to my parents."

❧❧

Later he led her out into the busy street. The snow was falling and mingling with the soot on the sidewalk to form a dirty slush; passersby seemed every one in a hurry. Cars tied up in long lines in Boston's narrow streets, were honking vociferously like angry geese, the sleek black taxis making most noise of all and showing themselves likewise the most adept at easing into the least of openings.

"That's all I need," said Leonard. "To get hung up in traffic. Mom can't stand my being late."

"Will they like me?" Carla asked anxiously.

"Ellen will be there," he reassured her. "And Agnes. My other sister, you know. She's a Trotskyite, but we still speak. As a matter of fact she speaks too much, though Ellen does tone her down a bit."

In a comfortable home in a suburb to the southwest of Boston a not unrelated conversation was in progress. "I hope she likes us," said Henry Engelstein as he struggled with his handsome new tie.

"I hope she doesn't," retorted his wife, giving a final pat to her hair. "I don't know what's with Lennie, getting mixed up with a shiksa."

"What if we like her?"

"How could we?" Esther Engelstein bustled off to oversee the kitchen where her two daughters were at work, for though the Engelsteins had hired help, when it came to the cooking, Esther trusted no one outside the family.

It was already dark when Leonard and Carla arrived. Ellen met them at the door and after the briefest possible introductions hurried Carla off to the privacy of her bedroom.

"I'm so excited," she said softly. "Leonard never brings girlfriends home to visit, I mean, unless it's really serious."

Is Ellen talking about marriage, wondered Carla. What else could she mean? It was strictly a family dinner, the immediate family, Mrs. Engelstein's brother Barney, and Carla. It was the most argumentative dinner Carla had ever experienced.

Mrs. Engelstein, a handsome dark-haired woman, big-bosomed and firm of opinion, knew how to maintain an expressive silence, but when she opened her mouth, she commanded instant attention. Her comments were laced with expressions in some foreign tongue, mostly Yiddish, and after translating for Carla's benefit, she would add, "But you could never understand." There was no getting past that "You could never understand."

Leonard's father was of different temperament. He was a man of medium height and extended girth whose soft brown eyes looked out of a jolly round face with paternal benevolence toward everyone. He had come from Russia as a young man and had prospered in America in a moderate way, but he still identified with his native land and had therefore to consider himself a revolutionary. Ah, Russia the beautiful! And with the Czar overthrown yet! He raised his voice to break up an angry argument between Leonard and Barney. Barney was an enthusiastic Zionist, and Leonard could not abide such reactionary nonsense. "Barney, Barney," Henry Engelstein said. "We never worried about Zionism when we were boys together. Do you remember the meetings we went to? Do you remember Bukharin?"

"Do I remember Bukharin? How could I forget? And Zinoviev and Radek. Oh yes, we knew some big shots, that we did."

Agnes, the older sister, a sharp-featured little woman, leaned forward and cried angrily, "And where, I ask you, is Zinoviev today? Where is he?"

"In prison," said Barney, suddenly calm and thoughtful.

"He's in prison, Trotsky in exile, the victims of the most vicious charges," said Agnes.

"Guilty of the most vicious acts, you mean. Hitler's secret agent." Leonard's tone was cold steel.

"No, no, no," shrieked Agnes. "And what of the millions of peasants starved to death in 1933?"

"There was a famine," cried Leonard.

"Did not Stalin's own wife protest about his abuse of the peasants? Just before she shot herself? The revolution, I say, has been betrayed." Agnes rose like a rider in a saddle, brandishing her fork like a weapon.

"Come, come," said Henry. "Just because we mentioned Bukharin."

"He'll get his too, the right-wing toady!" predicted Agnes, sinking back in her seat and using the fork to stab her meat.

Now even the placid Henry grew angry. Bukharin was the greatest leader of the greatest revolution the world had ever seen. How dare she, little snip, talk so of Bukharin!

"You're blind," retorted Agnes. "Even Stalin hates his guts."

Henry was silent. There was some trouble, yes, Bukharin was in trouble; it had to be cleared up; if only he could go there.

"Bukharin, smukharin," said Barney. "For Jews what matters is to get a national home."

That brand of fat was in the fire again. Esther asserted that they already had a national home, but Carla couldn't tell if she meant the Soviet Union or America.

"What we need is to rise above our rootless cosmopolitanism," Leonard began.

"We're kicked in the teeth," shouted Barney, "kicked in the behind, kicked from pillar to post, and he calls it rootless cosmopolitanism."

Carla sat in amazement. How could they shout so at the dinner table and about things so far away?

"You have to look at it dialectically," said Leonard haughtily.

"Dialectically!" snorted his uncle. "That means cock-eyed."

"Eat yet," said Esther. "The chicken is getting cold. And what I went through to get a good one. Those butchers, such cheats!"

Ellen had sat quietly undisturbed. Now Henry turned to her. "That Lowell of yours," he said. "I'd hoped he'd be here tonight."

Ellen smiled gently at her father. "Oh he would have, but he's working on a case, had to see someone."

"Him and his cases!" snorted Leonard. "Petty bourgeois lawyer, money grubber."

Now Ellen's face flushed, and she answered sharply, "He's a good man, don't speak of him so. Oh he's no revolutionary, but I'm not dedicated or disciplined like you, Leonard. I want money, not money for its own sake, but a comfortable life, a family, a home like Daddy provided us."

"I should hope!" said Esther. "At least this one is in her right mind."

"If she wants her Lowell," said Leonard, "that's what she'll have. Of course, Ellen, you know I'll still love you."

"How he looks down his nose!" said Esther. "You'd think she'd turned Catholic, at least." Then remembering Carla she said, "I hope you're not Catholic?"

"No," said Carla. And then with spirit, "I'm also not Jewish."

Esther sniffed. "That's obvious," she said.

⚜

Without the slightest encouragement from Leonard, Carla began to harbor wedding thoughts more and more, and this gave her mother's projected visit an unusual importance. On the appointed day she stood on the station platform, smelling the coal dust, hearing in the distance the whistle distorted by the surrounding mass of buildings. She edged forward and peered down the narrowing parallel lines of the track until pulled back by a worried old lady.

"He'll see you soon enough," said the old lady. "Better in one piece."

"Oh I'm here to meet my mother," answered Carla.

Just my mother, my poor little mother. Oh she did hope Leonard would like her, not find her ridiculous. There had been a time, she remembered, when this little woman had been her world. How Carla had sobbed when taken away! But coming back had been a thudding letdown. She could have explained, and did in her own mind, that the bonding of parent and child had been disrupted and after two years could not be restored, yet there remained a residual guilt at her coldness toward the mother who so dearly loved her.

The smell of burning coal intensified. The sound of the engine rolling along the steel rails, and then the whoosh of the brakes could be heard even before the train pulled into sight. The engine passed Carla, a couple of cars followed, then the train came to a stop. Thirty feet away a blue-coated conductor placed a stool by the steps of a passenger car. Abigail, dowdy in a brown coat too long for her, and wearing a hat perched in a way that hats weren't perching that season, stepped off the conductor's stool onto the platform. She was as excited as a child and talkative as all get out. For once Carla welcomed her mother's chatter, for she hardly knew what to say to her, what to reveal and what to hide.

That night Carla lay awake trying to plan for the coming week. Mama wanted to go to church, she wanted to see where her daughter worked, she wanted to visit historic buildings, she longed for memorable incidents. As for church Carla hadn't been for ages, she'd be greeted as a stranger, and what would Abigail think of that? And if Abigail went to the office, what would she make of Phoenicia and Francis? And in the evenings, how on earth could Carla take her to her kind of meetings, she wondered. Of course she couldn't. She'd have to plan day by day.

One thing was obligatory, a dinner at the apartment. It was scheduled for Saturday, the day after Abigail's arrival. The purpose was to introduce Leonard. Saturday morning passed quietly, with Abigail sleeping until eleven and then keeping up a steady chatter for an hour and a half. Soon Carla was elbow deep in preparations for dinner. The table was brought from the kitchen into the living room. The setting had been left to Abigail, and she completed that task neatly and with dispatch. No, Carla didn't need any help with the cooking. Abigail took her dismissal with an inward sigh but outward good grace. She sat down on the couch and began to thumb through the magazines in the rack. Carla saw that she'd picked up an old copy of "The Lighted Match" and groaned inwardly. There were those not-too-tasteful cartoons drawn by Francis, and Abigail was so old-fashioned. Carla moved over to where she could see the page. The magazine was open to an article, no pictures on the page. Carla moved closer, something about the imperialist Roosevelt. Well, Abigail was a Republican, that was some comfort. Ah good, there was Leonard.

Oh dear, the living room seemed crowded. The straight chairs were clustered around the table, the easy chair had gotten barricaded, and the couch was shoved far into the corner and under a shelf, so that it required great care to avoid bumping one's head, and there sat Mama, her nose in a magazine.

Leonard paused. He'd looked forward to this meeting with considerable curiosity. Somewhere he'd gotten an image of the inhabitants of the backwoods state of Maine as slightly larger than life-size, square-jawed swingers of axes, drivers of horses, iron men on wooden ships. And Carla, certainly taller than most women and with good looks which were handsome rather than pretty, had done nothing to dispel that image. Her mother, no doubt, would be a larger and cruder version of Carla. But there she sat, a round, plump little woman with an old-fashioned hairdo, a lavender dress, gold-rimmed glasses, and her nose stuck in a magazine.

When her attention was gained, Abigail rose hastily, bumped her head, was obviously embarrassed at having bumped her head, recovered, stepped forward to greet her daughter's friend, and in extending her hand reached across the table and upset a waterglass. She very quickly regained her composure while Carla busied herself sopping up the water, covering the wet spot and altogether acting much too uncomfortable.

Leonard and Abigail found places on the couch and sat quietly, each waiting for the other to begin a conversation. After a moment he asked, "Do you mind if I smoke?"

"Oh do, I love the smell of a pipe, but thank you for asking."

"I smoke cigarettes, but only if you don't mind?"

"Not at all."

He must be really ill at ease, thought Carla, to reach for a cigarette so soon, but was it from something that happened before he arrived or was it just meeting her mother? Abigail gave her little time for speculation. "Are you the Mr. Engelstein who edits this magazine?" she asked.

Oh dear, thought Carla, *why didn't I put them out of sight?*

"I must plead guilty," Leonard answered.

"Well, I never," Abigail was off and running. "I never thought I'd meet a real editor here in my daughter's apartment. I'm really thrilled. Not of course that I approve of everything or even most of what's in the magazine. Some of the language!"

"We use strong language because we feel strongly."

"It's not the strength so much," said Abigail reflectively. "It's more the ineptness."

"Ineptness?"

"Yes. Now take this, 'obscene, imperialist Roosevelt.' Obscene in this context has no real meaning. Just small boy name-calling. You should not write that way about our President."

Not bad, thought Carla. But what next? Carla could hardly believe her ears. Her confirmed Republican mother was defending Roosevelt the Democrat against the attacks in the magazine, the attacks made last year and surely not to be repeated under the new orders.

"Some of his policies—" Leonard began.

But Abigail, always prone to interrupt would not hear him out. "I don't care if he is a Democrat," she cried. "He has shown himself to be for the common man including the farmer, even if he doesn't really know how to end the Depression. You have no business to call him the tool of Wall Street. Wall

Street hates him, you should know that. Fair is fair and truth is truth even in politics."

"There's something to what you say," replied Leonard. "That's not a recent issue."

"Last August."

"We now recognize a certain tension between the President and Wall Street. Ask Carla to show you the latest issue."

"And this 'Defend the Soviet Union.'" Abigail continued. "It says Roosevelt is plotting to attack that country. Why he was the first American President to recognize them!"

"You're right, but—"

"Not that I want you to think," Abigail veered onto another tack, "that I am defending his recognition of that godless regime."

Oh, oh, thought Carla, *here we go.* What has gotten into Mama? Abigail, as a matter of fact, had been going to the Megunnaway Library and cramming so as not to disgrace her daughter with her ignorance.

Leonard puffed silently on his cigarette. "Mama," cried Carla, "will you come and taste the goulash? I'm not sure if it's seasoned right."

"Goulash? What do I know about goulash?"

"Come, it's a kind of stew. Please come and taste it."

Reluctantly Abigail rose, and with some difficulty avoiding the furniture, came into the little kitchen. "Strange young man," she whispered.

"Here, taste!"

"Needs more pepper," said Abigail.

The dinner went very well, the food was excellent, the quarters cramped enough to be intimate but not enough to be uncomfortable, and the conversation, thanks to Abigail's chattering, lively. Abigail was amusing in her accounts of the littlest Mills boy, who was quite a pet of hers. But energy flagged, and they finally resorted to the latest in the day's paper. Front page headlines had dealt with a vicious murder. A man had been arrested and would be tried. They were united in being against murder and fortunately did not get onto capital punishment. Carla knew that Abigail was firmly convinced that most, if not all murderers, should be hanged, but Carla had no idea where Leonard stood on that subject.

"Let's have another cup of tea," she hastened to change the subject.

The conversation took a literary turn, and Carla sighed with relief when Abigail began reciting Whitman. Leonard solicitously encouraged Abigail to discuss Whitman and to move on to her favorite Emerson essays.

The evening continued, but the conversation eventually lagged, and it seemed almost breaking up time, when Leonard said, "Mrs. Wingate, did Carla tell you that we've asked her to become Assistant Editor of 'Light'?"

New life welled up, new excitement. "How wonderful!" cried Abigail. "Oh dear, my little Carla an Assistant Editor! Why didn't you tell me?"

"Because I haven't decided to accept. And it's just part-time."

"Carla, you goose," cried Abigail, "how can you hesitate for even half a second?"

"To be a real assistant editor?" Carla looked steadily into Leonard's eyes. "To actually have some say?"

The mobile side of his face twitched as if in pain. "My dear," he said, "you'd better be more specific in your description of your responsibilities."

"Could I have charge of the book reviews?"

"You'd certainly write some."

"That's not the same."

"No, it's no use," he admitted.

"Then I wouldn't have charge of that section?" Carla tried to pin him down.

"Well—"

"Would I select the poems?"

"Poems can be dynamite," Leonard hesitated.

Deliberately Carla poured tea for everyone, and finally she said, "If you don't mind, I'll just do the typing."

The insistence that she accept was loud. Both Abigail and Leonard made their pleas. Great opportunity, recognition, name on masthead, surely, surely, surely. Carla remained quietly firm.

The party came to an end, and Leonard rose to leave.

He settled his overcoat on his shoulders, shook hands with Abigail, then turned and kissed Carla on the cheek.

The minute the door was closed Abigail faced her daughter with the question, "Just what is that young man to you?"

Carla blushed. "Mama, I don't know, I honestly don't."

So it's reached that stage, thought Abigail. And is stuck there. No good will come of it.

The days of that week passed with Carla working and Abigail taking walks, visiting historic sites, and eagerly awaiting her daughter's return each day as the darkness crept in. They went to a movie one night, and Carla remembered how she and Ray had so often done the same. The main feature was about a priest in the slums, a good and witty man, and to Abigail at least as real as life. The second picture was about baseball, a subject of no interest to Abigail, but they sat through it. Baseball, thought Carla, Ray had loved baseball. How he used to listen to it on the radio! She'd heard no baseball, no football, no basketball, no hockey since his death. She missed it. She'd never thought she would.

Baseball reminded Abigail not so much of Ray as of Howard. "Why doesn't he write?" she asked Carla.

"He will in good time, Mama," said Carla. "You know how he is."

On Friday Carla took her mother to the downtown shopping district. Abigail was fascinated by the crowds of people and the lovely dresses in the display windows. Frightened at first by each automobile which approached, she was soon doing as others did, and when the sidewalk grew crowded, marched boldly along in the street, challenging the automobiles' right of way and only retreating to the sidewalk when the crowd thinned. But much as she admired the clothes in the windows, she never suggested going in. "With such fine stores," she said to Carla, "no wonder you're so stylish."

Next Christmas, thought Carla, *I'll buy her something expensive, something with class. I'll save and save for it.* Abigail was talking away, now about all the mittens she'd knitted. "If you have old sweaters," she said, "send them to me. Mrs. Mittens must have yarn, you know." She seemed proud of this Megunnaway nickname.

They visited the library and the Museum of Fine Arts, which Abigail found sufficiently impressive. They didn't get to church, Carla having found transparent excuses on the first Sunday, and as for the second, Abigail's train was leaving at nine in the morning. As they stood in the station, Abigail hushed Carla's apologies for the lack of church; she understood the time schedule and she had church at home. But Fanueil Hall, that she'd counted on, and they hadn't seen the Old North Church or the Old South Church.

"Next time," said Carla.

"Do you ever hear from that friend of yours, the one Howard wrote about. Dear, dear what's his name?"

"Friend? Howard wrote about?"

"Yes, yes, Howard met him when the shoe workers had that strike."

"Oh, you mean Roger Thorfinnson. Why yes, he's studying electrical engineering at Purdue. We write, well, once in a while."

"Howard said he's a good man. Said he's in love with you."

"I certainly agree he's a good man, a very good man."

"Howard said nothing will come of it because you're too highfalutin.

"Howard's mistaken, Roger's not in love with me."

The conductor came striding down the platform shouting, "All aboard, train for Newburyport, Portsmouth, and Portland. All aaboord!"

Abigail hung on for that last minute. "I'm worried about that magazine, those politics."

"We used to be too far out, but no longer."

"And that Leonard. No good will come of that."

"Are you against him because he's a Jew?"

"How can you say such a thing! Carla, our Lord was a Jew."

"Forgive me, Mama. Leonard's a good friend to me."

"He's more or he's less."

"Come, the train will be leaving."

Abigail hesitated. *I'm sure Carla is having an affair with that man. Yes, that is the word—affair. If I admonish her, she'll be forever estranged. How can I call her to her senses? I am caught between the devil and the deep blue sea. Lord, teach me to swim.*

"All abooaard!" the conductor was becoming impatient. Abigail let him hustle her up the steps. She turned and with trembling voice she cried, "Oh Carla, come home! Carla, come home!"

Carla sighed and thought, *I cannot return to a lost innocence. The only home I've ever known was the farm.*

"Good-bye, Mama," she cried. "Good-bye."

TWENTY-ONE

Carla, of course, did not go home to Megunnaway, not in body nor in spirit, nor yet was she fully at home in the life she led in Boston. *He's too much on my mind,* she scolded herself as she hurried along the snowy walk and in the front door of the Attlebury house, wondering if he'd be there to greet her. Phoenicia and Emil sat at the table while Mollie, heavy with child, padded about the kitchen. How homey it was, that big old kitchen with its billowing yellow and whiteed check curtains. A fire burned, small and decorative, in the old fireplace, before which sat Francis in a low chair, toasting his feet and puffing placidly at his pipe. The aroma of coffee and cinnamon rolls drew Carla at once to the table. She glanced at Emil and at Phoenicia. What, she wondered, does Phoenicia expect? Emil, she assumed, was following the main chance along with a little espionage. But he might decide his best bet was to settle in here and play his role of Phoenicia's knight for years or even decades.

"Leonard's late," said Phoenicia.

Carla glanced at her watch but said nothing, not wanting to betray the ridiculous trend of her daydreams. What if she and Leonard had a home like this and their own fire and at day's end shared bread and peace? What if it were she padding about heavy with child? She took a deep drink of the coffee. *Wake up,* she thought. *We'd never have a home like this.* But what did that matter? They would never be able to endure demeaning poverty such as she had known, but voluntary poverty as they labored at their mission was quite another matter. They'd have to fit the baby in somehow. She drained her cup. What nonsense!

"While we're waiting, come to my study, Emil," said Phoenicia.

"Does that man live here?" asked Carla.

"No, but he might as well," answered Mollie. "Sure makes himself at home."

Francis meantime had sat gazing at the coals. He laid his pipe aside, glanced up and said, "It does her good. Don't be stuffy about it."

Carla joined Phoenicia and Emil in the study. She was at her desk, he roaming about examining the books on the shelves. Carla took her place at the typewriter where a pile of yellow handwritten pages awaited her. Her hands played swiftly over the keys.

"I started this as a proletarian novel," said Phoenicia. "As a matter of fact I got much of the background from Carla, pumped her dry I do believe."

Decent of her to mention it, thought Carla.

"Ah yes, Nicia," said Emil. "Now give me a rundown on the plot."

"First there's a lot about the hard work and the poor pay. That's already done. And the heroine, because she's beautiful and clever and a somewhat talented artist, painter, I mean, attracts the attention of the boss."

"Yes, yes, go on."

"After some obstacles she marries him. There's a union trying to better the conditions of the workers, and he's against it, I mean dead set against it. She remains true to her working class origins, but there I'm stuck. I thought she might leave him and he'd, well what would he do?"

"Good question. Find another wife, I suppose in the real world, but that wouldn't please the publishers I had in mind."

"I'd thought they might quarrel, a really deadly quarrel. He could attempt to use police brutality to stamp out the rising tide of working class solidarity. But I don't know? Should I really have her kill him?"

"Mmm. Maybe that's coming down a bit hard on the class struggle aspect. Would have been fine a couple of years ago. In today's climate, I don't know."

"Perhaps he could see the light, become a benevolent employer, sign a union contact."

"What would make him see the light?"

"Maybe a trip to Europe, to the Soviet Union."

"Has possibilities," said Emil thoughtfully.

"But I don't know anything about the Soviet Union, I mean local feel, that sort of thing."

"What difference would that make?"

"Sincere descriptions are always effective. Maybe I could have him get acquainted with the union organizer. Maybe a visit to a worker's home."

"Not convincing. And besides there you'd have full-blown class collaboration with your heroine disgustingly subservient."

"You're right. I hadn't thought of that."

"Better have her kill him. Make him some kind of a fascist, a Nazi sympathizer. Does he have a German name?"

"Isn't that too violent, verging on the melodramatic?"

"Perfectly natural sequence of cause and effect. Serve him right. He's only a money grubber. Let her kill him and use his fortune to further her own dream."

"It's out of character. She's not a killer type."

"Does she have to come out on top?"

"Of course."

"Let me think about it."

They were startled by a scream from the kitchen, and Carla jumped up at once. Emil was about to follow her, but Phoenicia's wail, "Oh dear, I just can't work, it isn't flowing. Don't leave me, please don't," kept him at her side.

In the kitchen Carla found Mollie sitting at the table, holding her swollen body with both hands while Francis hovered over her with a cup of coffee which he insisted she drink. Mollie motioned him away. "Just let me rest," she said. "I'll be alright in a minute."

"Carla," cried Francis, "tell her to drink the coffee, there's a dear."

Carla sat down beside Mollie, took her hand, and said gently, "What is it, Mollie? Have the pains started?"

Hanging her head so that her face was half hidden, Mollie nodded. "I am afraid they have."

"Call her doctor," said Francis.

Mollie gave a muted laugh. "What doctor?" she said.

Carla turned to Francis with an appeal in her eyes.

"You watch out for her," cried Francis, excited as Carla had never seen him before. "I'll make some phone calls. What doctor! We'll see about that" And he hurried into the hall to the phone.

After a while he came back and asked, "How frequent are her pains? The doctor wants to know."

They spent the next hour in great perturbation, Mollie refusing to sit still, convinced that she must get on with her cooking, Francis still certain that the occasion called for her to drink the coffee, and Carla insisting that Mollie must walk about with a good vigorous stride. Emil came in once, then hurried back to Phoenicia. At Carla's urging, Mollie managed to time the onset of the sharp contracting pains. Every twenty minutes. Oh, thought Carla breathlessly. This is it. Oh the wonder of new life and the wonder that Mollie felt no fear. Emil came in to report that Phoenicia, who'd been informed, was in hysterics; they'd better manage without her, he'd take care of her. Back to the phone lumbered Francis and soon returned with the announcement that Mollie was to go to the hospital.

"How'll I pay?" she wailed. "And how'm I to get there?"

"Come, woman," said Francis. "Put on that hat and coat and get in my car!"

"But I've so much to do. Look at the dough all rolled out!"

"It won't be improved by you having a baby in the midst of it!"

Another sharp contraction wrung a cry of pain from Mollie. "I give up," she said. "Help me!"

Francis helped her into her hat and coat and tried to lead her out, but she hadn't completely given up. When Carla announced she'd go too, Mollie was adamant. "No, you stay here and finish them little cakes, got to have them for tomorrow. You promised when my time came you'd—Lordy, Carla, I can't lose this job, not now."

"You don't think?" Carla began.

"Who knows?" said Francis. "Carla, would you mind doing just what she asked?"

Leaving Carla to cook or not to cook as she might see fit, Francis piloted his handsome Buick through the streets he knew so well. It wasn't right that this woman should have had to come to work, that she should fear for her pitiful job, that he and not her husband should be taking her to the hospital. Something wrong somewhere, but Francis wasn't sure what. For one thing, his sister should take some of the compassion she had for the world at large and pour it on the troubles right under her nose. The husband should not have disappeared, or if he had to disappear, perhaps he should have stayed disappeared. But Mollie wouldn't like that, no way would she like that. Something wrong somewhere. He kept glancing at the woman's face and saw upon it a kind of peace. *Good heavens,* he thought, *she's relying on me!* He pulled in at the emergency entrance of the hospital and helped Mollie out of the car. A couple of nurses came rushing with a wheelchair and whirled Mollie away. A third nurse, in a hurry to clear the entrance, pointed out the appropriate parking lot, then gave detailed instructions for finding the waiting room for the obstetrical ward.

If Francis had been his normal self, he would have thanked her with an added graciousness for she was young and pretty, and then he would have gotten in his car and, having accomplished his mission, driven about his own business. But he had in that brief passage at the hospital been taken charge of, and without volition he followed the young lady's instructions, drove through the snow to the parking place, sloshed back, went through the emergency entrance, walked down the white corridor, took the elevator as he had been told, got out on the second floor, and walked down another long corridor to the designated waiting room. It was rather small, furnished with a dozen chairs, both hard and cushioned, and a big coffee table covered with stale magazines. The prevailing color was buff with an occasional touch of green. A half dozen men were there, a couple smoking. A young man, surely not more than twenty, sat with his eyes, if not his attention, riveted on a magazine which he clutched as if it were living and might escape. A middle-aged fellow in painter's overalls was turning over the magazines on the table and scowling. He sighed. Seeing Francis standing there rotating his hat in his hands and looking quite bewildered, he said, "Your first?"

Francis, hemmed and hawed, shook his head vigorously and hurried out the door.

"Awful nervous chap," said the man in overalls, "considering it's not his first," and went back to searching among the magazines.

The encounter had startled Francis back into control of himself. The whole thing was utterly ridiculous: it was utterly ridiculous that he should have been the one to take Mollie to the hospital; it was utterly ridiculous that they were planning that bash for tomorrow night, that Emil had spent the previous night at their house and then had tried to convince everyone that he'd been in the room everyone knew he hadn't been in. He ought to go to the office, thought Francis, but he had an idea buzzing in his brain, an idea in pictorial form, since that was the natural form for his finest ideas. He drove back to the big house in Brookline. Phoenicia and Emil were in the kitchen, diddling around the stove, and she was giggling. Carla was rolling out some kind of dough. He hoped she knew what she was doing. He hung his hat and coat in the hall and hurried to his easel which stood in the living room. He sat down and began to draw. At last he showed it to Carla, a sad and lovely portrait of Mollie, a mother Mollie cuddling a little brown baby, and in her face he'd caught both love and worry, while the babe lay peaceful and unconcerned in the mother's arms.

"Why Francis," said Carla. "I've never seen you do anything so fine."

"I thought you liked my other stuff."

"Oh, oh, I didn't mean it that way. But this! She'll love it."

"She'll love it? Oh yes, of course."

"You did mean it for a present?"

"If you say so. I thought people gave little shirts and bootees on such an occasion."

"If they can't do any better."

Leonard came in, kicking the snow off in the hallway, then going at once to look for Carla. She stood admiring the mother and child on the easel. He put his arm around her and then saw the drawing. "Why Francis!" he cried. "You captured it, the feel, motherhood. What do you know!"

They spent the evening preparing for the following day, for there were to be big doings, a tremendous party for Mobilization, a high-class party with name people for both entertainers and guests. The big front room, which looked rather like a vacant warehouse, had to be turned into a festive ballroom. Cakes and cookies had to be finished, a last minute order phoned to the caterer, the bedrooms tidied, Fiddles brushed, the kitchen floor washed. But Francis rebelled at the mention of sweeping the snow off the big front porch.

"I'll do that tomorrow," he panted. "Now I have to make a phone call."

The others continued arranging the plants which were to mark off a little area for the musicians. Phoenicia stood in the doorway, eager to overhear Francis on the hall phone but not wanting her eavesdropping to be obvious. "Oh, it's lovely," she cried. The predominant colors were green and gold, appropriate for mid-March, fresh green with glistening gold.

"Now for the buffet tables in the dining room," said Emil.

"It's come already!" cried Francis. "Oh I want to get drunk! It's come already, the baby, a boy, shortest labor ever." He dashed over to his easel on which the drawing stood. "The baby's here!" he shouted at the picture. "It's here!"

Phoenicia and Emil exchanged amused grimaces. But Leonard went over and stood silently by the side of the big, flabby, sentimental man. "The miracle of miracles," he said. "I'll take Carla home now. The work can wait till tomorrow."

Sitting close to Leonard in the car, driving through the snowy streets, Carla found herself talking about the baby. "You know, Leonard," she said, "it could happen to us too."

"We take precautions."

"I know, but I wonder, shouldn't perhaps, shouldn't we go back to being just friends?"

"You talk nonsense. Or is it that you no longer love me?"

"Oh Len, how could you think that?"

Inside her apartment and alone, Carla glanced at the kitchen table and saw there an accumulation of the week's mail. Hastily she looked through it. There was a letter from Abigail, a package from Howard with a California address on it. And a letter from Roger. She opened the package first. It was Howard's wooden recorder, neatly packed in a dark blue box. Wrapped around it was a note: "Dear Sis, Please take care of this for me. It might get broke where I'm going. Howard."

Oh no, she thought, what now? Maybe Abigail knew something. But Abigail's letter was full of quite commonplace, newsy items about people who were part of Abigail's life but not of Carla's, and then at the end, a bit of a sermon. "I know you mean well by what you are doing," she wrote, "but don't forget what's paved with good intentions. Love, Mama."

Carla leaned back. Abigail and her proverbs! If the wish is father to the thought and the thought is father to the deed, must not good intentions lead directly away from hell? Philosophical musings! Something to write to Roger about, he'd be bound to have an unusual comment. She hadn't written to him for ages.

❧❧

Roger's letter was brief. "Dear Cousin Carla: I'm coming to Boston. I'll be at your place on the 22nd. God bless, Roger."

The 22nd, next Wednesday. She sat there for an hour, re-reading the letters, fingering the softly colored wood of the recorder, and thinking too of Leonard. She wondered if he was thinking of her. And then back to the letters. "Keep this for me. It might get broken where I'm going." But he'd carried it wrapped in his bedroll from coast to coast, from mission shelter to job to hitchhiking journey, and he'd never worried about it's getting broken. Where on earth was he going? And Roger would be in Boston on Wednesday. There was something restful in the thought of Roger, good old reliable Roger. But why on earth was he coming to Boston? His last letter had mentioned plans to get a job in California. Wednesday? After the Attlebury party. The party would have been such a fine way to introduce him to the grand new life she was leading. He was so frightfully casual; he hadn't said what time, nor how he'd arrive, nor how long he'd stay. Anyway she was glad he was coming. It was high time he and Leonard met.

On the big day Leonard paced through the living room, straightening a plant, picking up a paper from the floor, moving a lamp. The picture which Francis had drawn of the mother Mollie rested on an easel not far from the wide entrance door and Carla stood gazing at it. Leonard came to her side. He hoped her longing, her nesting instinct, was hidden deep in her subconscious. Freudian rubbish. He knew full well it was close to the surface. Ah yes, if only— "If this fundraiser is a success," he said, "this and some other deals, I hope to get a bigger apartment." She glanced shyly at him.

Emil Korvanen came in, straightened his bow tie, and rubbed his hands together in a congratulatory gesture. Yes, everything had been taken care of. He had proven his ability as a manager and gloried in it. He was particularly proud of the musical program: the brilliant pianist; the big bass-baritone capable of that amazing jump from "Ole Man River" to Beethoven's "Ode to Joy"; the Hollywood sex symbol who sang a cutesy pie popular number; and the quartet who played for dancing. They were all big names. Talent without name would have given him no satisfaction. Then there were the celebrities who were not part of the program but would be very much part of the scene.

Later as he piloted one after another from conversation group to conversation group he glowed with pride. There was a Congressman, not too well known outside his own bailiwick but with some promise; a personal friend of the President's wife; a poet of considerable renown and possessed of a craggily handsome face that might have made him a screen favorite had he been so inclined; a middle-aged actress at the height of her career. And Phoenicia's books were enjoying an upsurge in popularity so that she too was a "name." And there was the cause which enhanced the emotional impact, the general horror brought about by the madman Hitler and a shared feeling that something must be done, though less than perfect agreement as to what. There were even genuine refugees from Hitler's Germany, Pearl and Sam Friedman. She was willing to talk while Sam stalked glumly behind her, not a bad combination. Even having Carla come in her character of shoe worker union leader had been a good touch. True at first she'd balked at wearing a dark plaid skirt, plain light blue blouse and flat heel shoes, but she'd capitulated and like the game girl she was, had dug deep into her closet. It gave her some distinction, for the other women were dressed in either evening gowns which reached to the floor or smart, little black nothing dresses which were perfect foals for scintillating jewels. Of course Carla's hairdo was too smart, gently curled, piled high upon her head, every hair in its place. Emil reproached himself for not having done something about that. Furthermore she wasn't promoting herself at all, leaving that to him and to Leonard, who wasn't much help.

Leonard, handsome in black tuxedo, moved easily among the crowd, entering conversations, leaving them, now with Carla, now by himself. He like Emil was impressed by the publicity value of the guests and not indifferent to their money value. In Phoenicia's study copies of an appeal for funds for Mobilization had been left carelessly on the desk and a pile of envelopes near a basket for the convenience of anyone moved to donate. By evening's end the basket was overflowing with envelopes, each with a sizable check. Ah yes, a most gratifying evening. After years of wandering in the wilderness, the communists were at last advancing in a way that a year ago Leonard wouldn't have believed possible.

For Phoenicia the most memorable thing about the party was Emil Korvanen dancing attendance on her, flitting about seeing to arrangements but always coming back to her side to seek her approval, gazing at her with admiration, speaking to her softly and gently with—yes, she would use the word—with love. She was, she knew, looking her very best. She wore a long black taffeta skirt gleaming with golden threads and the blouse was gold lame. Emil had positively vetoed anything with even a hint of green in it. In place of the tousled wig which she usually affected she wore her own hair, softly curled and upswept, in color very much like the gold of the wig but with here and there a strand of silver. Her cheeks were flushed, and her eyes were bright, and when she caught a glimpse of herself in the mirror, she knew that though

her next birthday would be her fiftieth, there still remained a lighthearted love-
liness that would well have become a younger woman.

Francis had a part too. Supplied with blocks of drawing paper and a box
of charcoal he sat at an easel making portrait sketches of whoever was willing
to sit for him. What fascinating faces, he thought. Such diversity, such peculiarities. He knew enough to tone down the peculiarities just the right amount.
He sat there in his tweed jacket, puffing at his pipe, honored and busy
throughout the evening.

In the midst of the glitter of names and jewels, Carla found the one person
she'd really looked forward to seeing, Pearl Friedman, the woman who'd
taught her what Hitlerism was all about. Pearl Friedman, the genuine refugee
from Hitler's Germany, had entered shyly as if not sure she really belonged.
She wore a tailored, dark blue, floor length dress with long sleeves and highcut
round neckline, suitable display for jewels, but she wore no jewels. Happily
she greeted Carla, tried to stop and talk, but was whisked away by Emil
Korvanen. Guided by Emil and flanked by her somber husband, she moved
about with dignity and spoke simply in answer to questions, sometimes at
considerable length, while Sam remained silent. Emil was able to convey the
information to every single guest that here in their midst was an actual refugee
from Hitler, indeed two refugees, the woman in plain blue and the silent man
who walked by her side. A portly middle-aged man, whom Carla knew slightly
as the owner of the building in which Mobilization had its headquarters,
approached Sam and engaged him in conversation. Carla could see the down-
cast expression of Sam's face and went to rescue him.

As she drew near, she heard Sam say with a certain scorn in his tone, "If
you think that way, then you're in dangerous company." Well, at least his
English had come back to him.

"I'd work with Satan," said the man, "to help fight Hitler."

"So I'd noticed," retorted Sam.

The portly man gave him a withering glance and stomped away. Carla,
hoping to divert the landlord's irritation, approached him and received a blast
from his wrath. "That man's a renegade," he said loudly. "A suspicious element." He glanced angrily at Sam, who was standing quietly, looking at the
floor.

Carla might have calmed him, would certainly have tried, not even dis-
daining to turn on the charm, had she not seen at that moment that Pearl
was approaching and had obviously overheard. Leaving the portly gentlemen
to his own devices, Carla hastened to intercept Pearl.

"Pearl!" she cried. "I haven't had a chance to talk to you all evening."

"What's to talk about? I have to get Sam out of here. He didn't want to come, came to protect me. I couldn't tell Leonard I wouldn't come. Sam, a renegade indeed! These parlor Communists, they know nothing."

"Sam did speak rather sharply to him."

"Sam knows this is a communist controlled outfit, meaning no insult to you, and knows them all too well."

"But Sarah and Meyer—"

"I know, I know. We fight with them constantly, or did until we moved. I think Meyer's worse than Sarah. He was on us every minute," Pearl said. "Sam couldn't open his mouth without a string of insults from Meyer. Renegade wasn't the worst, but the most persistent. *That* I heard from dinner to bed, till I thought I'd scream. And I couldn't get Sam to keep his mouth shut."

"Keep his mouth shut?"

"Well you know that Meyer is a communist, thinks he is anyway here in this innocent country. And Sam hates communists! That's putting it bluntly, also mildly."

"Why should he hate communists?" Carla asked.

"One of the men who beat Sam was an old comrade of ours from the communists."

"Then he was a turncoat, a traitor, he'd gone over to the enemy."

"That's what I say, but did you ever try to talk to a man who's been beat over the head?"

"Where do you live now? And how are you doing?"

"We live in Boston. I'll give you the address. I didn't want to work in the shop in Laurel with Sarah, so I got me a job in Boston. I do the work pretty good now."

"And Sam?"

"His English came back to him. He gets occasional jobs in men's clothing stores. Selling, doing alterations, whatever. He needs a steady job."

"Surely some of these people could help, or maybe Phoenicia or Leonard."

"They could, but I'm not stupid enough to think they will. Certainly Leonard won't. I talked to him."

"I'll speak to him."

"Don't. We live, and the boys—Willi is fine and now is called Bill. Max broods too much, but he does well in school. Ah yes, we manage. Now if only I'd hear from Mother." She hesitated, then compulsively repeated the old question. "You remember her picture? She doesn't look like a Jew, does she?"

"I remember well. No, she doesn't."

"Maybe someone hid her. Sometimes my only hope is she died quickly."

"I'll pray for her." Carla promised then suddenly thought, strange words for one who'd forgotten how to pray!

"It will do no good. *You* have no faith."

"I hope to see you again."

"It won't be here or any place like it."

They went to where Sam stood waiting. Pearl hurried him away without giving Carla even a minute in which to talk to him. Indeed he seemed to have no desire to recognize her.

Leonard came over and stood by her side. "Too bad!" he said.

"Yes," said Carla. "They're having a rough time."

"Too bad he turned sour," said Leonard. "The woman might be salvaged still, but he's beyond hope."

Carla felt uncomfortable with his attitude but said nothing. The evening continued: Phoenicia starry-eyed, Emil filled with energy, Leonard pleased in a calm and cynical way, and Carla pouring tea from the graceful silver pot. Emil came over and scolded Carla for letting the Friedmans go. "Why," he said, "they were the guests of honor. They were to speak at our little program." Carla, glad that they'd escaped, smirked and gave him her country kitten look.

The next day, which was Sunday, Carla went to visit Mollie. She lay there in the bed, her dark face outlined against the white pillow. "They's so good to me," she said. "And you're so good to come to visit me."

When she saw the picture which Francis had sent, she burst into tears of joy. "To think Mr. Francis would draw my picture!" she cried. "I'll treasure it all my life. My momma will be so proud. But you must go see my baby Tom. I've named him Tom, after his daddy. You like that name?"

"Tom's a lovely name," Carla said. "Can I go see him now?"

In a minute she was standing in the hall in front of a big glass window behind which twenty or so bassinets cradled as many infants. There was no trouble finding Baby Tom Jackson for he was the only brown baby in the bunch, and he was screaming, his mouth opened wide, his eyes closed, his little hands waving in the air. At Carla's request a nurse picked him up and brought him to the window, and for a moment he quieted, and Carla gazed on the ever-new miracle of life, the delicate cheeks, the tiny head covered with soft brown wool, the perfectly formed hands. Then he started screaming again, so loudly that even through the glass Carla could hear him.

Mollie laughed when Carla told how the baby had screamed. "He's hungry," she said proudly, as if hunger were a great accomplishment.

Carla left not long after, and the last thing Mollie said was, "That baby sure has a lovely appetite."

Leonard came to visit Carla that night. Yes, yes, he was sure Mollie's baby was adorable, glad to hear Mollie was doing well. But there were two other topics on his mind. The fundraiser had been a great success, and he was actually going to receive his nominal salary. "I'll be able to get a bigger apartment," he said and looked intently at Carla.

"Do you need one?" she asked.

"Bigger and better," he said.

What was he leading up to? Apparently nothing much for he went on to upbraid her about her friendliness to Pearl. "I met her through you," she reminded him.

"They've changed."

"I don't care."

"You should. They're reactionary renegades. When will you ever understand?"

Oh dear, these strange political quarrels! She'd have thought he'd have grown out of them. She felt a tenderness for him. He needed her to lead him to a broader view. She kissed him gently and she fed him and she flirted with him and she sang songs with him until in a better mood he drew her to him and kissed her willing lips. At a very late hour he left.

Oh dear, she thought, *I forgot to tell him about Roger.* She rushed to the window, tugged to open it, that she might shout to him as he left the building. She leaned out as he stepped onto the sidewalk. Suddenly she realized the inanity of her position. She couldn't very well stand there bawling into the night that Roger was coming. She gave a low whistle, and he heard and turned his face up to her. Gently she blew him a kiss, and he took off his hat and bowed low to her, then with a quick tapdance routine went round to the driver's seat of his car. The tires squealed as he took off with exhilarated speed. At least she'd made him happy! Roger wouldn't be there till Wednesday. The two men would meet when they would meet. She was silly to think so much about it.

TWENTY-TWO

It had rained, but now the sun shone in golden light upon the trees. Carla approached her apartment house in the late afternoon, and there near the spruce tree was Roger.

"Oh, hi," he greeted her. "I've been waiting an hour, thought you'd never come." He took her outstretched hand, moved close to her, kissed her gently on the forehead.

She looked earnestly at him. He'd grown, not exactly older, but indefinably more mature. They went up to the apartment, he threw his sweater carelessly on the couch, went into the bathroom and washed up, came out into the kitchen, still wiping his face on a bath towel. He'd laid aside his glasses, his heavy eyebrows had been rumpled in the washing, his dark brown hair fell over his forehead. No, thought Carla, he's not handsome but how good he looks. And he was adding her up too. Smart new hairdo, a neatly tailored dress, shoes with heels. Getting to be quite the young lady about town. He went back into the bathroom, combed his hair, smoothed his eyebrows, put on his dark-rimmed glasses and came back to the kitchen whistling gaily. Carla had never seen him in such a happy mood before. And he felt it too. Just one glance at her lovely face, one touch of her hand, and he was filled with joy. He started to sing the words: "You're the purple glow of a summer night in Spain, I forget what's next, you're a symphony by Strauss, you're Mickey Mouse."

He came over to the sink, stood close beside her, continued humming, singing, "mmm, you're the steppes of Russia, you're the pants on a Roxie usher. What's next?"

"Here, put this on the stove."

"After dinner, we'll go to a music store and find—"

"But Roger, I have to work."

"You a union woman, working in the evening?"

"Volunteer work. I promised Leonard. You must come with me."

"Any friend of Carla's," he said lightly, "is a friend of mine."

Facing each other across the table, they were as intimate and at ease as if he *had* been her cousin or, as she sometimes said, foster brother. She told about the place she worked, about Phoenicia and Francis, Mollie and Mollie's baby, Emil who'd once been Professor Zero, about Mobilization which was growing by leaps and bounds and about "Light" which Leonard edited. Roger talked about the university from which he'd be getting his Masters in June, about his flight to Boston, and about the walk in the park he'd indulged in while waiting for her. He hoped she remembered the park they'd gone to? Yes of course she did. And did he remember Howard? Certainly, what was the latest? She got up and brought out Howard's package and note.

"What do you make of this?" she asked. "Where could he be that a wooden recorder wouldn't be safe?"

"Mmm. Doesn't sound too safe for flesh and bones, does it? Let's see the postmark."

"Fresno, California. No address."

Roger was grave, considering the matter. *Thank goodness,* she thought, *he doesn't tell me not to worry.* When at last he spoke, it was of his family. His grandfather had been ill, had recovered, but was failing. "Can't even sit and read," said Roger sadly.

"I remember how kind he was to me. And how he loved his books!"

"I'm just beginning to appreciate what a fine collection he has. I'm an educated man now, my dear. The books are mostly American history, several original documents, a few old manuscripts which have never been published."

"What will you be doing after you get your degree?" she asked.

"I'll find a job somewhere. On the cutting edge, I hope. When I think of the developments taking place in my field! Why, in a few years we'll be sending pictures as routinely as we now broadcast sound, and we'll be developing almost unbelievably concentrated sources of power. A trip to the moon is no longer science fiction, it's a project to be worked on."

"And you still believe in God?"

"Of course. Whether I lift up my eyes to the heavens or I gaze at the microscopic complexities, I see the mark of the Master Designer, the great creator. Oh Carla!" And he found expression in song, "He's got the whole wide world in his hand."

"Mollie sings that!"

"And you, Carla?"

She got up hurriedly to clear the table.

In due time they reached the Mobilization Hall. A half dozen young people, who were gathered around the table at the rear engaged in earnest discussion with Leonard, stopped abruptly and stared at Carla and Roger. Gus, who was one of those at the table, recognized Roger from the strike days and greeted him as a long lost friend. The arrival of Roger and Carla had either coincided with or caused the end of whatever had been going on. Soon everyone except Leonard had left.

"Are you the young man Carla grew up with down in Maine?" asked Leonard.

"Up in Maine," Roger corrected him.

"Whatever. She's told me so much about you. How you saved her from being crippled."

"Well, in a way I suppose, but really—"

"He's always modest about it," interposed Carla. "You know, Roger, when I couldn't run."

"Ah yes."

"I'm glad you two are meeting," said Carla. She went and stood beside Leonard, and he put his arm around her waist. She smiled lovingly at him then reminded him that she'd come to do some typing.

"Yes, yes. Roger, come on into the office."

Roger followed, studying this new complication. Strange face, intense, even on the frozen side. A man of strength and purpose, that was easy to see. And quite possessive toward Carla. Carla had never said anything about being engaged. Until she did, he'd assume she wasn't.

Carla set about typing, her eyes and fingers so well coordinated that she hardly had to think. She could hear an occasional word from the other room, and then there was merely a rumble of voices. Soon they were no longer talking but singing. Roger was still obsessed with the Cole Porter number. She heard him repeat, "You're the purple glow of a summer night in Spain," then stop, but she heard no response from Leonard. In a few minutes it was Leonard who was singing, the song from "Porgy and Bess," "Oh Lawd, I'm on My Way," and Roger was joining in. *Strange,* thought Carla, *I'd have thought that would be Roger's song, I never heard Leonard sing it before.* They both had deep baritone voices. There was a pause in the singing, but just as she was finishing her work they were back at it, this time "I've Got Plenty of Nuthin'." Leonard always sang it with a firmly sounded "g" at the end, "nothing."

By the time she had gathered her papers, placed them on Leonard's desk, and joined the men, they were no longer singing. "I do hope you're not a pacifist," she heard Leonard say.

"Certainly not," retorted Roger. "Though maybe, all things considered, you should wish I were."

"Come the revolution, you'll see that everything I say is true."

"Come the revolution, I'll be hiding out in the hills, and you'll be liquidated."

"That's just redbaiting."

"Love to bait those reds," said Roger.

Thus they met, Roger and Leonard, and it was Roger who wound up taking Carla home.

"Your Leonard has his good points," said Roger as they were seated once more at the kitchen table eating cookies and drinking coffee. "But his politics! Abominable, simplistic, wholly lacking in logic. Which is a fancy way of saying stupid."

"You don't have to look down on him for having different political views."

"We all more or less look down on those with different views. I'm sure he does. He reminds me of the students at the strike. Nice kids, but mostly studying social sciences. If only they'd gone into something useful!"

Carla was aghast that the great Leonard should be compared to those kids. "Leonard is an economist," she said huffily.

Roger snorted. "He would be! But of course he's a jolly good fellow, only so delightfully wrong."

Carla gave up. "You're impossible," she said. "Let's forget about politics."

"Righto. I keep thinking about your brother Howard. I may go out to California this summer and if so, I'll go to Fresno and see if I can pick up a trail."

"Why California?"

"To look for work. That is if I don't get the job I applied for here."

"So that's why you're here. Why didn't you tell me?"

"Why didn't you ask?"

"I don't know. When do you have to leave?"

"Tomorrow morning." He rose and said he guessed he'd better get back to his hotel. Then he held her in his arms, and he kissed her as he might have kissed a sister.

"I have to get that job in Boston," he said and left. *That Leonard*, he thought as he walked along, *is bad news*.

Leonard in the meantime had gone home much impressed and not a little worried. That Roger, blown in by some wind from out of the west, was certainly a ruggedly attractive young man. What exactly was he to Carla? *He's not her stepbrother or foster brother*, thought Leonard, *certainly not her brother, who, I gather, is somehow missing. He's not her cousin, and he apparently isn't even the hero of some dramatic rescue, like pulling her from under a horse's hoofs. What then is he? Too impertinent for one thing, and a threat, even if he's not in love with her, and how do I know he's not? And since she loves him like a brother which he's not, Leonard, my boy, something must be done.* Something drastic. What but marriage? That was a lot of bourgeois nonsense. Marriage was out of the question. Was there no other way? She'd complained a couple of times that they had no real tie, no real commitment, and when he'd said it was enough that each knew what was in his heart, she'd sniffed a huffy little sniff.

The very next Sunday, when after dinner in his apartment he was urging her to spend the night and she was sitting on the couch beside him kicking at the rug like an embarrassed child, he broached his plan. "We neither of us accept the bourgeois state and neither do we accept the pretensions of the clergy, but let us nonetheless be married, let me take you for my wife, dearest Carla. I love you so."

She stared at him in surprise, and the nervous foot no longer abused the rug. Her clear gray eyes grew soft with tears, just one tear in each eye. "Oh, Leonard," she whispered.

"We'll get an apartment, live openly as man and wife."

He drew her to him and enfolded her in his embrace. How dear she was to him, how terrible it would be to lose her! Her arm brushed against the wool of his jacket, her breasts felt the warmth of his body, his lips were on hers with a lover's demanding kisses. Drawing back she looked into his face, into the dark eloquent eyes, at the strange face, so sensitive on one side, so rigid on the other, at the lips now quivering and seeking hers again.

It was much later that night before she realized that while he was being quite literal about getting an apartment, there was no wedding in his plans, not even a sterile justice of the peace marriage. His mother would collapse in grief, her mother would insist on a religious ceremony which was out of the question. Their comrades would accept them as a couple; they were too politically mature to do otherwise. "You're my woman, Carla," he said huskily.

"It's—oh—not right."

"After the way we've been together these many months? Does going home at two in the morning sanctify our love?"

Nothing was settled that night. The next night she lay in her bed and wished that there were a god to whom she could speak. Ray was gone, her married life ended, but the strong urge of life was far from in the grave. It was true that the comrades, once they knew Carla and Leonard were sharing an apartment, would quite readily accept their new and special status. But his family! And Abigail! And her own deepest heart!

Leonard was insistent that they get on with the move. He was swayed by both his desire to tie Carla to him and an appreciation of the practical advantages, shared expenses, a better place than each had separately, a place where they could hold certain small meetings. Through May and June he kept a careful curb on his tongue about the practicalities and spoke eloquently of romantic longing. Not too surprisingly, early in July they went as might any engaged couple to look for an apartment. They bought furniture secondhand, with Leonard earnestly and vocally cursing the capitalist system which denied them the joy of buying expensive new furniture. However, they thoroughly enjoyed making their purchases and took delight in the sturdy design of the chest of drawers, in the lines of an old rocker, in the solidity of the table, and the expanse of the bed. They were full of plans for refinishing the chest and the table, and spent an hour in a hardware store discussing the relative merits of three brands of varnish remover and of substances to be used in refinishing the wood. Linseed oil would require hours of rubbing but would bring out the natural beauty, a lacquer would give a hard brilliant surface, shellac would be easy to work with. In the end they bought the linseed oil. They found themselves worrying about what the apartment manager, a smart youngish man, would think of the odds and ends they were having delivered. They would have to invite him in after it was refinished.

On moving day the young man gave them the keys and disappeared. Tenants were no big deal to him. Carla and Leonard, after a meal at a nearby restaurant where the food wasn't good enough to be memorable and not bad enough to be ridiculous, strolled along the street. It was a moonlit night, and the air was soft with the warmth of summer, and Leonard walked with his arm around her shoulder. Carla was silent. She must write to Mama, but what could she say to her? To Howard if she ever saw him again? To Roger? When they entered the vestibule of their building, she saw a couple of baby buggies. *What are we doing,* thought Carla, *in an apartment house for families?*

Leonard threw his jacket and tie onto a chair and started pacing the floor. "We're going places, Carla," he exulted. "You and I."

"Going places?"

"I'm not always going to be just the editor of a two-bit magazine like 'Light.' There are bigger things in store for me, there have to be."

"Bigger things?"

"The day is coming when the imperialist rulers of America will reign no more, when the racist overlords will no longer ride high and mighty."

"No longer ride high and mighty?"

"The war in Europe draws closer and closer. Out of the war will come vast changes."

"Vast changes?"

He grew impatient. "Don't stand there echoing my words."

"Scuse me. Bathroom, right out."

Alone in the blue and white cubicle, she held fast to the washstand, her head whirling, afraid she would faint. "I hate the revolution," she muttered. Hate it, hate it, hate it."

The door was open but Leonard didn't hear.

✣

Carla's next letter to Abigail was full of news and said nothing. What could it say?

Everyone around the "Light" office treated the momentous event as humdrum, no big deal. Carla had rather expected to be extolled by her comrades for her iconoclastic courage, but the only interest shown was by Phoenicia.

"We need to decide what name you should use," she told Carla at work the next day."Carla Engelstein has an inappropriate dissonance, won't do for a pen name and since you are doing book reviews for 'Light,' you really must have a nom de plume. A good American name would be better than such a Jewish one, not that I care, but we must realize there are prejudices. Really Wingate has a better sound than Putnam."

"But it was Carla Putnam who was the Joan of Arc of the Shoe Workers," Carla countered.

Phoenicia laughed and said, "Nobody remembers that! Besides, perhaps Leonard would rather not have you use the name of a former husband."

Maybe, thought Carla, it wouldn't be fair to Ray to give up Putnam. Carla had a sudden vision of her father berating her, reviling her, even threatening her, not the drunken father nor the man in the fire, but the tall, stern, bearded man who'd insisted on those long black stockings. But he was gone. Mama was one who wouldn't make light of it, that was some consolation; but Mama mustn't be told, it would kill her.

"I'd better get on home," Carla told Phoenicia. "Company coming, have to tidy up."

After dinner Leonard would be using their living room for a special meeting, so special that not even Phoenicia was to be given an inkling of it. Leonard insisted Carla must stay in the kitchen or bedroom. She guessed she could go to the bathroom, she wasn't sure. The guests were four in number, and the first to arrive was Dan McDonough, a middle-aged dark Irishman, well-known as a radical leader in Boston, a carpenter by trade who spent little time in construction these days but liked to represent himself on all occasions as a leader in the Carpenters Union.

The others soon arrived. Carla, still in the kitchen, could see them as they walked through the hall. The first was Sam Morris from New York, whom she'd seen several times before. He was a power in the movement. Following

Sam was a younger man with mischievous elfin face, who was quick to greet Leonard whom he obviously knew, though he was a stranger to Carla. Leonard called him Jack, spoke of not having seen him for some time. The third man looked quickly about, then spoke in a language Carla did not understand. The mischievous young man translated, then hastened to add that Peter understood English, though he wasn't fluent in speaking. Did any of them speak Russian? No? They'd manage.

Carla slithered down the hall into the bedroom. Leonard came and shut the door after her. *My,* she thought, *he's really monitoring me. She could hear only the sound of voices, sometimes a deep rumble, sometimes the excited tenor of McDonough, and on occasion all five men talking at once.*

It was two o'clock in the morning when the four men left. Still awake when Leonard came in to bed, she hazarded a couple of probing questions, but seeing that it only angered him, she stopped.

She went the next evening to "Light" and worked doggedly at her typewriter, still hurt at his lack of trust, keeping her eyes fixed on her work. Even when she heard footsteps she did not look up.

"Carla!" cried a hearty woman voice. "How nice to see you here."

"Tanya!" responded Carla. She sat staring at her old acquaintance. How much she had changed! She'd grown heavier, not fat, just sturdy. And she'd developed an aura of authority. "Tanya! Did you drop from the sky?" she asked.

"I came by train," was Tanya's matter-of-fact answer. "I'm an organizer for the Shoe Workers Union in Missouri. I wanted to get into basic industry, but being a woman, I got stuck with Shoe."

"Sort of basic."

"Next thing to it. Things have been humming. I'm doing an article for 'Light,' did you know? I have to talk to Leonard about it."

"He'll be in soon. How long are you staying?"

"I don't know. I'll have to see Leonard first." Her expression softened. "Tell me, Carla, how is he?"

"Oh he's, he's wonderful." She blushed. "He and I are well, sort of married, did you know?"

"Let me wish you all the best."

"You're not angry?"

"Don't be insulting. We'd broken up long before you came on the scene."

"Do sit down and tell me all about yourself."

Tanya complied most readily. She'd had such adventures. Yes, there had been a strike, and yes they'd won it. And Tanya had landed in jail; she was rather proud of having been sent to jail. When Leonard came in, she rose and greeted him with a hearty handshake.

"Tanya!" he said, "how good to see you!"

"I came to talk about that article for 'Light.' But don't let's go into that now. Send out for some coffee and let's catch up with all that's happened in our lives."

"If only I could! But I must go to New York tomorrow. We'll have to go over whatever you've prepared right now."

"But why must you go tomorrow?" Both women had wondered, but it was Tanya who asked.

"They're beginning to recruit for an international brigade to go to Spain. There's a meeting tomorrow."

"To go to Spain!" exclaimed Carla. "Oh dear!"

"I must seize this opportunity."

"Opportunity?" Carla again.

"Don't sit there repeating my words. Yes, an opportunity. Mark what I say. A communist government will come from the anarchy in Spain, and I'll be there. Spain is where the action is. Tomorrow I go to New York."

"It figures," said Tanya. "You would. I mean you would want to go."

"Do you think they'll let me?"

She looked him straight in the eye and answered, "I very much doubt it."

"Do you have any say in it?"

"Not the least. If I did, I'd probably agree that you can't be spared from the work you're doing." She paused then continued, "I'm going to ask to be brought back to New York. I don't hold out much hope for that either. What do you want to bet they won't let you go to Spain?"

"I never bet against myself."

"Not even for old times sake?"

"Come into my office and show me what you've written."

They went in and closed the door. Carla turned to her typing, and the tune her fingers tapped out was: Spain, Spain, fighting in Spain, dying in Spain, lost in Spain. Her typos increased, and giving up, she wandered out into the city night.

Spain! thought Carla, even after she was home. War in Spain! War toward which Leonard turned his steps. She saw whole battalions of dying men, neatly arranged on hospital beds, for she dared not think of battlefields. Men screaming in pain and men in silent stoicism bearing their pain, soon to have screams silenced and pain eased by death. Leonard would be one who would bear his pain in silence. And on the battle-field—no, it was too terrible. Why did he have to go? The answer was clear. Leonard was a true soldier of the revolution. Even while she grieved, she was proud that he had not evaded the call of duty. Had not her grandfather volunteered to fight in the Union Army and by so doing gained honor for himself and indeed for his children and in diluted form for his grandchildren? Leonard too must soar like the eagle.

On the day of Leonard's expected return from New York, she received a letter from Roger. She was too emotionally drained to feel the slightest interest, but because she was an orderly person, she opened it.

"You left something out of your recent letter, please trust me." The note contained but the single sentence. There was not even a date, or salutation, only the signature, "As ever, Roger."

She should have known he would spot the omission which she supposed he fairly well understood. She should write and tell him. What had she to hide, what to be ashamed of? She and Leonard needed no seal of approval. He was hers and she was his, proud to be his. She trembled as she heard his hand upon the doorknob. After a perfunctory kiss, he went into the bedroom. Carla could hear him moving about; she wanted to go in, but something in his manner made her wait.

"What's going on here?" he shouted suddenly. "Every one of my shirts has a missing button."

It certainly wasn't true, maybe one, certainly not all. Going into the bedroom she busied herself with sewing on a button. Poor dear! She supposed this was the way men going off to battle were likely to behave. How was he to know what a day she'd had with that addle-brained Phoenicia?

"Why are you doing that now?" he asked. "Go fix something to eat."

She made no retort, simply went to the kitchen, and hastened to prepare food. To save time, she opened cans of spinach and lima beans and patted the ground beef thin so that it would cook quickly. But she forgot the coffee.

"Carla," said Leonard, "do you expect me to eat *this?*"

She stared at him. While politically he was most particular, he never complained about food. What had they done to him? And why did he take it out on her?

She went to him and put her arm around his shoulder. He responded to her tenderness by pulling her down onto his lap. He crushed her lips with his. "Forget the food, I need you," he whispered lustfully. Angrily she leaped to her feet and went over to the stove. If he thought that would atone for his rudeness, he didn't understand much about her feelings. Hero or no hero, he was being impossible; she would not put up with it.

"Okay," he said. "Make me some coffee."

"Make your own coffee!" she cried in a rage. "You're a cruel, self-centered nobody!" The words were hardly out of her mouth before she was horrified at having said them.

Leonard sat perfectly still. "That is no description of me," he said icily. "You must be thinking of some other friend of yours."

Seven kinds of fury welled up within her. It took but a few steps for her to reach the door and slam it behind her. Down the stairs and out to the sidewalk she ran.

The sun was low in the west, and the sky was brilliant red with slashes of purple. A few leaves still remained upon the trees; every now and then one would flutter to the ground or to the gray concrete sidewalk where it would lie clearly outlined and alone, waiting some busy broom.

"Hello, Mrs. Engelstein," a child's voice greeted her. It was Bettina, a lively eight-year-old with tousled brown curls and sparkling dark eyes.

"I'm learning to roller-skate," the child announced proudly. She was wearing one skate and she whirred its little wheels on the sidewalk with a grinding noise, then careened along the walk to show Carla.

"You balance very well," Carla assured her.

"If you'll hold me, I can go on two skates."

She sat down on the step and with Carla's help put on the other skate. Soon she was wobbling along with Carla holding her hand. Then she got the feel of it, she moved ahead swiftly, Carla had to run to keep up with her, and they both soon tired.

"Will you help me again tomorrow?" the child cried eagerly.

"We'll see," said Carla and turned to go back to her own apartment. She and Leonard were on edge, but surely there was nothing their love could not overcome.

Halfway up the flight of stairs she met Leonard coming down. "I have an errand," he said and passed without touching her.

She saw that he had put the dinner dishes in the sink. It was an apology, she supposed. But what had he meant by that "You must be thinking of some other friend"? She went into the bedroom and saw that Roger's note had been moved; it lay carelessly thrown on the bed. Certainly he hadn't meant Roger? Roger was far away and like a cousin to her.

She glanced around the room, which had been decorated entirely in accord with Leonard's wishes. The walls were an off-white. The drapes and the bedspread were a deep blue and made of nubbly, heavy cotton. The easy chair had been upholstered in forest green and the cushions on the rocker were of the same color. The wood of the chairs and the chest had been oiled and rubbed until it glowed with a soft warm tone. Above the chest was an unframed mirror of heavy plate glass in front of which stood a tall green bottle, that same green bottle which Carla had carried about as a talisman ever since her last day on the farm. Beside it sat a squat jade-green bowl, the bowl into which she'd tossed the letter from Roger. She and Leonard had talked of getting a candle, one an inch and a half thick and maybe six inches tall, to stand in the bowl. Carla had suggested salmon pink, and Leonard had said he'd bring one back from New York, where there was a candle store far superior to any in Boston. But he hadn't brought the candle.

She picked up the letter and reread it. That Roger! Maybe Leonard *was* angry about the letter. Quickly she went into the bathroom, tore letter and envelope into tiny bits and flushed them down the toilet.

Her anger against Leonard had become anger against herself. It was she who was a nobody. He was Sir Galahad, a true believer. They should have had it out about Roger. Yes, they could handle that. But could they face the fact that his dream of a world revolution had come to seem to her an empty vision if not a nightmare? How terrible that his noble nature had become so ensnared! She heard his step in the hall, hastened to plug in the electric percolator, and stood waiting anxiously to gauge his mood. He was tired, subdued. He was carrying a small package, which he handed to her. "I forgot the candle when I was in New York," he said. "But I found one tonight."

Eagerly she tore off the white paper, then went to place it in its destined niche. It was just as they had decided, an inch and a half in diameter and six inches tall. It was not, however, a salmon pink but a bright red. She set it upright in the shallow dish and stepped back to see how it looked. "I got red," Leonard said softly, "because it's the color of our flag."

"It's a lovely touch," she said. The green and red were Christmas colors; they could never say anything else to her. She smiled and held her tongue.

Back in the kitchen they sat facing each other drinking the coffee and eating buttered pumpernickel bread, the mood sufficiently calm that she could ask, "What happened in New York? Do you go to Spain?"

The mobile side of his face quivered. "No, the idiotic bureaucrats! I'm not allowed."

She suppressed a sigh of relief and hurried to talk about "Light."

❧❦

They went back to the old routine, but she had not forgotten Roger, and she wrote him several letters, which she carefully and thoughtfully burned in the kitchen sink. She simply could not tell him she was living with Leonard.

Roger wondered that she failed to write. Though he had nothing concrete to go on, he was nonetheless positive that she was hiding something from him. He came to suspect what her secret was. And he, with his scientific training and complete lack of empirical data, grew more certain the more he thought about it. Even a scientist, he knew, made his greatest discoveries through an intuitive leap into the dark. Black anger at Leonard filled his heart, and he walked the floor and raged. At last his sense of justice forced him to admit to himself that he really didn't know. But he could find out. He'd go back, he'd see Carla, he'd know. Could they be married? If that was it, then that was that. He'd respect it, he'd stop seeing Carla, forget what might have been had he not been ninety-nine kinds of an idiot. Poor Carla! Why poor Carla if that was what she wanted? Poor Roger! Left stranded with the self accusations which accompanied his growing knowledge of Carla's place in his heart. There was, however, one plan directly relating to Carla that he'd had in mind since his visit to Boston and he decided to go ahead with it. He would go to Fresno, California, and find that brother of hers. When he went back to Boston, that would be the gift he'd bring. And if she were not accepting gifts from him, he'd do it for Howard's sake. Likable little cuss, that Howard.

He set himself to making deductions. Howard had said he was going where a wooden musical instrument would be in danger. What could that place be but a prison? Surely there must be some court record, some newspaper account, or some person who would know the details. Not for a moment did he doubt his ability to locate that brother of hers. Funny little guy, here today and gone tomorrow. Quick-tempered, maybe too much so for his own good, but a decent chap. And sending the wooden flute to his sister to save it from danger!

There was a job opportunity in Burbank that he wanted to check out, and Fresno wasn't a million miles from there, he guessed. Driving his still serviceable car, he set out on the long journey from Indiana to California. He marveled at the broad plains, the lofty mountains, the cool desert night, and at last the low-lying city in the midst of the great agricultural plain, Fresno, in the Central Valley of California. Although it was late in October, the sun beat down, a fireball in a cloudless, blue-gray sky, and the temperature hovered in the high eighties. Roger drove down the level street, looked out upon the vast fields, breathed the dusty air, and wiped the sweat off his forehead. His body cried out for rest. The next day he found the newspaper accounts he sought. Howard had indeed been placed under arrest, tried and sentenced. Roger was allowed access to court records, and he learned that Howard had been sent to state prison. He talked to the arresting officer who encouraged him to visit the prisoner. "He's not a criminal type," the man said. "But he did break the law, can't allow that. And he did resist arrest."

"Oh?"

"Certainly did."

Yes, Roger supposed he had. That was in the court record, and this officer was too sympathetic to Howard to have made it up. Roger also found, quite by accident when he went to church on Sunday, a minister who remembered the case very well. It seemed a parishioner of his, a middle-aged woman, had been a juror on the case, had voted to convict, and had been worried about it for weeks after, so that she contacted the minister for counseling. "She was in a real state," the minister confided to Roger. "But she'd only done what was right." He made time in his busy schedule for a long talk with Roger. The jurywoman was no longer in Fresno or he might have arranged for Roger to talk to her. He might, he wasn't sure. Roger rather thought he wouldn't have and indeed wasn't sure he wanted to see her. What he must do next was see Howard.

He left Fresno early in the morning, in order to travel in the relative cool. By the time he neared his destination, it was broad daylight and heating up, though the sky was overcast. The narrow black road to the prison, carefully marked with a big green arrow, went straight along the level ground for a quarter of a mile, then veered to climb a steep hill. At the top of the hill Roger pulled over to the side of the road to refresh himself with coffee from his thermos. They'd told him he'd be able to see the prison from this hilltop, but the valley was filled with mists rising off a small lake. The gray curtain of mist obscured the building, yet he could see faint outlines. Tall evergreen trees rose like spires through the vapor which was blown about by some slight breeze. The prison towers rose above the mist, square towers, manned no doubt by guards. It was like a medieval castle, except that a castle would have been on the heights not in the depths. There it was, the prison the very name of which, as the minister had said to him, strikes terror into the heart of the less hardened criminal. And the minister with worldly cynicism had added, "But the more hardened are terrorizing rather than terrorized." Roger wished the minister were with him.

He got back in the car and drove on. The sun shone more brightly, evaporating the mists; the grass in the fields was brown and the leaves on the few trees hung dejectedly wilted. Now the prison could be seen clearly, a huddle of gray concrete three-story buildings with several towers, the whole surrounded by a high chain link fence. The buildings grew larger until they no longer lay small in a valley but towered above the road. In the parking lot he hesitated, then plunged on into this labyrinth of unfreedom. He proceeded to a small building set into the fence and approached a guard standing just inside the door. Roger cleared his throat and, following the Fresno minister's advice, gave the name of the prisoner in whom he was interested and asked to see the Chaplain. The guard thought a minute, made a phone call, then took him in tow. He was a big sandy-haired fellow dressed in clean suntans, with just a little slouch to his shoulders. He kept muttering something under his breath. Roger walked beside him, tense and ill at ease.

"This here's the Chaplain's office," the guard said at last. "Wingate's in the hospital."

"The hospital! Why is he there?"

The guard made no answer. They were already facing the Chaplain, a tall man, with a countenance that at the moment expressed nothing save a benevolent attitude toward mankind. Roger gave Wingate's name, said he was a friend, was sorry to hear Howard was in the hospital, wished to visit.

Soon they were seated at the desk. The Chaplain was meditating. The guard had taken up a post at the door. Finally the Chaplain spoke. "I'm glad you came," he said. "We have somewhat of a problem with your friend."

"Why is he in the hospital?"

"He's been injured."

"What kind of injury? How bad?"

"Well," the Chaplain began, then sat there contemplating his desk. The guard standing by the door cleared his throat and shuffled his feet. He seemed about to take it upon himself to answer the question, but at this point the Chaplain again found tongue. "You must understand," he began, "that in prison men are under a great deal of tension."

The guard was muttering under his breath, Roger was tapping impatiently on the desk, and the Chaplain went on. "Under these circumstances it is regrettable that certain incidents do occur. Your friend has been injured, rather seriously though he's improving, in an assault the cause of which is difficult to pinpoint."

Filled with horror, Roger could only sit and stare. At last he was able to mumble, "What do you mean?"

"What happened," the guard broke in, "is that one of our esteemed boarders kept badgering Wingate until he swung on the big ape and got beaten to within an inch of his life."

"Yes," said the chaplain, "I'm afraid Wingate did, as you say, swing on him."

"Begging your pardon, Reverend," the guard continued, "and not wanting to upset you, young man, Wingate was being picked on something awful. That polecat Eddie Means spends half his time figuring out how he can hurt some other prisoner, and the other half doing it. That's the way it is, and it shouldn't be prettied up."

The Chaplain sat quietly through this tirade, his faint smile of benign compassion undisturbed. "There's something to what you say, Mr. Monroney," he said. "The important thing, or rather the two important things, are: One, Wingate is doing quite well. The fractured arm is healing normally and so are the three broken ribs."

"Broken arm! Three broken ribs!" cried Roger.

"And the second thing is what the fight tells about his mental attitude."

"That sounds okay to me," observed Roger. "Spunky little guy!"

"He lies in bed and curses," the Chaplain went on. "Lies there and threatens what he'll do to Means. And keeps moaning 'Butch Brown all over again,' which I don't understand."

"The problem is," said the guard, "he's such a little guy."

"That's not the main thing," the Chaplain argued. "He must try to understand. He must overcome this hate within him which can only end by destroying him."

"You must keep them apart," cried Roger.

"No doubt some effort will be made along those lines," the Chaplain said blandly, "but there are administrative difficulties."

"You mean Howard will be thrown back—"

"They might be separated or they might not, that is not the question," the Chaplain answered. "We bring men here to rehabilitate them, and they have to learn to accept each other."

"Some can't be rehabilitated," said the guard. "Except by hanging."

"As I sit here and study the records," the Chaplain went on, "I read of the lives some have led from childhood. It gives me great compassion."

"That's nice," said Roger, anger at the man's complaisance burning in him like acid. He rose to his feet. "Now can I see Wingate?"

"Yes, yes, certainly."

The guard led Roger into the gray-white hospital ward with its pervading odor of disinfectant. Roger looked the length of the ward but saw no Howard. There was one place, however, separate from the others, an open-ended cubicle into which he could not see. The guard led him there, and there he found Howard, sitting up in the white bed, dressed in a hospital gown, his arm in a cast, his hair neatly combed back, his chin clean-shaven. But how wild his eyes were! He was perfectly motionless except for those eyes, like a forest animal hoping not to be seen.

TWENTY-THREE

Fixing his eyes on the guard, Howard began coldly and clearly swearing horrible oaths. Monroney stood there deadpan.

When Howard saw Roger, he became silent, he could not speak, he struggled, he made a sobbing sound. Roger hemmed and hawed, then proceeded with a rambling account of his journey west, dragged out to give Howard time to get used to his presence.

"What did the Chaplain tell you?" asked Howard.

"I guess you know."

"I fought back, and I'll get that skunk if it's the last thing I ever do."

Roger swallowed hard. "You're right, of course," he said. "The only question is how to do it." Feeling a presence at his back, Roger turned around and there stood the Chaplain and a second man dressed in white cotton coat and pants. He was carrying a pail of soapy water to wash the window.

The Chaplain shook his head sadly. "Dear brothers," he pleaded. "Can't we cleanse our hearts of this spirit of hatred and revenge?"

The window washer turned quickly. "Brother Reverend," he interrupted. "You're talking nonsense."

"Brother Douglas," the minister replied. "I respect your devotion to God, but—"

The man paused in his work and stood facing them. Though his movements were those of a man in his forties or fifties, his hair was completely gray. "Reverend," he spoke slowly. "The Lord Jesus knows about me and Means, but He don't shush me, no sir, not the Lord Jesus."

"Perhaps you could work at the other end of the ward."

"Okay, going directly." Then looking at Roger he said, "Don't you worry. This here boy's going to be all right. That trash that done it to him will live to regret it."

"We must understand—" the Chaplain tried to get in a word.

"I understand that scum," Douglas interrupted, "you'd better believe. And what he done to me, I'll never forgive."

"Never is a long time," said the Chaplain.

"My daughter, my youngest daughter, my baby, what he done to her—" He was clearly saying this for Roger's benefit. "Always singin' and laughin' and making jokes, the most innocent, the most trusting. Till he got her hooked on drugs, got her hooked on, oh I can't even say the word, the worst. But some day we'll both be out, and when that day comes, I swear to God, I'll kill him. No matter what happens to me, I'll do it. Next time I'll make sure."

"Elisha Douglas!" said the Chaplain sternly, " 'Vengeance is mine, saith the Lord.' "

"He said that about Cain," retorted the prisoner, "on whom God put his mark. But that Means ain't got no mark of God on him. He ain't never been near God." Having said his say, Douglas picked up his bucket and left.

Roger turned to Howard. "Will they put you back in there with whoever it is?"

"They don't tell me nothing."

Roger bowed his head in his hands. All that he'd been taught concerning the sinful nature of man came sharply in focus. Is there no end to the evil in this world? his heart cried out. He raised his head and his face was controlled.

"I'm not sure," interrupted the Chaplain, "that your visit will have a calming effect."

"I want to help him."

"He's refused to talk about his family. Do you know them?"

"I intend to marry his sister."

"Oh, in that case. Another half hour. I have others in the hospital to visit."

"I always figured that's the way it was with you and Carla," said Howard.

"She doesn't know yet," Roger confessed. "Now, Howard, I want your whole story."

Howard sat upright, his eyes misted with tears. Just when he thought he hadn't a friend in the world, here was Roger, almost a brother-in-law. After ascertaining that his prized recorder was safe with Carla, he began his story.

"Right off the bat," he said, "I want you to understand I done just what they said I done."

"Start at the beginning."

"Holy mackerel! Where did it start?"

For years there had been a four-legged skunk, to use Howard's term, who seemed fated to pop up wherever Howard went. Butch Brown, his name was. And he was forever insulting a guy, making fun of him, and daring him to do something about it, he being a muscular fighter type. Howard had worked with him in a restaurant in Baltimore, then had left to go West and had half forgotten him when whammo, there he was, big as life and twice as ugly. Howard had come to California hoping to pick up some work in the fields or the orchards, and on the way he had made friends with a young Southerner, Monty Bannock, good guy, honest as the day is long, a little quick to lose his temper, drank too much, but a good buddy. They'd heard of a job in an orchard not far from Fresno and hitched a ride to somewhere near, then walked the rest of the way on a hot autumn afternoon and arrived around three, sweaty but hopeful. "Foreman's over there," a skinny Mexican told them, and they hopped on over to the shed.

"I'll be hanged if the foreman wasn't Butch Brown, face tanned, hair bleached, shirt sleeves rolled high like he's looking for a fight."

He recognized Howard all right, but he said he guessed he could use two more hands. He had to have something to poke fun at, and what could be better than the Alabama accent of Monty Bannock and the Maine twang of Howard Wingate. Butch, a native of Ohio, talked standard American with some dirt thrown in. Of all the bad luck, thought Howard, to run into *him*. Still it was a job, and he and Monty were broke, so they took it. They got in several weeks work and were on their way out, thinking perhaps there'd be something doing further south, around Bakersfield perhaps. First they decided to make a night of it. They went to a movie, a rip-roaring Western, and then to a bar.

The bartender-owner Bob something or other welcomed them as he always did. They'd never given him any trouble, just a middling amount of business. He was a sturdy man with a face strongly resembling a russet potato, both in color and shape, willing to talk when anyone wished, and equally willing to be silent. As he said, he made a good living minding his own business. There were several other customers, a couple in one of the booths, at the bar three men who appeared to be together, a young man playing the jukebox and favoring country Western. Howard and Monty took the other booth and sat there studying a road map. It grew late, Howard wasn't sure how late. Bob was alone behind the bar, the waitress had gone home, and the other customers had left. Then in came Butch Brown. He'd been drinking, and he swaggered up to the bar and gave his order in a voice which could have been heard three ranches away. Bob served it. Butch took a swig, spat it out, snorted, "Bilgewater!" Bob shrugged, screwed up his small eyes even smaller, rolled his sleeves even higher than they'd been, and said nothing. Butch downed the rest of the drink and looked around. Spotting Howard and Monty, he came over and greeted them. "Hiya, Yo'-all and Yank. Guess I may as well join you."

"We're just leaving," said Howard.

Butch Brown followed them out, insisting they'd insulted him, were getting too big for their breeches, he'd take them down a peg; then suddenly he grabbed Monty by the shoulder and demanded to know why they refused to drink with him. Monty, like Howard, had been working under this man for four weeks, had been shortweighted, cussed out, and ridiculed until he like Howard was rubbed raw. And here he was, grabbing hold of Monty, a man considerably smaller than he, but of strong, wiry build. Bob stood in the doorway. "If you guys have to fight, get out of my driveway, go back there onto the parking lot," he shouted.

"We could have left," said Howard. "I don't reckon Butch would have followed us. But we dug in our heels."

They headed out onto the parking lot, deserted except for Bob's car, and Monty and Butch stood facing each other. Monty got in the first blow, ducked when Butch came back at him, slugged the bigger man again and this time Butch staggered but did not fall. Howard could see his big fist doubled, drawn back, but believing in fair play which forbade two against one, stood by, ready to pitch in if Monty couldn't handle it, but Monty was not unprepared. Cold steel flashed, blood flowed, Butch fell back upon the pavement.

Monty and Howard stood there, not sure if Butch were dead or alive, not sure which they hoped. Bob was fifteen feet away. "Just what he deserved!" he shouted. Then turning to Howard and Monty, he ordered them to leave.

When they hesitated, he continued, "I've had it up to here with that bigmouth. I didn't see nothing."

Howard and Monty ran down the street, then slowed in order not to look suspicious, came to the drugstore a block away and stopped to admire a sleek brown roadster, the very latest model. The keys were in the ignition. "Just what the doctor ordered," cried Monty.

Howard slid into the driver's seat, and they were off. Ah what a baby! What a smooth-riding, smooth-handling, quick-on-the-uptake car. Miles after miles they drove, heading north for no better reason than that they had been planning to go south. Later he learned that the car belonged to the owner of the drugstore, a young bachelor, who, on discovering that evening after closing hours that his supply of hair goo or something was low, had gone at once to get that essential. Of course he phoned the police. The whole story came out at the trial. Bob had reported a fight; he didn't know who started it, but it was between this fellow lying on the parking lot with a knife in him and a tall skinny dude in a white sweater. He'd heard shouting and come out just in time to see the skinny dude streaking away. Needless to say neither Monty nor Howard wore a white sweater. Yes indeed, Bob had been decent about it. However, it didn't take much imagination to connect the missing car with the murder. It wouldn't have mattered which way Howard and Monty had gone, they'd have been stopped.

"Unless we ditched the car," Howard said thoughtfully.

"Why didn't you?"

"Maybe," said Howard, "because it was right that we should be caught."

Howard had been charged with grand theft auto and resisting arrest. He'd put up quite a fight. Monty had been booked on the same charge, but it wasn't long before murder was added, his fingerprints having been found on the weapon. Howard had pleaded guilty, and they sent him to serve his time. Monty had pleaded not guilty and was cleared of car theft, but they'd found his prints on the knife. He'd landed in a different pen and they hadn't seen each other since. They didn't even write.

"Do you still want to marry my sister?" asked Howard.

"Why not?" replied Roger.

He went back to the Chaplain and then to another man whose title he wasn't sure of and asked what it would take to get Howard out of jail. With a job, Roger was assured, Wingate could be paroled in a couple of months, maybe three or four. Would it have to be in California? Since he had a sister in Boston, it could be there, if she'd accept responsibility. The Chaplain would recommend Wingate's being with his family, yes, definitely. He supposed this prospective brother-in-law would be going to join his betrothed.

It took only a day for Roger to return to Fresno and arrange for the minister there to get an attorney, visit Howard if he could, talk to the prison authorities. Roger himself must get back to Boston. They shook hands like old friends, and Roger headed east.

It was mid-November when he arrived in Boston. He went at once to the address Carla had given him. *Mmm. Neat family-type apartments, children playing on the sidewalk.* In the front hall was a row of brass-plated mailboxes and under them the electric bells to each apartment. On the mailboxes were apartment numbers and name plates. *Ah, here it is: "207 Engelstein - Wingate." Yes, she'd told me she was using her maiden name, but Engelstein! Maybe it was Leonard's sister Ellen. Why shouldn't she and Carla share digs? And if it were Leonard?* The very openness half convinced him that she'd gone and married that fellow. If he could have retreated and gone into solitude to meditate he might have, but he had a message from Howard, and he had to plan with her how to achieve Howard's release.

Carla met Roger at the top of the stairs. There she stood in the hallway, her brown hair swept up in the smartest style, her navy blue dress in the best of taste, her height added to by the heels of her shoes. She was alone and she invited him in. Soften it as he might, still he had to tell her that her brother was in a California prison. She didn't break down and cry, she just sat there in the living room on the sofa, staring straight ahead, then she looked up, and her gray eyes were the same as Howard's—wild, frightened eyes.

"Is it very terrible there?" she whispered.

"Yes," he said. "We have to get him out."

"Oh Roger, I've just sat and worried and never even tried to find him. How did you do it?"

He didn't answer her question. Instead he rose to his feet, his eyes solemn behind his dark-rimmed glasses. She rose to face him. "Carla," he said, "I wrote you a letter. I said there was something you weren't telling me. Who lives here with you? Are you married?"

She turned scarlet red. "No," she said in a low voice, "I can't tell you that I am. But we live together, Leonard and I."

"I feared as much."

"Do not think," she said, "that Leonard is not everything in the world to me, and I to him."

"What will you tell Howard when he comes here?"

"By then it may be straightened out."

"Do you believe that?"

"No."

"Miss Carla Wingate Putnam, you've got yourself into a real quagmire."

At that moment Leonard came in the door, suave and self-controlled. "Going home for the holidays?" he asked Roger. "I hope you can stay and have dinner with us."

"Thanks, but no," Roger answered. "I just dropped by to give Carla a message from her brother."

"Oh yes, that's right, she does have a brother."

It was not until late at night after they were together in bed that she told him where her brother was. "We must get him out," she said.

"He'll get out in time anyway," said Leonard blandly.

"But he's a little guy, with a quick temper. He was in the hospital with a broken arm and three broken ribs when Roger saw him."

"He'll have to control his temper."

"You must find him a job," Carla insisted.

"What can he do?"

"He was working as an agricultural laborer."

Leonard snorted. "How am I to find a job for some unskilled laborer who isn't even class-conscious? Anyway how do we know he could be paroled?"

"Maybe Lowell could help." Lowell Beichman, she meant, Ellen's betrothed, son of the head partner and now himself a partner in the prestigious law firm of Beichman and Beichman.

"Let's not keep demanding things from Lowell. We don't want to over-load him."

"You didn't worry about that when you took those other cases to him."

"Those were different. This is just a straight criminal case."

"True this wouldn't be political," Carla snapped, "just helping a poor working stiff who's in trouble."

"You don't have to be sarcastic. Stealing a car was stupid. And a barroom fight! Dumb stunt."

"Well, he *is* my brother."

"Lilies grow in mud," he replied pulling her close to him.

"My family is not mud," she retorted, then got up, found a blanket and went to sleep on the living room couch. Mud indeed! Well, maybe they weren't the greatest. She wasn't much herself. With tears flowing she sang softly the spiritual, "There's no hiding place down here, Went to the rocks for to hide my face, Rocks cried out 'No hiding place.'" Had Leonard heard? Her voice grew loud and anguished. "There's no hiding place down here." If Leonard heard, he gave no sign. Why should he, she thought, why should he?

Roger went home for Christmas, taking the train because the roads were too blocked with snow to make driving practical. He had not repeated his visit to Carla, had not called her nor written, yet she had not ceased occupying his mind to the detriment of all other forms of mental activity, including his planned review of the highly technical book which he held open before him. The train pulled out of the Boston station and moved swiftly north. Past miles of Christmas card drawings it went and on through scenes that may well have been the models for dozens of Currier and Ives winter landscapes. Gray houses snuggled against the white snow blanket and dark green trees stood guard. As a high school boy he'd been sure he was madly in love with Carla, the sad little girl who'd come and left like a dream. It was romantic to love like that and a protection against the too-aggressive girls of that growing up period. Later in college he'd still remembered, and there'd been that strange encounter in the midst of a strike with Carla the heroine. A rabble-rouser. Or was she really? The book fell from his lap with a kerplop, he bent over to retrieve it, straightened up and was in the midst of the present.

True it wasn't a marriage, but it was a something with this Engelstein creep. Somehow he didn't condemn Carla for it, only the man. No, she was simply being foolish and in need of being rescued from a folly which was bound to lead to catastrophe. But did he have any right to do the rescuing, or even the standing by to pick up the pieces? One thing he must do was to spring that brother of hers from jail and get him into some kind of job, not just because he was her brother but for the sake of the man himself. Poor

Howard! Heaven only knew what might happen to him in that monstrous jail.

The train moved on, whistling a lonesome sound across the fields, slowly wheeling into the towns, sounding a sharp warning at each crossing. The familiar scenes of West Hambledon thrilled him; thoughts of the welcome he'd receive filled him with happiness. He brushed aside a momentary pang that he hadn't written as often as he should, hadn't come home for Thanksgiving, had really told them so little about himself. He'd make it up, oh he would, and what a joy to be here in the midst of snow and dark pine forest and modest houses, white with dark roofs and red brick chimneys. The smoke from the chimneys told of warm firesides, and he'd soon be by his own. Off the train, protected from the sharp wind by his overcoat and fur-lined cap, he ran toward his father who stood waiting, tall, rawboned, clad in brown mackinaw and woolen pants, silent, smiling just a little, extending a mittened hand.

"Sleigh's over there," he said. "I come in alone."

"Mom's not sick?"

"No. Busy at home."

The sleigh bells jingled as the horse, bred for sulky racing, trotted nimbly along the snow-covered road. Roger breathed deeply and pulled the lap robe over his knees. "Well," he asked, "how's everything?"

"Horses doing okay. Market's holding up. Feed prices outrageous as usual."

"And Mom?"

"I told you she's okay. Busy, always busy, you know her."

"And Grandpa?"

There followed a silence, not really long, just a trace too long. "Failing," said Ward Thorfinnson.

"In what way?"

"Every way."

"Gets tired easily?"

"Yes."

"A little deaf perhaps?"

"No, not deaf."

Roger decided if he was going to have to drag it out like pulling teeth, he'd wait until he saw his grandpa for himself, but after a quarter mile the father spoke again. "I'd better tell you," he said. "His mind's not what it used to be. Imagines things."

"Has he had a stroke?"

"Two."

Roger sat sunk in gloom. Grandpa tiring or deaf or even blind he could accept, but Grandpa with a weakened mind, oh no! He thought of all the stories, all the wisdom, all the manifestations of mind which had been his grandpa's gift to him. And now?

Julia Thorfinnson came running out. She hugged Roger and nodded to her husband and said how cold they must be, hot tea was ready and ginger-snaps. "Always your favorite, you know, Roger."

Grandpa was resting in his room and must not be disturbed; he'd proba-bly wake up in an hour or so. Yes, the tea was boiling hot, and Julia hadn't forgotten to have lemon, and the gingersnaps were super, and the dog a mira-cle of obedience once you got his attention. And Roger sat numb with fear of what he would find had happened to Grandpa.

The old man was frail and weak, had to be helped from the bed into the wheelchair which gave him some mobility for he could, as he showed Roger, push it about by himself. Ward had horses to attend to, Julia had supper to prepare, Roger was left alone with Grandpa.

"I knew you'd come, I knew you'd come," said the old man. "Let's go back to my room."

"I always come for Christmas," Roger reminded him.

The old man looked about vaguely. "Christmas already?" he said.

"A couple of weeks."

"Who was with you just now?"

Roger's heart sank. "Why that was my father. Ward."

"Oh. He's changed. Or maybe it's my eyes. But where's your wife?"

"My wife? Grandpa, can't you see me? This is Roger."

"I know it's Roger," said the old man impatiently. "But where's your wife?"

"I'll have to admit that though I'm six feet tall I don't have one yet."

"Nonsense. Yesterday she was here with you."

Roger sank down onto the bed. Then he saw his mother in the doorway. "Come into the kitchen a minute, Roger," she said.

Roger followed his mother into the kitchen. She stood there, very straight, her face lined with sorrow. "Didn't Dad tell you, didn't he?"

"I didn't understand."

"Just go along with whatever Grandpa says. You mustn't contradict him, he gets in a rage. Yesterday he thought that I was a hired nurse and he fired me. And I've been so good to him." The cheerful, uncomplaining mother he'd never seen cry was standing there with tears in her eyes. "Go back in and talk to him. God will guide you."

Roger went back in, but at first he said nothing, he just sat in the straight chair by the bed, looking about the familiar room. How many times he'd sat there with Grandpa, listening to the old man's stories, listening to his wisdom. How many times he'd sat there doing some study of his own while Grandpa was lost in his books. Grandpa had somewhere along his life journey become enthralled with American history and had undertaken to collect rare books on the subject, rare books and unpublished manuscripts. The walls of the room, which was of good size so that the bed occupied a mere corner, were lined with books, mostly bound in brown. The few touches of bright red and royal blue stood out in vivid contrast. In front of the shelves stood two oak filing cabinets which Roger knew contained the prized manuscripts. What a learned man Grandpa had seemed to him as a boy. And yes, Roger supposed, he was in a way.

The old man began to talk about his books and how difficult it was for him to see to read them, even with his glasses. "I'll read to you," cried Roger. "Whatever you want."

"That way we both might learn something," grunted the old man.

He was still the old Grandpa, who had in his youth raised horses because it was a living and who had in his early old age gladly turned the farm over to his son so that he might spend whole days in his study. Not that he'd been a recluse. Far from it, he'd many friends of like temperament, and he'd always time to spare for his grandson and his grandson's friends, and he'd done what work had been needed, and at family gatherings he was the great storyteller.

"Your coming has been so good for Grandpa," said Julia later. "Good for me, too, because I've lots of things to do."

Grandpa had forgotten nothing about his books; he knew exactly where on the shelves each volume could be found; he knew exactly which one he wanted Roger to read to him. Roger thoroughly enjoyed fellowship with the old man. Once he tried to take him for a ride in the sleigh, but they got only as far as the door, when Grandpa protested vigorously, said he didn't want to go to Manfred's, they shouldn't make him, though who or what Manfred was Roger couldn't find out. Roger, considerably shaken, agreed that they'd better forget about Manfred and go back and read some more.

"What shall I read?" asked Roger.

The old man sat silent in his chair, looking about from shelf to shelf. "Roger," he said at last. "When I die, I want you to have these books. You and Carla."

"Carla? What Carla?" He was amazed that Grandpa remembered one he'd known so little.

"Carla your wife," the old man said impatiently.

"Grandpa, I'm not married."

"What are you waiting for? Don't tell me you're not sweet on that girl?"

"Maybe she's not sweet on me."

"Nonsense. Why, she's the most levelheaded girl I ever saw."

Levelheaded was not exactly how Roger would have described Carla, but

Mom had said not to contradict Grandpa, and anyway he didn't want to argue that point. What he longed to ask was why Grandpa talked of Carla and in connection with him. For a moment he almost believed in mental telepathy.

"I never saw a kid," the old man went on, "who took such an interest in my old collection of history books. Not even you. Ward and Julia don't care two cents for them. You go call them in, I want them to know."

Since both his father and mother were in the house, Roger had no excuse not to call them, but having no desire to do so, he remained silent. The old man grew angry and began to shout, whereupon Julia came running in.

"Where's Ward?" cried the old man.

"I'll get him," said Julia and in a minute there he was, in his mackinaw and fur-trimmed cap, standing silent, waiting patiently.

"I just told Roger I want when I'm dead—"

"But Father," said Julia, "you'll live a long time yet."

"When I'm dead," the old man ignored the interpolation, "I want him to have these books. You can have the horses, but I want him to have all these books."

"Don't get excited," said Ward. "It's fine with me."

"I figgered so," said the old man, and then as Roger began to breathe more easily, he added, "him and his wife Carla."

"Carla! His wife? I should say not!" Julia could not refrain from an emphatic denial.

"Now run along," the old man said. "Roger's going to read to me."

"What's Julia got against Carla?" Grandpa asked after they had left. "Whatever it is, don't pay it no mind."

"Shall I read more about the Norse settlers?"

"Yes," the old man said quietly. "You know I've often wondered if we're descended from that Thorfinn who came here in the 1100's. Oh I know they went back to Norway, and our family didn't come here until around 1800. I never was able to find out exactly. I don't know, I don't know, but one likes to be part of history."

"Aren't we all, in one way or another?"

"No," said the old man. "Go ahead and read."

"You've done Grandpa a world of good," said Julia as she bade her son goodbye two days after Christmas. "I wish you could stay longer."

It was a long ride back to Boston, but not long enough for Roger to get his thoughts in order. Why on earth had he told them at the prison that he was going to be Howard's brother-in-law? Well, he'd done it to help Howard. But why had he let Howard believe it? For of course it was hopeless. He'd muffed it, diddled and dawdled till it was too late. Now he couldn't even see her, or at least he didn't think he should. On the other hand—

At his apartment he found a letter which gave him an answer. It was from the prison. They thanked him for his promise to find Wingate a job and would like to know what progress he'd made. They also wanted the address of next of kin. Why on earth, wondered Roger, hadn't Howard given it to them? Perhaps Howard didn't have it. He could rectify that easily enough. But wait, did she want her address sent? She'd had three weeks in which to send it herself; surely she'd written Howard. Perhaps they meant the mother's address, and that introduced a new complication. It was clear he'd have to have an understand- ing with Carla before he could go on with his plans for Howard. He must see her again, had to, no doubt about it, once more so that he could go on with his plans for Howard.

Roger, approaching the apartment house, stamped along like a determined stallion. He felt the elation of one who challenges another to a duel. Leonard, beware! It was preposterous that he, Roger, had had any scruples about seeing Carla. He began to pity Leonard, the poor benighted heathen. The ice on the deciduous trees gleamed crystal clear, clinkers on the sidewalk eased his passage, and he neared the horseshoe of the apartment complex. Children were building a snow fort on the space in front and every one had a touch of red in his clothing, a cap, a scarf, and one of the smallest was red from head to toe. Roger stood watching them for a moment and they, being used to having strangers around, paid him no attention. Humming, who knows why, "God Rest Ye, Merry Gentlemen," he walked briskly to the big front door, entered to a not uncomfortable warmth and pushed the button of the electric bell, then waited for the buzzer which would announce the opening of the inner door. But there was no sound. The inner door opened and a rosy-cheeked little girl came out. She held the door open and stared at him. "You're Mrs. Engelstein's cousin, aren't you?" she said.

"Not exactly, but I did come to see her."

"She's away," said the child, Carla's friend Bettina. "But he's home. Sick in bed."

"Could he get up to open his door if I knock?"

"Oh no. He's bad. But the door's unlocked."

"I'd better go see him."

"He's cross as an old witch."

Roger bounded up the stairs, entered the apartment and finally into the bedroom. The drapes were closed, the chamber dimly lit and under the blue coverlet lay Leonard Engelstein. The color scheme was cobalt blue and milky white with an accent of color furnished by a red candle, some green glassware, and a few books with gaudy jackets. The steam radiator proclaimed itself with a sibilant hiss and overheated the room. Leonard pulled himself to a sitting position. His dark wavy hair fell untidily over his forehead, his face was flushed, and the effort he'd made caused him to break into a prolonged fit of coughing. Roger went at once and pulled up the pillow, gave him a hearty whack to ease the coughing, then laid a cool hand upon his forehead.

"My goodness, you are sick. Feverish. What can I do for you?"

"It's nothing, touch of the flu. Complicated by cabin fever, it's maddening here alone."

"Where's Carla?"

"Gone to Maine to visit her mother. Due back today."

"What do you know? I just got back from Maine myself."

"Oh now, did you? Perhaps you saw her?"

Roger's heightened sensibility detected a note of suspicion. Good, he thought. But the man was really sick. "I'd better call a doctor," he said.

"No, no, no. Doctors are mostly quacks."

Roger took off his hat and coat and laid them on a chair. "Nice day out," he ventured. "Bunch of kids playing in the snow."

"Kids all over the place, brats, every last living one of them."

"Yeah, they can be pests, but I'm indebted to one little girl for getting in to see you."

"Oh, Bettina. Only eight and already a regular busybody."

It was, thought Roger, like talking to Scrooge about Christmas, but if he talked politics, they'd surely get into an argument. However Leonard didn't leave it up to him. "What," the sick man asked, "do you think about Roosevelt's policy in regards to Spain?"

Roger frowned, giving it some thought, mainly wondering how to change the subject. One didn't argue politics with a fevered man.

Leonard went on, "It makes me sick to think of it."

"Leonard, for Pete's sake, you know you can't convert me, and I don't expect you to change."

"We can at least discuss. We don't have to be enemies, not for the moment, though in reality I suppose we are."

"Why not just agree to be enemies? Come the revolution I'll shoot you, if your comrades haven't already liquidated you. Have you had anything to eat?"

"I'm not hungry, just dying of thirst, sore throat's killing me."

"Hot lemonade's the thing for that." Roger started for the kitchen.

"Why do you run from an argument?" cried Leonard.

"I've found the lemons," said Roger. "Don't see any sugar, I'll use some of this honey."

"Okay, enemy. Just don't put cyanide in it."

It came out forced and unnatural. Roger, having more of a temperament to joke, answered calmly that they were fresh out, he did believe, of cyanide. "But," he added, "I've something that ought to do as well."

The drink in the brown glass mug was steaming hot, fragrant with lemon; a round slice like a dainty yellow wheel floated enticingly on the surface, and Leonard smiled faintly as he raised it to his lips. Then he let out a scream and would have dropped the glass had not Roger caught it. He was choking, coughing, his face redder and redder. Roger thumped him on the back, and he was able to speak. "What on earth?"

Roger laughed. "It's good for what ails you. Nothing like cayenne for a cold."

"And there's nothing like eating hay when you're faint," Leonard replied and this jest floated, so that they both laughed, and while Leonard drank the lemonade, Roger went back to the kitchen for an icepack.

"Put this on your throat," he advised.

"First you burn me, then you freeze me."

It's hard, thought Roger, to hate someone you're tending to. He sat down and proceeded to entertain the patient. Roger decided it was time for more lemonade and fixed another glass, using the last lemon. Leonard sat in the bed alternately pressing the ice to his throat and gulping the hot, hot lemonade, and he and Roger were silent.

Roger watched him carefully. There was a lot to him, one had to admit. Courage and dedication and an agile tongue. Good looks too of a striking kind, black hair, flashing eyes, eagle nose, strong jaw. Roger could understand what Carla saw in him. The old anger returned for a moment, and Roger wanted to hate him, to utterly and thoroughly hate him, but unfortunately the poor fellow had the flu.

And Leonard wanted to hate Roger; it was clearly his political duty to hate him. And there was something personal to clear up. "I gather," he said, "that you've known Carla a long time?"

"Sure thing, I taught her to run."

Oh, thought Leonard, some kind of track coach, but Carla never ran, not even when she should; he'd never understood it. To give himself time he rambled on. "You've a strange name, Thorfinnson," he said.

"I guess so. I've been told so. Though in the town where I grew up there were more Thorfinnsons than Engelsteins."

Leonard stiffened, not sure if he should take offense.

Roger noted and bridged the awkwardness. "But my middle name is really odd," he said. "Snorri. Roger Snorri Thorfinnson. Did you ever hear the like?"

"No, I never did."

"Of course when I was a boy, I concealed that middle name as if it were a mortal sin."

"Properly understood, no name is strange or odd."

"That's what I always say."

"What nationality is it? Finnish perhaps?"

"Norwegian, I believe."

"I suppose you're Norwegian?"

"Me? Oh no, I'm an American." The conversation amused Roger. How stupid people were when they had nothing to say and felt they had to talk. "A real Yankee-Doodle-dandy-born-on-the-Fourth-of-July American."

"But your cultural background?"

"Oh. I'm a Christian."

Leonard gave a snort of disgust.

"Come, come," said Roger. "You oughtn't to feel that way about it. After all we have a common background. Judaism, you know, is a sect of Christianity."

"Christianity is a sect of Judaism!" snapped Leonard.

"Golly," said Roger. "You're right."

"And both are evil, exploitive, falsifying, stultifying, obscene superstitions, to be wiped out come the revolution."

"Guess I poured water on an oil fire."

Leonard looked hard at him, annoyed that he continued quite unflappable. "Excuse me for not making allowance for your conservative tendencies," he said to Roger.

"Conservative tendencies? Why, I'm downright reactionary with real capitalistic ambitions," Roger laughed.

"Somehow I get the impression that you're not from a working class background?"

"Oh but I am. Race horses. Those beasts are, believe me, work. Though of course we own our place. We raise the kind that pull sulkies, you know, sulky racing."

"Sulky racing?"

"Little two-wheeled carts. Workers love 'em. And you? Background, I mean."

"Bourgeois, I must confess. My father, who came here as a poor Russian immigrant, has done fairly well manufacturing shirts."

"Too bad. And you try to compensate by being a red-hot radical?"

"No, no, I am communist because I understand the dialectic of history."

"The dialectic of history, I have noticed, takes a dim view of America."

"Of America as it exists today, yes, of course. I'm an internationalist. But you really love this country!" He shook his head sadly.

"Of course."

"Can't you see the degradation, the exploitation, the racism, the evil?"

"I see many things I don't like, but just as my family doesn't have to be perfect for me to love them, neither does my country."

"Could either one be so bad you would hate them?"

"Good question. I guess the answer is that I'd grieve but never hate. For if I hated family or country, what would *I* be? I would be like an uprooted tree, and I would die."

"Carla feels this way too, doesn't she?"

"I suppose so. Don't you know?"

"I'm afraid she does. She's old yankee like you. She's never known rejection the way I have. A foreigner and a Jew."

Roger was silent for a moment, then continued the dialogue. "You said your father had done fairly well. How does he feel about being an American?"

"He's far more American than I."

"I wouldn't be surprised to learn he's also more Russian or Jewish than you."

"More Jewish certainly. The melting pot idea is a chimera, you must realize. He may be more American than I, but he'll never be one for real."

"With due respect to the religion of which we are a sect, I submit that only Christianity can make one nation out of many."

"There we're back to religion. Superstition, when it's not a con game."

"Yet the cloth graces many of your platforms of late."

"Idiots!"

Roger laughed. "Touché!"

"Here, I'm through with this glass, and the ice pack is beginning to leak."

"You look much better. Could you eat something?"

"Yes, I think I could."

"Chicken soup? If there is any."

"There's usually a can or two. I don't know where she keeps things. Fix yourself a bowl too."

Thus it was that Carla came in to find them both in the bedroom eating chicken soup, Leonard leaning over the bedside table and Roger balancing his on a little table which he had brought in from the living room.

"What on earth?" she cried.

"Just a touch of the flu," answered Leonard. "No, no, don't come too close to me, don't want you to catch it." He was taken with a series of sneezes.

"I had a letter about Howard I had to show you," Roger explained under cover of the sneeze barrage.

Quickly she read it. "Is there any real hope of getting him out?"

"Oh your brother," Leonard gave a disgruntled snort.

"Of course we must get him out," said Roger. "Will you write and give them your address?"

"It'll be in the mail tonight. We'll have to keep in touch, try to coordinate."

"Are you sure you didn't coordinate your trip to Maine?" Leonard spoke petulantly.

"Oh you've been to Maine too," Carla said eagerly.

"Yeah," replied Roger. "And Leonard's right, we should have gotten together."

Leonard groaned.

"I'd better be going now," said Roger.

"Do you have to leave?" asked Carla.

"Yup," said Roger. Then looking at Leonard he added, "Got to go join the National Guard." Hastily he donned his coat and headed out the door.

"Your friend is certainly strange," commented Leonard after he heard the door close. "Weird."

"Roger? Weird? Oh dear no."

"He said he was going to join the National Guard. Do you suppose he really meant it?"

Carla, fresh from a week back home in Megunnaway, found it easy to suppose that he did.

"I'm certainly glad you're here, Carla," said Leonard, "though Roger took care of me even if he does hate my guts. But I've another worry. You've simply got to do something about Phoenicia."

"Phoenicia? What's with her?" Carla asked.

"Gone sour, that's what. Totally out of control. Won't accept the Party's authority—says anything she wants."

Carla laughed. "Worse than me?" she wanted to know.

"Is cayenne pepper good for a cold?" he changed the subject. "Or for the flu?"

"I've always heard it was."

"Oh. Maine folkways?"

"Why do you ask?"

"I'd never heard of it," he said. "Are you positive?"

"Why yes, yes, I am."

He should have been reassured, but he wasn't. Reactionary idiot, he thought of Roger, son of the devil, curse him! But there was no hell, no power to curse, not even hexes. For the likes of Roger there should be, decided Leonard.

TWENTY-FOUR

Leonard awoke the next day in a foul mood but otherwise considerably improved. He had been unjustly used by his superior officers, and it rankled. He suspected that he'd been mocked by that imbecile Roger. Carla's indifference to all his problems, including his concern over that ninny Phoenicia, was hard to take.

Carla went to the kitchen and made the call to Phoenicia as Leonard had asked, or ordered, but the line was busy. Carla sat in moody silence and drank her coffee. She was weary of Leonard's political squabbles, wanted nothing to do with them. Oh she was against Naziism and glad to hear of trade union successes, but even these matters were remote, outside of her life.

The week at Megunnaway was what mattered, the week of listening to Abigail's happy chatter, living with her in that one miserable room. The familiar pictures were still on the wall: the shepherd in the snowstorm, the struggling woman in the water reaching for the cross upon the rock, and the El Greco "Toledo," in which the threatening storm seemed so real that she shivered and held her breath waiting for the flash of lightning and the crash of thunder. But no flash had come and no thunder, just a week of walking on eggs, watching every word lest she say something too revealing. Abigail sat in the evening knitting bright blue mittens and green mittens and striped mittens while chattering happily of the children who'd wear them as they played in the snow. Children and snow! What a merry combination! But only if they wore their mittens! Once in a while she would steal a look at the moody face of her daughter and yearn to help her, but make no comment, only wait. She too looked at the gathering storm in "Toledo" and said a prayer that God would save them both. Mrs. Mittens, however, had no time to brood, she had to get those mittens done.

Leonard snapped Carla out of her reverie. "Well?" he said. "I thought you were phoning?"

Phoencia answered the phone herself. "Oh Carla!" she cried. "How sweet of you to call. See Leonard? No point whatever. Anyway I'm much too upset to see anyone, I've cried until I'm a fright. Monday? If I have to see Leonard, make it Tuesday." And she hung up, gently, no bang, just a break in the connection.

On Monday when Carla arrived, Phoenicia was at her desk. The light from the office window fell unkindly upon the crow's feet around her eyes and outlined the wrinkles around her mouth, yet the face was lively, energetic, womanly. Carla noted that she had discarded the blonde wig and wore only her own short hair which was about equally golden and silver, tightly curled, a close-fitting cap. It was becoming, Carla thought, much more so than the frazzled wig.

After putting away her outdoor clothing, Carla approached her employer waiting for her instructions. "Could you help with this copy?" said Phoenicia. "I simply cannot think."

Carla sat down and was studying the information—special sale on skis, skates, and toboggans. "Let's see," she said. "Phoenicia, how about this, 'Let our experts help you select the perfect ski for *you*. Wide range of lengths, widths, ski bindings. The very best, designed by leading European masters of the art. Prices reduced.' We'll need to get the names of designers."

She had been writing as she spoke, and now she raised her eyes to see how it was being received. Phoenicia was sitting there with that faraway look, and tears were beginning to run from her eyes. "Oh Carla," she cried, "he's left me. I may never see him again."

Carla had always supposed Emil would leave. What comfort could she give? "You'll probably see him sooner than you expect," she said. "In the meantime think about the good times you've had with him."

"Such a short, short time," moaned Phoenicia. "And I thought he really loved me. He didn't have to leave me behind. I'd have gone with him, I begged him to let me. Yes, forgot my human dignity and actually begged him in a way I've never begged a man before."

"Where did he go?"

"He went to Russia, I mean the Soviet Union, at least that's what he said. And oh, I needed to go. We'd just gotten to the place in my book where the heroine is going to kill the factory owner, her husband you know, only he gets a whole new outlook on life and is so changed. And how does he get the new outlook? Why by going to Russia."

If Professor Zero said he was going to Russia, the odds were he went elsewhere, thought Carla. "I'm sure you'll be able to work out an ending," she said.

"It isn't the book. It's him. He's gone forever."

Somehow they got through the hours. Carla did most of the copy writing that day. It wasn't the first time she'd had this added to her duties, but though it set her back in her other work, she rather enjoyed sitting at her typewriter pounding out words, even words about subjects she wasn't interested in and not too well-informed about. She'd done some real writing that year on her own, actually finished two short stories, which she'd shown to none of her acquaintances but which she'd sent to a couple of magazines, only to have them rejected. She'd written one article for "Light," and though Leonard had called it namby-pamby, he'd printed it. She counted her personal letters among real writing, for she weighed each word and struggled with the phrasing and took pride in the results. But now she no longer wrote to Roger, and her letters to her mother were clouded by deceit, and those to Howard inhibited by the fear that they would be read by a censor. Now here she was enjoying this silly copy. She hurried to show it to Phoenicia who nodded listlessly. Then she took it to Francis who puffed on his pipe and said, "Good girl, Carla, hang around while I do a sketch to go with it."

Phoenicia went out to lunch with a prospective client and came back in a considerably livelier mood. She'd landed the account, and it had been one they'd almost despaired of getting. She settled down at her desk, started reviewing the work which Carla and Francis had finished, called a conference to tell them what was wrong with it, ordered them back to work, kept interrupting every ten minutes with some new command, and by five o'clock had them both in a state approximating rebellion. Then, like the suddenly clearing sky after a storm, she smiled and said to Carla, "Forgive me, please. I know I've been nasty. But tomorrow is another day. I promise it is."

Tuesday morning Phoenicia showed up once more in a golden wig, but not the old wild one, no indeed, a smooth, close-fitting, ever so ladylike wig. Phoenicia was pleasant enough to Carla, but she admitted she'd been shrewish again to Francis and didn't expect he'd come in.

Leonard, neat in dark blue overcoat and suit, white shirt, neatly knotted tie, perfectly composed countenance, gray hat in hand, came in for his appointment with Phoenicia. He came right to the point. "I understand that in your last speech at the Writers Club, you gave an in-depth evaluation of the situation in Spain."

"I certainly did," she replied.

"You shouldn't even be discussing Spain—" he began angrily.

"Leonard!" she interrupted him. "You don't know what's going on over there."

"I beg your pardon. I do know. I demand you stop listening to those white-slave, drug-trading, illiterate slobs you use as your sources."

Carla had never heard him more furious. Phoenicia was comparatively calm. "You're too dogmatic," she said.

"Phoenicia, surely you understand the need for complete control by those who know what they're doing."

"I say we should hear what's going on. You should run a symposium in 'Light.'"

"You're demented to even suggest such a thing."

For a half hour they batted the words back and forth. It ended with Phoenicia yielding somewhat and saying perhaps she had talked too openly. She'd think about it. "You know, Leonard," she said at last, "I'm so upset these days, sometimes I hardly know what to think about anything."

"That's another matter," said Leonard. "Did I hear right that you've been saying Emil has gone to Moscow?"

"Yes, of course. What's more he refused, absolutely refused to let me go with him, though I really need to go. For my book. One of the characters, a real bourgeois character, goes there and is completely reformed. But how can I write about it? I've never been there."

"What difference does that make? Read up, use your imagination. I'm not objecting to your wanting to go. I'm objecting to your blasted tongue. If he did go, and I'm not saying he did, it wasn't something he wanted talked about. Didn't he tell you that?" Yes, she believed he had. She was contrite. Sometimes she was a silly girl. Politely Leonard took his leave, bowing to Carla as if she were a stranger.

"What an intense person," said Phoenicia after he'd gone. "Don't you find him difficult at times? But I'm glad he came. He put things in a new light."

"You mean about Spain?" Carla asked.

"Oh no, about Emil. If he has some secret mission, perhaps he couldn't take me. Oh how thrilling, to think of him engaged in such important matters! To think of my Emil actually talking to those who have power, bringing them information, helping make decisions. To think I was so angry with him."

❧❦

Carla got home before Leonard, and he came into the kitchen where she was preparing dinner. "Do you suppose Emil really did go to the Soviet Union?" she asked.

Leonard gave her a hard sharp look. "Emil went where he was ordered to go," he said. "You and that Phoenicia with your clacking tongues! Shut up before you get us all in the soup."

She sighed a lonely sigh, but could not be silent, for silence would be a chasm between them. She tried talking about Howard and how she looked forward to seeing him and even said she hoped Leonard would be a brother to him.

Brother indeed! thought Leonard. Carla and her talk of family ties! She was altogether too eager to drag him into stuffy domesticity where he'd first have to take on responsibility for her relatives and later suffocate in the steam of milk and diapers. And what was Carla in terms of his career as a soldier of the revolution? He suspected that it was because of her that the higher-ups weren't sending him on the real missions. Yet when she would come striding into the "Light" office on those lovely long legs, her eyes twinkling with mischief, fresh color in her cheeks, her hair blown about, her whole being suffused with that enticing innocent energy, what else mattered? Surely, surely, he could win her back to the shining path he followed. That was why he had invited Ezra Winter, who was coming to Boston for a speaking engagement, to spend the night with them. If anybody could straighten out her confusion, it was surely Ezra Winter.

To Leonard, Ezra Winter was perfect—a pleasant, entertaining guest, good-looking in a rugged grizzled way, and possessed of a fund of stories, most of them dealing, not with the steel industry where he had worked, but with the waterfront. Between sips of tea and bites of cake he regaled them with tales of heroism and guile. Once he slipped easily into matter-of-fact discussion of strategy. "By organizing basic industry," he said, "including transportation, we establish a stranglehold. In case of war or revolution we will have total control."

Oh no! thought Leonard as he hastily forestalled Carla's outburst by insisting that he needed her help in getting the bedding out for Winter. The three of them labored silently converting the sofa into a bed. It was a task which Winter went about with agile ease, for he was used to this kind of accommodation in comrades' homes. After Carla had gone to her room, he turned to Leonard, "Was I too open?" he asked. "I mean, isn't she sound?" What could Leonard say?

Carla had mixed feelings about her political disagreements with Leonard. On the one hand, she found them interesting. However, they were definitely harming their relationship. Also, Leonard's politics made it difficult for them to relate to either of their families. She couldn't be honest with her own mother, and Leonard was constantly fighting over politics with one member of his family or another.

When Ellen's wedding day came, Carla stayed home, but Leonard attended. When he returned, he reported that his parents had made a real production of it. "Yet," he admitted afterward, "Ellen seems happy. Though why they had to have a wasteful and vulgar display is beyond me. I really should not have gone."

"Your going was not a cardinal sin."

"Of course not," said Leonard. "There's no such thing as sin." And that was that.

There is too, thought Carla, *such a thing as sin. His family and my family know it. And because they know it, Leonard and I are at odds with our families, will always be at odds.*

It came to a head one overheated Saturday several months later. The day started routinely enough with the usual household chores. At eleven o'clock the first visitor arrived, the first of three unexpected callers.

She opened the door in response to a firm knock, and there stood Mr. Engelstein, Leonard's father. He was in shirtsleeves and light summer trousers, but sweat stood in drops upon his forehead, and he was breathing hard as if the flight of stairs had been too much for him. Further there was a strained, anxious look to his countenance, so that he was quite unlike his usual jovial self. "We have to have a talk," he said.

"Come on in. Leonard's in the living room." She had flushed a hot red, blushing that he had found her there.

They went into the living room, and Leonard turned off the vacuum cleaner. "Why Dad!" he cried. "You catch me being useful."

The elder Engelstein was in no mood for small talk. "We have to have a talk," he repeated the words he had used to Carla.

Soon they were seated in the living room, the older man on the sofa and the young couple in chairs facing him, and each with the ritual cup of coffee.

"I'm glad you came," said Leonard. "I've noticed you don't attend Mobilization meetings any more."

"No. Some of the things I hear there send my blood pressure up, but I send contributions."

"We appreciate that, but why did you stop coming?"

"I just told you. Of course I'm against fascism, Naziism, what Jew could be otherwise? About Spain, I don't know. And I'm frankly worried about Russia."

"You call it Russia now?"

"Okay, the Soviet Union." The older man set his cup upon the coffee table, drew out a large and spotlessly white handkerchief and wiped his forehead. "I don't know, I don't know," he said sadly. "Anyway that's not what I came to talk about."

"What then?"

"Would you rather I left?" asked Carla.

"Definitely not. I came to talk to both of you."

There was an embarrassed silence. Mr. Engelstein's face grew red, he coughed, and then the words came rushing out. "It isn't right," he said. "Leonard, it isn't right the way you and Carla are living."

"Father," said Leonard, "I love and respect you, but I have my own life to lead. Carla and I sincerely love each other. I'm sorry you can't accept that."

"I do accept that. And Carla, I didn't come to talk against you, but for you. Leonard, settle down, get married. We'll make it right somehow with your mother."

Carla's heart was thumping wildly. But she had a firm hold on reality. "That's impossible, surely you know it is," she said.

"You're a good girl. She'd forgive you anything for a grandchild."

"Even if we were married, that would be out of the question," Leonard was definite.

"We didn't either of us know that you were living together until a week ago. Actually Mother still doesn't. I got it out of Ellen. I swear I didn't know before."

"Now that you know?" queried Leonard.

"It's not right. It's not fair to this young woman. It's not personal, Carla, you know, with Esther. With her it's her religion. As for me, I'm not religious, though we keep the holidays, of course. I don't suppose Esther's God will worry about details so long as you are a good girl and keep the Ten Commandments."

"Which," said Leonard, "we certainly don't."

"Carla," the old man continued. "I don't suppose you'd be willing to convert? For Esther's sake, I mean?"

"That has nothing to do with it," Leonard answered. "Don't badger her. Talk to me."

"To you? Of you I'm ashamed. What kind of life—"

"A life dedicated to the cause."

"What kind of dedication is it that makes you act like a heel?"

"You've already said what you came to say."

"Think about it, don't just brush it off," the father urged. "For now, I may as well go."

Carla rose and went to the door with him. "Thank you, Mr. Engelstein," she said as he stood in the doorway, looking back sadly. "You're a good man."

"If I can ever help—"

"Nothing can help," replied Carla.

She stood there watching his heavy figure as he walked to the stairs. Suddenly there was a commotion in the hall below, and up the stairs bounded an excited Bettina. "Carla, Carla," she cried. "Your brother's here."

Carla hurried to the top of the stairs, and there coming up was a broadly smiling Roger and behind him the slighter figure of Howard. Oh it *was* Howard! He had his head down as if trying to hide his face, but it was, it was. Mr. Engelstein, standing a couple of steps further down, made a most natural mistake. Seeing the tall, dark-haired, self-possessed Roger and hardly noting the self-effacing figure behind him, he stretched out his hand to Roger and said, "Well, Carla's brother, it's about time you got here. You see if you can straighten them out."

"I'm only a brotherly friend," said Roger, proceeding to introduce Howard.

Mr. Engelstein shook Howard's hand and assured him he was glad to meet him. He gave him a shrewd appraising glance, but what he would have said to Roger, he refrained from saying to Howard. He didn't think it any use.

Leonard remained in the living room, and they found him still sitting in a straight chair scowling ferociously at the empty coffee cup in his hand. He looked up, he even stood up, listened to Carla's excited announcement, and acknowledged the introduction of Howard. However, Leonard went out soon after on what he said was urgent business, though Carla suspected this was an excuse to leave her and Roger and Howard alone with a joy he did not share. Ah, what joy! Her brother had survived, he had been released, he was there, she had a brother, once more she had a brother, at least for the moment.

Howard stood there flushed with embarrassment, and yet there was defiance in the set of his mouth. He was silent, listening to footsteps going down the stairs, and when they could no longer be heard, he turned to Carla and demanded, "What's with this Leonard fellow?"

Carla scorned to pretty it up. "We live together," she said.

"Oh no," he groaned, but what could he say? He'd forfeited his right to judge or advise.

"We got a job for Howard in a Cambridge restaurant," Roger hastened to interpose.

"Never mind talking about the job!" Howard spat out the words. "I hope he drops dead!"

"And a place to live. It seems he can't stand apartments, but we found this shack."

Howard had regained some measure of composure. "Yeah, I guess you could call it that," he said. "It's like the place in Megunnaway. Only smaller. You'll come and see me?"

"Of course."

"Good, because I won't come here again."

"Is Leonard invited?"

Howard hesitated.

"I'd say yes if I were you," Roger advised.

"Okay."

It didn't matter, for later that night when Carla reported the invitation Leonard grunted and told her to go by herself. "I suppose," he said as they prepared for bed, "that your brother is on the same kick as my father, marriage, I mean."

"Certainly not," she retorted. "He hopes you'll drop dead."

✖❀✖

The muggy heat of August gave way to the crisp, clear autumn days and these in turn to dreary November and then the sparkling snow of December. In mid-January Tanya, still very much the union organizer, came again to Boston. Carla went into the inner office at "The Light" and found her there, close to Leonard, intently studying a typewritten paper. She glanced up, for a moment almost the old Tanya, thought Carla, the same light-hearted, singing Tanya who'd nearly been her friend. Then the sparkle vanished from her eyes, her brow wrinkled in a frown, she took a puff on her cigarette, in an instant she was hard as nails.

"You had some question?" Leonard asked.

"It will wait," said Carla.

Yes, she and Leonard were growing farther and farther apart. It wasn't personal, she told herself. It was political, but with Leonard there was no separating the two. It was easier when they stayed off politics, and this they both tried, most of the time, to do. When he jumped on her for not knowing how to make good red beet borscht with sour cream like his mother used to make, Carla chortled with glee. It was so conventional, so nostalgic, showed such longing for family life, was so highly indicative of a nesting instinct. She threw her arms around him and promised to learn. He laughed and hugged her. *We're two minds,* she thought, *but one flesh.*

One morning in February when she was breakfasting at the Attleburys' she felt suddenly ill. Even the tangy grapefruit was nauseating. She put down her spoon and looked up at Mollie, who stood watching her.

"What's the matter, honey?" the older woman said at last. "Morning sickness?"

Of course, of course, thought Carla. How wonderful! She asked for and got a week off from her job, and she spent many hours walking along the snowy streets and through the park, pondering this new mystery which had overwhelmed her. Every day she saw young mothers, bundled up against the cold, wheeling their equally bundled up babies out for fresh air. How rosy the little cheeks were, how proud the mothers! She saw others in the park gently helping toddlers to walk on the hard-packed snow. She saw tiny tots dash gaily into the snowbanks, saw the mothers help them make snowballs, saw the mothers hauling them on little sleds. How good these women were and how happy! Dear Father Engelstein had spoken wisely when he said she and Leonard ought to get married and have children. She saw herself and Leonard becoming a conventional family with children and a house in the suburbs and a dog or two. She saw them planning for the children and sometimes remembering with nostalgia the wild romantic days of their youth. It was a road which they must travel step by step, and the first step was to share with him the knowledge which was hers.

Of course it had to be documented by a doctor. Eagerly she made the appointment with the high priest of childbirth, the same man who'd treated her for flu and sundry other minor ailments. He was a crusty old gentleman, the kind where one senses without difficulty the soft heart beneath the shell. "Yes," he said. "You're pregnant."

It was one thing to daydream, another to face the reality of giving this news to Leonard, and fear washed over her. The doctor looked at her thoughtfully. "You don't seem exactly jubilant," he said.

"We hadn't planned it," she murmured.

"Oh you'll get things straightened out. And you're well-built for it, should be no problems."

When Leonard and she met at the apartment, her first thought was to tell him at once, but the words wouldn't quite fall into place. Besides he himself had news, or at least tentative news. "There's a possibility," he said, "no, that's not adequate, there's a probability I'll be going to New York." He went at once to hang up his coat, while she returned to the kitchen.

He was humming an unfamiliar tune as he came back. He hugged her, planted a kiss on her cheek, moved away to free her for her work. "New York!" he exulted. "They'll call me tonight, make it definite. And I'll be sitting waiting for the ring, waiting like a lonely-hearted girl." He laughed gaily.

His being in a jovial mood didn't seem to help, particularly since Carla was quite aware that he had said, "I'll be going," not *we*. They ate dinner and she washed the dishes. He was sitting on the couch smoking his cigarette and reading "The Partisan Review," which always made him angry. *I can't tell him now*, thought Carla. *I'll wait for the phone call. But I must tell him! I can't bear to wait!* She sat down beside him still groping for words. Then totally without buildup and almost involuntarily she made the flat statement. "Leonard, I'm pregnant."

He dropped his cigarette as if it had suddenly burned his hand. It took him a minute to scoop it up with the edge of the magazine, for his hand was trembling. The lines on his face deepened, and even the frozen side had a look of dismay.

"That," he said harshly, "is impossible."

Carla was silent. She had been too abrupt. Would it have mattered how she told him? The situation was utterly hopeless.

"It's your fault," he said.

This was too much. "Yeah," she snapped. "I raped you."

He struggled for self-control. "Carla," he said. "There is no need for us to quarrel over it."

"I see you find no cause to celebrate either."

"Right."

The phone rang. Yes, she saw by his face that it was *the* call. She went at once into the bedroom that he might not accuse her of eavesdropping. At last he called her back. She sat facing him, trying to read his countenance. Elation, she saw there, but also anxiety.

"It's come through," he said. "I'm to wind up here, and I'm to leave in a week."

"You are to leave? And I?"

"This will give us a chance to be apart."

"Apart? *Now?*"

"Nothing can make it like it used to be," he replied. "What's the use pretending?"

"You mean?"

"Don't worry. I'll take care of you, one way or another."

"One way or another?" There'd been too much talk about abortion in their circle for her not to know what way he'd arrange.

"Can't you see that it's time for us to go our separate ways?"

"Tanya?"

"It isn't really that. You and I have just grown apart. Something's gotten into you. You're no longer the loyal comrade you used to be."

"No, I guess not. Though I did think I was the same loving wife."

"How can you be one without being the other?"

It was useless to talk, she realized.

"I'd hoped we could break clean, no recriminations," he said. "No tears."

She got up quickly. "There will be no tears," she said and went into the kitchen.

The next morning around ten Carla, unable to stand the apartment, walked to the park. It was a cold and blustery day on which none of the mothers ventured out with their little preciouses. Carla had rather counted on seeing them, but perhaps it was better so, perhaps it would have been too much for her to endure. She walked back to the apartment house. There were no children about, the older ones being at school and the others confined to the house. She went inside, put away her hat and coat, made a pot of tea. She hoped Bettina wouldn't come calling this day, but one never knew; Bettina visited in her own good time even on school days. The doorbell buzzed. It couldn't be Bettina, who always came to the door, knocked and called out. Carla pressed the buzzer to open the front door, then went into the hall.

A man came puffing up the stairs, slowly, step by step. At last his gray hat reached the top. "Why Mr. Engelstein!" she cried. "Do come in."

He was unusually solemn and for a while said nothing beyond asking when Leonard would be home, which Carla didn't know. Then he leaned toward Carla, and his voice trembling he said, "Stalin killed Bukharin! Did you know? He killed him!" The Communists have turned on one or their own fathers and killed him!"

"I did hear it on the radio."

"It's true. Don't you understand what this means?"

"I suppose I do, in a way."

"They've killed the best of the revolutionary leaders. They've betrayed the revolution. What's left is a monstrosity. I can no longer have anything to do with it."

"Did you come to talk to Leonard about this?"

"Yes, I did. And to you. I came because I had to. I have to try."

He sat there absent-mindedly drinking his tea and eating his muffin, a bald-headed, round-faced, elderly gentleman dressed in conventional dark suit and white shirt, his whole life shattered by the death of an old Bolshevick whom he'd known many years before. "I've been worried for a long time," he said. "But this clinches it. It was wrong, all wrong from the start. I've done nothing but mislead my children. If only I could start over again."

"You could talk to Ellen."

"Ellen I don't need to talk to. Her husband understands, he can talk to her. And Agnes flits from one thing to another, and it doesn't matter, poor Agnes. It's Leonard I grieve over. And you."

"Leonard doesn't see it the way you do. And he doesn't listen to me."

He jumped up, quickly in spite of his corpulence, and he planted a kiss on her forehead. "My dear, my dear," he cried. "You and Leonard simply must get yourselves straightened out, get married, raise a family, lead a normal life."

"He and I had a dream together, and now I've lost it. We can't go on together. They've some plans for him in New York. He doesn't tell me."

"Oh no! My son, a fanatic like those who killed Radek and now Bukharin!" he wailed. "How can he be a son of mine?"

"Don't say that. Love your son and believe in him. He's like you and I were before, only he's more dedicated. I love and respect him."

"Then why must you separate?"

"We've already separated. Tanya—"

"So that's it! Esther will be delighted, but not I. Tanya's too calculating, too hard."

"She'll never lose the dream."

"But what of you?"

"It's settled. He's moving to New York."

"Aren't you going too?"

"No, I won't be going."

"What if there's a baby on the way?"

Carla remembered Margaret asking that same question, eagerly, hopefully. No doubt this good man also hoped, he and Margaret alike in their longing for grandchildren. But it had been different then, there was no child. She answered Mr. Engelstein as she had to answer him.

"There'll be no child," she said. "It's better so."

"Perhaps. I'd sometimes thought, forgive me, that if—you know this does happen, that then you and Leonard—"

"Forget me and remain his loving father."

"Leonard has a responsibility toward you, and therefore I do too. What relatives do you have?"

"You met my brother."

"Yes, and pardon an old man's frankness, think of me as your father-in-law. He didn't seem up to much more than looking out for himself."

"He's had hard luck, but he's doing fine now."

"Maybe. But it's not right. I'll wait for Leonard. I'll talk to him."

"You did once before."

"I will again. It'll be different. I'm different."

"Please say nothing about me."

They could hear footsteps coming up the stairs, along the hall.

"Okay for now, but if you change your mind. Anyway I have to talk to him. Really lay it on the line," expostulated the old man. "Does he know they've killed Bukharin?"

The door opened and Leonard entered. "Yes," he said. "I know they've killed Bukharin. I thought that would set you off."

Mr. Engelstein's face flushed with anger, he sputtered and could not speak. Carla rose to leave, but he pulled her back into her chair, then turned and faced his son.

"Leonard," he said. "This once you're going to listen to me."

Leonard tossed his coat onto the couch then came to the table.

"I don't deny they're ruthless, I even applaud it," Leonard proclaimed.

"Was it for this, great God, we ceased to worship You? Come home, son, and make an honest living producing shirts. I'm old, you can be a partner, whatever you want."

"Me? A businessman?"

"Go ahead sneer! But I predict these masterminds who find plots with Nazis will some day themselves march shoulder to shoulder with those very Nazis along the same road to perdition," Mr. Engelstein warned.

"When that happens," said Leonard, "then I'll enlist under some other flag."

"Enlist! Enlist!" cried the old man. "Who knows under what you'll enlist?" He rose, demanded his hat and coat, then turned in one last appeal. "What is the purpose of it?" he cried. "What?"

"Once you knew," replied Leonard.

"Once I was an idiot," said Mr. Engelstein and left.

Leonard turned to Carla. "Did you tell him?" he challenged.

"Certainly not about the—" she couldn't say the word.

"He'd forgive my politics, he will indeed forgive. But this, never."

"This?"

"I have arranged through a doctor I know for an abortion." He threw out the ugly word as nonchalantly as he might have mentioned a tonsillectomy. "Right away, tomorrow. Getting it that soon wasn't easy, but the earlier it's done the better, and I want it over with."

She sat half fainting. He didn't ask her opinion, and she was too profoundly shocked to give it. Oh in the past they'd talked about abortions, there were times when she hadn't been sure, thought maybe it was morally acceptable; under some circumstances. The previous evening she'd understood his hint and then had rejected the understanding. Now he spoke as if it were immutably settled. No! Something within her cried out no, but she silenced it.

He laid a folded piece of paper on the table. "There is the address," he said. "You're to be there tomorrow at noon. I'll put two hundred dollars in on the chest. That's what he charges. Now I'm going to pack."

"Are you leaving tonight?"

"Certainly not. I must wait until you've seen the doctor, and I know you're okay. Do you think me completely heartless or irresponsible?"

You'll kill our child, she thought, *but I mustn't think you heartless or irresponsible*. She was silent, confused, in love with him, anxious to be fair to him. It was not for her to judge him, she told herself. She went into the bedroom and stood watching him as he folded shirts and packed them in a suitcase. She hadn't remembered he had so many.

TWENTY-FIVE

Busy with bitter thoughts Carla saw the folded paper only when she chanced to glance at the green bottle, which was serving as a paperweight. She opened the folded paper and read the name Dr. Weisel and an address. Below that was a scribbled note: "Joan," it said, "I'll see you this afternoon, L." Why had he used the old nickname, almost forgotten of late? Joan of Arc of the Shoe Workers! Yes, that had been splendid. Wasn't it better to die young?

She set out in mid-morning. It was unseasonably warm, and the snow was melting into dirty, gray slush. Leonard had said his father would never forgive him this. No more would Abigail forgive her, nor would Howard. Oppressed with shame, she slunk along the street, her eyes fixed on the sidewalk, hoping she would meet no one she knew. A trolley took her downtown, and there she waited for another. The sky was overcast, and there was a feel of rain in the air. Though warmly dressed, she shivered and her stomach made audible sounds of distress. At last she boarded the streetcar and sat upon the hard wooden bench. The iron wheels ground along the rails, transmitting the impact of every bump directly into her aching back. She sat close to the window, looking out to hide her face from those who rode with her.

She'd said once that Abigail would never forgive her living with Leonard, but now she realized that Abigail could have forgiven anything but this which she was about to do. Howard must never know. And Roger must never know. The sense of defilement deprived her of strength, the conviction that she was trapped kept her chained to the jolting streetcar. Trapped, yes, trapped. How could she raise a child alone? Did she not know the horror awaiting a fatherless child? And the suffering for its mother? It would be far worse than anything Abigail had known, for she at least had had a husband the first few years. What if Abigail had drawn back from giving birth to her? But that was impossible. How could one think of abortion and one's mother? Would she and Papa have been able to make it with only one child? Or what if they'd had neither?

Poor Abigail, she worked so hard in that sweltering kitchen. Her letters had grown shorter and shorter as if she were too tired to write. But Leonard had said there was no other way.

Through the dark brown crowded places she rode, through the brick-red crowded places she rode, and with her rode fear and guilt. Looking out she saw that the red brick buildings, still four stories high, had narrow spaces between them. Here and there a tree struggled, its frame of branches, bare of leaves, straggly and gray as death. The buildings were all of a pattern, four stories high with short flights of stairs leading up to their front doors, which were of dark wood. The windows were tall and narrow and covered with dirt. She had no difficulty finding the number she sought, for it had been painted on the door in figures three inches high and startlingly white. She got off by the rear exit and feeling that she was about to vomit, stopped and leaned against a lamppost. In a minute she was able to walk back down the street.

She forced herself to climb the short flight of stairs. A small brass plate by the door read "Dr. M. J. Weisel, Room No. 7," and another indicated that the office of a dentist was located in Room No. 4. She entered a dimly lit hall. On her right was an open door through which she could see a dentist's chair, but there was no one in the room. Further on and to the left was a heavy wooden door with Dr. Weisel's nameplate. She hesitated. No sound came from the room. Did one walk in or was it more proper to knock? Just beyond was the Ladies Room, and she went in. She could hear a strange squawking, then a cry of pain. The squawking became louder. Good heavens, it was a parrot and it was saying over and over, "Shut up, doll; shut up, doll; shut up, doll."

Carla went back into the vestibule. A streetcar rumbled by. The parrot kept up his shrill command. Dr. Weisel's door opened wide and out walked a sturdy middle-aged woman dressed in white and carrying over her arm a black coat. "What are you doing here?" she demanded harshly.

Before Carla could recover her composure, a man in a white smock came hurriedly through the door and closed it behind him. He stood there glaring at her, and then she recognized him, though she'd known him by a different name. He'd been at many Mobilization meetings, even some of the rather intimate house parties. He turned angrily to the nurse. "Why the fuss?" he demanded. "This is the young lady I told you I was expecting."

"It's not time for her," the older woman said.

"Neither is it time for you to leave," the doctor replied. "Coffee every ten minutes! This is a preposterous time to walk out!"

"I have a headache," the woman said. "I'm taking off the afternoon."

"No, no, no!" the doctor screamed, but the woman ignored him and walked briskly down the hall. "That woman's a fiend!" he cried, then turning to Carla he smiled a nervous smile and with a gesture invited her to enter through the door he had just opened.

She walked into an office, neatly furnished with light oak furniture, a table strewn with magazines, an ordinary enough room except that the glass panes of the window had been painted an opaque white so that it was impossible to look out.

"You are early," the doctor said. "Just be seated."

Carla did as directed and started to thumb through the magazines. Dr. M. J. Weisel, hmm. She had known him as Dr. Judson Morris with a practice in Malden. She even knew a patient of his. So this was what he did on his day off. At least he was a genuine doctor. Dr. Weisel opened the door to an inner room, and as he did so, Carla heard a low moan, a steady low moan. The parrot, which was in that inner room, resumed his chant of "Shut up, doll; shut up, doll; shut up, doll." The door closed behind the doctor. Carla could still hear the parrot and now and then the moan. She took off her hat and coat and laid them carefully on one of the chairs, then went back to thumbing through the magazines, seeing nothing.

What if Ray had lived? And they'd had a child? Why, oh why, did her life always have always to be defined by a man? To think she'd quarreled once with Ray over picking up trash from the floor, had become angry just because he put it on the table instead of in the wastebasket. Resolutely she chased Ray from her mind, only to have memories of her father come flooding in. Those awful long black stockings he'd made her wear as a child! Made her wear out of modesty. Had he had some perception of her passionate temperament? Had he foreseen her bent for making a fool of herself over some man?

How evil men were and how good! Leonard's father, how he loved his son, and how he'd have loved a grandson. And he was so sufferingly right in his repentance. Ah that folly, that political folly of which she, even as Mr. Engelstein, had been guilty. She couldn't blame that on any man; it had been of her own making, already well-advanced before she met Leonard. Any way she looked at it, she'd been two kinds of an idiot, two kinds of a sinner.

The moans continued, now suddenly punctuated by a scream, and she could hear the low rumble of the doctor's voice but could not distinguish his words. *Of course it hurts,* she thought, *but the pain doesn't matter.* She believed her guilt would be wiped out by suffering. There was that screeching parrot again. How sick she felt, nauseated, dizzy.

She was snapped to attention by the sharp voice of the doctor. "Carla!" he cried, "Come in here and help."

Through the door she could see lying on the long table a body covered with a white sheet—a woman—young, blonde hair curling around her face,

face distorted with pain, a young face, little more than a child. "No, no," cried Carla. "I can't!"

"But you must," insisted the doctor. "The thing's dead anyway. I have to get it out of her."

She followed him into the room, washed her hands in the corner washstand, and all the while the girl was moaning and the parrot was squawking.

"Stand there," the doctor directed. "You must, you must. We have to save her."

The girl's feet were in stirrups, her knees bent, her body now writhing, now still. Seeing no way out, Carla took her place at one side as directed by the doctor while he proceeded with his task. "Force her knees apart," he instructed, and although the woman cried out, Carla forced apart the knees with both hands, stretching to reach the one on the far side, but because she was tall and long of arm, she was able to do so. *Yes, I can handle it,* she thought, *if only I don't vomit all over the woman, doctor, floor, and everything in reach.*

"Okay," said the doctor. "You can let go of her knees and take what I hand you. Just put it in that receptacle." He pointed to a metal white garbage can two feet tall which stood near the table.

Carla looked down, saw the container, noted that it was lined with a plastic bag, noted that the cover had been removed and lay beside it. Automatically she stretched out her hand toward the doctor, felt him put something wet and squishy in it, looked down and saw that she held in her hand a tiny bloody arm. She screamed a scream that on the open street could have been heard a block away and stood there unable to move, unable even to drop that tiny bloody arm.

The doctor turned purple. "Quiet! Stop that screaming this minute!" He was furious with her. "You're worse than that nurse of mine."

"Shut up, doll; shut up, doll; shut up," screamed the parrot.

The young woman lay there sobbing incessantly. She started to sit up.

"No, no!" cried Dr. Weisel. "Lie down! I'm not through with you." He turned to Carla. "Drop that thing!" he ordered.

Carla closed her eyes and held her hand over the garbage can. Her fingers relaxed. She heard a soft plop.

"Go wash your hands, then stand by her head and sweet-talk her."

"I can't."

"She needs your help."

Carla washed her hands and went to the head of the bed, gently stroked the girl's forehead, smoothed her hair, said softly, "It's almost over, honey. Lie still, there's a good girl, lie still."

"Carla, I really need you," said the doctor. "Come back where you can reach what I hand you. Here, this is the second arm. Try to keep track."

Carla looked at the doctor's extended hand. He wore pink rubber gloves, sharp metal shone in his right hand and in the extended left was a miniature arm, like the one before, two inches long, bloodstained, soft firm flesh, perfect fingernails. Oh perfect fingernails! Her hand, without any instruction from her brain, took the tiny arm and dropped it in the container. Bit by bit she received the mangled baby, felt the blood upon her flesh, kept track of the pieces as she was ordered, dared not stop for the sake of the moaning girl upon the table.

"Take her feet out of the stirrups," commanded Dr. Weisel. "Then go wash."

Moving automatically she did as he said, then returned to stand by the girl, who lay with eyes closed, face flushed, breath regular and even. Dr. Weisel stood by her side, his rubber gloves removed, his hands washed, his face calm and professional. He listened to the girl's heart with a stethoscope, he took her blood pressure, inserted a thermometer in her mouth. The girl stared at him, silent now, her big blue eyes those of a badly frightened child. The doctor talked consolingly to her, apologized for having to proceed without his regular nurse who, he said, had been taken ill rather suddenly, oh nothing catching he was sure, she had a chronic condition. He assured her that all had gone well, just as he had told her it would.

She lay still and stared at him with those frightened big blue eyes.

He turned to Carla. "I'm going into the next room," he said. "I want you to get her ready to leave."

"Leave?" Carla demanded. "She's not able to leave!"

"She must leave," Dr. Weisel said blandly, "can't have her here. Use the sanitary pads which you'll find in that cabinet and her clothes which are hanging in the closet. And get her dressed and out of here."

The girl seized Carla by the hand and now for the first time she spoke, not to the doctor but to Carla. "Help me dress," she pleaded. She said not another word until fully clothed she stood there, a slender young woman of perhaps nineteen, rather short, decidedly pretty, neatly dressed in low-heeled shoes, gray woollen coat. She looked into Carla's face and said, "I had to. I really had to."

"I'd better take you home."

"Thank you, it won't be necessary. My boyfriend—there's someone waiting in a car for me."

"I'll take you there." By now they had reached the office, where Dr. Weisel sat at the desk.

"No," said the girl. "Please don't." She hurried through the door.

Carla sank into a chair and looked at the doctor. "I'm sorry," he said, "for what may have been an unpleasant experience. It should have been done sooner. I can assure you that you will have no problems."

"Was it safe for her to leave?" Carla demanded.

"Her young man was waiting for her. Anyway she had to leave. I trust you know there is a certain risk in this business. I have to get patients out as quickly as possible. And now, my dear, you. Do you have the money?"

Carla rose and started to put on her coat.

"Do you have the money?" he asked again.

Carla nodded.

"Good. I need a few minutes to prepare. You may go have a cup of coffee," said the doctor, "but do not eat. Give me the money and go have a cup of coffee to calm yourself. I'll get things ready."

She felt herself trembling with fear. She opened her mouth to say yes, she'd like to go for coffee. To her surprise the fear vanished the minute she looked straight at him and she heard herself saying, "I am *not* coming back."

"Wait a minute!" he cried. "I've set aside time for you, not my fault you came early. I've taken the risk of having you come here; it's not my fault you're getting jumpy. Okay, I'll give you an hour, be back in an hour."

With quiet determination she said, "Not in an hour and not ever."

"Leonard expects it," he threatened her. "You'll be alone, you don't realize the difficulties."

"God will take care of me," she answered.

She walked down the stairs to the street trying to understand, trying to accept the fact that words had been placed in her mouth. How could she say that God would take care of her when she didn't even know God? Why hadn't she simply left and given herself time to sort things out? Yes, that was the rational thing to do, but she would have been filled with fear. The surprising thing was not what she had said but that total absence of fear, that blessed assurance. Was this the religious experience that pious folk talked about? It couldn't be because she had no faith. How could it be? But it was. She knew it was.

A slow drizzle had now commenced and the streetcar was picking up passengers. She boarded and sat next to a poor, weary-looking woman with a sleeping child in her arms. Carla thrust her hands into her coat pockets and felt the envelope with the $200. Over the rough tracks she rode, past long lines of buildings, through town. When the time came to change to another streetcar, she handed the woman the envelope and left the car quickly without a word. She boarded a car heading in the direction of her apartment house. Leonard's car was parked in front when she arrived. She didn't want to talk to him, but she was not afraid. Leonard opened the apartment door for her, then began pacing back and forth. Carla went to the kitchen and started making lemonade. Why lemonade? She didn't know, she just wanted lemonade. The pungent fragrance of the lemons filled the air. Silently Carla stood reaming out the juice.

"Did you go?" Leonard asked.

Carla, who might not have carried off a direct lie, looked calmly into his face and answered, "Yes, I went."

"How do you feel?"

"As might be supposed."

"Answer! How do you feel?"

"Strong as an ox."

He heaved a sigh of relief. "Good. You know, Carla, I have always admired your courage, your strength of character."

"Oh?"

"It seems to me that since I'm to leave, I should go at once. If you need money—"

"I have a job," she turned back to the kitchen counter.

He moved close to her left shoulder and asked, "One last kiss?"

She whirled to her left and buried her clenched right fist in his diaphragm. "Tomcat!" she hissed.

Leonard doubled over, struggling for the breath she had knocked out of him.

Carla calmly turned back to making lemonade while he gasped for air. In time he recovered enough to get to the front door and out to the hall. She listened to his receding steps, but she did not turn around.

Thus it ended. And deep within her lay the babe—safe.

He was gone. It was over. She shouted "Yes!" and laughed. She'd taken control, and he'd run from her. She felt a heady sense of being in charge, she'd rescued her baby, she'd cut forever any tie with Leonard, and now she must wind up her old life, break completely with all of Leonard's associates, get a new job, leave Boston. Yes, she must leave Boston, how wonderful to leave! She recalled random lines from a Whitman poem and shouted them aloud.

"'Henceforth I whimper no more, postpone no more.'"

"'Afoot and light-hearted, I take to the open road.'"

"'Listen! I will be honest with you; I do not offer the old smooth prizes, but offer rough new prizes.'"

Whitman always made her think of Abigail. She went into the bedroom to look again at the snapshot her mother had sent a few months before. Abigail's hair had grown thinner so that the Gibson girl roll was flat and the bun more prominent. The sun reflecting off her glasses concealed her eyes, her face was round and had few lines, and she was looking straight ahead. Her arms were folded, she stood straight, her long dress reached almost to the ground. What a dignified, patient, old-fashioned woman! Carla pressed the shiny paper to her lips, then whispered, "Thank you, Mama." The tears began to flow.

Snap out of it, she commanded herself. *Stop this whimpering, get on with what you've got to do.* Phoenicia would be in Brookline and so would Mollie. The steady roll of the streetcar wheels had a calming effect, and the breeze as she walked along the street was just brisk enough to be invigorating. She passed beautiful homes, saw children running from school, came near Phoenicia's, pulled Fiddles out of a neighbor's garbage pail, and arrived out of breath at the kitchen door just as Mollie came out to call the dog.

"Bless my soul!" Mollie cried. "What you doing here? She said she couldn't locate you."

"I have to see her."

"She's gone to the store, back any minute. You go on in and sit down, and soon's I finish with Miss Fiddles, I'll get you coffee. Say, you look like something had happened, now I aim both eyes at you."

When Mollie came in, Carla, still in hat, coat and overshoes, sat in the breakfast nook folding a paper napkin into tiny squares.

"Before you say another word," said Carla as the big colored woman took her seat at the table, "I must tell you why I came."

"Yes?"

"Leonard and I have split up, for good, for keeps, for ever."

"Mmm," mused Mollie. "But I was right about that morning sickness?"

Carla nodded, unable to speak, the bravado having lasted but a moment. She leaned forward, seized the other's hand. "Mollie, he must never know."

"Now honey, you mad now, but you stop and think. It ain't right to not let a baby's papa know."

"Not even if—"she could go no further.

"Not even if you and him's split as split can be. No, Ma'm."

"But if," Carla was crying now. "Mollie, he doesn't want the child, he sent me to—" she bowed her head on the table, sobbing uncontrollably.

"In that case," Mollie came and put her arms around the wretched Carla. "Honey," she said. "One thing you can be sure of is I won't never tell nobody unless you say for me to."

"Oh thank you, thank you." Carla sat up and wiped her eyes.

"But it ain't a thing you can keep secret forever."

"I have to quit my job, get work somewhere else."

"Ain't going to be easy," warned Mollie.

"I'm sure you know."

"You'd better go to your brother."

"How can I?" Carla asked.

"You've got to have someone."

Carla was silent for a moment.

Looking very serious Mollie said, "There's something you don't know."

"What are you talking about?"

"You kept the books at the agency?"

"Why yes."

"Then you know it wasn't making much money."

"Some months we lost, and Phoenicia had to put money into it."

"Now she's in a bind. Some bank or other lowered the boom, that's what Mr. Francis said. They've got to sell this place to raise money. And fire me to save money."

"How will they ever manage?"

"I'm more worried, how will I ever manage."

At this point Phoenicia came bustling in the front door, stopping only to remove her overshoes before hurrying to where she heard voices. She seemed unusually excited, lifted out of dull routine with some new idea or some new project.

There were still signs of tears upon Carla's face, but Phoenicia was too excited to notice. "My dear," she cried. "Everything is in a whirl, oh a delightful whirl! I want you to come to the office and help me straighten out the books."

"Everything is up to date."

"I know, I know. But we're in a receivership, we don't know if we're coming or going." She sounded as if being in a receivership was the most delightful adventure imaginable. "We're selling the old house, and Francis and I will get an apartment, hopefully keep the agency but if not, he can easily find another job. He really is a top-notch commercial artist."

"Indeed he is."

"I might even get to take that trip to Russia after all. Emil has written to me. Sort of cryptic. I'm not sure what he means. I think he's being held there for some political reason. And if I read between the lines correctly, he needs money, and he needs it hand delivered. Oh dear, real intrigue, I suppose. I do hope I go. It'll be the making of my book. What we'll do about your job, I don't know, it's really not in my hands now."

"Oh but I came to tell you I must quit."

Phoenicia gave a sigh of relief. She asked no questions.

Carla rose and buttoned her coat. "I guess this is good-bye," she said.

"Surely I can call on you to come in if I need you?"

"I'll be leaving Boston."

"I do want to see you again, auf wiedersehen, au revoir, not good-bye. I know I won't have the house, and I know you've gone sour, now don't deny it, it's pretty obvious, but I do want to be friends."

Carla looked at her thoughtfully. Yes, in her own way, Phoenicia had been a good friend.

"Can you come in to the office tomorrow?"

"Phoenicia, there's really no reason for me to come in tomorrow."

"Well then," Phoenicia tossed her head with an angry gesture. "I'll write you a check for what we owe." She took the checkbook from a drawer and in silence wrote out the correct amount. "Good-bye," she said coldly. A final, angry good-bye, Carla noted. Gone was the offer of friendship. Going sour she could forgive but that *and* not coming in tomorrow was too much.

That ended that. It was a clean break. And it had hurt. She remembered that night at the motel and the meeting where she had impersonated Phoenicia. If only they'd had one last good laugh!

I could go out West, thought Carla the next morning as she drank her morning coffee. *Yes, that is what I must do. I'll have a new name, I must get truly lost.* The West was still remote, strange, frighteningly far away. Howard had been there, she must see him. She must see him anyway for the one way to get him on her trail would be to fail to say a proper good-bye. The canary began to sing, a sad caged song. Leonard should have taken the bird, perhaps she could call him and have him come and get it. No, no, no! She must purge the days with Leonard from her memory.

She packed her clothing, her books, the green bottle with its power to evoke the memory of a sparkling brook. A clear brook and a father and a mother and a brother. A brother. She repented her arrogance toward him. Even as a child she'd looked down on him as stupid and ungainly. True she'd stood by him when he was far away in jail, but after his release when he lived not far away, she hadn't so much as gone to see him, though he'd urged her to. She would go now and talk humbly with him and accept his rebuke and tell him very little. She would stay only the night and ease her heart and be for that one night not so terribly alone.

By late afternoon, the furniture had been sold to a secondhand dealer, the canary had been given to Bettina, a trunk and a box had been entrusted to the apartment manager to be held until called for. Carla was free to pick up her suitcase and leave. It was already dark when she got off the bus in Cambridge, but the streets were well lit. She walked by apartment houses, by a few individual homes like islands in the sea of multiple dwellings, and past a small corner grocery store which was still open for business. Howard might like a treat, she thought. She stood by the meat counter, felt faint, steadied herself with one hand on the counter, rallied, made her purchase. Awkwardly juggling the suitcase and the grocery bag and her purse, she struggled down

the street until she came to the two-storied house which he had described as
being in front of his cabin. An arrow on a picket fence indicated the way to
his street number. She went along a narrow walk which led from the street
past the big house, found the cabin just as he had described it, read by the
dim light the narrow white board with H. Wingate neatly lettered in black.
A gray tiger cat came and rubbed against her legs, and she wondered if it were
Howard's. Fancy the wanderer Howard with a cat! She set her suitcase down
and knocked a couple of times. Getting no response, she did the sensible thing
and tried the door. It was unlocked.

In the meantime Howard was winding up his day at the cafeteria. "Coffee
and danish? Yes sir, coming right up. Milk and doughnuts? Plain or sugared?
Here you are. Vegetable soup? You got here just in time, ma'm, we're just
closing but the soup's still being served. Say, this just about empties the container, but you got a real full bowl." The last flurry of business, time to hustle
everything off the steam table and into the kitchen, then time for a cup of
java and a look at the paper in the peace of an empty restaurant.

Howard wasn't much of a reader, but he did relish the evening newspaper.
After a perfunctory glance at the sports page and another at the comics, he
turned to the front page. More about Germany's invasion of Austria, another
protest by the British government. In New York a mechanic working on a new
type Army plane at Long Island Airfield had been arrested as a spy. He was a
native of Germany, six feet tall, with old scars on both cheeks, and had recently
visited his homeland. A World War I law had been invoked. World War I.
And now World War II was coming, coming sure as preaching. America would
be in it, no two ways about it. *Should* be in it as a matter of fact. They'll need
men in the Army, he ought to enlist. Perhaps they wouldn't want him, for
he had a jail record, he wasn't very smart and he wasn't big. During the short
bus ride and the walk to his cabin he kept turning it over in his mind. There
really wasn't any reason he shouldn't enlist. Poor little Tigress, who would
look after her? He guessed she'd have to take her chances for he didn't suppose
the DeSapios would want her back. Maybe Mollie Jackson would like a cat.
Certainly little Tommie would love to have Tigress. Maybe he'd go visit them,
hear news of Carla, stretch his legs. It wasn't a long walk, just long enough
so that he'd never have known them if Carla hadn't told him they lived in the
general neighborhood and eventually given him the address. Now when he
wanted news of Carla, he had to go to Mollie. That Carla! She could at least
come once in a while or even write, but who was he to complain? People in
glass houses!

He thought about the things he'd done to fix up his cabin. He'd cleaned
out the wood from the shed and now kept it outside covered with a tarp, and
he'd made a bin with a hinged cover for the coal. He'd finished off the walls

of both the cabin and the shed with paneling that looked almost like brown stained wood. He'd built a shower stall next to the toilet and had a plumber hook up the water. And he'd replaced the solid outside shed door with one which had a window in the upper half so that he had another room, which he had furnished with a bed, chair and small table, though what he needed that other room for he didn't know. Yes, it was home, and he'd have to give it up. He had a three year lease, two years to run, and he wondered if he were to enlist, would he be held liable? No way he'd have money for the rent. He pondered the question, but nothing in his experience had taught him the answer. Maybe Roger would know, but Roger had gone up to Maine for his grandfather's funeral.

Exactly what would Army life be like? He'd never cared much for being ordered around, but on the other hand, one always did get ordered around. That was his experience on every job he'd ever had, and he didn't see how you could run a big farm or factory or even a small restaurant any other way. During the worst days of the Depression he had steered clear of such things as the Civilian Conservation Corps, but he guessed that was because they were charity. Oh they'd said the CCC wasn't charity, but he hadn't been taking any chances. He'd had a bellyfull of charity early in life. The Army most certainly wouldn't be charity, and it wouldn't be any picnic. Still others put up with it and he guessed he could too. He wondered how he would look in a uniform. Those sailor suits were silly, but the Army, neat khaki, short haircut, soldier cap. It didn't matter much, he supposed, for he was no beauty out of uniform, and he wouldn't be much better in uniform. He wasn't cut out to be a hero, he had to admit that. He scared too easily, but no more he supposed than most. Yes, he could be a soldier, slogging through the mud, shooting the enemy. He guessed he'd better stop going to those bangbang movies. But it wasn't really the movies that had set him off; it was that six-foot German spy with old scars on each cheek. With his mind so fixed on his future in the Army, he would not have been the least surprised to see a khaki clad recruiter posted by his door, but as he drew near his cabin, he saw something that did startle him. His light was on, and he could hear someone moving about inside the house. Then he saw Carla.

"Smells like you're cooking steak," he said, playing it cool. "I haven't had steak in a dog's age. Neat rig, that electric plate, heats in a jiffy."

Carla turned toward him and for a moment said nothing. Good grief, he thought, she looks as if she'd lost her last friend. She made no explanation, just went on with her cooking.

The steak and string beans and rolls hit the spot, but they didn't stop him from wondering what was up. Carla, however, just sat and ate rather listlessly and talked about the weather.

Howard could stand it no longer. "What's happened?" he asked.

She left the table, slumped down on the couch and turned her face away from him that he might not see the tears, but she could not keep the sobs from her voice. In spite of her resolve the whole story came tumbling out. She told him of her learning that she was pregnant, of the trip to the abortionist, even about the little arm, the parrot with his "Shut up, doll, shut up!" Yes, Leonard had sent her. She hated his guts.

"The scum! Monstrous scum!" Howard ground the words between his teeth. "I'll horsewhip him to death, kill him by inches!"

"Calm down," Carla sighed. "You can't do anything to him and you know it. I'm going out West. It's best that way."

"Sis," Howard came over and put his arms around her. "That baby may not have a father, but he'll always have an uncle."

Now she was able to sit up and face him. "I didn't come to be a burden to you," she assured him. "I just came for the night to pull myself together."

"You must stay, not just for the night, not just for a few days, for keeps."

"No, it won't do. You have to think of your future."

"What future?"

"Oh I don't know. Maybe I mean the present. Howard, I don't even have a job. I have to strike out, find some place I've never been, build a new life. You ought to understand. You've done it."

"You can't do it. A man alone can. Not a pregnant woman. Why the first thing you know you'll be faced with a choice of letting your kid starve or taking to the streets."

"I'll disappear, find work a thousand miles away."

At that point Howard jumped to his feet, drew himself up to his full height and said emphatically, "You'll do no such thing." Howard, put upon, beat down all his life, heretofore a marginal person, stood firm, a man, and faced the sister of whom he had been in humbling awe all his life, and he laid down the law. "You're staying right here," he said.

"I'm leaving in the morning," she replied. "I'll take care of the child somehow, even if I have to place her for adoption."

He stood looking at her, at the sister who'd done his homework as a child, the sister who'd been favored and kept by the mother when he was sent away, at the sister who'd been a union leader, high upon a platform, and now the sister who crouched in unutterable sorrow there before him. "You'll do no such thing to any nephew of mine."

"It'll more likely be a girl."

"It'll be a nephew."

"Niece."

"Nephew."

"Niece."

"Okay, have one of each, but you're staying with me till they're born, and if you can't or won't take care of them, I will. Don't think you can give me the slip. I'll track you down, so help me, I will."

Then because he knew how harsh his voice had been he sat down beside her and spoke gently. "Do you remember that last day on the farm? The brook? The school?"

"I still have the green bottle."

"And the time we went to see Papa?"

"We should have stayed." Carla sighed.

"There was no way we could, but you can stay here."

"No," she said firmly. "I leave in the morning." With that she went into the bedroom and shut the door.

He took his recorder off the shelf and started playing, slowly at first, then picking up tempo and ending with "Turkey in the Straw." The recorder proved inadequate as a vent for his emotions, and after a while he sensed that she was calm enough to be left alone. He stood by the door for a few seconds listening to be sure she could safely be left. Hearing no sobbing, he went out and struck off across the field in back of the house and ran for a hundred or so feet, that being the width of the field, and then he ran back. He couldn't enlist in the Army now. He was no longer alone; now he had a family. Maybe it was well that Leonard and Carla weren't legally married since this way he could never have any claim on the child. The skunk!

When he went back into the house, Carla was washing the dishes. "Howard," she said thoughtfully, "maybe Leonard ought to know the baby is going to be born."

"Don't be an idiot!" he exclaimed and retreated into the room in the shed to keep from saying more.

Five minutes later she followed him and found him lying down reading the paper. "You were right," she said. "I'll never let him know."

The next morning she came to the kitchen and found him frying bacon. They had breakfast together, he cheerful and she lethargic. Warmed by love for her and uplifted with pride in himself, he looked confidently to the future. She was pulled in two directions. The growth of new life filled her whole body with serenity, but at the same time her mind was troubled, so that she hardly knew what she felt. The only reality was that she was tired to the point of fainting. That day she'd rest; her journey could be postponed a day.

After she'd finished her chores, she went out to the road. The landlady, resident of the house in front, Mrs. DeSapio, fresh in blue-checked gingham and white sweater was standing on the porch. She was stocky of figure, gray-haired, round faced, smiling, the perfect grandmother.

"Good morning," she said. "How nice you can visit your brother. That is, I guess you must be Howard's sister?"

"Yes indeed!" replied Carla.

The landlady thought for a moment. "It's good to have you here," she said at last. "Your brother told me about you, but somehow I'd been under the impression you were married."

"We separated. But I'm only here for a day."

"Well, as far's I'm concerned, you're welcome to stay. Howard's real neat for a man, but he forgets things like putting out the garbage, could attract rats that way. A woman remembers things like that."

How ridiculous to be standing there talking about putting out the garbage. Carla sighed, went back into the house and lay down upon her bed. Howard had insisted on giving her the bedroom he'd been using and moving his things into the room in the shed. He'd said she'd find the bedroom warmer, she needed to keep warm. Perhaps it was warmer, but even though there was a stove, she felt chilled. The chill gave way to fever and she had a sore throat. She crawled in bed and lay there tossing and turning and worrying. What if it were German measles, she thought. That might cripple the baby. If it were pneumonia she might die. *If I should die, Mama would cry! But if I live?* The room whirled and she was unconscious. Then Howard was lifting her up and offering her tea.

"Tomorrow I'll go," she mumbled.

"Shut up and drink this," he replied.

She was better the next day but still feverish. For a week she spent most of her time asleep, waking when Howard came, eating little, drinking alternately hot tea and iced ginger ale, and adamantly refusing to have a doctor called. Then one day she was stronger, restless, but not quite energetic enough to leave the bed. The cat Tigress jumped up beside her, and Carla hardly had strength to chase it off. Tired by the effort, she slept once more, and when she awoke, Tigress sat on the floor staring wide-eyed at her.

"Good kitty," she said, reaching out to stroke the animal. Her voice was a croak. The cat sat there and stared for a minute and then began to meow.

Carla got up, opened a can of cat food, went outside and filled the cat's dish. It was a beautiful day, the sun was shining, the air was fresh but not cold, chickadees hopped about on the remnants of snow and pecked industriously at the bare ground. Carla cleared her throat and tried to sing, was able to finish a line or two before the voice cracked. Howard came in during his afternoon break and was greatly relieved to see her up and about.

"Now I can do the housework," she said.

"Don't overdo."

"Howard," she asked, "do you ever see Roger?"

"Of course," he answered. "Didn't I tell you he'd gone to his grandfather's funeral? He's staying a few weeks to help his folks."

"I'd better leave before he gets back, I can't face him."

"If you hadn't been an idiot, you'd have married him before you ever met that Leonard."

"He never asked me."

"If he hadn't been a ninny, he would have."

"Stop talking nonsense. Anyway it's too late now."

Howard sighed. Yes, he agreed that it was. Until now he'd kind of thought maybe. Thought it the very first time he met Roger, was sure of it when Roger came to visit him in prison. Now, as Carla said, it was too late.

"You look tired," he said. "Hadn't you better get back in bed?"

"No, no," she answered. "I'm getting well, I feel it deep down and in every part of me. I really am."

Indeed she really was. Her illness was over. She was like a boat put up in drydock for repairs and now scheduled to slide into the sea. Or as Ray might have said like a car ready to leave the garage. Ah yes, and take to the open road, the long road, the dark road.

She was stirring something in a bowl on the counter. Round and round the spoon went, and Carla gazed into the distance. Howard watched her intently. She's got some bee in her bonnet, he thought. And that's not good.

TWENTY-SIX

Yes, Carla had a bee in her bonnet. She was going to leave, go out West, probably hitchhike. Howard squashed that bee flat. "If you try that kind of crazi-
ness, I'll hunt up Leonard and tell him about the baby," he threatened. "Yes,
I'm desperate enough to do even that. I don't know what he'll do, but then
neither do you."

She hesitated.

"I'm determined. I know what's out there. And Mama—"

She gave a deep sigh. "You win." When they were children, it had always
been she who'd won. "But I'll get a job."

"Okay, okay," he said gruffly.

A couple of days later in the dawn of a sunny day, they walked together
to the bus. There was pride in Howard's heart and in Carla's a newfound
feeling of respect for this humble man who insisted on being her protector.
The bus bounced along, gathering passengers. They passed houses and apartments and came to a block in which the buildings, big and rectangular, were
set back behind a lawn covered with the emerald green of emerging grass.
"Con-Ray," said Howard, with somewhat of a proprietary pride in his voice.
"Roger's place." After all he did know Roger rather well, and while Howard
wasn't quite sure what Roger's job title was, he knew it must be something
important. "You'd ought to try Con-Ray first."

"Neither first nor last," Carla replied.

After a hasty breakfast at the shiny clean cafeteria where Howard worked,
Carla set out, trembling with anxiety, in pursuit of a job. *Why, oh why,* she
thought, *can't work ever come looking for me?* She walked a block and made a
right turn as Howard had directed and came to an old gray building, the first
of the shoe factories on her list. Hanging by a leather cord looped over a hook
on the "Employees" door was a small cardboard sign, with the gray empty
side outermost. Gingerly she turned it and saw that it read in crude hand let-

tering, "Stitchers needed." She hesitated. Had the sign been turned over by the wind, or some careless hand, or had it been turned over by the foreman who no longer needed stitchers? If so, why hadn't he removed the sign altogether? A short, stocky, dark-haired woman came bustling along and stopped to talk.

"They hired coupla women yesterday," she said.

Suddenly Carla felt dizzy, and she leaned against the wall. She couldn't go in like this. "In that case," she said, hoping the woman hadn't noticed, "maybe I'd better try some place else."

Thoroughly frightened by the dizziness, Carla tried to walk, found that indeed she could walk, discovered that she felt better walking. She went back to the main street, found a bench and gratefully sank upon it. Hoping it meant no more than that she hadn't quite gotten over her recent illness, she sat there for about a half hour, then resolved to give up for the day, only for the day. She had to get a job, she couldn't lie idle. What if it meant she might miscarry? Wouldn't that be for the best? No, no, it might not make sense, but she desperately wanted the life inside her womb to continue, to grow and in the fullness of time be delivered. It was her child, it had arms and legs, it was already a boy or a girl, most likely a girl, it had a heartbeat. She wished she knew if it were a boy or girl so that she wouldn't have to use the impersonal pronoun "it." *Little person,* she thought, *my baby person.* A soft warmness flooded over her, and she smiled so that a woman going by turned and looked and thought what a pleasant face.

Back in the cabin she was still weak and lay down to rest, but when Howard came home, she got up and busied herself with baking a cake. She told him exactly what had happened though not all that she had thought, certainly not reopening that argument about boy or girl and not wanting to sound mushy. She brushed aside his suggestion that she see a doctor, but promised to wait until Monday before going again to the factories.

"I hope that cake you're making is chocolate," he said. Soon they were bending over the cookbook trying to figure out how to turn what had started out to be a white cake into chocolate. She turned it into a chocolate cake, though not the greatest, not having risen quite as it should.

Half of it remained the following afternoon, and they were debating what they had done wrong when they were interrupted by a knock at the door. In walked Roger Thorfinnson, casual in light sweater and brown pants, his hair slightly mussed by the breeze, very much at ease, and not too surprised to see Carla, for after all, it was her brother's home. Carla trembled, could hardly control her voice.

Roger sampled the cake, said he knew Carla could do better, and settled down to coffee and conversation. He became serious as he told how he had been called home for his grandfather's funeral, had known that it was a blessed release, yet found it hard to accept. His parents were well, bearing up bravely; it was a good thing they were busy.

"Carla," he asked, "do you remember the books in Grandpa's room?"

"Why yes, quite a collection. He was a real history buff."

"He willed them to me," Roger said.

"Some of them, I believe, were rare old documents."

"Yes. He never forgot how interested you were in those books."

"He was such a dear old man," Carla murmured.

"Yes, when his temper wasn't up."

"Carla's looking for a job," said Howard.

"Oh? What about the Attlebury lady?"

"Things are in a mess with her," was all Carla would volunteer.

Roger looked sharply at Carla. If only he could talk to her alone.

Howard glanced at his wristwatch. "Time for me to get back," he announced as he stood up and grabbed his jacket. "See you two later."

"Would you like another piece of cake?" asked Carla the moment they were alone.

"No," he replied. "And I also don't wish to discuss cake. I want to know what's going on."

"What's going on?"

"The air is full of it. Why must I pretend not to notice?"

"You always seem to arrive when there's a crisis."

"I arrive on many occasions, but you notice me more when there's a crisis."

She blushed scarlet. "Howard thought you might help me find work," she said. "But I certainly had no intention of asking you to."

He leaned forward, looked intently into her face, then said gently, "Don't you know I'd do anything I could to help you? That you should have no more hesitation asking me than you do asking your brother?"

"But you're not my brother."

"I seem to have blundered into a blind alley," Roger sighed in frustration.

"I didn't mean to make a secret of what certainly isn't one. I'm living here now."

"Since you'd baked a cake for your brother, I'd guessed as much."

She was silent, hardly understanding Roger, who seemed to her to be going out of his way to be stern and harsh with her.

Roger, buffeted within by his love for Carla and his feeling of hopelessness, having wanted to get her forever out of his mind and now struck with an intuition that this was no longer necessary, sat helplessly feeling for words. "Carla," he said at last, "let's don't play games. Tell me all about it."

"Don't ask for details, please don't. Leonard and I have separated."

"For good?"

"For evermore, certainly. That's the one thing we're agreed upon."

"There's politics involved?"

"Isn't there always with Leonard?"

"Have you really—?" He hesitated, not knowing how to phrase it in an acceptable fashion.

"Come to my senses?" she asked, using the words he'd suppressed.

He laughed. "Why yes, that is my question. And you've given the answer."

They were both eager to steer the conversation back to everyday talk. "What," he asked, "is this bit about Miss Attlebury? You're no longer working there?"

"I quit just as Phoenicia was about to fire me. She's so involved with Leonard, I didn't want to stay."

"But she's so much older than he."

"Oh no, no, she's not the other woman. I meant she's involved politically."

"What are your plans?"

"Stay here and find work in a factory."

"And Howard thought I might be able to get you into Con-Ray?"

"Yes, he did, but that was strictly his idea."

"I wish I could, but—"

"Don't explain and for Pete's sake don't apologize."

"I don't apologize, but I must insist on explaining. I'd have to to Howard if I didn't to you."

"Now you're getting mysterious."

"Yes, and melodramatic. The truth is that Con-Ray has undertaken some pretty hush-hush national defense contracts, and we need security clearances."

"Which I couldn't get?"

"Well, Carla, you know."

She lowered her eyes, tears began to run down her cheeks. "Yes, I know," she said. "Of course they're right, but oh it's too terrible. To be suspected of being disloyal, a spy."

"That's not exactly what I said."

"A couple of weeks ago Howard was reading about a German arrested for espionage, a mechanic at Long Island airfields. And oh how he raged! Why he still goes into a tirade over it! And now I—"

"Now you nothing. Did Howard rage at you?"

"No."

"He knows about your wacky politics, but he also knows your character."

"Don't say my politics! That's past, washed down the drain. Oh dear, perhaps I should be past and washed down the drain too."

"Carla, Carla, forgive me for my lack of tact."

"How else could you have put it? Does the choice of words make any difference? What matters is that I've been a traitor to my country."

"That's putting it rather strongly."

"Roger, you shouldn't be seeing me, it could get you in trouble, cast suspicion on you."

"I don't think so. I'll take the risk."

"I don't want you risking anything for me, it's preposterous. Why should you even remain friends with me?"

"We became friends just when I was becoming me," he answered

"A long time ago."

"I know something of what you and your family have gone through; I understand your rebelling. I've prayed that in time you'd see that your new friends were your enemies, and I had faith."

"I don't need your charity."

"We all need charity."

"I'm so ashamed."

"A whole new life opens up for you."

"It's knocked the conceit out of me."

"But not the awareness of your very real gifts, I hope. Do you remember your talk about writing an American history series for use in schools? Did you ever start it? Research or anything?"

"I, who can't get a minimal security clearance, write an American history?" scoffed Carla. "Once an age ago I did try doing some research, using the resources of the Boston Library, and then I moved to Laurel, and there was the strike, and the first thing I new I found myself in a new life with new ways of looking at everything."

"Marxist?"

"Er, yes."

"Like the North didn't really fight to free the slaves? And the American Revolution was not really a revolution?"

"How do you know all their arguments?"

"I learned them thanks to you, Carla. They were forever being dinned into the audiences of Mobilization, and Leonard was always willing to spend a half hour enlightening me."

"Don't mention his name, Roger. If you knew how I hate him!"

"Hmmm. You need to achieve indifference. Did he leave you for another woman?"

"Yes, in a way. Though he would tell you that I had already, as they put it, gone sour," she paused, then added hastily, "I have another reason for hating him."

Roger puzzled over this for a minute. "Of course I always knew you'd see the light," he said at last. "Won't you tell me just how it came about?"

"I think there was a night which was a dividing line; before that night I'd been questioning, but after that I knew. There was a party to raise money for the cause at Phoenicia's and there was a couple there I'd met before, Sam and Pearl. Refugees from Nazi Germany, Jews, with the scars of persecution on their bodies and on their souls."

"They were the guests of honor?"

"On display, I guess you could say. Leonard quarrelled with Sam. Then he upbraided me for being friendly with Pearl. And something inside me snapped. I tried to defend her."

"She needed defense?"

"At that moment, yes. Against the self-righteous arrogance of the whole gang. They couldn't disagree with anyone without spitting on him. I don't remember the terms Leonard used about Sam and Pearl, but I remember their hurt."

"Sounds like living in a pressure cooker."

"And Stalin was God Almighty. And speaking of God, mention of the real God was enough to send shivers of disgust the length of a twenty foot table. Even when I was most in agreement with communism, I never felt that way about other people, or America, or about religion."

"But you had lost your faith?"

"In a way, yes. God the Creator is obvious enough to anyone, I mean, should be obvious. But a God who had anything to do with me, or any other person—yes, I lost my faith."

"That was the real trouble."

"What do you mean?"

"It seems to me that the real question for the twentieth century is the struggle between two philosophies: one the elevation of the man-made state to the role of deity; and contrasted to that the worship of God who created man and gave him a soul."

"Not democracy versus totalitarianism?"

"Democracy is the form without substance, the empty bottle. 'Where there is no vision the people perish.'"

"You never talked like this to me before."

"No, I guess not. I find myself sounding like my Great-Uncle John, a missionary, who froze to death in Alaska. He used to visit before that. Such a happy man! And such a daylong preacher! Grandfather's funeral brought him back to me, a veritable living presence."

"Do you remember in the park before you went away how you talked of nothing but electrical fields, protons, neutrons, electrons."

"Vaguely. I suppose I was wrapped up in it. Maybe at that time it was my false god. Oh forgive me for not talking then." For not talking of love, he thought. What if he had? And now? No, not now, not yet, he must not take advantage today of her freshly wounded heart, today let her do the talking. "You said there was another reason for your anger at Leonard," he continued. "Could I ask about that?"

"I don't want to hide it from you, but I'd rather let Howard tell you."

"I won't listen to any one else."

"Roger, I'm pregnant."

The words were like a blow. Carla saw his face pale, saw his lips quiver, then heard him speak in his usual pleasant voice. "Shall I assume that Leonard is the father?"

"Thank you at least for that assumption."

"Carla, forgive me, oh I don't know what I'm saying! But since I'm in this deep, bear with me, know I speak only out of my love for you. Since there's a child, don't you have to see Leonard again?"

"Oh Roger, it's too disgraceful."

"I don't understand."

She bowed her head upon the table, and through her sobs she told of Leonard's insistence on an abortion, of her trip to the doctor, of the tiny arm covered with blood, of the young girl who'd walked unsteadily out to the waiting car, of her flight from the doctor's office. "So you see," she concluded, "why I must never see Leonard again. And why I hate him."

"Yes," he said softly.

"You're not going to say I ought to go back to him or let him know about the baby?"

"I don't know, I don't know," replied Roger sadly. "Certainly you should stop hating Leonard. And despising yourself for having loved him."

"The old truth—hate the sin and love the sinner."

"Yes, the old, old truth."

"I've confessed to you almost as if you were my minister."

"Today I am your minister. But there are consequences to be drawn from that."

"Yes?"

"You must continue to confide in me. And I'd like to help you find a better minister. Come with me to my church tomorrow. I'll drive over for you."

"Oh no, you mustn't be seen in public with me," Carla insisted.

"Let me worry about that."

"There's a little church near here," Carla's eyes filled with sadness as she spoke, "which reminds me of the one in Megunnaway, same simple Christopher Wren kind of building. I walked by there yesterday, stopped for a minute, and if it had been open, I'd have gone in. I actually cried a little, homesick for a home I can never go back to."

"May I go there with you?" Roger asked quietly.

"I'd rather not."

Roger sighed, sympathy for her overwhelmed him, but he spoke lightly and changed the subject. "My grandfather willed his whole collection of books to me," he said. "And the last time I saw him he made it clear he wanted me to share them with you."

"He remembered me?"

"Yes, my dear, he remembered you very well. I have a few of the books in my apartment, and the rest are still at the farm. Some day I'll bring you a sampling."

"Why oh why?" Carla cried out. "What good will it do to bring them to me?"

"Carla, I'll make a deal with you. Go on hating Leonard if you must, but stop hating yourself."

"It might be easier to stop hating Leonard," she said slowly. "Not that I'll ever see him again, of course. I keep thinking of his father who'd been political like Leonard, but had experienced a complete change of heart because they'd killed a Russian hero of his."

"Do you think Leonard could change?"

"No he won't. And remember the child he sought to kill."

"From his point of view, is that so terrible? Isn't it accepted in his circle? Didn't you, even you, go right to the last step?"

"Oh Roger, I did. How could I? How could I? Yet I did draw back. Oh if you knew the depths of my repentance!"

"Could he not also repent?"

"No, he won't. He never admits mistakes."

"Surely there is for everyone," said Roger, "the possibility of repentance."

With that, he rose quickly and left. He was afraid that if he stayed, he would allow his personal feelings to overwhelm his Christian beliefs.

When Howard came home shortly before ten that night, he found Carla just then eating her dinner.

"Why so late?" he asked.

"I had a lot to think about," she replied.

Carla finished her food, got up, came around and put her arm around Howard, gave him a hug and said, "Thank you, Howard, for everything."

"Don't mention it," he answered, and he meant it quite literally, or at least he thought he did. He'd had so little experience being a brother, and here he was an uncle. Kind of staggered a fellow! He wished Roger hadn't been such a ninny.

Could he have entered into Roger's thoughts that moment he would have cursed vigorously and called him ten times worse than a ninny. In agony of soul Roger had come to the conclusion that Leonard ought, as a matter of right, to know his child was still alive. He had only to close his eyes to see there before him his Great-Uncle John fervently declaring the sacred duty of man to place the doing of God's will before personal danger, to endure the greatest deprivation, to face even ridicule, but always to do what he knew to be right. If only he could take Carla by the hand and lead her to Leonard and stand as her support while she talked to him, divulged to him the truth. What would happen then? Certainly he risked the end of all his dearest hopes, certainly such a step held out no promise of happiness for Carla, but are we placed here for happiness? Or supposing that Leonard rejected her, still rejected her? *Do I*, he wondered, *have the love and courage to make her mine, both her and the child?* "What," he cried aloud, "am I called upon to do?"

When Roger opened his eyes to the morning, he no longer felt the presence of Uncle John. He was alone in his comfortable Beacon Hill apartment, and a soft breeze was blowing the fragile curtain at the open window of his bedroom. He got up, bathed and shaved, had coffee and toast, read the morning paper. The world, he noted, was in a muddle. He sighed. All he could think of was Carla. *How can I help her do what's right? Do I even know what is right? And what does she think of me?*

He tried to break his preoccupation by setting out paper and pen and starting a letter to his parents. They'd taken Grandpa's death rather well. Now he was all they had. He wished he'd had a brother to love the farm. He sighed and finished the letter. He included the information that he'd seen Carla; after all they did know her.

It was almost noon when he finally went out to mail the letter. A plan, yet something too vague to be called a plan, was developing inside his mind. He couldn't see Carla again with things the way they were, and he couldn't stay away from her. He felt, quite illogically he was sure, that by seeing Leonard he could resolve this dilemma. He thrust the letter into the slot on the corner mailbox and walked over to Boston Common and across the Common, seeing little more than his own brown shoes, so intently did he look down as he walked. The Mobilization and "Light" headquarters were not far away, and he headed in that direction. Cars jockeyed for position in the hectic traffic, men and women hurried along the sidewalk, but he was oblivious to them. Alone, he walked along the busy street.

Leonard, he'd always believed, was one of the better sort among the radicals, not that that was saying much. He was a true believer and on some subjects an intelligent observer. Roger remembered that day he'd found Leonard down with the flu. He'd enjoyed Leonard's sharp wit and appreciated the strength that didn't leave him even when he was laid low. He saw before him Leonard's face, handsome on the right, twisted on the left, and he wondered what effect that accident of birth had had upon the man.

Suddenly there stood Leonard before him, not surprisingly since Roger had by now come right up to the Mobilization headquarters. "An unexpected meeting," said Leonard. "To what do I owe the pleasure of this visit?"

Roger hesitated.

"Don't think too hard," said Leonard. "I suppose Carla sent you. No need to work up to it diplomatically."

Roger became angry. "Carla most certainly did not send me!" he cried.

"Allow me to take the liberty of doubting that. I was sure you'd be sneaking around," sneered Leonard.

"Where I go, I go quite openly!"

"You don't deny seeing her then?" Leonard demanded

"I don't discuss it."

"I trust she is well," Leonard's voice was hard. "You can tell her that I've seen her doctor, whose care she left so abruptly. Perhaps her indisposition will cure itself. That often happens. In any event she has no claim on me. Do you understand, no claim? Be so kind as to tell her."

Roger looked him straight in the face, and the dark brown eye on the right was as fixed and cold as that on the left. They understood each other. "I'm not in the business of delivering messages," said Roger. He turned on his heel, and quickly walked away. "He knows!" Roger muttered furiously, "he knows, and it means nothing to him—not Carla, not his own child!"

Roger walked on. Since Leonard knew and talked as he did, then not only did Carla have no claim on him, he had no claim on her or the child. *What happens next*, he mused, *depends on how strong a man I am*. That he didn't know.

His impulse was to rush at once to Carla and comfort her, pull her close to him, let her lean upon his strong shoulder. His second thought was to go home and thrash it out within himself. Then he realized that he had been taking it for granted that Carla would welcome that strong shoulder. How conceited could a man get? And if she saw in him merely a port in a storm, was that something he could accept? Oh he'd loved her so long. And she'd liked him. Pretty cold stuff from a high-strung girl like Carla.

He went inside and got out some papers he'd been working on before being called away for his grandfather's funeral. He sat at his desk staring at the white paper covered with black lines and letters and digits. Even that refused to make sense. What was this world coming to when he couldn't even work out a simple problem in electronics!

TWENTY-SEVEN

Carla told herself she didn't think of Roger at all, except as a childhood friend. There was no harm in going that far. What might have been? Even Howard had given up talking about that. Her thoughts were about Fit-Rite Shoe, where she worked, and how to dress to conceal her condition. And she thought of her mother, particularly on Easter morning as, still in pajamas and robe, she went into the front yard where the three lilac bushes were in full bloom. Lilacs! Abigail's favorite flower, thought Carla, as she struggled to cut a few clusters without destroying the symmetry of the bushes. With the bunch of flowers in her arms she walked along the edge of the house until she could see the daffodils which formed a golden border around the three outer edges of the DeSapios' yard. What a variety! Single and double, deep yellow, and white, and even pale green. Mrs. DeSapio had spent years gathering them, tending them, loving them, and she knew each variety by name, knew a long history for many. *What will that dear lady think of me when she sees me out here in robe and slippers,* thought Carla. She scurried back to the cabin, getting inside just before Tigress came to impede her. Carla found a glass jar in lieu of vase and carefully arranged the lilacs. Yes, Abigail's favorite flower. Carla closed her eyes and strove to recall the words.

> "When lilacs last in the dooryard bloom'd,
> And the great star early droop'd in the western sky in the night,"

She wondered if the great star had indeed set early last night in the western sky, but most of all she wondered if she would ever again hear Abigail read that poem. Regularly Carla wrote to her mother, and resolutely she withheld the great encompassing fact of her pregnancy.

She had no time to think of Roger, though of course when he was there in the flesh, she couldn't exactly be unaware. And she'd better think of him now, for he was coming to take her to the little church she'd mentioned to him. She stooped to pick up a paper which she had pushed off the chest. Just a piece of paper, a crude drawing of a girl figure with oval face and a boy figure with square face, the two hand in hand, lacy doodles around the edge, the valentine she'd kept these many years. Hastily she tucked it into a book and set about getting dressed for church, though she wasn't sure just why she was going to church, was indeed surprised that it she was. Hadn't she "abandoned her faith," and wasn't that the unforgivable sin? Roger said no, he said the unforgivable sin was to have so hardened one's heart that he was no longer capable of repentance, and he knew how bitterly she had repented. Yes, repented of being untrue to her past and to her family and to her faith. She'd repented, but the faith hadn't returned. What right had she to celebrate the Risen Christ? She continued getting dressed. She had promised Roger.

He'd been a regular visitor since that day when she'd broken down and talked to him. "I'd think he was courting you," Howard had said, "except that all you ever do is sit and argue."

Yes, they sat and argued, quite amicably. Low key, no passion, just logic. Roger was so incontrovertibly logical. When he wasn't arguing, he was trying to explain something technical, much to her confusion. She'd finally gotten through her head what was meant by the Base 2 numerical system. Quite simple, Roger had assured her, once you'd rid yourself of preconceptions.

She went to the closet and took out her dress, a simple shirtwaist style, cut rather full, with three quarter length sleeves, a soft delft blue. Abigail's color was lilac, blue was Carla's. She maneuvered the dress into place, pleased with the perfect fit of the shoulders and the fullness over the waist and hips. Carefully she swept her hair up, brushed it back. Luckily it had a natural wave, and she didn't have to spend money on beauty parlors. She arranged her hat, pulled on her neat white gloves, took her handbag, and walked out past the lilac bushes toward the street. There was Roger's dark red car. He was early. He was standing by the white picket fence talking with Mrs. DeSapio. In his hand he held three fine daffodils, about which he and Mrs. DeSapio were chatting like old acquaints. The coat of his dark brown suit was unbuttoned, his striped necktie blown askew, and he wore no hat so that his dark hair was disheveled, which didn't in the least disturb him. That's Roger, thought Carla, always himself no matter what the circumstances. She found herself blushing for no reason at all.

"Good morning, Carla," he said. "Did I get here at the right time?" And before she could answer, he went on, "Why don't you take these in and put them in water for me? I'll pick them up when I bring you home."

What do you know? thought Carla. Mrs. DeSapio had never offered her any of the precious daffodils. Carla took the flowers and went back to the cabin. What a way Roger had of charming people. He'd always had that easy manner, even back there in the schoolyard when he'd been able in a single recess to bring her into the gang; and again during the strike and later with her radical friends when, without in the least concealing his own conservative views, he'd moved smoothly and affably in that strange milieu. How, she wondered, does one acquire that poise? Or is it inborn? Certainly his childhood, son of a stable and respected family, had something to do with it. Yet that alone could not account for it. It definitely could not account for his attitude toward her. It might more logically have been expected to make him draw away from her to protect his own respectability. But Roger never did worry about his respectability. She found a pickle jar, smelling of dill and vinegar, rinsed it, filled it with water and placed the daffodils in it. Taking a spray of lilac from the other jar she thrust it in among the daffodils, stood back, rearranged them, stood back again, was not quite satisfied, but there was no delaying.

Roger was standing by his car, holding the door open. "Hurry up," he said. "Don't want to be late. Everyone will turn and stare."

"If that frightens you—"

He laughed. "It rather intrigues me," he said, "but it would make you blush."

This ease of manner, she thought, is nothing but a tough skin, an arrogance, a self confidence so great that nothing ruffles him. For one so sure of himself there's no risk in being kind. They arrived just before the service began. Several people greeted Carla, though all were strangers to her. There were men in proper suits and new neckties, women mostly in light colors, little girls in ruffled dresses and straw hats walking primly by their mothers, boys rubbing fingers inside uncomfortable collars and brushing back with furtive gestures unruly locks of hair. "What would happen," Carla whispered to Roger, "if I were to cry 'Christ is Risen' the way they do in Tolstoi novels?"

"All the Russians in the crowd," he answered, "would kiss you. Then I could too."

"Roger!" Carla glanced around to see if anyone had heard him.

He guided Carla into the sanctuary. Inside the door they paused. A dozen potted Easter lilies lined the edge of the platform on which the pulpit sat. On the left the sun shone brightly through the stained glass windows, which were predominantly pale blue and golden yellow; while similar windows on the opposite wall, in the shade, let through a delicate glow. The choir, robed in white and consisting of five men and twice as many women, were sidling into their places in the choir loft.

The minister, robed in black, wearing a resplendent purple stole, took his place and stood beaming happily at the congregation. He was a middle-aged man, his dark hair just beginning to gray, his figure portly, his countenance expressing perfect serenity. The prelude drew to a triumphant close, and the organist folded her hands in her lap.

"The Lord is in His holy temple: let all the earth keep silence before Him," intoned the minister.

The silence was broken by a baby's cry; the minister beamed brightly. "Ah yes," he said. "Time to make a joyful noise. Let us sing Hymn Number 154, 'Christ the Lord Is Risen today, Alleluja.'"

Carla stood close to Roger, sharing a hymnal, singing the words so familiar to her, yet words she hadn't heard for years. She felt a sob rise in her throat; she was unable to sing. She remembered Abigail's plea that she come home. Mama, dear Mama! "Soar we now where Christ has led," she managed to get out the words, then choked again. *Dear God,* she prayed, *I'm coming home, coming home to you.* She had sufficient control of herself to join in the final "Alleluia, Amen."

The minister was continuing, a pleasant, even voice. The congregation was seated, all were bowing over their hymnals reading the General Confession: "Almighty and most merciful Father: We have erred and strayed from Thy ways like lost sheep. We have followed too much the devices and desires of our own hearts. We have offended against Thy holy laws. We have left undone those things which we ought to have done, and we have done those things which we ought not to have done. But Thou, O Lord, have mercy upon us." The tears were blinding Carla, the letters became a blur, she could not read, she could only listen to the gentle rumble of the many voices. Roger slipped her a big white handkerchief, and after wiping her eyes, she was able once more to join the unison reading. "And grant, O most merciful Father, for His sake, that we may hereafter live a godly, righteous, and sober life; to the glory of Thy holy name. Amen."

Heads were being raised, a young woman seated next to Carla reached over and gently patted her hand, and Carla flashed her a smile. Composed now, she sat and listened: to the choir singing "Up from the grave He arose"; to the minister reading the 28th Chapter of the Gospel according to Matthew, the resurrection story, ending, "and lo, I am with you always, to the close of the age." Then they were standing, singing mightily "Glory be to the Father, and to the Son, and to the Holy Ghost."

There were no longer tears in Carla's eyes and no longer tears just under the surface. The Easter joy was her joy too. She listened to the sermon but afterward could not have told you a word that the minister had said, yet somehow she was comforted by it and by the rest of the service, the pastoral prayer, the announcements, the efficiently taken offering, the final hymn, and then the Benediction, pronounced by the minister, who was now at the back of the sanctuary: "The Lord bless thee and keep thee. The Lord make His face to shine upon thee and be gracious unto thee. The Lord lift up His countenance upon thee and give thee peace."

They mingled with the congregation flowing out. Roger shook hands with the minister, introduced himself and Carla, promised to come again, easy and matter of fact as he always was. Carla found herself blushing as she shook hands with the minister and mumbled a few words in response to his kind welcome. She was still blushing when Roger helped her into the car, and she knew that she was blushing, and the more she strove to overcome it, the worse it got.

"I'm staying for lunch," said Roger as he took his place behind the wheel. "Do we need to stop at the store?"

"No, no need to stop."

"You have something you can fix quickly? I don't want you to waste a lot of time on cooking."

She reassured him, and indeed quite honestly, for she had roasted a chicken the day before, and with cold roast chicken on hand it's easy to whip up a lunch. What, she wondered, did Roger have in mind that he didn't want to waste time? He showed no clue, certainly he didn't seem to be planning on going anywhere. After lunch he asked her to come outside.

"I want to snap your picture," he said. "I'll get my camera out of the car. I think I'll send a copy to Mom and Dad."

Oh no, thought Carla. The Thorfinnsons would not be pleased. Roger got his camera, an expensive 35 millimeter type, and went about the practical business of setting up his shot, choosing the best background, rejecting the lilac bushes as too busy, deciding on a shot of Carla coming out the door, all the way out into the sun. She stood there on the walk.

"Face just a trifle more to the left, ah that's great," he said. "Elegant!"

He snapped the shutter, and she came striding toward him. "Me elegant?" she laughed.

"Yes, you, silly. But when you walk, that stride is pure country girl."

"I could practice."

"Don't you dare. Country girl is beautiful, particularly elegant country girl."

"May I take one of you?"

"Sure," and he showed her the precise way to handle the instrument.

"It's lovely out," she said.

"Yes," he agreed, "but we, my lady, are going inside."

"Carla," he began once they were inside with the door closed. "Don't you know why I came today?"

She smiled mischievously. "To worship the Lord?"

"Even in my Back Bay neighborhood," he replied, "we can do that." He drew her toward the couch. "Maybe you'd better sit down."

"You frighten me," she said as they sat side by side on the couch but not touching.

"It *is* a serious matter," he said. "Carla, I've come to ask you to be my wife."

"You're so good." She began to sob. But she couldn't accept his sacrifice. "So very, very good."

"Now, now. Don't exaggerate my goodness. There's meanness in me too. And hate. I hate Leonard for what he did to you."

"You tell me not to."

"Together we could overcome it. Oh, not to the point of ever wanting to see him again. Let's keep our feet on solid ground. Just to place him in the past."

"How can we place him in the past?" cried Carla laying her hand upon her abdomen.

"By your marrying me. By our becoming one."

"Are you doing this to give a name to my baby?"

"I want to give my name to our baby."

"Oh, Roger! You're so good," she repeated her earlier words.

"That's not what I'm trying to say. Don't you know how much I've always loved you, how much you've always been in my dreams? I don't want to be just any port in a storm. I want your love, your wild passionate love."

Wild, passionate love? Roger talking of wild passionate love! Was there any such thing left in her? He drew her to him, he sought her lips, and the longing of a strong man flowed into that kiss. She felt him tremble as he drew away. "Carla," he whispered, "my longed-for bride."

"But I haven't said—"

"The electricity was there, my sweet." She couldn't deny it.

"Your parents will never forgive you, they'd never accept me."

"You're wrong on both counts," he insisted.

"It's not fair to you."

"Let me worry about that."

"Why did this have to come so late, after so much. Why not when we met in Laurel?" she cried.

"I was still wet behind the ears, and you already a woman, but dearest, we're ready for each other now."

She was crying again, and she wasn't sure whether from joy in his love or from grief, for she must say no.

"Let me kiss away the tears," he said gently but the kiss was upon her lips. And she yielded and clung. "We must be married soon," he said.

"Before the baby?"

"Of course," he replied calmly.

"Everyone will think—"

"Of course. And that's what we both want. Isn't it?"

She looked up into his eyes, gazed at his strong-boned face. "Oh Roger, Roger!" She ought to say no, but there was no way she could.

"Will you come with me tomorrow to pick out an engagement ring?"

"I don't want any ring except a plain gold band."

"Then we'll pick that out. Not even one little diamond?"

"No, not even one."

"Good. The plain band now, later I'll buy something elegant."

"You keep using that word, elegant."

"Because you, my love, are elegant. With your tall, graceful figure, and your wavy dark hair, and your perfect complexion, and your classic features and intelligent eyes. Don't laugh at my clumsy way with words. But you're elegant; even in rags you'd be elegant."

"In spite of the country girl stride?"

"That makes it perfect."

Carla was silent and thoughtful, amazed that anyone should see her as elegant. To Leonard she'd been Joan of Arc of the shoe workers, beautiful in an uncultured way, a non-precious stone to be worn for a while.

"I'm glad you want just a golden band, because I really can't afford an expensive ring now," Roger was his matter-of-fact self once more, "but changes are in the offing that will up my income. Even so, I kind of like just the gold band. We need to save for a house."

How casually, thought Carla, he says he can't afford it. How Abigail had hated to admit that. And Leonard had flourished it like a badge of honor. But Roger was casual. "Why oh why did I have to get mixed up with that gang?" she cried.

"I suppose part of it was that you found revolutionaries romantic," he said.

"Romanticism is stupid."

"Maybe, I'm not sure. I can see the excitement generated by the wild dreamers who seek to rebuild the world. Though, of course, they're gnats on a bull's ear. What I do has far more impact on social development than all their grandiose schemes. Their storming the barricades is nothing beside seizing the very elements, grasping the lightning bolts, learning to ride on the wings of the morning."

"Who's being grandiose now?" she laughed.

"They grub away in a dingy office and I in a maze of wires, but it's my engineering that transforms the world. One thing worries me. Can we retain the timeless spiritual values in this changing world?"

"Worries you?"

"Yes, but that's where you come in. You, with your work on that history, your work in the church, in community organizations—"

Howard walked in, and Roger jumped to his feet, seized Howard by the hand and cried, "Howard, congratulate me. We're getting married."

"It's for real?" asked Howard.

It didn't take long for them to assure him that it was, nor for him to decide he had to go somewhere, he was rather indefinite about where. They didn't argue with him.

Roger held her close with tender affection, and this was what she needed. "We've lots of planning to do," he said.

"Your parents—"

"We must be sure they can be here and your mother too. As far as I'm concerned, it doesn't have to be formal, but we certainly want our families here."

Relieved, Carla agreed.

"I'll write my parents immediately and talk to the minister. How does early June sound?"

"Whatever we can arrange," she agreed.

❧❦

Carla looked forward to the wedding with joyful anticipation but also some anxiety. They would be at the church, she and Roger at the altar, and the minister would say, "If there be anyone who knows any reason why this man and woman may not be lawfully joined in matrimony, let him come forward now or forever hold his peace." What if Julia Thorfinnson, at that moment fixing her eyes upon Carla's body profile, were to shriek, "No! No!" It seemed impossible that the wedding would actually proceed as other weddings did. Roger grew angry at such talk. There was also Carla's own family. She hesitated about writing her mother, and even Howard seemed reserved and ill at ease.

Carla looked anxiously at him as they sat at dinner one night soon after the remarkable Sunday which had brought Carla finally into Roger's arms. A worried frown sat upon Howard's face not to be dispelled even by his favorite chocolate cake. As soon as they'd finished dessert, Howard hurried out.

Carla followed her brother into the yard. "What's the matter?" she asked. "I know the dinner wasn't that bad."

Howard kicked the dirt, hemmed and hawed. "What," he finally asked, "is going to happen when he knows?"

"Howard!" she cried. "Do you think I'd let it go this far without telling him?"

"And he proposed after that?"

"Yes, my brother, he did."

"He really did!" exclaimed Howard. Roger's car pulled up and Howard cried, "Speak of angels and hear wings flap."

"Or devils and smell brimstone," Roger gave the response. He put his arm around Carla. "Let's sit out here awhile," he said. "Howard, for heaven's sake, don't think you have to run."

"Two's company, three's a crowd."

"We like a crowd, don't we, Carla?"

"When it's this crowd."

There was an old wooden lawn chair, weathered gray and littered with stray leaves, and Carla wiped it clean with a kitchen towel, then at their insistence took it for her seat while the two men squatted on the doorstep. The three of them sat there in the tiny yard between the two houses, enjoying the freshness of the outdoors. They talked about the day's news, Howard having read the paper while the other two had not.

"Europe's a mess, and it's only a question of time till America's in it with both feet," predicted Howard.

"You could be right, said Roger.

"I've thought of enlisting."

How awful, she thought, to talk of war while she sat thinking only of her wedding. She felt the sting of a gnat on her brow, brushed it away, but there were more. The tiny insects became more and more numerous, and soon Carla led the retreat to the house, where Howard buried his face in the newspaper, and she and Roger did the dishes.

"It's still early," said Roger. "Want to take in a movie?"

She was tired, she had to get up early the next day, and there was unreality enough for her in her own life. Roger kissed her gently and left. He went at once to his own apartment and found that Chad, his roommate, was not at home. Roger had now been engaged for more than a week, he couldn't put off telling Chad. He supposed Chad would offer to move and give up the apartment to the newlyweds; Chad was like that. Maybe they'd let him. Telling Chad would be easy compared to striking the right note with his parents.

Roger sat down at his desk where lay a supply of writing materials neatly positioned in the upper right sector and undertook the letter he'd been postponing. He hoped his father would accept his engagement; he knew that his mother would not be pleased. She'd been frigid toward Carla upon her return to the Hubbards' those many years ago, frigid as he'd never seen her toward anyone else. She had certainly not encouraged Grandpa in his talk of marriage, not even her desire to humor the old man could prevent her from showing her displeasure. She had even made catty remarks whenever Carla's name was mentioned. And there was the baby. Roger flung down the pen. Perhaps a walk would clear his head.

He went out, passed the State House, went down the street and entered Boston Common. It was dusk and the street lights were just beginning to glow. There were sauntering couples and single men roaming about, but room enough to walk briskly and think. Of course his parents must never know it wasn't his child. In a way that was unfair, but it couldn't be helped; that's the way it would have to be, and there would be other children later. He returned to his apartment and positioned himself once more at his desk. After several crumpled sheets of paper, he managed a letter of sorts, which definitely announced his engagement and took their presence at his wedding for granted.

When Roger came to the little cottage the next day, he found Carla sitting on the doorstep in the sun. She looked up lazily, the picture of contentment. Her face was filling out, there was a new serenity in her manner, she was the very picture of young motherhood.

The minister, when Roger visited him, was all benevolent smiles. Of course the church was available, so happy they planned a church wedding. "My, how very well we're doing in June. Two other weddings. Both the first week. That's all I can work in that week. Then I have to be at Conference. Maybe the third week. "How about the 18th?"

"The 18th is perfect," said Roger hastily.

"And when can you come for the counseling, maybe this next week, before we get into the June rush?"

"There's something I must confess," said Roger, looking the older man squarely in the face. "My bride is with child."

"Oh dear!" the good man said.

"Must I bring her in for counseling? Can't it just be with me?"

"I have only one concern. And not really that, for I've seen you two together. But I must ask. Are you marrying only because of the child?"

"God knows that is not the case."

"I'm glad. Actually I tend to think that the child alone would be a good reason, but the latest thinking is that it really isn't. Gives a marriage a poor chance of success, you know. Or at least so they say, the evidence is not overwhelming."

"Shall I come in for counseling or could we make it now?"

"Are you familiar with the marriage ceremony?"

"I know the vow, 'for better, for worse, for richer, for poorer, in sickness and in health, to love and to cherish, till death do us part.'"

"Does she know the vow?"

"She is a widow, young as she is, she's a widow, husband killed in a car crash."

"Oh! Do you both subscribe to the vow?"

"We do."

"Let us pray." The good man bowed his head and asked God's blessing on this couple, thanked God for their commitment to each other, asked God's blessing on their child. And said Amen.

The two men sat there in solemn silence for a couple of minutes. Then the pastor rose and said in his everyday voice, "Saturday the 18th of June. In the afternoon. Would two o'clock be acceptable?"

"Yes sir, be there with bells on."

When Roger saw Carla he skimmed over this conversation in a hurry, eager to get to his other news. "I'm being promoted," he told her. "They think I'm managerial material."

"I can see why."

"Thank you *very* kindly, ma'm," he said. "Of course what they have in mind would mean going to California."

"To California!" She sounded terrified.

"Con-Ray has a branch there being managed by our old man's brother-in-law, who's a crack salesman but no kind of production manager."

"Won't he resent your being placed over him?"

"He's been begging for it."

"How soon?"

So that was her concern. "They want me to take some courses in business and management at Harvard before I go. It'll be another year. You can have the baby here. Though they do say California is really quite civilized."

"Howard says it's dry and dusty, a lot of irrigation farming."

"There's a lot of everything, including an expanding electronics industry. We'll be going to Gutierrez near Los Angeles."

"He says out there they call San Francisco 'The City' and Los Angeles seven villages in search of a city."

"I'll take the seven villages. I've been to L.A., don't remember Gutierrez. The city's spread out, lots of individual homes. Gutierrez, they tell me, is in the foothills. In the mountains there's snow."

"And Northern Lights?"

"No, but how many times have you seen Northern Lights in Boston?"

"I was thinking of Megunnaway and the way the hill slopes down to the river or up from the river. As kids we used to climb those hills and over the hills, the sky would be a vast bank of brilliant lights flashing on the crystal snow."

"We had that in West Hambledon too."

"I'd forgotten, maybe I didn't notice."

❧❦

The days passed, the weeks passed, and finally Roger's parents arrived in Boston by motorcar. And after getting thoroughly lost and finding themselves in a busy thoroughfare which was like a narrow canyon between two cliffs and so overrun with pedestrians that Ward hardly dared drive, they were finally rescued by a kindhearted motorcycle policeman who guided them to their destination.

"Fancy picking up a police escort," Julia Thorfinnson laughed as Roger came running out to meet them. "What a quaint street this is, the houses all one against another, but each different."

Dear Mother, thought Roger. Dear, lively Mother! He took them out to dinner, choosing a small Italian restaurant, which met with their hearty approval.

"When will we see Carla?" asked Julia. "I'd hoped it'd be tonight."

"Tomorrow at the church," said Roger. "You haven't seen her for years, have you?"

"Rather a coltish girl," said Ward.

"From him, that's a compliment," said Julia.

"She's an elegant lady now."

Julia was silent. Somehow elegant wasn't quite the description she'd expected. It was hard to imagine the diffident, awkward girl as elegant. Roger said no more about Carla to his mother, but after she'd retired, Roger detained his father in the living room. And there he made his father acquainted with what in any event he would know on the morrow, that Carla was with child.

"Of course I can't approve," Ward tried unsuccessfully to look stern. His blue eyes twinkled in his weather-beaten face, and only by an effort did he hold his lips in firm line. "Maybe I won't have to let the farm go to strangers after all," he said.

"This may be a girl."

"I suppose."

"I promise we'll keep trying till we get you that son. Though I can't promise he won't be an engineer."

"Maybe even a girl if brought up right."

"Mom's going to have a fit. Do you think you can get her out of it by tomorrow?"

Ward laughed. "That woman of mine," he said.

"It's no laughing matter," Roger objected. Dad was not a laughing man. What had gotten into him?

"For two hours on the way to Boston she's been bending my ear with laments that that Carla would certainly never have children."

"Why on earth?"

"Oh I don't know. Because she's an egghead, because she's been married and had none, because—I do believe Julia wants grandchildren so bad she's afraid to hope."

Roger made himself a bed upon the couch, where he lay thinking. He'd promised his father a son, and indeed in all fairness there had to be one, one of his own blood, his parents' own blood. But how did he know it would come to pass? His family had dwindled so. His grandfather had been one of three at a time when three was a small family, his father one of two, and he an only child. Was it creeping sterility that would find its culmination in him? Oh dear God, he prayed, don't let that happen. Not daring to bring his other concern to God's attention, not being sure but it were wicked, he lay there hoping Carla's child would be a girl. The next one should be the boy.

He was startled early the next morning to get a phone call from Carla. "Mama is here," she said. "And she insists on seeing you this morning, before the wedding. What shall I do?"

"According to Emily Post we really should have met before. But let's make it at the church. I could get there early."

"No, no. She insists. She's all upset."

Roger found the three of them, Carla and Howard and Abigail, sitting around the table, staring morosely into their coffee cups. Carla got up at once as Roger entered the open door and came to his side, putting her arm around his waist. "Mama," she said. "This is Roger."

Abigail rose, a little woman, dressed in lilac, her gray hair combed up to the top of her head in Gibson girl style, her brown eyes peering through gold-rimmed glasses, her whole countenance serious as serious could be.

"I know you and Carla first met in those dreadful years when we were separated," she began.

"Yes," said Roger gently. "When we were children."

"When she wrote you were to be married, it seemed so right."

"It is right."

"But now I come and find, well, you know what I find."

"Yes, I know." He felt Carla's hand tremble, and he took it in his and held it firmly.

"It's true," Abigail continued, "that we've fallen from being a prosperous farm family down to the very depths. My father was a hero of the Civil War and Carla's father had his own farm. He was in politics, he talked with presidents, or at least with one president. Oh we don't come from nowhere, and we've our pride."

"Which I respect."

"It's a pride that will have no shotgun weddings in our family." The tears were streaming down her cheeks, but bravely and without a break in her voice she continued. "Carla can come home with me, or she can stay with her brother. We assume full responsibility for her. You don't have to marry her."

Roger winced. "Don't have to marry her?" he cried. "How can I make you see how I've longed for this day? From the first moment I ever saw her. If you're angry with me, I don't blame you for that. But for heaven's sake, don't talk about shotgun weddings."

"You first came back into her life several years ago. Why just now the wedding?"

Carla answered firmly. "The delay was my doing," she said.

"Then let me say to you. You don't have to marry him. Howard and I can care for you."

"You told me that last night. Haven't I convinced you?"

Abigail sank back into her chair. "Oh dear, I'm weak as a rag. What shall I say?"

"Congratulations and best wishes," suggested Howard.

"It's not the way I expected."

Roger went and put his arm around her. "I swear to you, I'll be a good husband to her and a good son to you."

Abigail sat there, weak but determined. "I repeat what I said, and Howard stands with me."

"This whole thing," said Howard, "is beginning to sound like a mellerdrama."

"Melodrama, my dear," said Abigail, making the correction automatically.

"Whatever," said Howard.

"Goodness!" said Abigail. "What am I talking about? I should be glad you're enlarging your vocabulary."

"Now we're drifting into comedy," said Roger.

"Comedy!" cried Abigail. "That, at such a moment, I cannot stand."

"Just so it's settled and stays settled, and there's no more nonsense," said Roger.

"Anyway, I've done my duty," said Abigail.

"Yes, Mother," Roger answered gravely as he put his arm around her. "And I love you for it. Now I've got to go get into my fancy pants."

He hurried away, and Abigail sat there looking solemnly from Carla to Howard and then at the door through which Roger had left. "Oh you young people," she said at last and her face relaxed. "You young people!" She sighed and wished that she were young again.

With the groom gone, after all he had no business being there that morning, they got down to preparations. After dressing, Carla and Abigail rode to the church in a taxi. Howard, who had elected to walk, arrived soon after. He had in his hands a box from the florist and in the seclusion of an ante-room he pinned on Carla's dress a buff and yellow orchid, the first orchid she'd ever worn. For each of the other women he had a yellow rose, and in the buttonhole of his neat blue suit he wore a tiny rosebud. "I brought a rose for Roger's mother too," he said. "Was that right?"

"Oh so right," said Carla.

He went outside, and when Mrs. Thorfinnson finally entered the room, she was already wearing the yellow rose. She went at once to Carla, extended both hands to her. "My daughter," she said.

She was exactly as Carla remembered. Her face showed only a few wrinkles around the eyes; the large dark eyes were soft and gentle as they had always been; her dark hair which she wore in a soft bob was untouched by gray. Carla took the proffered hands, she let the older woman kiss her, but she was ill at ease. Overcome with emotion she grew dizzy and hastily went to sit upon the sofa, which was away to the side in a secluded nook.

"My dear, are you ill?" Mrs. Thorfinnson was sympathetic and worried.

"You're so good to me," Carla began to cry.

The tears fell like rain. Julia Thorfinnson sat beside her and held her close. Carla felt as if she had been lost in the forest and had wandered alone for days and days and just at the moment of collapse had been discovered by the rescue party. Oh how she hoped this was for real, that she was truly accepted by Julia.

Carla moved as in a dream through the ceremony. Since it was a church wedding, the members of the congregation felt free to attend and a round dozen had elected to do so, mostly elderly women. There was the long walk with Howard down the aisle, the vows, oh the vows, "till death do us part." And Roger was holding her hand, she could feel the warm pulse of blood, and he fitted on the ring. Then it was her turn to place the plain golden band on his finger. He held her tightly by the hand. There was a prayer, which Carla listened to but did not hear, but clearly she heard the minister intoning:

"Forasmuch as Roger and Carla have consented together in holy wedlock, and have witnessed the same before God and this company, and thereto have pledged their faith to each other: I pronounce that they are husband and wife. Those whom God hath joined together, let not man put asunder. Amen."

Roger gently touched her face, lifted it to him, placed on her lips a loving kiss, and they turned to accept the greetings and congratulations before adjourning to the yard by Howard's cabin for the reception.

Roger noticed that his mother was missing. He went into the house. There upon the couch she sat, her head bowed into a cushion and she was sobbing.

"Mother," cried Roger, "it's the mother of the bride who's supposed to weep. And she's out there happy as a lark, entertaining everyone with one story after another. Come, don't be sad on this happy day."

Carla, who had also noted the absence of Julia Thorfinnson, came into the house just as Julia raised her head and said, smiling through the tears, "Son, they're tears of joy, purest joy."

TWENTY-EIGHT

On the evening of a muggy August day, Carla and Roger and Howard sat together in the living room of the new apartment. It's very soon, thought Roger, any day, any hour. Carla sat on the sofa, and on the coffee table before her were sewing implements and bits of yarn and cloth and batting. She held in her hands a small stuffed pony made of rough brown upholstery fabric, and she urged the others to look at her handiwork, calling particular attention to the face which she had embroidered on the toy.

"Let me have that donkey," said Howard.

"Pony," Carla corrected him.

He took it, looked carefully at the face, turned it over. With a puzzled frown he said, "The eyes are not the same."

"I was being playful," Carla laughed. "I made one eye closed, one open. He's winking, don't you see?" An amusing toy. Doubly amusing. Amusing to a baby by reason of its soft nubbly texture and amusing to adults because of the wink.

Howard stared at the pony, his expression unwontedly severe. He gave back the toy head first and for a moment she saw what he had seen, a face distorted, with one side, that with the open eye, calm and peaceful, the other frozen in an expression of anger. *If I'm so haunted,* she thought with horror, *by the image of a distorted face that I imprint it on a toy animal, who knows what's happening to my child.*

Howard left soon after and Roger decided to walk out with him, but Carla didn't join them. "You looked at Carla's poor toy," said Roger, "as if it were a ghost."

"I guess I saw something there that wasn't," replied Howard. "Something that had been on my mind.

"Carla saw it too. What was it?"

"There's no getting away from you, you'll worm it out of me. It was just that the two sides of the face were different. You know."

"I do indeed," Roger said gravely. "And then I wonder why should I worry? Fear of being caught in deception, I suppose. I expect some resemblance."

"But not that, not that," said Howard fiercely.

"And if it is?"

"It's not likely. Carla says none of his family—"

"She's talked to you about it?" Roger demanded. "But not to me?"

"But you'd thought of it?"

"Of course."

Roger walked aimlessly for a while, then slowly returned to the apartment. He must bring it out in the open with Carla in order to reassure her, but he found her already in bed and half asleep. He picked up the toy. She'd done a good job, flowing tail, thick mane, face with expression. No, it wasn't at all like Leonard. Why did Howard have to see what wasn't there? But the fear was there, present with all three of them. *Oh God*, he prayed silently, *give me words to bring comfort to Carla*.

Not long after, Carla awoke and thrashed about, as if hoping to create a cooling breeze in the stifling room. Even Howard's cabin would be cooler than this, she thought as she tossed about in the big double bed. She didn't mean to complain; by the time the baby could walk they'd have their own house; Roger said they definitely must. At this juncture the baby gave a muscular kick.

No, thought Carla, that's not it. Not yet. She's been doing that for months. It was reassuring, proof that the infant was alive and well. Carla could feel the warmth of Roger by her side, and she knew that he was asleep. She waited, hoping the baby would give another kick, it would be company in the night. She was half asleep when she felt an unusual movement. She drew her breath in, she gasped for air. She was conscious of a new sensation, a pain, not severe, actually more the harbinger of pain than actual pain itself. It subsided, she thought she might even sleep, but before sleep overcame her, there came another gentle pain. Mollie had said to time the pains, but was this really a pain? The doctor also had stressed timing the pains. "It is of importance," Dr. Greenbaum had said, "to start timing at the first indication."

She raised her arm to look at her watch, which she could not see to read. No need to turn on the bedside lamp yet. She'd wait until they got more intense. It could be only false labor. The cloud of pain became a stab, and she turned on the light. Roger was awake at once, hugging her and kissing her, and then going at once to pull on his trousers.

"Oh dear," said Carla as they passed along the hospital corridor, "it's like a factory." Anything could happen to her here. She refused to give in to her fear and stalked along like a tragic queen. In the end the affair proved more of a comedy, but of this she had no intimation.

They were met by a gray-haired nurse, who sat Carla in a wheelchair and started off briskly with Roger trailing behind. In an elevator, out of the elevator, along a corridor they went, into a small room with a hard bed and one chair. The nurse seated Carla on the bed, while Roger teetered on the edge of the chair.

"How often are the pains now?" the nurse asked.

"I've lost track," Carla confessed.

"We must know the intervals," the woman said sternly. She turned to Roger. "Wait outside," she said.

Competently she got Carla into a white hospital gown and did the necessary preparation. Then she smiled a very human smile. "Your hubby can sit with you for a while," she said.

Carla lay on her back on the hard bed and Roger sat by her side, holding her hand, stroking her brow, saying words of love, whispering a prayer.

From then on it was like a dream. Dr. Greenbaum was there, talking gently, checking her, telling her it would be a while longer, then leaving. The pains grew more severe and more frequent, sweat cooled her laboring body, she held tight to Roger's hand until Roger was sent away. She was transferred to an even harder bed with wheels and was whirled along. She was lifted onto some kind of a table, and a dark-haired nurse she hadn't seen before was taking her pulse. A slender young man dressed in white was leaning over her. "This is Dr. Rafferty," the nurse said, "the anesthesiologist."

"We'll make it as easy as we can," he promised.

It wasn't easy, but in due time the nurse laid the baby in Carla's arms.

Still overwhelmed with a floating sensation, Carla lay and stared at her precious child—red of face, squinty of eye, with perfectly formed features and a head of dark hair that must certainly be a wig, no infant could have such hair. "We'll take you to your room," said the nurse.

"Roger," Carla murmured.

"He's in the hall wearing out the floor," said the nurse.

Roger continued pacing with long steps up and down, up and down, wonderful corridors for pacing. Someone came and told him about the waiting room, and he thanked them and remained in the hall, pacing back and forth. "Dear God," he prayed, "take care of Carla." He found himself hoping that it was a girl, hoping it wouldn't have a twisted face. Surely that was developmental not genetic, but nonetheless, *dear God, help me know what to do whatever kind of face.* Back and forth, back and forth he went, until at last a tall, red-haired nurse came up to him and led him to a huge plate glass window through which he could see rows of tiny bassinets, three dozen he guessed. The red-haired nurse went to one in the back row, scooped up a white bundle and came over to the window. Smiling as proudly as if she had produced the baby herself, she held it up for Roger to look at. "A lovely girl," she said. The baby was beautiful! And a girl! The son who just might inherit the farm would indeed be his parents' grandchild. That is if there ever were such a son. And if not, and in any event, this was his child, his daughter. He and Carla had agreed on the name Julia if the baby was a girl.

The rest of that day passed for Carla in a peaceful haze. She yielded herself to Roger's fervent hug, and she let him go when he was told to leave, and she did whatever she was told to do, and mostly she slept. The next day was quite different. She was excited about everything, nursing the baby, congratulating her two roommates, both of whom also had girls, and finally getting out of bed and finding herself quite able to walk unaided, though a plump little nurse insisted on steadying her. The morning passed quickly what with breakfast, a visit from Dr. Greenbaum, talk with the roommates. Then there was the red-haired nurse with baby Julia!

"Here's your Jezebel," she said as she placed the baby beside Carla. She spoke in a soft Scottish brogue and in spite of the horrid name she used she spoke lovingly. "I call all my baby girls Jezebel," she explained. "And all my boys Butch."

Carla laughed, not only at the names but also at the pronoun "my." Carla wondered if she had children of her own. "Here," said the nurse, "take Jezebel."

Carla lay peacefully gazing at the little pink face, the tiny hands with their fingernails, and the glossy hair which was certainly no wig. When the nurse returned, Carla reluctantly gave the baby back to her, and turning on her side went promptly to sleep, and woke as promptly when Roger came to visit.

"Mother's arriving tonight," he told her. "Possibly your mother too."

The next day Carla was up at six o'clock. After pulling on her robe and putting her feet in her slippers, she went out into the hall and started walking back and forth. Finding this good she accelerated her pace and soon was going at a jogtrot. The short plump nurse came and insisted she stop this at once.

"I'm fit as a fiddle," insisted Carla, and added, "I'm going home today."

"I don't know," said the nurse doubtfully. "I believe you're to stay ten days. As a matter of fact, I know you are."

"No way," vowed Carla. She went to her room and got Roger on the phone. At four o'clock he pulled into the parking lot with three passengers, the two grandmothers and Mollie. "Wait here," he said. "I'll see if I can spring her."

Roger came in to Carla's room to find a spirited argument in progress. "I most certainly am leaving today," Carla insisted.

"Certainly not," argued the plump nurse. "It's unheard of."

Dr. Greenbaum came in and stood at the foot of the bed, rubbing his chin thoughtfully. "But you'll need rest, my dear," he said.

"That I think," said Roger, "we can provide."

"But Mr. Thorfinnson," the doctor was not convinced, "going home in two days!"

"Wait right here," said Roger. "I'll show you my household staff." He hurried off to get the three women. He returned with them marching single file behind him, Abigail first, then Julia, and finally Mollie. Dr. Greenbaum, busy as he was, had remained.

The three women lined up solemnly by the bed, itching to congratulate Carla, to see the baby, to hear the details, but holding this in check and retaining a dead serious mien as Roger had instructed. They stood there, Abigail, short and sturdy, in neat lavender gingham; Julia, tall and smiling, clad in spotless white even to her shoes; and Mollie, big and competent in her blue maid's uniform complete with white apron and little white cap. They stood in a row by the bed, silent, waiting.

Dr. Greenbaum threw back his head and laughed, a tremendous laugh. "You win," he said. "You win. Quite irregular, but you win!"

He needn't have worried. This was what they needed for perfect bonding. The family knew quite well how to take care of things, and Mollie knew when to stay and when to make herself scarce. The parents got too little sleep and the grandmothers made too many plans, and Howard said too many silly things to the baby. And Baby Julia slept and ate. It worked out beautifully.

Unburdened by care for the future, Julia thrived, Julia the fragile baby, the little dark-haired, round-faced, greedy baby who cooed and gurgled and howled in the middle of the night.

The days passed, summer giving way to fall. Howard came often and smiled sheepishly when Carla said he came only to see the baby. He'd extend his finger for her to grasp, he'd hum a tune for her, he'd talk to her in an almost inaudible voice. And sometimes loud enough for others to hear, but always softly. "I'm your Unk, Julia Baby, your Unk." Following this declaration would be promises of wonders to come, of piggy-back rides and gifts of toys, a teddy bear, a doll.

Carla laughed. "A teething ring first," she said. The very next day he brought a teething ring.

"I guess I'll have to send the doll to California."

"We'd hoped you'd travel with us."

"I have plans," said Howard.

At Christmas all three of the grandparents came to Boston on the train and stayed a week, crowding into the apartment and finding the tight quarters no hardship. They even had a Christmas tree, oh a very small one, no more than three feet high and fitting neatly on top of a bookcase which was pulled out from the wall to accommodate its branches. They were sure the baby noticed, that it was making an indelible impression on her little mind.

As a background to the happy melody of the lives of this family, there growled the contrabass of the developing world crisis. It was Howard who kept bringing it to the fore. He would come in waving a newspaper, he would hasten to the radio, he would listen eagerly, he would shout over and again, "The world is going to perdition in a handbasket." And once he corrected himself. "No, no, rushing in a racecar driven by a maniac."

The weather went on as if nothing unusual were happening. January was mostly sunny but cold; in February the temperature rose to just a little below freezing. For Julia there were more and more rides in her carriage, and Howard was often the power behind it. Then came March, and the winds were cold and blustery, and Carla feared to allow the child out in such weather. The baby didn't mind. She was thoroughly good-natured indoors or out. She was crawling now, all over the apartment, and was particularly fond of the low kitchen cupboards where there were lovely metal pots and pans which she could bang and arrange and rearrange, put back and take out, and if she didn't get caught at it, drag into the living room to hide under the couch. Howard had bought her a doll, said he'd be blessed if he'd wait till he had to bring it to California. It was a tiny thing, no more than seven inches long, soft and cuddly, a stuffed blue plush bunting with a pink plastic face staring out from the hood. Julia hugged it and cooed over it and would not sleep without it. She'd shown no such interest in the pony made by Carla, which had found its way to the bottom of the toybox. And her three adults were silently happy with her choice of object, seeing in it foretellings of strong maternal inclination. No danger, thought Roger, of her wanting to run the horse farm. The farm should go to the next child; that was only fair to his parents. There had to be a next child, there had to be.

On a typical day late in March, Carla and Roger and Howard were in the living room and it was evening. They'd had a pleasant dinner together, it having been a day when Howard got off work early. Baby Julia had been well exercised by her uncle, who had played creeping tag with her in the apartment and then had taken her out for an hour's carriage ride and then played a rampaging game of horsey. After that Julia had been fed by her mother, and finally, hugging her cuddly doll, she had fallen asleep in the middle of the living room floor. Tenderly her father bent over her and gathered her in his arms and placed her, still clinging to the doll, in her crib. The three adults sat in that blissful peace that ensues when the beloved infant is at last bedded down.

Howard had to hear the news. "No danger of her waking," he said. "She's out."

The excited tone of the reporter riveted their attention and silenced their small talk, their eyes were fixed on the radio as if that would make the words more intelligible. Neville Chamberlain, Prime Minister of Great Britain—they could see in their mind's eye that willowy figure with the tightly rolled umbrella; they could see the sharp-featured face, the bristling gray moustache. How many times it had stared at them from the front page of the daily paper! That very day this Chamberlain, who for so long had labored for conciliation beyond conciliation, had surprisingly enough firmly announced that in the event of any action threatening Polish independence, "His Majesty's Government would feel themselves bound at once to lend the Polish Government all support in their power." His voice was clear, quiet, determined.

"That's it, war," cried Howard.

"I'm not so sure," said Roger. "Even Hitler ought to shy away from tackling England, France, and Russia."

"But he's crazy," said Howard. "I have a gut feeling."

"Does that mean you're still eyeing the military?" asked Roger.

"I don't know as they'd want a jailbird."

"They'd snap you up so fast you'd be dizzy from the air current."

The weather grew warmer, the trees were covered with leafbuds, narrow strips of ground and spacious yards were filled with the pink and the pale blue and the lemon-yellow of spring flowers, and the air carried their perfume. Carla had Julia outside much more now, in the carriage and out of it. Julia could toddle along in a strutting kind of walk, and it was hard to tell who was more proud of this amazing feat, the baby or the three adults.

Spring gave way to summer, and Roger's courses at Harvard had been completed to the full satisfaction of Mr. Addison. Roger would definitely be going to California. He would end his duties in Cambridge on Friday, September 2nd and would report to the Gutierrez office on September 18th. He turned in his sedan and got a station wagon, big and heavy, with real wood reinforcing the sides, with easy seating room for five and another seat that could be pulled up for three additional passengers or folded down to add luggage space, this in addition to the large cargo area which alone could hold three times as much as the trunk of their old car. Even the middle seats could be folded down if they needed the space, but they decided that the seat up provided the ideally buttressed spot for Julia's car bed and also for her ingenious car seat, made by her father. She could be strapped into it, and thus elevated, could see through the windows. Mollie came every Thursday to help with the packing and accomplished wonders.

Carla sat down wearily. "Oh Mollie, I don't know how I'll manage without you."

Mollie turned to her. "You do look a bit peaked," she said.

"Just tired, I guess."

"Do you suppose Roger could get my oldest daughter, Claudia, transferred out there? She's been pestering me to ask."

"But do *you* want her to go so far from you?"

"Lord love you, girl. If she went we'd all go. With her having a job we'd manage till I pick up work."

"Oh, Mollie, think of it. Having you there with us!"

Glory be, thought Mollie, if only Roger would arrange it they'd all go to the Golden State, and who knows what great things would happen to them? And there was just as much chance of her seeing her Tom again out there as there was in Boston. More maybe, he'd always liked warm weather.

The world continued, to use Howard's phrase, going to perdition in a racecar. One day when Carla was alone with the baby, Howard came rushing in as if the devil were after him. "They've gone and done it," he cried. "The Commies and the Nazis have signed an alliance. It figgers, they're the same kind of polecat. Now Hitler can rampage all over Europe. Until Uncle Sam stops him."

Julia came toddling over, and Howard swung her above his head. "Unk's going to be a soldier," he said. Carla trembled, but Julia just gurgled something that sounded like "Unk" and kicked her chubby feet and laughed.

Roger came in. "You're just in time," cried Howard. "Look what I brought." He went to the kitchen table and returned with a brown earthenware bottle. He carried it over to the bookcase and set it on the top beside his sister's green bottle.

"What's that for?" asked Carla.

"There may be a mystery to your bottle," he answered, "but in mine there is a celebration, a good old-fashioned celebration."

"We thank you, Howard," Roger began.

"Don't you drink it," Howard cautioned. "It's not for that."

"For what then?"

"I'm going in the Army," replied Howard, "and it's just a question of time. The Army is going into war, and by then I'll be nicely broken in, and they'll be shipping me off to battle. If I come back whole, we'll celebrate, and if I die, hold a wake for me and store my ashes in the jar."

"But Howard—" Carla began.

"Don't laugh at me."

"Believe me, we're not," said Roger. "Whatever we have to leave out of our boxes, you can bet your bottom dollar we'll find room for that bottle."

"Good! I don't reckon I'll see you again before you leave. There's a visit I have to make."

Abruptly he left.

TWENTY-NINE

Howard found his mother in the midst of a stream of men and women coming from the Blodgett Mill, walking with another woman. He stood still and waited as they approached him, two women clad in cotton print dresses, walking wearily in silent companionship.

Abigail caught sight of him, stopped, dabbed at her glasses with a handkerchief, straightened them, looked again. "Howard!" she cried. "It *is* you!"

As he approached, he saw fear in her eyes. "Oh nothing's wrong," he reassured her.

"This way," said Abigail. "I'm a boarder now at Twin Pines." She laughed as if it were a joke.

He noted that her hair was in disarray and her face sweaty. Poor Mama, he thought, she works too hard. And her plans for moving had evidently fallen through. A cool breeze blew from the river, and Abigail brushed her hair back and took a deep breath. "What brings you here?" she asked.

He took his time answering. At last he said, "You know about the war in Europe?"

"We have newspapers even here," she responded sharply. "And radios."

"Yes, I know. Mama, I've something to tell you."

"Yes?"

"I'm in the Army. Report for duty in a couple of days."

"And you connect that with the war in Europe?"

"Don't you?"

They entered the lobby of the Twin Pines, which didn't look nearly so big to him now as it used to. Mrs. Hembonny came from within, and she too didn't look nearly as big, nor as imposing as he remembered her. Her hair had grown gray, her shoulders slightly stooped, her figure less portly. "Your son?" she said. "A room? Of course."

"Abigail! Howard!" cried a woman's voice.

Howard turned, and there were Margaret and Barclay Putnam, Margaret all angles and vivacity, and Barclay sadly surveying the world in silence.

"I met Nancy from your place, Abigail, and she told me your son was here. Oh how nice to see you! Both of you!"

"He's enlisted in the Army and come to say good-bye."

Barclay, who'd seemed hardly aware of Howard's presence, now came forward and extended his hand. "Well, well," he said, "so you've signed with Uncle Sam?"

"That's right."

"Should've gone Navy. I was Navy, World War I."

The Putnams had only time to say hello and goodbye, and Howard was alone with his mother. Washing up and going to dinner was a diversion, and then they sat in Abigail's room, each uneasy with the other. "Will you sit on the bed or this chair?" she asked.

He opted for the straight, stiff chair and sat looking around while she fumbled in a straw basket and pulled out red yarn and gleaming steel knitting needles. "May as well keep my hands busy while we talk," she said.

He noted the pictures on the wall. They'd had them in the farmhouse and in the cabin where he'd stayed such a short time. There was the Jesus leading the flock through a blinding storm, and the woman tossed by the waves struggling toward the rock upon which stood a wooden cross, and the dark gloomy landscape with the winding road and the unearthly light. "You've still got the pictures," he exclaimed.

"You remember them!"

"Indeed I do." They'd been apart so much that it surprised them both to find they had a common memory.

"Carla always notices them too," said the mother. "Oh Howard, I try not to complain, but why do they have to go so far away? Why must he take her all the way to California, where maybe I'll never see her again?"

"I suppose they have their reasons."

"It isn't right. He shouldn't do it." Abigail spoke angrily.

"If you knew the whole story—" Howard too was angry, angry that anyone should have even the slightest critical thought of Roger. To Howard, Roger was the best man who ever walked God's green earth.

"I do know the whole story!" Abigail retorted.

"You don't."

"Then you should tell me."

He hesitated. He ought to hold his tongue, but this wailing was too much for him; he couldn't stand it. "Roger," he said, "has done for Carla what no other man would do."

"If you mean got her with child and then married her, that is only right. And I told him clearly he didn't have to, you and I could care for her."

"He gave her his love, he gave the child his love, but Mama, it wasn't his. The father and many of his friends live in Boston. Roger and Carla do well to move, and the opening happens to be in California. And now, don't you ever let me hear another word against Roger."

She buried her face in her hands and shivered and sobbed. "Oh dear," she cried. "I never do anything right, I never understand anything."

"They'll skin me alive if they ever find out I told you."

"But I'm your mother, you should tell me." She raised her tear-stained face. "No," she said, "I have no right to make such a claim. I never did anything for you. Whatever I tried turned out wrong."

"You started me out right," he answered. "Taught me to honor my father and mother."

"I don't deserve to be honored, but I do want you to love me."

He put his arm around her, poor suffering little mother. "Oh but I do. I thank you for the many things you taught me, even with a switch on the legs."

"Such a little switch," she said. "You were always easy to correct. That Carla, once anyone touched her she fought like a wildcat."

"She'll be okay now," he comforted her.

"And you?"

"I'm a man, not much of one perhaps but enough that I must act like a man."

"I won't say I'm not worried," said Abigail. "I know the danger. But son, I know you're doing what you think is right."

"Don't you think so too?"

"Yes, son, I do. Only it's hard for me to face it. But I'm proud of you, and Grandfather Benson would be proud."

Grandfather Benson, hero of the Civil War. She could give no higher praise. So he, poor worthless Howard, had made her proud!

She had found her place in the knitting, and her hands moved without her eyes watching. She looked carefully at Howard and though he was her son, she saw him clearly—a small man, his gray eyes sad with an unfulfilled longing, shy but not timid, wholly undistinguished in appearance, a mere mutt of a man, but a good man, definitely a good man, and if no giant, still possessing a wiry strength. And he looked into the appraising eyes peering through the gold-rimmed glasses and found acceptance.

"Son," she said, "you had a rough childhood. I wasn't much of a mother to you."

"I guess you did the best you could. Anyway, somewhere along the line a man has to stop bellyaching and get on with life."

She went over and put her arm around his shoulders. How hard and muscled his arms were! "I do love you, believe me, I do," she said. "And I must face it. I did do wrong, leaving your father. Can you forgive me that?"

Forgiveness, he thought was not his. But the words she'd spoken had broken down a barrier. He took her hand, pressed it to his lips. "I never was a good son either," he said. "Always running off."

She went back to her knitting, smiling through the tears. "Don't ever do it again," she begged.

"Not likely."

"Son, let me confide in you. I was terribly worried about Carla. Bad politics, for one thing. Even worse, there was, well, I'd suspected what you just told me. But I didn't want to believe it. Thank God for Roger."

"Wherever he takes her," said Howard solemnly.

"Wherever. And one of these days there'll be someone for you."

"Women don't cotton to me."

"Some day the right one will come along."

There was plain honesty in that tear-stained face. She would not have said it had she not believed, and because she saw this possibility for him, he saw it for himself. He loved her for it. At last he had a mother.

In the morning she walked with him to the station and waited there with him, for once in her life silent. The Southbound train pulled in, come to carry him away.

"No more disappearing acts?" she demanded assurance.

"Never again." He held his figure to its greatest height, not very great to be sure, and without turning back boarded the train. He found a window and waved, and she lifted her hand to her forehead and gave a salute, which he returned with snap and vigor if not perfect form.

She turned to walk away, her eyes filled with tears so that she could hardly see.

※※※

In Boston at nine o'clock the next night Howard was approaching a train with a group of other young men in assorted civilian clothing, each carrying a suitcase or bundle, waiting to be herded onto the train. A burly, khaki-clad Sergeant came marching along the line, shouting in rasping voice, "Move it, move it, move it!" Howard swallowed his resentment for the sake of the duty he'd sworn to perform and crowded up the steps with his buddies. He'd write to his mother from boot camp. She'd be proud to get the letter.

THIRTY

"Believe me," Roger had said, "whatever we have to leave out of our boxes, you can bet your bottom dollar we'll find room for Howard's bottle."

And indeed it was carefully packed in a hamper with other breakables and placed in the cargo area, and on the day they left Roger himself checked and verified that it was there in a safe place. Carla put Julia in the special seat Roger had made for her, strapped her in and fastened the buckle. Julia sat by the window crowing with delight at the prospect of a ride. It was early on a brilliant September day, the sun was shining brightly, the maple in front of their apartment house blazed fiery red, and the other trees in sight were beginning to turn, red and yellow and orange. They rode silently and were soon out of the Boston area and driving through open country dotted here and there with a farmhouse or other building. The big car moved swiftly westward. "And so," said Roger gaily, "they drove off to California and lived happily ever after."

It was mid-morning when Julia began to fuss and then to cry. "I'll give her a bottle while you get us some coffee," suggested Carla, laying aside the old brown book she had been trying, not too successfully, to read.

They pulled up at a very small restaurant where Roger purchased cartons of coffee and corn muffins lavishly buttered. They were all very quiet as they drank and ate, after which Julia went quite willingly into her car bed and fell asleep at once.

They resumed their journey, and the car rolled smoothly along the black highway. "Why so thoughtful, my dear?" asked Roger.

"While you were getting the coffee," she said, "a wonderful thing happened, a wonderful thing inside of me. Not exactly a vision, but yes, almost that."

"A vision?"

"I'm sorry you weren't able to be in our Sunday School class studying Exodus," she said.

"Somebody has to teach the kids," he responded, not all that eager to discuss Exodus.

"We studied about God's hand leading the Hebrews, and I kept asking myself why has He never led America? And then reading some of Grandpa's books it came to me, I began to have a glimmer." She held up the old brown volume. "This one in particular, I was reading it last night." The book was *Of Plimouth Plantation* by William Bradford.

"So that's why you stayed awake half the night."

"You don't get what I'm saying, the importance, the importance to me."

"Important in general of course, but specially to you?"

"To me it's important right here and now, a light upon my path. This is the key I've been seeking. I sensed it last night, but it was a filmy cloud which refused to take shape. But sitting here, thinking, it hit me, oh Roger it hit me! Every wheel in my brain is turning! Oh where is paper, I must capture it on paper."

"Here, take this notebook. I suppose you're talking about that history you want some day to write."

"Don't you see it? American history is one miracle after another. Squanto, for instance."

"Was that a miracle? After all they had landed at the Patuxet lands, and he was the last of the tribe returned from his wanderings."

"His being there was natural enough, but what of them? Of all the places along the coast, why did they land there?"

She'd caught his interest. "I never thought of it that way," he admitted, "but you've got a point."

"You mean you thought God didn't exist for America?" Carla asked.

"No, of course not. Obviously He was there. The Pilgrims survived because they lived according to God's law. And they were a healthy lot. But was it a miracle?"

"In Exodus freedom was possible only as the Hebrews followed God's commands," Carla explained. "Still time and again God did intervene, and it's been the same with America. Americans have lived according to God's Word, but sometimes God has intervened. It was a miracle that the Pilgrims survived. The unbelievable victory in the War for Independence was a miracle. There is a pattern, there *is*."

"Carla, my Carla!" he cried. "Here I've been trying to teach you love of God and love of country, and suddenly you run far ahead. I salute you, my love."

"You don't pity me any more?"

"I never did." He supposed he had in a way.

"You didn't marry me because you felt sorry for me?"

"Rub it in! I deserve it. Not that I for a moment admit anything. But I will stop calling your typewriter Carla's toy."

She laughed. "Good."

"You said this came to you all of a sudden, like a vision?"

"It's somehow been dancing before my eyes for a long time, but I couldn't really see until I got the blinders off."

"You mean complete disillusionment with that Marxist, atheistic so-called interpretation of history?" he asked.

"Yes."

"I guess I have some things to learn from you. Hang on to this idea, pursue it."

"It won't be easy," she warned.

"Let me help."

"I'll need your scientific logic to keep me from wishful interpretations. But enough of that. I have something to tell you," she announced.

"I'm all ears."

"Not here. Somewhere out in the country."

They rode all day, and they had lunch, and her tongue clattered, but she hadn't really talked. They went uphill and down and by nightfall were in flat level country speeding along a smooth straight road. Women! he thought. If she wants to talk, why doesn't she? At a roadside cafe where they dined by candlelight, she was humorous about the food and giggly about the dim light, altogether in a strange mood. Julia, who'd slept half the day, was embarrassingly noisy. Roger was tired and cross but maintained the poise on which he prided himself. Women and babies! Babies and women! He'd sure hate to have to go off to war and leave them to manage by themselves. Just outside the cafe were two phone booths, and as they went out, he lingered near them and suggested they call Abigail.

"Later," said Carla. "You carry Julia."

They passed by the phone booths and started down a dirt road. What now, he wondered. "Have you been here before?" he asked.

"No," she said. "But oh this space, I feel so free, unfettered, there are no longer mountains hemming me in."

The heavens were filled with the wonders of a starry sky and the earth with an expanse of stubbled plains from which the crops had been harvested, and they walked along a dusty road.

"Let's run!" she cried. "Oh I could almost fly!"

He put Julia on his back, where he could reach to hold her on, and he lumbered after Carla, who was a fast-moving, light-colored blur. Why she could run! He'd never seen her run before. How long, he wondered, had this been going on?

"Giddyup pony!" cried Julia.

"I," he said, "am a jackass!"

"Dackath!" piped Julia, and he laughed.

After a while he caught up with Carla. She stopped, breathed deeply, seized his arm to steady herself. "Now," she said, "secret-sharing time." There they were, in an open field, the three of them. Roger set the baby on her feet, where she stood hanging onto his pantleg demanding to be picked up.

"Okay Carla," he said. "Out with it. Whatever it is, I'll be able to stand the shock."

"How serious you are! Can't you see I'm happy?"

"I can see you're higher than a kite!"

She threw her arms around his neck and drew his face down so that she could kiss him, gently on the cheek. "Roger! My darling!" she cried. "We're having a baby."

He seized her and swung her off the ground and kissed her lips. "At last! About time," he said.

"Oh Roger!" She was suddenly subdued. "Can you forgive me for everything? I have so much of which to repent."

"Don't let repentance become self-hatred," he cautioned. "I won't have you hating the woman I love."

"I myself love her all too well," said Carla. "And I'm happy, wild, crazy happy!"

She broke away from him and raised her hands to heaven. "Oh, I want to dance, dance in the moonlight." Her feet moved swiftly, her body swayed in rhythm. He too felt wild emotion down to his toes, and he too was dancing. "Be jubilant, my heart!" he sang.

He held his hand to her, and simultaneously they realized that right before their eyes Baby Julia had gone toddling across the field in pursuit of a tremendous black-and-white dog. They had to run to intercept her. The dog turned, it had a silly grin on its face, it let the baby and the two adults approach, then lay down and rolled over. "Puppy! Puppy!" cooed Julia.

"Full-grown dog, you little imp," said Carla. "Doggie, go home."

The dog got up and trotted off. Walking slowly with Julia in Roger's arms, they went back to the phone booths. Roger took over one phone while Carla, with Julia tugging at her skirt, used the other. He called his parents, and she phoned Abigail.

"Isn't it wonderful, Mama?" Carla could hardly contain her joy. "And oh, Mama, little mother, I love you so!" When had she said that before? She could not remember, but today it came naturally.

"Oh Carla!" cried Abigail.

"We're so happy."

"Carla, you've come home, you've come home," sobbed Abigail.

Roger was at her elbow, eager to talk to Abigail. "We want a boy," he said. "We promised Dad."

"The nerve!" Abigail was laughing now. "Wishing for a boy! But Roger, I just remembered. Before Carla I wished for a girl."

"Dad isn't rigid about it. Just in case, he's helping steer Julia right. He promised a rocking horse for Christmas. But he's wasting his money. She's a little mother."

"Take care of her, oh do take care of her. Both of them, I mean all three."

"You bet. Here's Carla again."

"God be with you," Abigail said. "Forget about my foolish ambitions for you. Now you've a family, you're part of a family. It's worth giving up all else."

"I've given up nothing," said Carla. "I've just begun to find myself, to free myself."

"Oh my daughter, my daughter, God bless you and keep you, now and evermore." Gently Abigail replaced the receiver.

Roger and Carla walked slowly back to the car. "She knows," said Carla. "She knows."

"Knows what?"

"Everything."

"She told you so?"

"No, but she knows, I'm sure of it."

On the highway driving toward the West in a comforting blanket of darkness riding in the conical beam of illumination from their headlights, Roger and Carla rejoiced together while Julia lay still awake in perfect security in her car bed.

"We're on our way, we're on our way," cried Roger gaily. Carla snuggled against him and echoed his words. From the back seat Julia took up the refrain, "On a way, on a way." And the parents laughed happily at the cleverness of their child.

In Megunnaway, Abigail, overcome with the emotional turmoil of the day, grasped the handrail and pulled herself slowly up the stairs. Soon she was seated at her table. *Praise be to God, Carla has come home!* Abigail rejoiced. *No matter where she goes, she has come home. And Roger. It is right that there should be another child. And Howard knows my mother love for him; I don't suppose he ever has until now.*

Far into the night Abigail sat at her table and prayed her prayer of Thanksgiving. "My children, oh my children, saved by grace, dear God, by Your grace." And she included the unborn as well as the born. Another baby was another miracle in the great miracle of life and another chance that this might be that extraordinary one. Abigail, Mrs. Mittens of Megunnaway, still sheltered in her inmost heart her grandiose dream that from her should spring some day a shining genius. If not Carla and not poor dear Howard, then in the next generation or the next, time sifting the sands for the gleam of gold. She smiled serenely as the needles clicked in her agile hands. She wondered if the Army would let the men wear mittens. The needles clicked, and the mitten grew.

⚜

She lifted up her eyes and recited:

> "Give thanks to Him, Bless His name!
> For the Lord is good:
> His steadfastness endures forever,
> And His faithfulness to all generations."

Her fingers moved swiftly, without halt or error, as if the fate of the world rested on her getting those mittens done. The woolen yarn was brown as a new-plowed field in spring. It needed a touch of color; she reached for a skein of gold. It'll match his sergeant's stripes, she thought with easy optimism. And she had crimson for a line at the wrist. Tomorrow she'd get blue yarn for the baby blanket. What radiant color filled her world! Her heart could scarce contain her gratefulness.